THE ZIO

by

Mark Moiré

*Z'A*telier® Publications, Co., Franklin, TN

www.ZatelierOnline.com

A Division of *Z'A*telier® Productions, Inc.
Corpus Christi, TX

*Z'A*telier® Publications Books Edition: February 2008

 Published in the United States by *Z'A*telier® Publications, a division of *Z'A*telier Productions Inc., Corpus Christi, TX

LOC Cataloging-in-Publication Data has been applied for.

Moiré, Mark

THE 710 / by Mark Moiré. – 1st ed.
p. cm.
ISBN 978-0-9639906-4-8
2008

Library of Congress Control Number: 2008921673

*Z'A*telier® Publications ISBN: 978-0-9639906-4-8

The main text font face is Times New Roman.

Printed in the United States of America.

20 19 18 17 16

Published in conjunction with LSI, Lightning Source, Inc.

www.ZatelierOnline.com

*Z'A*telier® Publications, Inc.
PO Box 1586
Franklin, TN 37065-1586

Other books by Mark Moiré

The 515

The 612

To : Linda

"Passion in a lover's glorious,
But in a husband is pronounced uxorious."
(*Byron, Don Juan*)

Prologue – as prologues go

This is a book about a classy, very special and small town in Tennessee and if you read any reviews or even the cover, you'd know that. But life is circuitous, at least mine; so I feel my faithful readers (of my last book and/or even the one before that) deserve a brief explanation on how I arrived there.

Mark Moiré

Yea, that's it. I believe as prologues go that they should be brief and that's all I have to say for now.

Well, maybe another word about prologues. We both know the usual meaning, an introduction, yada yada. But it has a fascinating history and I'll rely upon our cyber and free Wikipedia to explain with the parenthetical italic incursions that are mine. Hence:

> In Attic Greek drama (*I have no idea what they are – maybe like skeletons in the closet*), a character in the play (*that's me*), very often a deity (*excuse me if I especially like that*), stood forward or appeared from a machine (*computer for now*) before the action of the play began, and made from the empty stage (*a mostly empty page will do*) such statements necessary for the audience to hear so that they might appreciate the ensuing drama (*that's my Franklin*). It was the early Greek custom to dilate (*yackey-yak*) in great detail on everything that had led up to the play (*a.k.a., my circuitous route*), the latter being itself, as a rule merely the catastrophe which had inevitably to ensue on the facts related in the prologue. The importance, therefore, of the prologue in Greek drama was very great; it sometimes almost took the place of a romance (*a concept that has been bothering me – as you will read*), to which, or to an episode (*say approximately 10 years*) in which, the play itself succeeded (*or not*).

OK? So let's begin.

What is she doing up there!?! Does she have to pee-pee?
OK – so who cares

CHAPTERS: Page #

My Own Personal Funny? No - Just Life.

The occasion was the first "contract." In Japan, a market one doesn't expect to crack for one to three years, the time necessary for the natives to get to know you and your sincere desire to be in their island market for the long haul. Japan is a place where familiarity is everything: whom you know determines your destiny in business. I don't know about the life side of that coin, probably the same. And I was just starting to meet the Japanese experience.

When one is initially successful after the time invested to be "familiar" to one's potential, indigenous customer(s), one doesn't obtain an "order" but a "contract." The order/contract difference is a "long term commitment" with the proviso that the product will be everything you told them it would be in price and quality. A person's trust is everything in Japan. That's why there are so few lawyers there, probably less than any one of our major cities in the US. You become a trusted family member versus just a vendor, sort of. And, of course, the onus is on the "outsider." In this case – me.

We, my trading company and self, obtained our first contract in only seven months. He, thanks to my publisher, worked for six plus months and I came in the seventh. Yes, one isn't presumptuous enough to enter the Nippon market without a go-between (one of their own, ergo Trading company) even if one is conversant with the language, laws, business protocols, and life shaping, indigenous customs. It takes the "trading" company partner to be one's interpreter, appointment setter-upper, person to make the appropriate introduction, entertainment director, (diners, lunches, gratuities, geisha, etc.). It's the trading rep, one of their own, that they will put their trust basically. OK, I'm not serious about the geisha thing; it just also started with a "g" and I like alliteration.

One of their many Japanese customs is to celebrate such a happy occasion, the contract, which the trade rep was anxious to set up in a celebratory, "first class" way. It was a forgone conclusion that he would be spending more of my money. But he wasn't taking advantage, he was just setting the stage for a mutually profitable future, a "promise" to the future for the six of us: his company and me, my company (publisher) and me, our customers (one and more to come) and me, and Japan and me. Is that still six? This is just the way it is and how can one complain when there are so many "me-s" in there?

The first irony, at least for me, was the rep's choice of restaurants. We're in Tokyo, the largest concentration of people in one place in the world; a place where there are ten's of thousands of eateries even a "district/ward" of restaurants (Roppongi ward) that is cut out of the city just like they have a distinct "electronics" section (Akihabara, also known as Akihabara Electric Town), a "department stores/shopping" section (Ginza ward and also the Shibuya), and more, there are twenty-three districts to Tokyo.

I'm expecting my rep to choose one of the best Japanese places and, low and behold, he chose a Chinese one maybe not realizing that from my experience in the states that our "Chinese" feed-places, while popular, were near the bottom of the food chain. I immediately wondered if this meant an "all you can eat buffet?" Trust me, the Japanese don't over eat.

My fears were dispelled when I saw the valet parking, doorman, an official greeter just inside the door, and the starched tuxedo of the Maître d'. My expense account surged to an additional page or two; at least in my mind, as I followed my controller trade rep up the green carpeting rolled out for late night business hours, the usual day's extension for doing business in Japan. I tried to relax and enjoy a "five star" occasion as I observed the highly polished, thick beveled glass panels in the ten foot high, gold framed doors. Already I was hoping he wasn't spending any of the minimal profits from my first contract that had been intentionally down-skewed in favor of breaking this new market-wall sooner-than-later let alone the pressure of the stiff negotiating skills that most native businessmen seemed to possess here.

Either they, the restaurant, thought we had importance or maybe my friend had some pull but we were next seated at an excellent, elevated tier table with a commanding view of the inside as well as the ornate floor to ceiling glass outside windows and the people passing by. Admittedly, it gave the other restaurant-people-watchers a look at us as we at them. VIP? Me? Fooled them!

Glass see-through tables with white linen place mats, real silver and fragile, multicolored China see-through China. Excuse the pun. Yea, I secretly am a pun as well as an alliteration guy. Each place setting was complete with crystal serveware, i.e., s & p shakers, sugar & creamer, bread, butter, and relish tray glass dishes, plus the appropriate crystal animal of the Chinese year. You know, the rabbit "Year of…snake, monkey, etc.

There were two waiters, also starchy dressed, that were in attendance for our table and two busboys standing close by. I refused to think of what my colleagues "treat" was going to cost me especially and by another one of their traditions, you squared accounts with your host before leaving the island, which was tomorrow as now scheduled. I began to wonder if he took plastic. Just kidding, the honor system meant I could bank transfer the balance after returning home.

Rep-san, they seem to put that after all their names; "-san," like we do Mr. before a name, must have ordered drinks with the reservation he had placed because a pseudo-wine smellier, white gloves et al suddenly appeared at the table's edge, parting the two waiters as he came. Rank, and Face, does that in the Orient; "pares/parts the lesser(s)."

The white-gloved gentlemen presented his treasure as if it was a red Mouton Rothschild or cuvee Dom Perignon, white Champagne. I said pseudo-wine-er because he wasn't a bartender or a wine-steward. He was holding, read caressing, a finely sculptured crystal bottle that I knew had to be a very fine Chinese whisky. It reminded me of the once a year, Christmas issued containers in the states for the better liquors. As a kid I remember some of the neat containers took the shape of locomotives, cowboys on horses, futuristic cars, etc. but more recently were more crystal or "prestigious" in design. I liked the earlier ones. OK, especially the cowboys.

The letter characters, logograms, on this particular bottle before me were more ornate than their Japanese counterparts, signifying Chinese (the oldest surviving writing system), and there is a distinct Japanese design style that permeates everything they do with in-country products, which this was not. Besides, the Japanese prefer the familiar black label, Jack Daniels No. 7, their "liquor of choice," and are the largest consuming group of JD outside of Texas. I just have to add that JD's distillery just happens to be in Tennessee, south of Nashville (Lynchburg, TN).

The hand ground, heavy, whisky glass felt good in my hand. The aromatic bouquet emitting from this golden liquid, our "man" (waiter) had poured and set on the table between me and my colleague was awesome smoothly awesome. Since I was talking this way, at least to myself and before I tasted this nectar of the thousands year old next-door, mother nation, the "Middle Kingdom," I knew I was ready for a good time.

China has been referred to as the "longest running show in our universe." Marco Polo was man's first astronaut in my mind, landing on a foreign, nay, alien soil and alien life the likes we won't see on the moon, Venus, Mars or anywhere else in our galaxy. It's an oxymoron but all people are equal in China. Of course all men don't rank very high in the scheme of things in their life underlying raison d'état. Where else have peoples lived through periods of "Great Leaps," "Blooming Flowers," numerous "Cultural Revolutions," and the more recent "Gang of Four." And westerners can, should, read that anyone living outside of China haven't begun to tap the rich art, theater, medicine, music, and yes – even Operas. We tend to think that gunpowder and spaghetti were the only exports from this alien place. We have no indigenous comparable pride that emanates from their thousands of years and living history.

The waiters had refilled our half full glasses; you don't pour your own drinks in Japan, and then the salads arrived. Elegant crystal glass and matching (the others at our settings) plates held crispy fresh lettuce something like Romaine and a myriad of vegetables that I didn't recognize but enjoyed.

I was a third of the way through eating this leafy dish when the two waiters rolled over a gigantic, probably 50 gallons aquarium with the biggest shrimp swimming therein that I had ever seen. Maybe they were giant seahorses, accent on the giant word. Fortunately I didn't call them shrimp before my colleague introduced me to the swimming "prawns," kind of like baby lobsters, and asked me how hungry I was – did I wish four, six, eight, ten or twelve, etc. It reminded me of picking out my own lobster, only slightly bigger, in New England some time ago. The only difference was that there one had to walk to the tank and here the tank came to you. Isn't there a "tank" saying like that somewhere? "If you can't go to the tank…have the tank come to you," or thereabouts? Tank you. Ahh, what whisky. OK, so I'm feeling good.

Since I had learned that the Orientals were already concerned with the quantities westerners, "gaikokujin," (I think I got that right) ate despite our size differences, I decided to be modest and order four. Once translated, the waiters seemed slightly disappointed that I wasn't living up to their expected eight, ten or whatever. My partner picked up on this and I know (without knowing) that he scolded them (in Japanese) in a stern voice all the while talking through a broad smile. And from the months we had spent together, I knew better than to ask what had just happened. He would have merely replied, "Just ordering" or something to that effect. I was never sure if such situations were to shield bad manners from outsiders, that he was posturing a rank of importance for a foreign guest, or that I should not question anything he did since, bottom line, it was his responsibility to "get the job done" with the least impingement on my standing, propinquity.

What happened next was unfathomable to me. And I guess I should mention that each of our glasses had been refilled probably three times during our leisure salad/conversation; filled meaning to just above half way. Well it was good stuff and I was enjoying this intoxicating aqua vitae as well as the building camaraderie.

The waiter standing nearest the portable prawn aquarium put on a pair of gloves that reminded me of my grandmother's big olé rubber oven mittens. This made me think that maybe prawns were mini-sharks in disguise and he was preparing for whatever came next. It also crossed my mind that one of the delicacies, in fact the most celebrated and notorious, in Japan was some sort of poisonous Pufferfish (fugu). That's lethally poisonous, the tetrodotoxin poison (how can I forget) paralyzes the muscles while the victim stays fully conscious and eventually dies from asphyxiation. There is currently no antidote. Maybe these prawn were something along those lines! Time for more whisky.

Also, by this time I had noted the elaborate temperature controls, aeration, and filtering system connected but mostly out of sight on the shelf below for this mini sea creature swimming pool. The water was crystal clear as one could see from the build in lights surrounding the top. I couldn't see but guessed there was a long extension cord reaching back to the kitchen (well it wasn't solar powered). I just knew I was going to pay for this manned aquarium even if all that I was going to get to take home was a receipt – and memories. So I decided to pay extra attention, surreptitiously.

The second waiter wheeled over another, expensive matching, glass and metal, serving gurney with two beautiful, Waterford Crystal type, casserole bowls complete with removable tops. I was noting all this out the corner of my right eye as I ate my salad, sipping my Chinese good-stuff since observing the obvious in Japan wasn't done, or kosher, or good manners, or something along those lines. Whatever…toast!

Please understand that curiosity is another "foreign-sin" in a culture where no one stares at events, even typical street happenings or especially at their fellow people. Such prying might impinge on one's neighbor's comfort level, a selfish, improper thing to do. Only last week, on a traffic-deserted side street in a small town north of here, I saw a Japanese middle-aged woman carrying a bag of groceries walking in the opposite direction and across the street. She slipped and fell. Her groceries didn't spill as she successfully juggled the bag, her purse, et al, but (and smiling) when she tried to right herself I could see that she had skinned her knee and it was starting to bleed.

My immediate reaction was to cross the street; bolt to her side, while my trade rep/interpreter colleague grabbed my arm pulling me forward verbally apprehending me with a quiet, almost under his breath, "Don't look at her and keep going." I countered, "We should help her!" He responded, "You'll only embarrass her and upset her for her clumsiness with its impact on two strangers." I keep on salad eating. And sipping the good stuff. And watching the show out of the right corner of my eye (or is that the corner of my right eye – or the right corner of my right eye. Right? Oh well).

The first waiter had picked up a two-foot long, silver prawn-prong in one hand and a matching, read just as long and silver prawn-tong, in the other rubberized oven mitts. Actually they, the tongs, were spring-action, grooved-jaws, handle locking, and prawn-tongs. It seems that the good whiskey was giving cadence to my thoughts. Groovy. Skoal, prosit, cheerio, down the hatch, here's howl!

Rather than say those things, "prawn-pong prawn-tongs" over in my head five times fast, I continued looking straight ahead, sipping my "luscious liquor" [Milton], and eating my salad (Julie Childs or someone) as if I ate like this every night. Doesn't everyone? Japan - what a great place.

The first guy, waiter, was now standing above the prawn-pool on a small footstool hovering, held by one of the busboys, over the fish tank trying to dislodge the happily swimming fish-things from their comfortable habitat, at least a few of them. After successfully nabbing one at it's middle with his tongs, I expected him to head-stab the critter with the prong but he only used this spear-like instrument to gently lift the squirming creature up and out of the crystal clear, warm water and into the topless bowl held by the second waiter now stationed at his side. As soon as the first prawn was deposited into the glass bowl, the top was summarily snapped back on as if the critter was going to be hopping back out on the rebound. The second busboy was standing nearby with a hand towel in each hand, I assume, in case the prawn things splashed any water, which I guessed was salt water.

I knew this prodding-prawn-procedure was about to be repeated several times and also knew that if this three ring circus act was taking place in any restaurant in America that a large crowd would be automatically gathering to watch the show, at least the little kids. I forked my salad and sipped my twenty or thousand year old liquid. I'm cool, not necessarily under fire, just under good whisky.

The first prawn seemed to be nonchalant about being in his new waterless home initially, seemingly all right with the breathing out of the water experience. Maybe he was just taking things in. I hoped he/she wasn't watching me. Maybe he felt he deserved this new, ornate, crystal palace and all to himself. Note how I am more comfortable with the masculine side of critters.

OK, so I had already noticed that both waiters didn't have on the expected spit-polished black shoes that would have gone with their formal outfits but were wearing soft, cloth, dark, foot coverings that couldn't have been too much more than ballet shoes with rubberized soles. For the life of me I couldn't remember if any of the hundreds of Japanese waiters I had already encountered wore similar shoes, sandals, or only socks. Were we supposed to take off our shoes before being seated? Nay, I would have noticed and followed the lead of my leader friend. Maybe these prawn things were like electric eels and these knowledgeable fellows were using protective, insulated footgear. More whisky yes but I can't gauge its potency so I really have been only taking small sips. Really.

The second prawn was quickly popped into the awaiting bowl only to disturb the first critter setting off a small joust between the two knights of the sea. Maybe theirs was a "territorial thing."

The third and fourth critters caused similar commotions with the others that increased with viciousness and with the activity starting to coat their transparent prison walls with a distasteful scum like film. Ditto for the fifth. Maybe I looked scrawny to them or that they were determined that I live up to their idea of the American Eating Habits. I knew I was going to pay for it, the fifth. Oh well. Parades of dollars flashed before my eyes.

The body long feelers that extended from each of their heads, the numerous spider-like legs, and their flashing fan-tails et al were now indistinguishable in this seething combat going on within three feet of my nonchalant salad eating, whiskey sipping. I was wondering if my companion, new-found-friend, at my left was more-eyeing me for a reaction than watching the live floorshow at my right.

A similar procedure was followed for my friends order of "Three;" into (his) (the) second bowl on the tableside four-wheeler cart. I wondered if he really wanted four but, in front of his countrymen, needed to be at least one less than this reputed over-eating American type guest. And they didn't give him an extra.

None of the sea-gladiators in either bowl seemed to be tiring when the second waiter reached down to retrieve another, exact replicated, only full, whisky bottle to the one I had been watching, slowly draining, on the table before me. This took me by surprise as I began to wonder if there was another custom I had missed, starting a new bottle when your guest's was more than half gone. I hoped I could afford such luxury, at least tomorrow before departing this island.

I needed not to worry since the waiter deftly popped the two tops, the decanter quality whisky bottle and the first bowl's lid. Next he liberally poured the sacred contents in and over the stunned occupants. He repeated the action in the second bowl quickly replacing the tops in both cases almost empting the bottle between the two sarcophagus. And with another sip I didn't even care if that last word served as plural or should have been sarcophaguses or something else.

Yes my attention was now riveted on the two bowls to my right. Code of the indubitable, foreign curious. So?

It was no less compelling than having two small 3-D televisions yet to be invented on an expensive TV-stand wheeled almost up to my nose. I hardly noticed, or cared, that the two waiters were in the background busy extracting the big aqua-cage with it's relieved survivors, at least until another prawn-loving customer wanted whatever it offered.

I knew that late night eating was chic on the continent, the other one - Europe, and I had eaten yesterday plus the day before. These factors plus and thanks to my velvet smooth, caramel-like tasting whiskey, I really didn't care if I was about to eat this night. The show to this point was quite enough.

The pawns had instantly become docile. I could see because the pouring of the whisky had the effect of washing the sides of the bowls. I mean they were now dead still while still alive. I could see their beady black eyes at the ends of their stalk appendages looking around as if trying to comprehend what had just happened to them. It occurred to me that they might have noticed me, noticing them, "another staring foreigner." Their legs were moving as if they were testing the temperature of this strange liquor shower that had invaded their harmless but sincere posturing altercations. I wondered if the healthy prawn males at their prime had similar brawls over female selections in the deep blue.

Maybe the whole restaurant jumped back, I can't tell you. I know I did and that was in a seat, which was, fortunately, a booth. I knew instinctively that my Japanese companion wasn't about to guffaw or even snicker at my surprise and subsequent action. And I would never hear about it in the future no matter how entertaining my "wide-eyed, out of my socks experience" appeared to him now.

I only thought those mini-dragons were active before. Now they were the equivalent of sixteen tomcats thrown into an oversized, industrial Laundromat dryer with six quarters inserted. There was so much commotion next to me, in those two bowls, that I was tempted to jump up and hold down the lids since our two waiter friends had retreated and were nowhere in sight.

I wouldn't have been more surprised if they had rigidly lined up in exact profile in a parade formation; pinkish-red pets that had been served up a new aqueous home. I wondered if they too were savoring this expensive liquid since each bowl had received approximately half of the now empty bottle returned to its original lower shelf on the cart. I watched with awe as each organism raised a feeler or two; possibly trying to understand what would probably amount to be their future, cooking base.

It was only the fleeting thought that "the waiters just might know what they were doing and it wouldn't be necessary" that saved me. Besides, good, leaded, thickly beveled crystal is heavy. Isn't it? It would have been like me jumping up in the middle of a formal dinner at some country's consulate to pin someone from the next table down on the floor and start giving CPR or mouth to mouth for a perceived ailment that obviously didn't exist.

No sooner had this happened then it stopped, the mix-master bowls' action/commotion. I pushed the plate with the few tidbits of salad remaining across the table and drained my glass. Despite his decades of innate training, or his peoples' millennium of tradition, my dinner companion couldn't wipe off the broad face smile off his face or the chuckle I could hear, that he fought desperately to control, as he reached to refill my glass even above the halfway spot thus draining the remaining contents of our own bottle. I didn't care and decided not to notice wanting more of that, hopefully, numbing liquid. But as I raised the glass to my lips I began to wonder what it was doing to my insides since I had profound evidence at my right elbow of it's effects on lesser creatures, very dead creatures I might add.

But the show wasn't over: two acts left! First: the waiters returned each in attendance to one of the funeral bowls. I casually asked San, "What happens next? Do they grill them?" "No. They're done!" was his response. I assumed, rightfully so, that he meant they had been sautéed a la whisky, "spiritized-sushi," and now they were about to be served. I just know you've heard of the "drunken chicken, well I was about to be served the drunken pawns.

Second: I had experienced the New England halved lobster served on a serving plate, the tail split in front of the stand-up rest of the body, large pinchers draped to the sides whereby one extracts the tail and pinches off the succulent claws too, adding them to one's own plate for a fabulous feast. But I wasn't prepared for my five staring, severed body prawns sitting in half-body positions, as if one eye was looking up at me with the other eye looking down at their whisky laden rent-in-two long tails on my plate in front of themselves while their terribly long feelers acted as supporting two legs of this gastronomic upsetting tripod, "gang of four plus one." And it didn't help that I had watched them all involuntarily relieve themselves into that expensive potion in their repulsive, futile death struggle. Prawn poopy. Fortunately the waiters hadn't scooped the whiskey from the bowls to "sauté" the entrees. So I am left with these five critters forming a North, South, East, West (and one in the middle) cross on the beautifully ornate, silver trimmed plate before me.

So what am I doing here? Do I need more drink? Will this luxuriant stuff embalm me too? Do I have to eat these self-de-veined/relieved, forlorn sea critters what have been placed before me? Will I be hung over tomorrow? Will my trade-rep-san take a credit card? Will I be able to read his "chit" by then? When does my plane leave? Thank God for the abundance of white-gloved driver/taxi here.

How did I get here? Japan? Those are two good questions for a guy about to go through the mid-stream thirties in life's seventies, the good olé 1970's. The short answer is, "I wrote a book." Actually it was two books and they were about the previous two decades that also happen to correspond with my last two decades but it was the second (book) that caught fire, enough to bring the first to the attention of my agent and publisher (and hopefully a lot of the public). But Japan?

I have always liked to read and my day-job, news reporter, coupled with my education, journalism, seemed to add up to trying my hand at writing. OK, two more things: small towns - I really like small town America. They're comfortable. So I chose to write about those. Actually, about the only one I had lived in the 1950's for my first book, and the second town for the 1960's book. And please don't ask me why there should be a market for such books, at least the second, in Japan. Maybe they're just curious although it does seem that they appear to be fascinated by anything American. That's based on my first trip, short that it was.

My second reason for writing was thanks to Kurt Vonnegut. I read his *Player Piano* (1952) since I had taken several years of piano with THE NUNS but that's another story. I liked Kurt's piano better; it played itself. Kurt was off the wall for a writer, not using the conventional styles, words, phrases, or story lines. It had great appeal to me even if I figured he'd never get to the bestseller status. That was all right, I didn't care. I said, "I think like he writes," and decided to try and write like I think. For better of worst, I may have a budding new career.

Hope can be repressive – but what else is there. Oh well, reporting the news is great too. No, I still have no guesses why the Japanese would be interested (and I forgot to ask if Kurt has a huge following there). You don't happen to be Japanese, are you? If so - please write. Thanks. But if you're a Psychiatrist or Psychologist – don't bother. Thanks also.

If you have ever written a book, there comes a defining moment when you have to choose a title. Of all the possible defining moments in my life, and now going into the third decade of it's own history, I came to my books-naming point's, with the idea that they, autobiographical, were best described by the physical places I stayed, i.e., the number of my street address at that time, which happened to correspond to the said decade. No, it's not like an egotistic, future, "George Washington Slept Here" wish. It's more like a "Nothing Else Better Describes or Captures the Essence" of my little life and it's little circumstances thing, in a little town. Besides, it seemed to beat Book #1, and Book #2.

Now, and from my experience of a third book (read: big deal or little depending on how many books you've written even if only in your head), one's own gut wrenching, soul-searching, writer's-block, defining-moment of the naming-thing isn't really important in the scheme of things. It only becomes the fodder for other's (read: agents, editors, publishers, critics, family, friends and even the general public), with their propensity to ridicule, reject, change, or at least criticize your choice(s). This is arrogance at its best since they weren't the one that had to experience the joys-and-painful moments behind your personally chosen, defined-moment-naming thing. I like hyphens – did you notice?

If you happen to be one of those that have read either (or both) of the first books, you probably (still) have a (good) question: How is it that a writer of the US-small-town-genre is in Japan? Hey author, "Is this your (real) day job?" So I like parenthetical remarks also. Alliterations, hyphens…whatever.

The answer is that an ambitious publisher felt that there was/is a substantial audience for my books there. This probably opens up more questions than I care to think about but suffice it to say that I don't have a bloody clue to the answers nor do I understand how we just received a contract for the first order of 30,000 copies each of my first two books especially since there wasn't the proviso that they should be in Japanese. (!?!) It's only the time spent here versus going on a publicity tour that has suited my personal needs. Yes, I truly shun personal publicity/aggrandizement. And now I will have to avoid the tour thing at all costs because you just know the first question, "Mark, what are the Japanese doing with 30,000 copies of your book especially since it wasn't translated into Japanese?" Or the second, "Mark, what was your mother like?" Obviously I don't have much respect for the intelligence of questionnaire-ers. Wait – that doesn't include my readership – really!

Besides, it is surprising that one can write a good deal on the thirteen hour flights to here despite the smoke laden, re-processed air (disgusting for a non-smoker like me). Also, one has enormous time/waits in the international airports between here and there (meaning the states). This, actually, is good news since I like to write and big blocks of time are needed to get the juices going (at least with me). So this is how I'm starting the new decade, the '70's (and my 30's) – so I'm writing again.

After all, we did land a contract, my rep-san really, plus this is a fabulous country, which I had no previous idea of enjoying so much. There's so much to this island nation that one never hears.

First, the Japanese coffee is absolutely great (beyond good) and I have never had a bad meal in any restaurant, the popular little street booths littering the public places in the bigger cities, or the soba noodle kiosks in practically every stop in the train stations. Add to this the personal fun things one can experience from investing one's time here.

Please don't write – all of you that know Nipponese. I know my spelling/phonetic pronunciations of this foreign language may be anything from the correct one and I know (from my little pocket English-Japanese, Jap-Eng dictionary that the correct word for noodle is nudoru with a long line over the u). But I know what I heard and I can't believe what I saw!

I'm talking about my first and numerous train rides there, a very convenient and typical way of getting around to most places and cities (and they are nothing like the very poor trains/subways in the states). It happens in the mornings (mostly) and mostly as the trains that are heading into the bigger cities from the outlying areas, the rush hours. Train rides are at least an hour away from the central, city stations for practically everyone since the real estate, the closer you come to the center of any city, is astronomical. Couple this with the low wages (if the translations, conversion rates were correct) and one understands why commuting is a way of life in Japan. Fortunately the well-maintained trains are everywhere.

It happens at practically every stop and they are numerous. Fortunately all the trains are extremely punctually, a necessary ingredient for what I'm going to tell you. The growing train-population that builds up with each stop closer to the city vacates the train at the next and succeeding stops when it pulls into the little train stations. Really. It's a phenomenon. "Why," you ask? I'll tell you but the first time this happened I figured that I had missed the recorded, stoic, Japanese language announcement of an emergency fire drill before the stop but then at the next stop - it happened again.

Hordes of commuters rush out of the doors to congregate at these little Soba-noodle-kiosks that are located up and down the track and continently/strategically near the train doors. The computers must have called ahead or the food-fare is all the same because the breakfast-noodle-shops-on-the-go all have rows and rows of hot noodles (buckwheat based) in Styrofoam bowls with plastic wrapped chopsticks all lined up. Maybe the commuters have given their rush-hour travel schedules for the week so that one's soba (noodles) order is conveniently waiting for them each day at the designated stop or stop (dependent on how hungry one is that day).

Understand, the stopover isn't exaggerated nor prolonged for these on-off-on-again hungry passengers but it is the exacting, dependable time slots of the Japanese train system that make their sojourns possible. I, after observing the trains for a while, have actually set my watch to them rather than depend on other sources such as the hotel or bank signs. To make this work, the soba slurping breakfast thing, I figure that each hungry commuter had to have the exact train token and the exact soba change ready before entering their home station for the morning's commute. I also figure that all the soba-fare is the same or maybe the "spicy" is on the left, the "mild" in the middle, or whatever. Then, since they read right to left, versus our way, maybe I have this backwards.

With the doors open, everyone, or at least anyone paying attention, sees and hears this slobbering, breakfast, eating exercise. I couldn't imagine working chopsticks so fast as to slurp up a bowl of noodles during just a train stop and repeating the show at the next stop without experiencing severe stomach cramps as soon I got to the office. Maybe the latrines at the city stations are full.

My thoughts revert back to my bland, Quaker Oats, unvarying, oatmeal, kid breakfasts that were a mandatory requirement in my mother's house. Those were mild by comparison.

I know you're going to ask me how many times each one of the commuters goes through this procedure, on again off again on again, or how many bowls on the way to work and is this a commuter tradition? And your answer is - I don't know. I haven't been that observant and besides – they all seem to look alike! But I have learned that they're serious about their soba. Maybe it's like the rice-thing, every different area thinks their rice is better, but the different districts of Tokyo make (slightly) different varieties. Maybe this changes but while I was there, Nagano soba was the reputed best. They even tried to coin a special (distinguishing) name, Shinano Soba. Don't tell but their secret variance is two parts regular (white) wheat and eight parts of buckwheat. Wonder if they'll let me back after I write this? Damn, might I lose my contract(s)?

Wow! Did you read what I wrote? No, not the soba-secret, the "they all seem to look alike" thing. Will the race-critics, book-condemners come out in droves? Will subsequent contracts be revoked when this comes to the fore? Have I lost my Japanese (to be) fans? Where have you heard that before? Another good reason for missing the "tour" thing.

You're wrong – it's not so much the facial appearance of these peoples but the fact that they're all, more or less, dressed the same: all the men, janitors, laborers called "salarymen," stock brokers, managers, executives, etc. are in dark suits, white shirts and ties carrying dark brief cases whether they work in a factory or office and the few women that are rush-hour commuters, are in dark shirts, white blouses with (typically) a dark sweater covering on top.

Come to think of it – it's seems to be more of a man-thing, the soba rush. And since it's a man's society – they don't expect to loose their seats. Yes, the men have preference in this regard on the trains and buses. In fact I was reprehended in this regard by my interpreter-rep the first time I stood to give my seat to a woman. But the embarrassing thing for me was that she didn't accept, only looked sheepishly at my companion (not me) slightly shaking her head as if to say, "Haven't you informed your foreigner of our ways yet?" So much to learn on a foreign land. Thank God my book won't sell on Mars or the Balkans.

Yes, the Japanese people seemed nicely homogenous. You can't believe the singularly surprising sight from the morning train window of twenty or thirty school children tramping off to their school especially in the rain when you can't (hardly) distinguish girl from boy, or any one of them since each have the same bright yellow hat, yellow coat, matching yellow boots, carrying the same yellow, same type school bag (or back pack). Well it's these children that grow up to all be dressed alike on the way to their work later in life. No, I don't know if the kids get soba at home before school or upon arriving at school. Maybe there are little soba shops on the street corners along their paths. (Just kidding). (But the raincoats might help).

OK, so there is a slight repose, a rebellious thing, along the growing-up-Nippon-life-way. It happens to the teens just before they have to graduate and take their first jobs or take the horrific "college entrance exams" for the lucky ones. They, the James-Dean-rebellious, are tolerated, walking the streets, in punk, pink hair Mohawks, chain belts, cowboy boots, or with hanging things pierced whatever or other westerner (assumed) fads. I'm serious.

You have to visit Harajuku Station and area, to experience the teenage, rebellious culture at its most extreme. The youth call it cosplay (costume play) and typically show up in anime character or punk costumes. They openly strut their stuff but instantly revert back to cultural conformity when it's time to get a job and don their black suits, white shirts, et al. And the "independent, experimental spirit," doesn't seem to appear later in life as a Japanese version of our Hell's Angel, or other late-life crisis neuroses. But then they don't have the anarchistic, independent spirits that we do (in America) let alone Harley-Davidson hogs.

Safely in my cramped tourist class plane seat, flying back home, I'm still thinking of Japan. It's possible the carefully manicured island, dramatic Geisha to Samurai history, friendly, polite people, quaint and enduring folk arts, Mingie, and crafts such as the paper origami crafts, Kabuki dolls, department store greeters, colorful Kimonos still gracing the streets, train station pushers, and struggling populous wishing to be world respected – has gotten under my skin, at least a little. Maybe a little of my heart and soul were left behind. Writing about it helps. I hope you like.

One scary moment I had coincided with the very first meeting we had with the largest publisher in the country. Please note that it was necessary to go first to their largest, so I was told. It would have been unthinkable to go to a lesser house (publishing company) and then approach the biggest. "As if they would know?" was my candid response. "They might and that would be it!" was the curt Japanese response from rep-san.

This was my first introduction to the small world, island mentality. But the scariest was after the meeting had started and I had been asked to speak, for them to hear my presentation of the books. Understand, I didn't think the opposite side of the table spoke English since my trade rep was handling everything and I certainly didn't speak their language. But for whatever reason, they wanted to hear me what I had to say via my interpreter.

I said "opposite side of the table" because that was the way we were invited to sit – the two of us on one side and the six of them on the other. The seating at this very large (maybe 20 chairs, rather common table with ten chairs on each side) was definitely skewed. I felt a little out numbered, uncomfortable. Then maybe that was their purpose, to have an "upper" hand but who knows. Actually I was beginning to think that my publisher just wanted me out of the country as if there was a real possibility of selling thousands of my (English) books about small town America here.

They were all men and all dressed alike and I had been prepared for no-woman thing in advance. Before the meeting my trading partner, who had spent several years in New York City, tersely and with some embarrassment explained that I might not run into any women in our meetings except the receptionists, and/or "tea servers," those bringing in the expected tea/coffee traditional meeting preamble.

Unfortunately I couldn't guess who was the head man to address directly and had to keep looking up and down the table at all of them because they were all dressed the same, no distinguishing one from another by the "cut of one's suit," more expensive silk tie, or any other visible clue. It wasn't until later that I learned about the "consensus decision making" part of their business and all businesses and business decisions made in Japan.

As it turned out there were a pressman, editor, typesetter, copywriter, Vice president, and the Managing Director (himself). These were the six sitting across from us. When six, not just one, first entered the room I thought that this was a "power" play, a show of "we're the biggest, we send in more people than you have, we already won before we have begun – who are you?" But…?

Anyway, I was slowing speaking, so that my companion could easily translate, dealing out small sentences that I felt would not overpower him with my extemporaneous, possibly cumbersome, soliloquies. Suddenly the table on which I had comfortably folded my hands since I had been pre-warned not to talk with them, the hands, started to shake. I mean the table begun to dance back and forth, slow at first then violently. My hands couldn't keep up. I calmly kept on talking trying not to miss a beat but watching my audience for any recognition of what the hell was happening.

My trading partner kept on translating even though he now had his own hands flat on the table in order to stabilize himself. My audience kept on swaying with their folded hands on the table, hopefully listening but nary a reaction – all of their eyes to the front only occasionally looking straight at me. At this point I realized the whole room was like it was at a Universal Studios' fun house tour, shaking back and forth. I tried to surmise it was some sort of Japanese publishing test for a new and naive author. I began to resent my good buddy for not preparing me for whatever was happening.

When finally the windowpanes made noise I calmly inserted into my speech (as if on cue and in only a mildly curious voice), "What's happening?" It must have been translated verbatim because there was some confusion and my audience started caucusing among themselves as the room still swayed back and forth. My companion put his opposite hand over his mouth, leaning over to me and said the following "aside" almost under his breath, "It's just an earthquake – keep on going" (meaning my speech). I was traumatized. I had never experienced and earthquake – and didn't want to now!

During those few moments the shaking suddenly stopped; no sirens went off, no buildings collapsed, no hordes of people went screaming into the streets – things I had surmised routinely happened during one of these "life shaking tragedies" but these happenings were not happening. (OK, so excuse the pun. Thank you very much. What – you missed it? Too bad).

I was scared and wanted to bolt as my trading partner simply paused, refolding his hands on the table, waiting for a cue from across the table to begin again. And the now nervously smiling talking audience, for the first time and only to their selves, paused with what now appeared to be the headman, the first to my left, the man who filed into the room the last and took the seat across from my buddy, speaking to my trader-interpreter.

I was very anxious to hear what he had to say. It came to me via the rote at my side, "They weren't sure at first what you meant. He says that it's just one of our many earthquakes, that there is no danger to you, and that you should continue – please."

I pictured myself as a war correspondent calmly standing before the camera March 16th during the final assault on the infamous Iwo Jima island hill during The Big One, WWII, with bullets flying everywhere since first landing with our troops February 19th, with the Fighting Leathernecks fiercely fighting back, forging forward foot by foot up the deforested hillside for the last few yards of this God forsaken place so that they could plant their treasured red, white, and blue fluttering tree at the top and I could record it for the world. Duty calls, damn the bullets, just a job, someone has to do it.

You know the movie – the one that Commander John Wayne got shot in the back by a Japanese foxhole sniper after he had led our forces from the shores to this last stronghold and had taken this last piece of real estate on that God forsaken island, Iwo Jima, only wanting to sit and share a cigarette with a fellow GI or two after a job well done.

I might be flying over that particular memorial, Iwo Jima, as these memories surge through my mind. I know I have to visit there someday although probably nobody ever does. I will cry there and I never cry. John, a.k.a. the Duke, dad, my uncles and my upbringing taught me never to cry as a man.

My uncle fought in that "theater," the Pacific one. He was the older of my two warring uncles. The younger, both my father's brothers, fought in the Atlantic theater. Neither of them, my uncles, were buried in another national memorial, the Arlington National Cemetery. After the war they wanted to distance themselves from that horrendous event, as if it never happened but especially that they never where participants. I don't think I could tell my Pacific theater, WWII uncle that I liked Japan.

Speaking of memorials, I think of John, The Duke, as being buried in the Arlington one. There was confusion after he was shot in the movie and the required transport back after the playing of the credits. He ended up being buried in his own memorial, The Tomb of the Unknowns at Arlington, along with the myriad of memories we, as a country, should never shed. OK, so it's only in my mind.

My dad is buried in The G. He never fought in any war but was worried that it was inevitable for me and wanted to mentally prepare me. Dad received a dispensation. I think they called it a deferment, for his "war-critical" industry/job. Dad worked in the food industry and didn't go to war as his younger brothers did.

I was eight? Maybe ten. I like to think eight instead of ten, since that would give dad two more years to live. I often wondered if my uncles, his brothers, wished they had started out as grocery clerks instead of pursuing engineering careers as they did. They went to engineer the war. Dad stayed behind to help feed the country.

Dad was the one who took me to the movie that played back in The B, *The Flying Leathernecks*. I saw the next Wayne war thing, *The Sands of Iwo Jima*, on my own. That was all before we moved to The G. I cried when my father died there. Sorry dad.

I didn't know it at the time but a guy by the name of Howard Hughes produced the1951 *Flying Leathernecks* movie. He also produced the Spruce Goose, the biggest wooden plane ever build. I saw it in California on my way to Japan. It had only flown once, in 1947, by Howard himself as pilot. He must have been working on both, flying-movie and flying-goose, at the same time.

I won't ever know about the war, their feelings, thoughts, or memories, not because they're all dead – it's just that we had this unspoken family rule: we never talked about The Big One, World War II, ever. I have a Big One memorial in my mind and lots of questions, "My Unknowns," are buried there in my own personal Arlington Curiosity tomb. I place it in my amygadala, the left one. The right is for my sex thing (but that's another story - later).

I think the Japanese have many unspoken memorials. I had ambivalent feelings going to the Land of the Rising Sun. Now I can't think of this people doing what history tells us they did in their, at least their leaders', Charlemagne-ic savage efforts to capture the world. I don't think they do or at least want to remember those times/things either. Except it seems there is no forgiveness for Little Boy and Fat Man despite all of their uncountable atrocities – just ask the Chinese.

What the Japanese set out to do had to be an ant-theory-disease that happened to have picked this tiny island, Japan, actually five main ones, islands, that only total 146,000 square minuscule miles all toll, at the time. That's (only) the size of Montana (with over a thousand square miles left over). I wonder if Montana might have world-domination ideas? Do ya'll think?

OK, so I don't really know if the sex thing is/happens in the amygadala, on the right. Or is it the prostate? Does the prostate have a right and left?

And the state that does (have such aspirations), our own California, is bigger than that Nippon land. I know California has aspirations of taking over the world but just in a leadership, follow-the-leader (weird) way? OK, so maybe Hollywood still does too, and has repeatedly tried.

My mom is not buried with my dad. She's still alive. She lives in The G, Gowanda, New York, keeping vigil over my dad's memorial. Credits, like epitaphs, are no way to end a movie or a life.

Mom grew up in The G, left for a few years and returned with dad and us in tow, has been there ever since and probably will be buried there. If that doesn't mean "home town," I don't know what does.

There is another memorial, George's estate. It's on the south bank of the Potomac, 16 miles down river, below Washington. It's called Mount Vernon. It's the same name as the (only) third place I ever lived in, The V, Mount Vernon, Ohio, my last town before now. Born in the B, Binghamton, New York, moved to The G, Gowanda, NY, and then The V, Mount Vernon, OH after college and now The F, Franklin, TN to where I'm flying back. Well, to The F via BNA, Nashville International Airport. I like to abbreviate the places I've lived but you probably already noticed that.

George and his wife, Martha, never flew and are buried at the first Mount Vernon, their own sacred place in Alexandria, VA. It's a beautiful place. The home, silly.

I had, and have, many more thoughts and memories of Japan, which I might share with you later but for now I'm back home, back in the good olé US of A.

"Home," it has such a good ring to it. I know, home is where you make it… Maybe we need that. But it may not be what you are thinking. If you recall from reading the last part of my previous book where I said that I had several pending interviews, that my landlords were about to sell my rental digs (theirs too), and that for several months I had felt that The V had given me all there was, thus my feelings/need to move on – I said that," I answered an ad for a Toledo newspaper job. I answered one in Texas, and Tennessee too." Well I did.

Toledo was almost eliminated before I hit the Maumee suburb, driving north into town from the V. I was flattered they had even heard of me but their enticing descriptions of Toledo being, "just a big-small town" was greatly exaggerated from my perspective. With due respect, The T is a small-big city with the predictable sprawl, problems and rather large population. News and journalism is quite different in a city versus a small town. And I don't want that. The "big." At least yet.

I appreciate that they were trying to lure me there but now I'm not sure they were being totally honest or that they truly understood the redeeming attributes of a real American small town. We didn't even get to the salary-interviewing stage let alone their generous offer to take the weekend to stay, looking around. The bucks were probably higher but I didn't want to hear what they were, their headquarters and offices were modern, the computers were modern even if I was still comfortable with the olé electric Selectrics or thc manual Royals, their vast resources and being tied into the radio and TV was beneficial, the (very) large staff seemed friendly (on a first-impression basis), and their archives were huge, organized, indexed and readily available to everyone. It's just that I'm still young, with lots of future ahead of me to go there now, at this stage of my journalistic life.

Having heard that, you're not going to understand taking up the invitation to interview with *The Tennessean.* Well OK, so they're in Nashville and said the same thing, little-big-town even though they add a couple hundred thousand people to the Toledo number and this was quite apparent as I flew into their substantial BNA, Nashville International Airport, but they have outpost-offices in the truly small surrounding towns or so they said. Anyways, it was while I was waiting to be interviewed there (tie, coat and all – but not with the news-feet up on anything) that I received the call from my publisher (I like the ring to that) regarding my books and even the possibility of a Japanese trip.

I had occasionally picked up one of those new lotto tickets back in Ohio and now figured that if a person had won and there was on a job interview like this that his confidence level, even the way the interview proceeded, would be quite different. And it was. My books were my lotto winnings.

The last one of those ad-interview places was Austin, Texas. Texas is next to heaven in my mind having grown up with TV westerns galore and ever since my dad made his first trip there coming back with a ten-gallon, wide-bream, soft-gray Stetson and before I checked the population. I just felt that Austin was the epitome of a small town even if it was on the large size of that equation. But I had several days before going there so I accepted the TN's invitation to stay over two days and "look around."

Lots of small towns around middle Tennessee and this was important since number one: I don't think I could hack the big city and secondly: I wasn't sure where or if my book-writing career would be life sustaining.

The TN small towns spread out in wagon wheel fashion with Nashville as the hub, at least in middle-Tennessee. The only thing was, most didn't have one of the paper's outpost-offices so I had to do some picking as to where I would go to see the area. (That's an apt word, picking, in this Music City seemingly mostly associated with at least one guitar in any of the many, many singing and musical groups).

The idea that one of the small towns, to the south of Music City, advertised itself as "historic" caught my attention when I cross-referenced the TN's outpost list with the towns. The second advertised point for this historic small berg was just as compelling to me since I had never had any prior contact with anything to do with our Civil War, like visiting Gettysburg, and this place, named after one of our founding fathers, billed itself as the site of the bloodiest five hours of the entire war with hollowed ground that saw the Confederates turn the corner to (eventually) losing the war. It was Franklin, TN named after Ben. I couldn't wait.

Franklin was and is truly awesome. Another small town that doesn't know it's own attributes nor do the busy people (seem) to appreciate the gold around them as they bundle off the kids to school, run off to work (probably in Nashville), hurry back at the end of the day, with mowing, grocery shopping and the million and one things people have to do to crave out a living and life these days. The Franklin visitor's brochure says something like, "*Visitors will find commemorative brick sidewalks, beautifully landscaped everything, lovely, historic, and stunning Victorian architecture for the homes as well as the office and retail buildings in the commercial district located in the heart of Franklin, a fifteen block historic town just fifteen miles down the road from Nashville.*"

Brick sidewalks remind me of the awesome brick streets back in The V, ones they kept up and repaved with red brick (when necessary) even to this day. And by-god, Franklin is the home of George Jones. I used to listen to George as one of the farthest away stations I could fine on my little bedside radio back in the G. As a kid, and not minding the parental "lights out" commandment, by XX times, I would haul the little wooden encased radio under my covers with my trusty little flashlight and either a comic book or a regular book I found stashed in boxes in the cellar from my father's growing up days. It seems the biggest radio tower in the world, maybe the highest structure in the US was located in another world called The Nashville Scene and put out "real, down-home" country with the most popular singer being

George Jones. And about George, they kept introducing him as the country singer who had the most songs on the country charts, more than anyone else.

George is the man. I'll have to look for that tower – maybe I should just look up.

I walked around olé Franklin and then drove around in my rental since it was necessary. God bless the town that gave one the impression of being small, forever, but secretly along the way they must have felt that they were going to be the Los Angeles of the East some day and had annexed (or somehow gained) every piece of land as the town's as far as one could see in any direction. Once out of the 15 square block area you're immediately into rural, ranches, farms, hills, etc. but still within the city limits. Wow, now that's optimism for a "town."

My one disappointment was the Tennessean outpost-office. It was small although that I didn't go in. I just knew there wasn't much staff, etc. I guess it was almost predictable since I have been picking up current and any back issues I could find of *The Tennessean* and was mostly at a lost to find articles on Franklin. After seeing the office, I began to wonder if it was a big city newspaper's ploy to plant offices in the surrounding, progressive, growing towns that at one point could start sustaining a town paper where the possibility was undermined by the big city one already established supposedly already covering the news. I don't know about such stuff (yet) but it crossed my mind. Nor did I know if I could get a posting at that particular office or for how long?

Well I liked what I saw in The F, knowing that if I did chose it that I couldn't live with The F as my own personal naming thing. But plans are good so I wanted to go forward and also wanted to see Texas via my last scheduled job interview.

On the flight back to Ohio and The V, I decided that I really, really wanted to see Texas, all of it (or as much of what I could). I was off the paper back there and had submitted a 45 day notice on the apartment, more to give me a deadline to move on then for the landlords who had moved on (somewhere, unbeknown to me) and were working through their attorney with the very generous proviso that I had as much time as I needed to fine a new place. How many times have you heard that from a landlord? Of course I kept up with my chores around the house as part of my rent.

Anyways, I decided to drive to Austin. I had the time. That would afford me to see a lot of Texas; Dad had done it. Big mistake.

First it was the car, my rusty, trusty, olé news mobile that I had named Walter in honor of one of my favorite newspaper guys, Walter Winchell. It was nearly the exact car my grandmother, Teenie, used to drive (when alive) except for two less doors.

Please note that I started calling my car Walter right from the get-go and before Walter died this year. Some critics thought of him more as a radioman because of his popularity but I knew his column was carried in more than 700 papers.

OK, so there's another reason I call the machine Walter that I've never told anyone. When driving alone, I practice my singing in Walter, named after a guy that started out as a singer. Really. Besides, my Walter doesn't mind (the name or my singing. And maybe the real Walter, now upstairs, gets a kick out of it too).

After I got back from Nashville, I took Walter to the local U-Haul place get a hitch, knowing that it was going to take a small trailer to cart my worldly possessions to wherever I was to get a new job. I knew the guys there and told them I planned to drive to Texas as a possible new home. The bad news they gave me was that Walter wasn't going to take a hitch of any kind, old technology I guess. The worst news was that Walter's 1949 undercarriage was so rusted out that it was severely doubted that it would make it to Texas anyways. I almost cried. Walter had become one of my appendages.

What's a guy, between jobs, homes, banks, Laundromats, and small towns to do? I didn't have enough money saved to buy a new car for cash and make a move with all the required down-deposits et al. Would you sell me a new car with those (little) credentials, and leaving town?

That's OK; I had a feeling that Derrick would. You know my good friend Derrick at the auto place? OK, so he didn't know it before but he was going to become my very good friend now. I had done a little op-piece on the dealership that they liked and had run into Derrick a few times at the Alcove Lounge, you remember the place, the ones with the naked mermaids. Derrick was single (also) at the time and enjoyed talking with us newspaper junkies a few times, before he met Ethel. Now Derrick has a wife, two rug-rats, a mortgage, and hasn't been at the lounge for the last few years (even though us office fellows went there religiously - waiting for him – or something).

I could never marry a gal by the name of Ethel. Not to worry, I'm not going to say that to Derrick.

Recently I read that Texas has the most pickups per person of any state. Maybe I should take a pickup off Derrick's hands. With a gun rack over the window behind the seat. I wonder if one can drive those things with cowboy boots. Well, of course they do – all do – in Texas. I need boots.

Love the small town where everyone knows everyone, the good, the bad (and a few uglys). All right, I saw Clint's 1966 Italian epic, I think they call them Spaghetti Westerners, so that my last comment wasn't exactly original. At least I'm an honest writer. Well then, a nice guy. Oh, forget it.

Good or bad, Derrick didn't have a pickup but said that he was confident something could be worked out. I felt I had to tell him about my beloved but defective trade-in, Walter, and I knew from walking into the car dealer showroom that I wasn't going to buy a current model car with the high monthly payments. Instead of calling it sticker-shock, they could call it Spaghetti-Pricing since it too was unbelievable.

Derrick diplomatically led me out of the showroom to his used car lot. Immediately, a blue monster Buick caught my eye that wasn't as old as Walter, by one year. Derrick said, "Sorry, not hitchable." It sounded right coming out of his mouth but I decided to look up that new word when I got the chance.

Next there was a 1970 Caddy convertible that I felt would really look good in Texas. Derrick said, "No Mark, not you." I wasn't sure what he meant; the cost or maybe it wasn't cool pulling a U-Haul with all you owned behind such a good-looking car.

I settled on a respectable 1970 blue Ford sedan, definitely a news car. Over signing the papers, I decided to name it Blue Tail in honor of one of The V's most famous residents (maybe after Johnny Appleseed) Daniel Decatur Emmett, of the song *Dixie* fame. And *Blue Tail Fly* fame. Read my book.

I patted Walter goodbye even if he/it only brought me $150 trade-in, got a $55 hitch installed for the future, packed some things and gave myself two days to get to Texas. Did you realize the atlas maps of the states aren't to scale with each other, da, the same size? Now I do.

It's not like crossing the Rhode Island state line and finding yourself in Providence. Texas is huge. You can drive for ten hours once in and still not reach another Texas state border or the gulf. Not that I did it but once through Texarkana, the city at the Texas/Arkansas border, it was like going through three states just to get to Austin.

Speaking of the border crossing, one of the very first signs I saw as I entered the lone star state was, DON'T MESS WITH TEXAS. I loved it even if I didn't know if the State Troopers put that up, the State Legislature, the mayors, environmentalists, garbage association, a Texan women's association or whoever but I loved it and wondered if you could get a bumper sticker like it. State Troopers? One whizzed by in a supped up Mustang with aerials, racing tires and I'm pretty sure the guy was wearing a cowboy hat but he was so fast, gone so quickly at an awesome speed, I'm not sure. Wow, I wouldn't want to mess with them. I bet they use those cars at the drag races and/or the racetracks on the weekends. And his dark, wrap-around sunglasses added a mystery. Wizzzz – and gone! Clint – take notice.

To get into the spirit of things, I stopped at the first small town I came across and bought a pair of cowboy boots. My first as an adult. The last pair was Hopalong Cassidy ones that I received for Christmas as a juvenile, one of the best presents I ever received. Hoppy was great, he was so good that he could wear a black or (the good guy's) white cowboy hats. I'll have to think and remember his horse's name. Trigger? No, that was Roy Rogers. Now that I think of it, Roy and Hoppy were Ohio born. But you wouldn't have recognized them from their birth certificates,

Leonard and William, Sly and Boyd respectively. Leave it to a newspaper guy to discover the facts.

My boots were Justin's. And the store didn't sell spurs, maybe never did. I remember Hoppy had them. Oh well, I'm not sure I could drive the Blue Tail with spurs anyways.

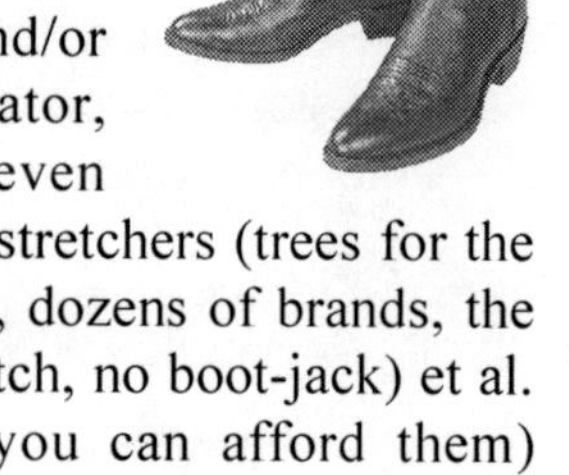

I though cowboy boots were cowboys boots that would come in brown or black. Wrong. Later I was to learn that the "last" (the foot–print) is everything and the first consideration. Then there's the different heights of the boot and/or heel, pointed toes, exotic leathers (alligator, Buffalo, eel, elephant, lizard, Ostrich, even Python), metal accessories for the toes, boot stretchers (trees for the serious) and then boot bags for the travelers, dozens of brands, the device for removing them (I think called a hitch, no boot-jack) et al. It's a science. I've also learned that (if you can afford them) Lucchese's are like leather gloves on your feet. It's pronounced Lou-Casey – just spelled in a Texas-way.

Most of all don't buy and wear any boots if you don't invest in thick, tall boot socks. My calves were chaffed by the time I got to the motel in Austin. That was from just driving. Yes, you see boots on the guys everywhere in Texas, in the offices, on the streets, in the restaurants, etc. That part is nice.

Austin a small town? Give me a break. You take Toledo (please), add the two hundred thousand more of Nashville, and you're still one hundred thousand short. I love the state of Texas and everything I hear including that Austin's on the throes of the Hill Country just to its south. That I'm anxious to see it for myself.

It was flat, very flat from Arkansas to here, Austin. And they don't have trees as we do back in Ohio. I wanted a cowboy-hated fellow that I met at a fast food place on the way in, to take my picture. He said, "Why don't you stand over near that tree?" I looked around, not meaning any offense and said, "You mean that tall bush?" After that I just knew my picture would be skewered or out of focus.

Lots of sun, awesome open skies and on the hot side, which doesn't bother me. I used to read that man was the most adaptable creature every created so as a kid I read desert books, artic books, jungle books, all the while picturing myself there "and adapting." So I was reared for the beautiful heat, or cold, or rainforest. I wonder if they wear boots all summer, these Texans?

I didn't go into the interview with enthusiasm (or boots, just chaffed calves) and maybe it showed (lack of keenness – not the calves, silly) so I got down to business explaining I really prefer small towns. They quickly responded you could cover a few of those for us – there are lots within a stone's throw. I wondered if their throws were as far as their roads.

They made me an offer anyways with twenty-four hours to look around and decide. Shucks, my calves wouldn't even be healed by then. But at their suggestion, I headed south to nearby San Marcos (just a stone's throw south but thankfully I was driving).

Immediately I liked San Marcos, small with many big old houses that reminded me of the V and the several I saw back in Franklin. It was too bad that it was cut in half by an interstate but on the positive side, it had a small quiet river running through it from an aquifer to it's north (whatever that was) that you could rent an innertube and float down. I felt I had to do it.

There's a little pub (maybe they call it a joint) on the little square in the middle of San Marcos and I was told to not miss the jam session on the weekend with someone called George Straight and his band, a local cowboy who had a great voice. But I wasn't settled in my own right and didn't want to watch someone else's career – on/in any stage of development. Oh well.

Yes, I asked about the aquifer. This is what I got: it's an

underground lake that forms the San Marcos Springs is an area of artesian outflow from the Edwards Aquifer along the Balcones Escarpment. Since I didn't know my artesian outflows from my escarpments I left it alone and went on.

There is a huge University there, alma mater of LBJ, the president even if his Pres-Library is in Austin, there were signs to that effect on the interstate coming in to Austin. And there's a little paper here, the *San Marcos Daily Record.* I felt I had nothing to lose by stopping in and checking whether they happened to be in need of a dedicated, small-town, ace-reporter. I was pretty sure at that point that I wasn't going to take the BIG CITY Austin paper's offer.

Nothing ventured, nothing…I hate clichés (and olé wives tales, and repeating the same word or words over and over and more) but I do like Texas girls in jeans (or is it girls in Texas jeans? Maybe both). No, there were no openings. Jobs. What were you thinking?

So now what? Thank heavens the Blue Tail is holding up just fine. Maybe it's time to take a float down the San Marcos River, to reconnoiter. I wonder if they allow a beer, sorry: a longneck. Maybe I should have waited to get to Dallas before buying my boots, hears' tell (local language) that they hand ya'll a longneck first off when you enter a boot store, before you even look at their wares.

No, I didn't bring a bathing suit nor was I, the possibly, unhappy, unemployed dynamite news guy, want-to-be international book writer, going to buy one. Maybe they had geese that bit your toes hanging over the innertube on the river anyways. And if it's spring feed, it probably is cold?

Wait, I saw a little paper in Franklin, Tennessee, *The Franklin Chronicle*, when I passed through. What do I have to loose. What do they have to loose? Maybe they know they need a dynamite newspaper guy to buck the big city newspaper threat. What's that area code and information number?

I reached the managing director directly back in Franklin. OK, so I said to the receptionist that this was a special call from Texas. After a brief intro and background brief, I heard the following singing tones in my ear – pure music, "When can you start?" Awestruck even for a seasoned news guy who has covered virtually every beat – well, small town ones, I said, "Shouldn't we talk salary first?"

Response: "What do you want?" So I told him wondering immediately if I was blowing it, a little on the high side, but wow, he accepted and I was on my way back to Tennessee via packing a U-Haul in Ohio. Damn, I forgot to ask if I was going to be able to put my feet up on the desk. On the other hand, they, he, sounded like a real news guy so I know it'll be OK.

Was he that astute? Sight unseen? Were they desperate? Could I have gotten more? Did someone just die there? Was that just a reporter answering, having fun when the director was off to cover a 4-Alarm fire? Well, I'm going back to Ohio anyways and hopefully the confirmation fax will be waiting.

Not to keep you in suspense, it was, and signed. No phony-baloney. Now I had a new dilemma, what to call my new home. I didn't like The F or Fran or Frank or even The Franklin. OK, I quickly settled on The Ben.

Life is good. Did I mention that The Ben has trolleys? Really! Awesome little town.

No, I didn't forget to call, turn down, but thank - Austin before I checked out of the motel the next morning and hit the road back to Ohio. But that call was confusing. I didn't infer anything but honesty - the Austin chap, when I told him I was taking an offer in Franklin, said, "The State?"

"No, Tennessee," I replied not knowing quite what to make of his comment. Had he been drinking a morning longneck? To which he casually said, "Well good luck, watch what you volunteer for and watch out for the Melungeons" and hung up. What? Texas talk? Texas-newspaper talk? Bats in the belfry?
Now I was in a quandary. He was a smart man to have reached his post especially in a big city, a big big city capital (of the state). I just know he wasn't being flippant or bitter. So – what was that all about?

All the way back to Ohio I kept going over and over in my mind: his words. As a trained newspaperman I was pretty confident of what he said versus what I remembered. But say-what? I was already missing the access to the archives I used to have back at my old job and/or the accumulative knowledge that filled the office especially from my old editor, Fred.

Wait, I get it – at least in part. Tennessee is known as the Volunteer State. Yes. Well, one out of three ain't bad – is it? OK, so I got that information at the state line as I was driving back. Their Tennessee welcome sign said, "The Volunteer State." What a book – no secrets.

Oh, sorry about the bats thing. Remember, as a clue, that I lived in The G that happened to have a state mental institution (better wording than insane asylum) at the north edge of town. Well, the Latin adjective *sanus* means healthy and the phrase "*mens sana in corpore sano*" means a healthy mind in a healthy body with the opposite "bats in one's belfry."

Sorry number two: I took Latin in high school and (finally) had to use it – the first time since school – anywhere – I think. Well what's a Catholic guy to do? I had to learn a smattering to be an altar boy but now they're doing away with it and saying mass in English. Did away with the fish on Friday thing, much to the chagrin of the fish markets. I guess I don't like any changes to the religion I was born into – it was the one thing that was suppose to remain (always) the same! Wasn't it?

Sotto voce is my favorite. The Latin thing. In a soft voice – translation. I should put it in gray and smaller type. I know, onward.

PS, my friend Kurt wrote *Slaughterhouse Five* (1969) to close out the 60's. It was one of the few good things that closed them out – my opinion. Awesome book. Now I'll have to read all of his works.

When I was young I has'd wait
On Massa sir an hand him de plate;
Pass down de bottle when he git dry,
And bresh away de blue tail fly.
- Daniel Decatur Emmett

Beware the Melungeons

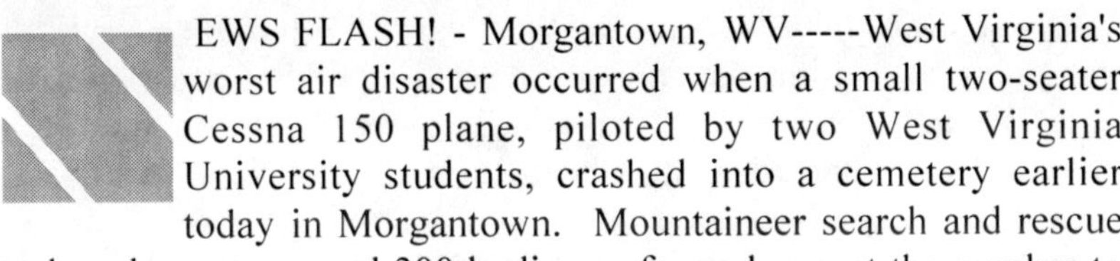

NEWS FLASH! - Morgantown, WV-----West Virginia's worst air disaster occurred when a small two-seater Cessna 150 plane, piloted by two West Virginia University students, crashed into a cemetery earlier today in Morgantown. Mountaineer search and rescue workers have recovered 300 bodies so far and expect the number to climb as digging continues into the evening. The pilot and copilot survived and are helping in the recovery efforts.

We have West Virginia jokes here in Tennessee kind of like the Newfies-New Foundland jokes in Ontario, Canada. Did you hear about the war between Newfoundland and Nova Scotia? The Newfies were lobbing hand grenades and the Nova Scotians were pulling the pins and throwing them back.

Nova Scotia is an awesome place that no one seems to visit. I think it's a wife turnoff since the province is shaped like male genitalia. This is the Newfies getting even.

"One day a Newfie goes down to the village carpenter and requests a wooden crate that is 1 inch tall, 1 inch wide and 50 feet long." When the carpenter asks what he needs it for, the Newfie replies "The wife snapped her clothesline the other day, and I have to send it to Toronto to get it fixed."

"One day a West Virginian goes down to the village carpenter and requests a wooden crate that is 1 inch tall, 1 inch wide and 50 feet long." When the carpenter asks what he needs it for, the Ridge Runner replies "The wife snapped her clothesline the other day, and I have to send it to Nashville to get it fixed."

See, it works, unfortunately there are three such containers in the USPS Nashville-Lost and Found but I doubt if Toronto has received any. Such is life.

My writing, the books, may have been due to my zealous reading, most of my life. Thinking about it now, maybe it started with comic books. I could lose myself on the pages, forgetting everything, imagining me within the story or at least most. Superman was my favorite and I had the number 1 and number 2 issues, long gone much to my embarrassment, valuable now. I guess the movies might be a little responsible too. Books and movies took me outside myself, completely/totally removed, from my little world, expanding it by leaps and bounds. I think the later was a Superman thing.

I didn't just read, I jumped into the pages and unto the brilliantly lit screen (especially easy from a dark theater) and lived in the new world I found. So maybe small towns are my new world, one that I can put my arms around, concentrate on, live anew and all the while knowing that the myriad of fascinating stories contained therein will never all be uncovered.

Phony-Baloney? Where did that come from - back there a ways? OK, probably the fifties and sixties. We had a lot of them. "Being in the family way." Curb feelers and steering knobs. "Wall to Wall." Percolator and (steam) Pressure Cookers (in the kitchen with Dina…err mom), "Rat Fink," Spectravision and Electolux (in the living room), Dynaflow, fender skirts, and Continental Kits (on the cars in the garage), Holy Ghost and confessions (in the church), and don't forget, everyone and everything is just 'Cool" (in the fifties) and "Super" (in the sixties). Of course for someone else in the same time, just in a different place, the words and/or meanings might be different. Life is like that.

Actually that old song, *Someone's in the kitchen...* should read Dinah (not Dina) I think. Dinah was a generic name for an African-American slave woman. Past life, not mine.

Anxious to learn about my second (possible) career, I kept calling my publisher regarding my books that I have written, Maybe he was reading from a script on his desk but the standard reply went something like this, "Cool your heels, Mark. These things take time." Maybe he's from the sixties too.

Are you going to the State (of Franklin)? Beware The Melungeons? I packed up the small trailer with the unexpected overflow of my stuff going into the Blue Tail. I said a few more goodbyes, made a TN motel reservation, and headed south to my new home, somewhere in "the historic" Franklin, The Ben.

The Ben is not nearly as far as Texas, by half and I arrived early afternoon. Before I get to the motel and I couldn't find one of those or a hotel in the "historic" 15 blocks, I note the numerous little black signposts in the yards of many houses. I guess they're serious about the "Historic" thing. Finally my curiosity got the best of me and I pulled over to see what these little signs were about and that wasn't necessarily easy with a U-Haul behind the Blue Tail, even as small as it was. The little signposts identify the house owners of 100 or 150 years (or more) ago. Wow, how quaint. I never saw that before and can't even remember the previous, cranky old maid owner of the 515 that my parents bought back in the G when it was a B & B. These signed-places in the Ben had to have outhouses back then. Didn't they?

I quickly settle into the motel room, use up another parking space for the U-Haul so the Blue Fly is free to wander the city since it's imperative that I find a place ASAP (to avoid overages on the rental vehicle). My first stop will be the Post Office at what the locals call 5 Points, the second center of historic Franklin with Mr. White, the forty three feet and eight inches high Vermont granite and confederate carved marble soldier statue a few blocks to the north. I wondered how high Mr. Brown had/is back in the V all the while being amused at them carving a confederate anything with the northern, Vermont marble. I think Vermont and marble are in my heritage, I vaguely remember someone saying. I'll have to look it up some day.

I park behind the PO at 5 Points only to see, hidden in the back, the Heritage Foundation of Franklin & Williamson County. Well I at least see their door all the while wondering why they aren't boldly out front, on the main drag or somewhere very apparent to visitors, etc. As a reporter I chalk that question up in the back of my mind to pursue at another time. Maybe there's a scandal or something there for an otherwise proud town.

It is already apparent to me that my new Ben didn't have such a thing as the two-hundred sixty nine stirring words that were delivered at Gettysburg only to immortalize the area. But Franklin's claim to being the bloodiest five-hour battle of the Civil War, with the biggest loses and the resultant devastation of the key Confederate Army, the Army of Tennessee, that started the beginning of the end – just ain't touted enough or this whole place would be bigger, more important than Gettys and overrun by those who have to be in historic spots for themselves. Two small signs on the way into town and a small write-up in a brochure or two if you search for it doesn't bring the crowds. Maybe there's a compelling reason. Another reporter question sewn away.

Yes the PO for an immediate change-of-address, not that I get that much mail and have all the bills current. Since I'm here, waiting in the expected, necessary USPS customer line (it's indigenous), I figure I have nothing to loose by asking if they happen to know any nearby rentals for an ace reporter (to be). If I could just nail this apartment/rental thing over the weekend, before starting my new job on Monday, I would be saving some and would feel somewhat established.

Mentioning Mr. Soldier White (statue), it's funny - the turns in life, especially since I just left a similar but opposite, Private Brown, the "Federal, blue, Union Army's" counterpart left standing in the middle of The V back in Ohio. Interestingly, Private Brown was facing south whereas Private White is facing East, I'm pretty sure. But no problem, I have my trusty camera with me so I'll take a picture. Are there west and north facing soldiers in other towns?

It was within the first year of my journalism career back in the V when I learned it was smart as a reporter 24/7 to have your own camera with you at all times (and not to depend on the papers' photographers since there weren't enough in a crisis, available without a time delay especially at nights and weekends). Then there was my "big chance" back at that job when I happened to be the only one at work one night when a police dispatch came over the radio regarding a murdered girl. Murders were/are unusual for small towns, at least the V. It was Linda Marie K...(something). She was a very young, once pretty, and a go-go dancer. I was one of the first on the scene and carrying my trusty camera complete with a flash attachment. Of course taking her face-up-nude body pictures wasn't an option even if it might not have been appropriate (or used by the paper) since I had forgot those funny little blue-dot flash bulbs for night photography anyway. So much for being an "ace."

After waiting for three others, in my postal-line, I walk up saying, "Hi, I'm just moving into town and I'll need a change of address form to send back to Ohio."

"There's moving-packets on the counter behind you near the door. Anything else?" At least he didn't say, "Next! Or you passed them dummy! Or aren't ace reporters suppose to be more observant?"

Now I know I'm going to ask the "something else" (to get something for my waiting-time). "Yes as a matter of fact, you don't happen to know any apartments for rent nearby?"

"Dorothy!" he yelled over his shoulder. I didn't know if Dorothy was a bouncer, the Post Mistress, or one of those small-town-very-informed persons that happened to work at the PO. I braced myself and went back over everything I had said, reviewing my facial expressions and inflections just in case. He didn't talk "southern," didn't have a "draw-er," so I was pretty sure he understood.

Thank God I asked. Dorothy, a slight, older woman that one couldn't imaging throwing mail bags into the truck out back, appeared at the corner. He repeated my question to Dorothy and she said, "Yes, Harry's just down the street. He just put a for-rent sign in his store window yesterday. Finally."

"Great! That would be...down which street?" I enquired in the middle of their 5 Points. Wondering what her "Finally" meant (before the building fell down? Was Harry dying? What?).

"Right here, on the Columbia Pike. Harry has the little sundry, general store on the west side of the street, only a block or two at most," said Dorothy.

"She means south on Columbia Avenue right out front so you can't miss it," my just-as-old to Dorothy, senior clerk added when Dorothy had promptly returned to whatever she was doing "back-there." I appreciated the clarification since any town's 5-point-corners place could be confusing to an outsider. Like me. Ace or novice.

If it hadn't been for the additional four waiting in line behind me, I would have gone for the doctor and dentist referrals but I figured my new landlord, Harry, might help. How's that for optimism.

No, I didn't ask for a street number since "the sign in the window" would probably be sufficient for me to identify Harry's place. The general store genre was another give away. I'll find it.

It worked, happy Harry, who had conducted business at 708 Columbia Ave. since his father died years ago, used to live upstairs with his ailing wife until she passed away two years ago. She wouldn't leave and Harry used to have to find doctors who made house calls, upstairs until her demise I was to learn. It took him awhile to leave "their" place but he had, getting the place cleaned and with a little remodeling such as new appliances. That was probably what PO Dorothy was "finally" referring to.

Harry's wife didn't want to part with the appliances and furniture that she was familiar with but they had greatly aged over time and with her illness. I was ecstatic that the place was furnished at all since I had forgotten to put that into my PO question.

The one thing Harry obviously didn't replace that appeared in his tour and that I liked immediately,

was the four footed old bathtub. He had, sometime ago, installed a shower curtain gadget for his preference, but I could just see myself luxuriating in the tub like the ones one occasionally sees in the movies. I can hear your mind, NO, not David's Death of Marat, thank you very much.

I just knew it was going to be a place of inspiration, a place I could knock out novel after novel, column after column. I would have to think syndication. But I will need candles and a tub-side table for my inspirational and liquor, Port. Or should I choose Sherry for inspiration. Maybe a phone was going to have to be installed nearby to conduct the necessary business of a successful writer and newspaper person. The walls look well insulated; I could probably practice my singing. Look out Walter Winchell, I might be the first Syndicated Columnist Novelist Country Singer that Tennessee has ever seen. Should I call it my throne? No, if I ever referred to it as The Throne Room, I know that the thinking would jump to (the commode) and they would miss the point. I knew I had to think of a naming – it's in my genes. Maybe I could sell tours – after I became famous. "This is where it all happened…" That's just clean-fun-thinking.

"Excuse me," Harry, having moved on and returning, was saying at the doorway, maybe having had to come back to wake me from my imagination for the second or third time. Harry was a great, nice guy and I had taken to him immediately. I knew he was much older but couldn't guess his age. It didn't help that he didn't have his share of gray or white hair for his age. I was sorry he lost his wife. And now that I think about him, he reminded me of the real Ben Franklin, at least pictured by the artist Duplessis. He just needed a bigger belly and those octagon shaped, wire rimmed glasses that I think they use to call spectacles in the old days. Didn't Ben invent them? Well, a higher hairline, longer hair, and maybe a few inches shorter but I'm not sure about the height-thing so Harry qualified.

Oops, I stand mistaken; it's a new tub he had installed in honor of his late wife who had an old, similar one. Harry said, picking up on my obvious interest, "Tis a new, sixty-six inch, vintage clawfoot tub kind of' like her old one or at lease the closest I could find except hers didn't have the silver feet."

"Very nice," was my reply as I was testing the naming of "Clawfoot Room" in my mind – and we moved on to the kitchen. I already knew I would take the place if the price were right. I also knew that it might be best to forget about his departed wife. I was hoping Harry wouldn't mention her name let alone her illness. No, I don't believe in ghosts except maybe one. And except the old church Holy Ghost and yes, they changed that too. Now we're supposed to call "Him" the Holy Spirit. I wonder if He knows. Do you think all those old prayers to Him went to the wrong address? Or the new ones get lost in the God's Dead Letter depot?

"Lance Jefferies, Editor in Chief," was my answer to his enquiry about my new job and possible references. "Oh, I've know Lance for years. He's a Mason too. Good stock. That's fine. How long do you want it?" was Harry's response.

Harry's quaint and very small neighborhood store was 708 and my entrance (did you hear MY entrance) was to the south side of his store and toward the back with separate stairs leading to the apartment. MY place was designated 710 and that was really much nicer than a 708a or 708-rear. When I answered his question about how long, I said, "Indefinitely but at least a year." All the while I was really thinking that the apartment might outlive his store or even Harry since I had researched an article back in the V on the life expectancy of a spouse after the other one dies, even if it never got to press. Guess – yes, it isn't very long before the "averages" take the other mate.

Guess what. No contract. Just a handshake. Just like in the western movies or Japan. Just like my arrangements back in the V, minus the handshake – not the style of "the girls," my previous landlords, which Harry never asked about come to think of it.

I guess my new Boss Lance was a good enough reference. Plus it was a small town so my new landlord was probably right - he thought that he would always know where to find me.

Mentally I thought about going back to the PO to thank them but remembering the lines, I decided to get the U-Haul turned in and settle myself with the rest of the weekend to tour my Ben. Or maybe lounge in my new tub, start a new novel, maybe buy candles, no – the Port would be first, they do drink in TN don't they? God, I hope this isn't a blue-law state. God, I hope that the hot water reaches the second floor.

Library or drive around? Decisions, decisions. Well, first I better check out of the motel, get the U-Haul over to here, unpack it, turn it in and then I'm free. And that "free" had a nice ring to it.

So I was overly optimistic getting to the free part. The rest (and especially climbing the stairs umpteen times) wore me out. I didn't even get to turn in the U-Haul since it became too late. Too much stuff as little as it was. I was so tired, I didn't make the bed, decided to sleep on top of the covers, which I did well.

So much for my first time in my thinking tub – it'll have to wait until tomorrow night since lounging there in the morning (with or without candles) was not conducive to accomplishing anything else for the day. I'll shower. Then take the U-Haul back and then be free to discover my Ben.

First morning impressions were that I was probably not going to need an alarm but that I was going to need earplugs. It's still dark but nobody told the numerous chirping birds that they shouldn't start singing until daylight. Hello! I like (love) nature but do they have to be so enthusiastic about starting their day so early? In the dark? I was sure that my Nana, my most favorite person/grandmother, used to keep her canaries covered until she got up because, "They won't start their day until I remove the cover and let the light in." Guess there must be a difference between a domestic and birds in the wild.

Gee, as a kid growing up in the G, I used to keep my window open at night just to catch the caw of the crows on the nearby hill behind the 515 in the mornings. I cherished those times. So, what's this? Am I aging? Well, just thinking about it has me awake. I might as well try the shower tub. Did I pack soap? Maybe shampoo will have to do – all over.

Showers are wonderful. I equate them to the old Superman phone booths where a complete transformation takes place. Someday I'll have to look for a phone booth shower curtain for myself.

Breakfast is usually next. Yea, I known, put grocery shopping on the "TO DO" list for today. Meanwhile I guess I'll see if there's a mom and pop's diner close by, within walking distance. I already spotted a laundromat just around the corner and that's good, very good. I'm pretty sure the huge brick building across the street from the PO, on the 5 Points and within easy walking distance, is a/the library – something necessary for a guy in my profession (as well as a guy that has more than his share of curiosity). That's good too. Life is good. "Hello Ben!"

As a new outsider, especially one having come from "the Union" (Ohio) I know I'm going to have to look into the difference of why the V had a blue suited statue and the Ben has a gray. I know the obvious part but that was over a hundred years ago. Do the feelings and sentiments change? Is that statue-difference an indication of indigenous or a deep-seated cultural separation? Don't people move on? Maybe it's just a case of spending monies not available for statue upgrades (for both towns), something not unusual in small towns civic improvement projects.

This subject/answer, seems to me, to be critical for interaction with a new job, new friends, new neighbors, writing for the paper, etc. That's right, how and why did this guy hire me without the first interview and without seeing my resume first? I'm happy and appreciative that he did, that this is all happening, but what the heck is going on? I've never heard of that happening to anyone else I have ever known.

Breakfast was not a problem, lots of choices just up the street with a morning constitution built in. Who said that? Was it Nana? Dad? Maybe Pops, my grandfather on my mother's side. Anyways, it's one's morning walk, the constitution, but sounds like something left over from New England or "the old country" not that any of the family has ever been there (except Pops, born in the olé Prussia before coming here).

Yes, that's another thing I have to do – send mom the new address, which is as good as telling all the family members. Not that communication is the best within the family, except a rumor and that spreads faster then wild fire. If it weren't for regular rumors, occasional weddings and the unexpected deaths – families wouldn't end up so close any more. Plus families aren't as big as they were. Nana used to tell me about the 8, 9, 10, 12 and even the 14 children-families within our relatively recent family history. Of course I don't seem to be perpetuating anything – at least in the immediate future.

Well, thanks to my bird friends that I can't hear or see even one now, it's early, too early for the library to be open so I guess it's time to drive around a little – and check my gas level, which I regularly forget to do. Time to rev up the Blue Tail and show her the new digs.

Did I just call her a "her?" I swear I think of her as a "him." Maybe it's just our American custom to calling ships et al a "her." Let me think; I did an article on the commissioning of the *John F. Kennedy* launched back in May of '67, the thousand foot, 30 knot, 75,000 ton

CVA-67 Kitty Hawk class aircraft carrier...But I can't remember if they called it a her or not. I can remember those figures and the CVA-67 thing (not remembering what that designation stands for) but can't remember if it's a him-ship? Go figure!

As least I remember that there is such a dictionary. Really – the *Dictionary of American Naval Fighting Ships.* I remember because I've been meaning to look up what Nana told me about one of our family members being a privateer, commanding the *Morning Star* during or about the time of the American Revolution. It's in my "TO DO" file.

First impressions? I'll mention two for now. Like my first impression for the V, I can't believe the number of churches all around. At 5 Points I counted not less that four and the phone book at the diner listed dozens, many more than the old V. Secondly, it definitely is a small town with most of the lawyers, dentists and doctor's offices in (former) homes. Of course this is not to exclude the antique places, interior decorators, dress boutiques, and you name it including piano sales and recording studios in former homes. If it weren't for the shingles out front, you'd mistake them all for residential homes. Did you catch the free parking? I love that. This is definitely my kind of place.

Hills? I said that I had been traveling around the pretty hills of Franklin this morning, in innocent conversation at the library, specifically at the Reference Desk. "NO," I was emphatically corrected and faster than I put this morning's earlier steaming coffee cup to my lips for my Java-spike at

the local diner downtown. Franklin and vicinity just has knobs (little hills thank you very much) she said.

I've heard of mounts, knolls, prominences, rises, tors, moors (England), knaps, kops (Africa), hillocks, buttes (Western US), foothills but knobs? Don't knobs happen on trees, drawers, doors, and appliances? So we don't have the Texas Hill Country, we have the Tennessee Knob Country nearby. I've heard of a knobstick weapon? I'm not proud of it but growing up the guys used to describe the just-flowering females with, "Yep, she's starting to get her knobs." That conjured up all kinds of images.

I was about to ask if one capitalized the K, partly in jest, when I was offered, "That the most famous in Franklin is Roper's Knob and it has the distinction of being one of the 71 registered Historical Sites in Franklin." Now that's something when in comes to your knobs. Trust me, I didn't say. Nor did I ask where and what for it was so registered but silently added this to my SHOULD DO mental file. Mentally I made the leap that their "bluffs" were just little knobs but didn't ask.

"Have you seen the Natchez Trace?" she, the ref-lib added. Her name is Dorris with two "R's." Now I think my out-of-state ignorance is being put to the test. "No, where's that," I returned (in place of "What the hell is that? Is that some southern-word/talk?").

"It's just to the west of Franklin. Go out the new 96 West and you can't miss it," was her response. Fortunately I didn't detect any condescending anything so I felt a little better.

I wasn't about to go on any wild goose chases except a brochure with the title TRACE on the shelf behind caught my eye. It featured the most awesome bridge I had ever seen. I decided when she wasn't looking to reach for it or check out the online catalogue. Meanwhile: hills called knobs and bridges called traces; knobs and traces, traces and knobs – what a place. Lots to learn I guess.

The sixteen hundred foot (plus) bridge rising about 150 feet above the highway is art, or at least one of the prettiest art forms I have seen. It was the first segmental concrete arch structure built in North America. I guess they strung a cable across the ravine and threaded the 50-ton segments, pushing them together. Some cable! And it wasn't just any concrete that made those segments, it was their/my Williamson County concrete. So there! Now I wonder if it connected two knobs or just bluffs?

If you're stupid enough to say, "I'm interested in the Civil War," to a reference librarian in Franklin, without being more specific, back off and wait for the forthcoming deluge. Trust me, you may have thought that Noah had a problem but you'll also going to need an ark. Their life is information and they must think that if they do a bang up job, they're successful. I call it overload. And that's what I got.

In my defense, I didn't want to say, "I'm wondering first, why on earth there was such a Confederate sympathy in Tennessee before and during the Civil War for a state so close to the north and secondly, I was wondering if these prejudices are still held by the populace here." Think about it, one would rather have a deluge to sift through, doing one's own research rather than being hung on Private White's granite phallic obelisk monument in the square.

That's another question; do they call that driving circle "the town square" like they do in New England for all their town-centers? Or is that centres up there? Questions and questions.

I was given two tables; normally for four people each considering the surrounding chairs, and both were piled high with Civil War stuff – all within twenty minutes (and the help of three reference volunteers). One table was devoted to THE BATTLE OF

FRANKLIN, which I learned in the process was actually, and technically, the Second battle of Franklin. And included references on local writers, the Carter House, the Carnton Plantation, the (killed at almost his own doorstep) young, confederate, Tod Carter, and what was reputed to be the largest (and local) independent Confederate Cemetery called/or having something to do with John McGavock's land plus a lot more including maps, books, and atlases of maps. The subject could be a college course – and maybe is.

Captain Theodoric (Tod) Carter C.S.A.

The other table, also piled high, was about the Civil War in general. I figured if they locked me in bringing in the occasional ration of salt pork and hard bread with the occasional beans, the standard for the CW soldiers (with the proviso that a soldier "with common sense" would shave off the excess salt and use it with other foods if one was so lucky to raid/find/get them; so that most soldiers had a good hoard of the stuff – until crossing rivers or a good rain) that I could comfortably finish all these materials in a short sixteen to eighteen months not taking notes of course because that would take extra time.

Actually, on the very top of the second table was this small (less than 50 pages and illustrated), 4 X 9 inches brochure/booklet called *A Path Divided* that virtually answered all my (immediate) questions. I read it in less than fifteen minutes being slightly distracted at the good answers all the while trying to figure out how to gracefully exit this place, preferable un-observed when I was done reading it.

During the 1861 to 1865 conflict, about 3,000 engagements were fought in Tennessee during which over 600,000 souls lost their life. TN, obviously in the middle of the N and S, and home of (already) two presidents, was the second most populous state in the South. It had been accumulating slaves, and the dependency on slave-labor, up until that time at a compounding rate and slaves were now about a quarter of the population. TN was also a key farm commodities and manufacturing state with many resources making it attractive to both North and South with trading ties to both. The principal north and south as well as east and west railroads ran through this state as well as the key rivers, the Mississippi, Tennessee, and Cumberland. When the big-decision time came, TN was the last to secede (and the first to re-join after the war). Obvious internal allegiances that resulted in conflicts even within families existed throughout.

TN furnished more soldiers for the Confederacy than any other state except Virginia and furnished more men for the Union than all the other (Southern) states combined. Once the conflict started, TN was a virtual war-zone without the benefit of any law (except martial law dictated by the occupying army, which ever one was in place, and/or "the law of the local brutes"). Not a happy place.

From this and before taking a personal survey of all my new neighbors, which I never intent to do, I think I understand. After all, a lot of us lean toward the underdog. I was a Brooklyn Dodgers fan for all the time they were (still) in Brooklyn, since 1883. Because? Because, and simple answer, they were never as good as the Yankees (still aren't; California wasn't the "it" they needed to get there and they've been out there since 1957).

So TN was in between, raped and pillaged, tramped on, spat on, run over, and virtually devastated with it's confederate sons trying time after time to win back their home. And they almost did a couple of times during the fracas including an almost brilliant romp over the Union/Federal forces just south of here on the Columbia Pike. Hey, that's my new address, err Columbia Avenue.

I just knew I was going to spend some time on this CW thing but not now. Blue Tail is waiting or my feet are aching to walk the downtown. So how do I get out of here? Maybe raise my hand to go potty? By the way, Franklin was only four-square blocks at the time of The Battle. Virtually every corner of it and miles around were in that one. Damn, I'm sleeping on sacred ground that was run over and run over by both armies just at different times. Wow.

Maybe the Dodgers never got over their earlier naming. You don't know? Well don't depend upon them telling you. It was all forgotten with the move but they were the Brooklyn Bridegrooms for several years, then the Brooklyn Grooms, Brooklyn Superbas (whatever that brings to mind, OK so add an "r"), the Robins, Grays, and then there was their first name, the Atlantics (can you believe that?). If you know Brooklyn (the borough without any trees) you just don't give them any guff or fodder for funnies – they'll drive it into the ground (with you with it). If the truth were known, Texas probably got their bumper stickers, Don't Mess…from the Blue and Gold Brookski (that's Dutch, not Polish). Oh yea, I have to go to the bathroom. Bye.

Walking and riving around a little more I have come to one conclusion (verifiable later) that there is only ten inches to one-foot of topsoil anyplace you are in these parts. Really but especially noticeable when you drive around the outskirts (while still in the extended town limits) where they had to carve out the roads. There's only about a foot of topsoil on top of solid limestone (or is it shale – no that's softer. Remember I never took the mineral badge tests in the six months I was a Boy Scout. But I think I'm right).

Another similarity to the olé V is that there are a few homes that have candles in the windows. Far less then back in Ohio but another common element to make me feel right at home.

I had just mentioned the many businesses in former residences here in the Ben. Walking around, I found a very interesting one that I've never encountered before, its Shuff's Music and Piano Showroom on 3rd Avenue North. I now know that I shouldn't take these walks without a camera.

There are lots of professionals including lawyers in former homes here with the added benefit that these establishments are being kept up very well. As I think I said, there were a few of these in the old V but they seem to proliferate here.

The most striking coincidence to my previous small town was the exotic named mansion on South Margin Street and Lewisburg Avenue (Pike) just a few blocks east of downtown that I discovered on one of my many "constitutionals" or walkabouts as the Aussie's refer to them and that I call my Benabouts. Hey, us writer-types can borrow anything. Can't we? Isn't that what they call literary license?

Maybe I should get one of the many specialty car license plates they have here in this state; one that would say, "Ben Writer." Sounds western too. I imagine "Ben Writer Ya'll" would be too long.

The little black yard sign for this mansion said, "Abbey Leix Mansion, formerly the Winstead Place, 1868" and there are acres to this well manicured estate right here in the middle of town. Wait a minute, 1868 was right after the Civil War and I know there were hardly, if any, building materials around let alone the stuff to make such an impressive place as this. And doesn't the term, "Abbey" have to do with monks et al? Damn, I just knew I wasn't going to be able to let this drop, which meant there was going to be a lot of research in my future. OK, with maybe the benefit of an article or two.

Looking at the main house, the Abbey I guess, it was clearly of the High Victorian Italianate or the Italianate Revival style and I know this from my last small town, The V. Really. It was different but clearly like the twenty-three-room, specially build home for my previous landlords when they were much younger (and before my time).

Their V Villa, without the benefit of any name that I know about, was specially build and was for their private residence – that is for my two sisters, French dancing landlords whose life sized erotic portraits still hang on other side of the stage in the (to be restored) Woodward Opera House on Main Street. The Villa on the V's only small hill north of downtown faced McKenzie Street.

As the story goes and as the villa was being build, the town reeled at the prospects that they might all benefit from the rich Italian gentry-suitors of these two hometown gals, the two Italian brothers (and entourages) whom the girls had lured back from the Continent on their summer visits to The V. Wedding prospects filled the air at the time but weren't meant to be. And no, I never asked them about any of this and no, they never lived there nor did I. My place was like their pseudo-servants quarters upstairs in the rear of another old house they owned on High Street in The V.

So how did I learn about that? Haven't you been paying attention to the benefits of a small town?

I almost missed the sign – Da – the sign next to the soldier-stack-wall entry starting the cobblestone drive-up, with the accompanying flagstone walkways, leading up to the mansion entrance with the nearby pergola-ed patio covered with native cross vines. I caught all that and almost missed the sign.

The Franklin Abbey Leix Mansion is the home of the O'More College of Design, an accredited college. I mean it – right here in Le Mansion (and other buildings here). To add insult, I missed that it's registered in the National Register of Historic Places. I caught the Magnolia trees with their genus dating back twenty million years and it being the state flower of nearby Mississippi, the Buxaceae boxwoods, the slow growing rounded and leathery leaved evergreen shrubs, the Hydrangeas, native to southern Asia with colorful flower-heads at the ends of the stems and even the evenly spaced Hellebones, the herbaceous perennial flowers especially known in the Balkans, and the simple but finely toothed deep sea green

Hollies with their very small vibrant red berries. But I missed the sign. Some Ace! Did I mention the many Evergreen and scale-like Thuja, commonly referred to as arborvitae? Yea - the sign. So what's the opposite of Ace?

The O'More College grounds with its courtyards and sensory gardens designed to provide a stimulating journey through the senses and created to be accessible and enjoyable by visitors are generously open to the public. One is encouraged to view our panoramic and historic Ben from the west side of their spacious eight acres, to wander through the white Annabelle Hydrangeas, to enjoy the blood red roses, and even to bring a lunch in order to picnic under the canopy of Magnolia trees. This was not the atmosphere of learning for my brick and mortar alma mater - trust me.

Talk about luscious gardens, there's one hall I'm anxious to visit, called Hieronymus Hall. For now I assume it was named after the heretical painter Hieronymus Bosch, this fifteenth-sixteenth century painter who turned the art world on its head with his evocative, iconographic works like his *Garden of Earthly Delights*. I loved this idea, shaking people out of the doldrums of sameness. He made critics wild. Do you think they have some of his works on display? That would be awesome.

Of course it might be named for St. Hieronymus or Hieronymus Peabody. Yes, I'm Catholic but know nothing about St. H other than I've heard the name. And yes, I made up the Peabody thing. Sorry.

Abbey Leix Mansion in Ireland

Of all the house collections I've seen, I can't leave this one alone. The Ben's library helped shed some light that the Mansion Abbey Leix was founded by Conogher O'More in 1183. It's real in County Laois, Ireland and exists today.

Also, an unusual character, at least for a small town, Mrs. Eloise Pitts O'More founded the college just in 1970 with a starting two or three-dozen students. She was born in 1907 in Fayetteville and wanted to become an architect from early age even knowing that only men were allowed into those ranks. Not to be deterred, she went to Paris and attended Le College Feminin, an interior design college, studying ballet on the side. Eloise married Colonel O'More, an Irish military man in the 40's, moving to the Ben in the 60's. The idea of establishing a similar design school in America as she attended in France never left her and she did just that with the O'More School of Design started in her own home. We're just lucky that she did it here. Maybe there should be an Art Appreciation course or two in my future.

No, I didn't leave the "NO MATERIALS AVAILABLE" thing alone and by following through I learned the involvement of the Winstead name. Le Mansion (and I think I got the Le vs. La right) was started in 1866 immediately after the war by William O'Neal Perkins. Enterprising Mr. P purchased a structure on our town square, dismantled the same, and had the bricks, doors, windows, etc. carted to South Margin Street to form the materials necessary to build Le Mansion on top of an existing basement, a basement that had been used as a morgue during the Battle of Franklin. It was probably the first residential constructions in Middle Tennessee after the CW. In 1887 the mansion was sold to William Winstead.

And for those astute readers with the question, "How does this William tie into our infamous Winstead Hill south of town, which served as the Confederate General Hood's headquarters during the Battle?" be assured, I'm still working on it. Do you think there are ghost stories – at least in the basement?

If you do visit our Le Mansion, don't miss the many panoramic murals detailing the palaces, monuments and scenes of the earlier Paris landscape painted by the prolific Eloise. She also painted many other murals in Nashville and the Ben that are still in evidence today.

Talking about similarities, my only other small town, the G, had beautiful big houses up on Maltbie Heights that I would have called mansions or estates at that time, the 50's, but they pale by comparison to what I have seen since and especially here. Funny - how life seems to evolve.

Walking back home on this very pleasant day, I pass by a gorgeous and grand, white, Victorian house in blue trim just off the square with a wee little sign in the high arched doorway that I have to stop to read and almost miss. It reads, Lillie Belle's and having just reminisced about exotic dancers, I'm not going to tell you what came to mine because I would have been way off base.

It's a Tea Room and light lunch place, maybe more. I guess that means High Tea and I guess it's the same place I've seen valet parking out in front when I have passed by a time or two. As it turns out, the name was to honor a farmer's wife that bore and raised nine children, just in another county. And you can get Brie en Croute with Warm Blackberry Preserves as well as Tennessee Pot Stickers and with Lemon Curd Tartlet for desert if you like. Now this is a first. Maybe we should change the name to Classy Ben instead of Historic. OK, Classy Historic Franklin. How about: Cosmopolitan Classy…Oh never mind, I'm not running for anything.

7:55 AM Monday morning sharp I walked through the door of my new job at the *Franklin Chronicle*. The building wasn't one of the many (really) old ones downtown, where it was and I could have walked to work since it truly wasn't that far.

Through the door, I thought I had better check on the office hours since everyone seemed to be in their places already. Maybe there was a longer lunch hour or an early closing.

It was very open for an office with only a receptionist desk to separate the public from staff et al. In the middle of the back was a good sized, glass partitioned office I was to later learn was affectionately called Lance's aquarium but to an outsider it looked like a messy office supply room with stacks of papers and files everywhere. You couldn't even see the desk, the several card tables and even a couple of the chairs, probably for meetings, were piled high with "stuff."

"Moiré's the name. I'm here to see Mr. Jefferies," I formally said to the young receptionist.

"Thomas Moore?" she replied with what might be a slight flirting smile or maybe a sarcastic, "You ain't from around here" response. I didn't know or really care. And maybe that was the extent of her education.

I get a lot of that, mispronunciation, misspelling and more-familiar-name substitution. Moiré is French and seemingly very unfamiliar to the American ear. "No he's at the Meeting of the Waters," I smiled and replied knowing she wouldn't know that I was talking about Moore's 1852 final resting place named after one of his famous ballads. Me…irritated?

Smile undone, our receptionist picked up the phone or intercom, pushed a button and said, "Mr. Moray here to see you." Silently I wanted to be one of those brightly colored, sharp-toothed voracious eels she just called me, living in the rocky crevices in the coastal places beneath her desk…

I noted the guy in the glass cage had stopped running around his office and had picked up the phone in response to my little helper's, who would probably be a receptionist twenty years from now, conversation. So I figured I had laid my eyes of my new boss, Lance Jefferies.

Continuing my smile I stood erect waiting for the Editor in Chief, err ED, EC, or maybe Chief (I was already into the naming thing) to come forth or call back to summon me. He did pick up the phone but my recept-friend's phone didn't ring nor were her buttons lighting up. No, I would never be interested in lighting her buttons – clear your mind. Besides, I was more interested in sizing up the dress code (not hers) and was surreptitiously surveying the place.

It looked like the area between the front and Chief's office was the bullpen, the area of staff reporters housing the desks, their typewriters, etc. It's called several different names (the hut, morgue, dugout, stockyard, pigpen, the factory, coop - think chickens, etc.) depending on where you find yourself but I think bullpen is the most popular for obvious reasons.

I knew The Factory wasn't going to be used here since there was just such a place here in The Ben. I've seen it, just haven't taken the tour. It's just north of town over the Harpeth River. In it's hayday and I'm not sure if that's one word or two, The Factory had been the 300,000 square feet site of the Allen Company, one of America's biggest kitchen stove manufactures. I think they sold under the Magic Chef name or maybe the Chief followed the Allen, I'll have to research it. But now I understand, sight un-seen, that it is given over to retail shops, artist studios, boutiques, and the like. And it's a Molly trolley regular stop. I saw them there the few times I was passing by.

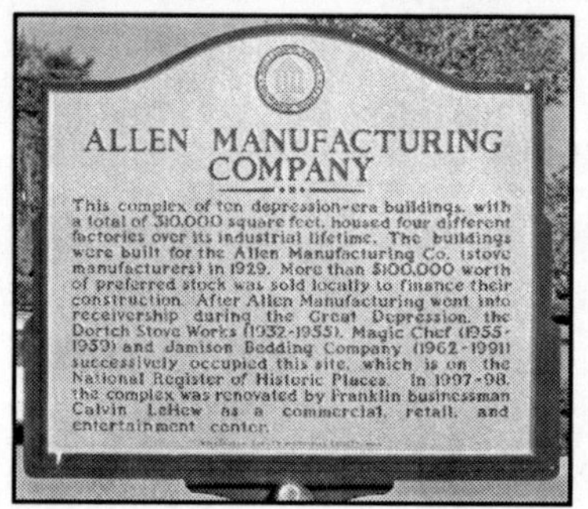

I have a folder and my trusty dictionary under my arm, one of the few items I'm bringing into my new job, at least the first day. A dictionary is something I rarely go without, even have a couple more at home, my 710 (now). That's right, I should probably invest in a new one for my Crawfoot. Oops, now I know I'm not going to live with that name.

Lance is a great guy, I could just tell. Firm handshake, he had come out to meet me and I liked that. Older, thin like many excited newspaper guys who have smoked and drank too much and lost a lot of sleep in his 24/7 job over the years/career but without loosing the enthusiasm for the very next breaking story. About my height, sincere but with a good smile, a down-to-business sort without being aloof, with deep-set and almost penetrating eyes, eyes that seemed to front a sixth sense. A guy that could give a talk to the seniors at the local high school about our fascinating business and stir dozens of new vocations our way.

"Your initiate is good, Mark. Welcome aboard," were his first words. This contrasted to, "Hi Mark, I'm…" And his next words, shouted words, were similarly pointed but not to me – just for my benefit.

"ATTENTION please, this is Mark Moiré, who is joining us today." And he got the name right.

That was it, introductions, short and sweet, were over, down to business. I liked the non-condescending "please" he had added in his address to everyone. I noted he didn't give out a title, job reference or anything else and I took it to mean that everyone here under Lance's direction was a team member. Maybe I should call him "coach." No, definitely "Chief," respect and all.

But I didn't have time to dwell on this because Lance had started back to his office saying on the way (to me), "Pick a desk or free office (both his arms making wide circles). Yellows (the standard, legal sized, small lined pads used in journalism all over – or at least the places I know about) are in the supply room back there (pointing right) so help your self. Liz (pointing the other way, left) will help you with the customary paperwork. She's over there – wave Liz (and she did). I just received a phone call (we had reached his office and he had turned around to face me without going in) and here's your first story to sink your teeth (handing me a folded piece of one of the yellows). Grab anyone you want in front (of his office – the bullpen) that might be free, to help you on background, directions, etcetera and go. Again Mark, nice to have you on board. I know we'll be good for one another." And he was done, shook my hand again and turned his back to me entering his office. Wow. This is all I have to say on that!

I had been given my marching orders so I couldn't dwell on anything else including handing over my formal resume or copies of my work in the folder under my arm (with my desk sized Webster's). Liz would have to wait – Lance was a "business first" guy. So I looked around stopping at the first face, the young one, looking at me, pointed to the guy and said, while walking up to him, "Hi, I'm Mark and I need someone to accompany me on this lead. Would you like to be that someone?" I couldn't say more because I hadn't even read the yellow yet.

Fortunately for me he responded positively, "Sure. I'm Clark and I'm free. What's the deal?"

Clark? No one but no one in the newspaper business has that as a real name and no one would ever choose it as a nick, short for Clarkston or something. I just know that's why Jerry used it. Jerry Siegel, an American writer and Joe Shuster, artist, created Superman back in 1932 - some of the trivia that fills my mind's archives probably taking up a lot of the room not devoted to females, women, girls and all that they involve.

I bet Clark gets more guff about his name than I do, especially in this business. Gee, doesn't he have a middle name he could go by? He seems intelligent maybe he's so self-assured that he doesn't care. He didn't hesitate to look straight at me when Chief gave that broad invite. There's got to be a reason.

Have I mentioned that I had the numbers one and two in my youthful hands and collection. The first and second Superman comics called Action Comics at that time. They're long gone, unfortunately, since you just know that there will be a resurgence and they would have been very valuable one day. I had a few of the early Batman's and the number one Wonder Woman too. All gone. Gone, even after trekking weekly on the city bus to the B's downtown cinema to see George Reeves in tights for most of the 104 episodes of the Superman series back in the fifties.

"Well, let's see," as I unfolded the yellow sheet Lance had given me. Now I wish I had left my suit coat in the car out front since the tie was good enough. The dress shirt and tie would have fit in to this crowd even just a sport shirt, not like the really big city offices where the dress code is business formal. Here is kind of what I had observed in Texas – except absolutely no ties. Did I tell you parking around the Ben is free! How many times do you see that? Yea, I guess I said that too.

“Deputy Sheriff Morris Heithcock was shot answering a disturbance call late last night…” I said as I tried to lower my voice and cut off reading the rest of Chief's writing. I knew better then to shout a lead in front of fellow reporters, let alone be the new guy with an obviously dynamite story in my hands. F A V O R I T I S M – not a good thing for a new guy.

Yes, there was the expected sudden silence and drawn eyes on me from anyone in earshot. Clark stood in a deer-in-the-headlight stance before me probably wondering why one of the more senior reporters didn't get this assignment. Or him. Clark was not senior but young instead, one reason for my picking him. But now I just knew I was going to forever think of him as a Jimmy, you know, Jimmy Olsen, the bow tie-wearing, red-haired, young, fictional character who works as a cub-reported and who idolizes his mentor, Clark Kent. Thank god, this Clark didn't have red hair – it would help me forget, and not call him Jimmy.

Lordy, is that why I'm a newspaper guy? Is my life due to my childhood fascination with everything Superman – with him hiding behind the newspaper facade? God help me, as a kid, I even had a makeshift cape that mom was good enough to make. She used to sew costumes for us too. No I only wore my cape in the house and mostly with my pajamas (we called them PJ's). Lordy, if I learn that this Clark also writes books. Even more if he turned out to be a singer (just kidding).

Admittedly, I was taken up with Superman everything. As a youth I built a soapbox derby racer at my father's urging. He was always gone, working, but noticed that I loved to tinker with his tools. He had showed me a few things and (must have) now felt that he could trust me not to kill myself in his absence/mentorship if I was to tackle such a project. I had built the required birdhouses and a ladder to get in and out of the kitchen window, my preferred entranceway.

Did I ever mention the time that mom was entertaining some company, another neighbor housewife, at the kitchen table one day, talking when I knocked on the window from the outside ladder? Someone had carelessly locked my special way in – probably older sis. Without missing a word, mom casually stood up, went over to the window, unlocked it and sat back down continuing her conversation as I entered via the window behind her and went merrily through the kitchen to the living room, on the way to my bedroom (read front porch).

Yes, of course I remembered to shut the window after my grand entrance but not locking it (for my return or another grand entrance if I happened to leave via the front door. I liked to keep my options open). I said "grand" since it was very apparent at least to me (and I don't know about mom) that her guest was stunned to see the "what" that had just happened before her eyes while cool mom and me just acted like every home with a youth my age accessed the house in a similar manner.

OK, if you read my (damn) first book, you know that I finished my racer in fine form never to let it see the light of day. I had built it in the basement, near dad's tools. The reason I abandoned it? Well, doing my own paint job on my masterpiece, I misspelled and called it Supperman much to the small amusement of mom who pointed it out but much to the grandiose guffaws of big sister for the next several years. I know she told all her friends and any stranger that would listen.

There's a PS to my racer episode. While dad was (typically) away and while building it (or was it my ladder) I did try to saw off my left thumb with one of dad's hand saws, fortunately not one of the rusted ones, saws not thumbs. I saw it happening and was fascinated until the pain hit. That was just after the saw had hit bone. But enough.

Overall I was in euphoria; job, apartment, new (used) car, new small town that I really liked and all. Yes, a little nervous with the new everything including the possible new resentment of fellow reporters for a nice assignment in my hands but I figured, at best, this would be a test for my new colleagues, knowing (as they should) that we rarely have a say in assignments, that's why there was a Lance B. Jefferies, Editor in Chief at the helm.

But the point that I was getting to was that the euphoria was on top, winning by far. So what I wanted to say to Clark when he asked, "What's the deal?" was: "Clark, bring your camera or get a photography guy for us we have the assignment of assignments. Chief is sending us out to the new Coventry Fair Pageant out at the fair grounds where they're staging the infamous Lady Godiva ride."

Yes, my humor gets me in to the occasional and/or colossal trouble and it's spurred on by euphoria bouts, like now. Yes, I don't really know if the Ben has a fairgrounds like we did back in the V. Yes, I was proud of myself for calling him Clark and not Jimmy." Yes, I showed some prejudice by saying "guy, photography guy, but in defense, most of the ones I've known are guys.

No, I don't know if Clark knew that the Coventry Fair was a real annual event carried on since the 1880's only in England and not anywhere here that I know. No, I didn't expect him to know some of my useless trivia - in this case that the name "Peeping Tom" came from this legendary ride in which a innocent, regular guy who happened to be named Tom watched, nay – stared, at the naked lady on horseback riding through his Coventry streets. Tom was stricken blind on the occasion, which one is to infer "because" of it (versus the Puritanical looking-away). Maybe Godiva chocolates would have come to his mind, Clark, and all my

senseless humor would have been missed anyways. Oh well, on to a Sheriff's death.

Women are unmistakably beautiful as objects, I just know this, it's self evident says the artist in me. They just shun being thought of or spoken of as that, objects not beautiful. They love the later. They are empowered by being told that they truly are beautiful. They take it personally when told, as if they are the only one. Their whole demeanor is changed, transformed when addressed like that. And I'm not sure where this came from or where it's going. Maybe The Ride did it. Anyways it ends here. On to death, violence, police action…the next great Chronicle front-page story. I'll make it happen. Jimmy will help, Damn, I meant Clark.

If I only thought there was an immediate silence around the bullpen when I was talking to Clark, I could have heard the proverbial pin drop when the following happened:

"So lets hit it Clark." And he responded, "I'll bring my car around." To which I innocently responded but a little too loud since Clark had grabbed pencils and a yellow off his desk and was already heading toward (what I assumed was) the back door, "No need Clark – I have the Blue Tail parked out front." Big mistake. And I knew it as the words came out of my mouth in seemingly slow-motion.

Dead, unearthly silence penetrated the entire office, maybe even the Ben. Lance B. Jefferies, Editor in Chief, even noted the difference in the office chatter/noise and looked up. I swear the phones stopped ringing. I caught this, the Chief, and was thankful it was only momentary on his part as the "all business" man looked back down continuing with his whatever.

I could have said, "Batmobile" with the same effect (from a crazy-outsider). Meanwhile, I knew my mistake, knew I wasn't going to be able to explain it to this attentive crowd so I merrily headed for the front door as if nothing had happened, been said, as if everyone should have known even if nothing like that appeared on my resume, the one still under my arm still in it's pristine folder, the resume Liz hasn't gotten yet. "So I'm an Ace newspaper enigma in a suit jacket, the last one you'll ever see on me," I said in my own mind, walking a little faster toward the front door.

Noting the glance of the receptionist as I exited and returning the same, the thought came to mind that maybe she wouldn't be so bad on horseback, dressed as The Lady. So maybe I won't eel bite her after all. "You're lucky day girl," I said outside fishing for my keys, hoping Clark was not too far behind.

And he was, on my heels. And he had gotten the Blue Tail thing seeing my blue car ride. So as we both settled in our seats he casually said, "So this is the Blue Tail. Nice." My simple response was, "You've got it. My trusty news car."

I reread the note and handed it to Clark as I started the car adding, "Where are we going Clark?"

"Friends call me just 'C,' Mark. And I guess I'm your navigator for now."

He started out saying a right at the next corner and we were on the way but first we found ourselves passing in front of the office. I wouldn't have mentioned this but there were five to seven people at the front window and door peering out as if Flash Gordon and Dr. Hans Zarkov or maybe the lovely Dale Arden were passing by in one of their many space ships. "Eat your hearts out – this is the Blue Tail and we're on the job," I said to myself, smiling as we went by.

Fortunately I didn't say anything out loud. It would have dated me beyond my youthful years. Flash was my father's or his father's thing, I'm not sure except I know Flash pre-dated WW II.

With C's directions coming at me in plenty of time to drive them, I asked, "So where are you from, C?"
"From here, my parents still live here too, always have."

Hmm, I figured he might be a good source on the town as well as the office. Hopefully he wanted a friend too. So I continued, "Why the newspaper?"

"I like writing, it's always been easy for me."

Now this short answer could have been a diversion or just a humble statement since I was hoping for his life history so I just had to test my new friend. "Any schooling C?" I was purposely getting used to his nickname, taking me farther from the Clark, Superman and Jimmy things.

"Yea, I went to Newhouse after UT." Seemingly a man of few words (which I like – like Duke, you know, Marion Robert Morrison…come on…John Wayne).

I was slightly stunned. "You don't mean the Syracuse University's Newhouse School of Communications, do you?" It was reputed to be the best journalism school in the country and I couldn't believe he had been shaving long enough to go there and graduate too. Besides, I didn't go there.

"Yea, I got my master's there." He kept busy with the piece of paper not offering too much and not asking me similar questions back. Masters? Did he say the masters-thing – that I don't have (yet)?

"Journalism or communication?" was my vocal response.

"Master's in journalism, take the next left," was his simple straightforward, matter-of-fact answer.

I was being trumped and re-trumped by this cub-reporter who was probably my senior – at least in education. The New York Times, Washington Post and the big city papers die for these credentials in a candidate. It's out of my league but there is probably a Journalistic Draft somewhere like the NFL for people like C. So what was he doing here? Is he academic savvy but possibly lacking "street-smarts?" Doubt it. We might have a future Scripps or Hillman winner (top, yearly journalism awards) or maybe a Peabody or Emmy. He might turn out to be a true Clark Kent at least in Franklin Metropolis. Oh yes, I forgot to mention that I did find out the square mileage of Ben. It's 41 (a little less than LA at 470 square miles – sorry).

"So the UT was University of Tennessee and not the University of Toledo by any chance."

"Yea, I fast tracked it and got my Psych there. We're here, lets find parking."

I knew he meant a degree in Psychology and I assumed the fast-tracking meant that he went through in less then four years. I was hoping that my stunned mind wasn't showing through my skull. Thank god for parking and the chance to review this new info in my mind. Maybe I should let C conduct any interviews. I might learn something. At this point I was glad that, as a true newspaperman, that I hadn't given up drinking. Speaking of which, did I decide on Port or Sherry for my thinking-tub. No, no-name yet (but I'm working on it).

The "here" was at the Sheriff's office, on South Columbia Street (or Avenue or are there two), south of 5 Points where Columbia is one of the intersecting streets, my street. I should have been paying attention to directions instead of being focused on C, but I just knew in my reporter's gut that there was probably a story right here in my car.

"Hi C. Who's the new guy?" was the first thing I heard going through the Sheriff's door…and knew I was going to take the second-seat on this one.

"Hi Brad, this is Mark. He just joined the paper. Mark this is Brad," not giving last names, which isn't unusual in small towns when everyone eventually gets to know everyone (and everything about them).

"Pleasure Mark. You guys are probably here about Morey. You should probably talk directly to Sheriff Williams. Let me see if he's busy. You do know we already got the guy," was the question he left in the air as Brad pushed a button to ring the Sheriff's office. C looked at me with the same puzzled face that I supposed I was wearing too.

"Fast work," was my quick response to C's look even if I didn't have any of the details.

"Yea Sheriff's free, go right in," said Brad. But as Brad was buzzing us through the door, C asked, "Has anyone else been here yet?" I was pretty sure he was talking about our competition and Brad seemed to know this saying, "No, you're the first." And this was good information since the first ones on a story seem to get better information and more time than Johnny Come Late-ly's when the interviewee gets tired of repeating the same olè thing over and over.

"Hi Flem." "Hi C, who's the new guy?" was the exchanged salutations, which I kind of expected at this point. Familiar is "Hi Flem" when his office door said, Sheriff Fleming Williams.

Copy (story): Deputy Sheriff, Morris Heithcock, only six weeks on the job having come over to the department having worked at the Ford glass plant previously, happened to live nearby when a call came in about ten o'clock last night for assistance from the Chief of Police, W.W. Mangrum of nearby Fairview. Of course Flem just said "Shorty," to his good friend C. I learned later (when C was translating for me) that Shorty was Chief of Fairview.

Shorty and another deputy had chased the suspect, Harry Ray Conley, 44, a Hickman County resident; through Fairview at speeds up to 110 mph. Responding Deputy Sheriff Heithcock was shot while exiting his vehicle at Conley's home. Shorty's windshield also took a shotgun blast but the Chief had jumped from his car and was not hit. State Police bloodhounds were brought it to chase down Conley who had fled into the nearby woods. They found him asleep under a tree about 3 AM.

I wondered but never asked if C knew of Conley and/or especially on a first name basis. Conley was in a holding cell with an arraignment set for tomorrow morning. I was thankful that C didn't ask but I suspect Flem would have let us, his good friend and me, see and interview our crazed suspect. There was more details but this is the story I'm writing in a nutshell, thankful that C didn't want any part of it, even to share a byline. It wasn't until after we left that I forgot to ask for a Harry Ray mug shot. And it wasn't until I filed the story that I learned we didn't get bylines. Team concept (only).

I must tell you about our conversation on the way back. "So C, you seem to know a lot of people."

"Yea, well…it's a small town and one gets to know most when you've virtually been here all your life. Not to worry, this isn't an 'uppity' town and you'll get to know most too. But take it slow with the oldest families and the few here today that were born here, like me. They might take a little longer, your accent and all."

Accent? What accent? I wasn't sure how to take all this information but I felt it was given in a positive vein so I merely thanked him but continued, "I'm curious, with your credentials you could be in any big city paper so why are you here."

“You’ll learn this someway so I’ll tell you now. Lance is my uncle. Or I should say, Lance is my favorite uncle and I might have the academia but I felt there was still a lot to learn about the business. Besides, this pleases my mother for now.”

I’m sure you remember who Lance is: Lance B. Jefferies, Editor and Chief, err boss man. Again C was forthwith so I merely added; “Well you’re probably smart for taking the time and tutelage from the Chief. And I’m very happy you were here today.”

Nice guy and a good, informed friend to have. I wonder if he drinks? I wonder if there is, even unofficially, a designated drinking-place like the Alcove Lounge we had back in the V. I wonder if he’s learned to put his feet up on desks like “real” newspaper guys do even if this privilege wasn’t in evidence at any of the desks I observed earlier. Everyone seems busy doing whateven they were suppose to be doing.

Yes, I found a desk in my new office and lots of nice and interesting people, seemingly team members all. A couple computers but not on everyone’s desk like I saw in Toledo. I also, disappointedly found no archive, disorganized (like my old one back in the V) or otherwise. Lots of the needed background stuff was learned from “talking to the people” whether that was the self-proclaimed town historians, the Heritage Foundation, the key people, the Masons, aligned people (like the law enforcement for those types of matters), etc. Archives are easier; at least for outsiders. I’m happy here and will tell you more about the people, job, office et al as we go on but I have to tell you something special, very special that happened to me.

Did you ever have something happen to you that you felt was more than a coincidence, that was seemingly unexplainable but nice – maybe something that could be taken as a “sign” that you were just meant to be in a certain place at a certain time? Well if you haven’t, it’s not scary necessarily and I’m not one to think it’s religious or anything weird. It’s just a good feeling, one of confirmation, verification, of authentication of you and what you're doing at that moment. Anything else – I'll leave to Freud, the priests, rabbis, psychs, or whomever.

With that introduction, let me tell you that on or about the Wednesday of the first week, there was a lull in the work efforts and I moseyed over to Lance's book shelves, ones we were told were his personal, Franklin, Williamson County, and Tennessee books and that we were welcomed to peruse or use as necessary as long as the borrowed item was promptly returned to its designated place. My own observation noted that this rule didn't seem to be hard and fast since there were a few books on the desks since I'd been there and there were corresponding holes on the shelves. Anyway, I had been in a quandary about the seemingly lack of indigenous architecture in the environs, the Ben, so I picked up this rather worn book, *Majestic Middle Tennessee,* since leafing through showed lots of pictures of houses and I assumed that that was the subject matter even if not clear from the title.

When I returned to my desk and laid it down (on an open spot, one of two) and put my feet up (on the second open spot and no - Lance was out of the office) I noted the book had opened to about the middle, pages 78 and 79. So I picked up the book and started reading right-page 79 of a pictured, 1840 build (and more recently restored after a hurricane) home that had been named Eventide. I don't know if all the old houses had names, if house-naming was a Franklin, and/or southern thing but I thought it was neat, until I looked at page 78 and stopped cold with chills going up and down my everything.

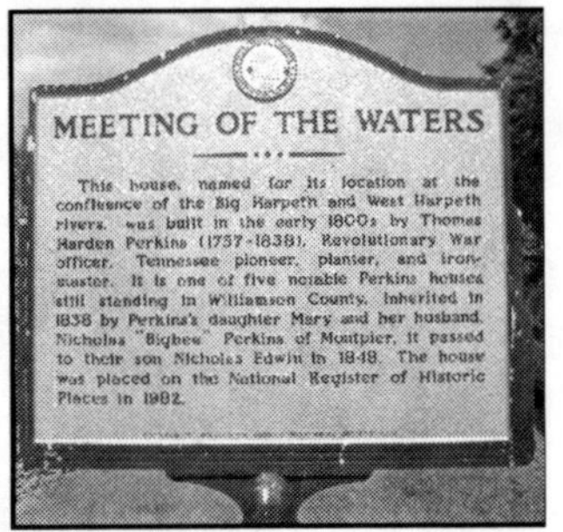

Remember my initial contact with this office and the recept calling me Thomas Moore with my response, "No he's at the Meeting of the Waters," (Moore's 1852 final resting place)? Guess what the name of the nine windowed, nine years in the making, circa 1810, brick house, on page 78 was. Yes, Meeting of the Waters.

Of course I put my feet down and looked around until I concluded that this is silly, no one can/could read another's mind. Call it fate or whatever but there it was (back) on my desk before my very eyes. I started to replay her, the receptionist's look at me after saying what I did and realizing there was kind of a blank stare that I interpreted as "dumb" but now thought could have been "confusion" (as if it were a possibility to her – there was another guy that was at a place familiar to her).

This Ben's Meeting-place supposedly was built with this name because of it's location at the "confluence of the Big Harpeth and West Harpeth rivers" but was it more, from an educated or at least "read" Revolutionary War officer, Tennessee pioneer, planter, and iron-master, Thomas Harden Perkins (1737-1838)? I knew Moore's place was named from one of his ballads but did it get its inspiration from here or vice versus? How does one find out about the first publishing date of an English Ballad? Will I ever know whether there was a possible connection or just a coincidence?

Nine years in the making? Well it seems bricks were rare commodities here at that time but Indians weren't so that Tommy had to find brick layers, "artisans" that could "work with a trowel in one hand and a rifle in the other" to build this "fine old Georgian house" his MEETING place.

And like many of the historic houses in the Ben, this particular one had a strange, fateful, Civil War story to tell. The house, at the time of the war, had remained in the family with the third "master" of MEETING OF THE WATERS, being Nicholas Perkins, "his right hand hopelessly crippled by a duel with a classmate during his old Centre College days." Therefore Nick wasn't in the soldiering but home during the Battle of Franklin when it became necessary to protect his abode because of the "flotsam of Yankee marauders" that spilled off the battlefield to rob and pillage his home. Told they planned to put MEETING OF THE WATERS to the torch once their haversacks were filled, he (Nick) grabbed up a sword with his good left hand, sent his family off to safety in an upstairs room and planted himself defiantly outside their door.

"Suddenly, there was a frenzied commotion below, From out of nowhere, a sabre-swinging Union officer had ridden up to the house and waded into the looters with a torrent of oaths that cleared the downstairs chaos within a few head-splitting moments.

"Out of deepest gratitude and sheer amazement, Nicholas Edwin Perkins would extend his good left hand to this noble Yankee officer – the selfsame Centre College Classmate who had put a ball through his good right arm so many years ago."

Maybe it's the MEETING's fate to cause untold "goofy-bumps" to some of her admiring parties. Whatever the reason, I now know how Nick felt.

"If walls could talk…" aptly applies to another, also a named house, here in the Ben. It's called the Harrison House. In September of that Franklin fateful year, the Battle, the youngest general in the Confederate army, John H. Kelley was brought up the front five steps of the Harrison House having been mortally wounded leading a charge of Wheeler's cavalry at nearby Parry Station. In November Johnny Reb was followed by another youthful Johnny Reb, the top one, the commander himself, General

John Bell Hood. Also wounded? Well, yes, most of his career and suffering accordingly.

John Bell started out as a second lieutenant serving in California, later transferred to Texas under the command of a Colonel Robert E. Lee. There, while fighting the Comanches at Devil's River he took an arrow through his left hand. He resigned the US Army immediately after Fort Sumter was attacked and joined the Confederate army as a cavalry captain. As his aggressive leadership and stubbornness became apparent, he was nicked name "Old Wooden Head" by his troops. He particularly distinguished himself by leading a brigade charge that broke the Billy Yank line at the Battle of Gaines Mill, part of the Seven Days Battles. He escaped being wounded here but was the only officer not wounded or killed.

Hood's arm took part of an overhead, exploding artillery shell at Little Round Top, part of the Battle of Gettysburg and, while not amputated, was never of use again. His right leg wasn't so lucky and was amputated four inches below his hip from the Battle of Chickamauga. The officiating surgeon assumed he would die and sent his severed leg along with JB in the ambulance-wagon so that they could be buried together. Yet this wound was lucky since it was while he was recuperating in Richmond, the Confederate capital, that he befriended President Jefferson Davis. This led to Hood being promoted to full general and given command of the army. At that age, 33, he became the youngest man on either side to be given command of an army. Of course his old superior Robert E. Lee, now a general himself, tried to prevent Davis' choice saying that Hood was "all lion - no fox."

Hood's Tennessee Campaign lasted from September to December 1864, comprising seven battles and hundreds of miles of forced marching in bad winter conditions (at least for this area). After failing to defeat a large part of the Union Army of the Ohio under Maj. Gen. John M. Schofield at Spring Hill, just south of the Harrison House, JB had successfully out maneuvered Schofield's entire army and was strategically camped between them and Franklin (their way to Nashville and other Union troops) beside the Columbia Pike. So was it his many wounds, relentless fatigue, bad communications and/or miss information, less aggressive field officers, a bitter cold and dark winter night when no one wished to leave the confines of a tent or whatever they could find to bundle themselves from the cold – no one seems to know till this day but Schofield's army silently, successfully and unimpeded crept up that dark freedom road, the Columbia Pike, to the safety of Franklin. Awesome and true.

So it was the next morning when Hood, looking much older than his years, was informed of this debacle, aging him even more. It was later that same morning that Hood struggled mightily and independently with his crutch to navigate the five steps of the Harrison House where he would make the fateful decision to attack the Union troops at Franklin.

Actually the very scene was the Harrison House library and reportedly, the air was filled with flaring tempers especially between Hood and his Chief of Cavalry, General Forrest who wanted to flank the Union (versus a frontal assault over hundreds of yards of open field against fortifications that were being build, reinforced, and reinforced as they argued). Hood finally pulled rank as the commanding general and Forrest stalked out, reportedly taking two of the front steps at a time, a meaningless protest but something he knew he could but that his superior would never be able to do.

At the Battle of Franklin Hood's troops were unsuccessful in their attempt to breach the Union breastworks and as they themselves recovered, the Union force withdraw, again unimpeded, toward Nashville. Hood lost six generals and numerous line commanders. The Battle is reportedly the bloodiest few hours of the entire war and estimates vary but no one argues strenuously against the figure of 10,000.

Two weeks later JB was defeated again, by George Thomas, at the Battle of Nashville, in which Hood's remaining army was virtually wiped out, thus making the Franklin-Nashville Battle one of the most significant Confederate battle losses in the Civil War. After the catastrophe of Franklin-Nashville, the remnants of the Army of Tennessee retreated to Mississippi and Hood resigned his temporary commission as a full general as of January 23, 1865, reverting back to lieutenant general. How in hell did he ever stay on a horse with only 4 inches of a right leg?

Near the end of the war, Jefferson Davis ordered Hood to travel to Texas to raise another army. Before he could arrive, however, General Edmund Kirby Smith surrendered his Texas forces to the Union and Hood surrendered himself in Natchez, Mississippi, where he was paroled on May 31, 1865. He died in the yellow fever attack in New Orleans in 1879. Fort Hood in Texas is named so in his honor. Today, John Bell's remains are in the Metairie Cemetery in Louisiana with remnants, if only memories, in our Harrison House just down the road here in the Ben.

Andrew Jackson was no stranger to the Ben. He wasn't born here, nor in Tennessee for that matter but once here, he called Tennessee home. Like me, maybe one's "adopted' home is more precious than if one is (merely) born here. Not that anyone listened to Andy who consistently claimed to be born just inside the border of South Carolina because there were many news articles (and later books) written that he was born in a couple dozen different places including foreign countries.

Andy (1767-1845) our seventh President made his official home (and final resting place) up the road about 30 miles at Hermitage, TN but those few miles didn't stop him from filling up his carriage with cedar saplings and bouncing down the road from the Hermitage to here and his good friend's son's new home building site, a house to be called Riverview, reportedly the first Franklin house "to have all the modern conveniences." He not only brought them he personally set about planting those trees, still here today, all around the site just north of the river and downtown.

Andy and Randal McGavock, Sr. had been close friends for years and therefore Andy wasn't a stranger to the Ben by any means or Randal and family to the Hermitage. Randy was a year younger than Andy and died approximately a year shy of him. Randy was Mayor of nearby Nashville, fifteen miles to our north, but built his home here and named his home after the McGavock family home back in Northern Ireland.

This new home was to play a key role in the Civil War and it stands today with thousand's of visitors traipsing through if for no other reason then to stand on the upper Greek Revival rear porches which served as an observation post for General Nathan B. Forrest, or for them to see the blood stains still in the floor boards from the hundreds of wounded carried there in it's new, makeshift role as hospital for the infamous five hour battle, the Battle of Franklin. It's called Carnton Plantation.

A postscript to Riverview and the Kentuckian first cousin bride of James Randal McGavock is that wife Louisa McGavock gave birth to ten children at Riverview. Unfortunately Jimmy died soon after the war started but his wife and many of those offspring were at Riverview as the two freighting hours of rattling windowpanes and shaking walls caused by the Federal guns at nearby Fort Granger signaled the start of that terrible battle and the demise of 10,000 souls.

Now I know what my new apartment needs – a Nana fern. Grandmother and favorite person in the entire world, Nana, used to specialize in two things, Canaries and ferns. Both were always a part of her home. The study of ferns is called pteridology and one who studies ferns is called a pteridologist.

Nana, more a West Virginia Ridge Runner than anything, was merely a successful Fern-grower. She would cut some of her fern fronds (read leaves), stick them in a glass of water, set it on the window ledge, let it grow roots, plant it and pass it around to a family member. We all had Nana-offspring-ferns in our houses and Nana would critic it when she visited suggesting more or less water, more or less sunlight, replanting, etc. And, God forbid, one of the ferns would die…the process started all over as soon as she got back to hers, the mother fern.

Nana's gone and I'm not going back to the G (or mom's) just for a cutting of her Nana-fern but the Ben has nurseries galore. I bought the biggest one I could find and I remembered to buy a water spray bottle – they like that daily attention. I'm going to call it Nana…and talk to it. I'm thinking that I should put it near my thinking tub…but I'm not sure if that's a healthy place for it. We'll see. Maybe I need to consult a pteridologist or the first fern-loving grandmother I come across.

I said Nana was a Ridge Runner because she always referred to herself as that. Correction: a West Virginia Ridge Runner…I'm just not sure of the capitalization. West Virginia, the state, was brought about because of the Civil War…to distinguish themselves from the rest of the Virginians, which they were before June 20th, 1863, a celebrated West Virginia Day in the newly formed state. WV is the only state to have seceded from another state (but may not be the last, i.e., Upstate NY from NY in the future. I hope).

West Virginia can be referred to as the southernmost Northeastern state, the northernmost Southeastern state, the easternmost Midwestern state as well as the westernmost Eastern state. Maybe this is why it was easier to say ridge-runner.

WV is virtually all in the Appalachian Mountain chain so if you threw a blanket over it you'd have peaks and valleys with lots of "ridges' in between. Yes they have knobs (too - like the beautiful Spruce Knob, often covered in clouds). I was just taking "writer's license" for the Tennessee knobs.

It may have a State bird that I don't know but I would guess it is a yellow Canary. Nana told me it has a State fish, her favorite to catch (anywhere), Brook Trout. Great tasting when pan-fried too. You just have to get through the bones. And WV is the only state I know of that has a State animal, the Black Bear, of which I've only seen one in the wilds, a cub or smallish one.

The WV peoples are and think of themselves as "down-home-folk." And because of Nana, I have to be very careful in any grocery checkout line because a sack or paper-bag is really a "poke."

She taught me how to play tiddlywinks when I was knee high to a grasshopper (another one of her expressions) and constantly took credit for the feat for many years. Too bad I lost my squidger somewhere along the way.

You might hear a lot about my Nana as we go forth. So I apologize in advance.

PS? I know, as astute as you are, there is a question about Hood's leg. Yea, Chickamauga, the battle, was no picnic and yes it's in Tennessee over by our Choo-Choo (read Chattanooga). It was the opposite of our Battle of Franklin since it was the most significant Union defeat (at least in the Western Theater as they called it). Unfortunately the Confederates were not able to capitalize on their victory and were soon routed across the nearby state line of Georgia.

The river for which the battle name was picked is the Chickamauga Creek. It had a prophetic Indian meaning, River of Death. 34,000 plus American casualties - an awesome number for any engagement. This one was only two days in length.

Today, the Chickamauga Chattanooga National Military Park is the nation's oldest, largest, and most visited one covering some 8,000 acres. And somewhere there, probably in the nearby cemetery on Bailey Avenue rests JB's right leg. It's near the remains of the infamous James J. Andrews and his Raiders of "The Great Locomotive Chase" fame. It was a significant part of the man, buried with reverence (as opposed to being deposited on the vast mountain of other soldiers' appendages) but not worthy of a grave marker – thus Tennessee has a piece of Hood still here, somewhere, down there near our Choo-Choo.

Err, knobs - in Tennessee!

Franklin is 41 square miles with 50 thousand (if you count the horses and cows). LA is 470 square miles housing probably 3 million (and you don't find any horses or cows). Of course the Greater LA area encompasses five counties (and lots more folk just not many country ones, except the visitors).

The Lost State

Talking about girls, as we seem to be doing that a lot lately, did you ever notice that from a guy's perspective, to get involved requires a whole new language. Bodice, thelarche, areola, derrière, crinolines, hair curlers, cosmetics (from foundation to lipstick and lip liners, concealers, rouges and blushes, mascara to augmentation etc.), bustles, falsies, hoop skirts (or are they out by now), menarche, menstrual cramps, syphilis, Midol, Women's rights (whatever they are), femininity, gynecology, suffrage, banshee, Paget's disease, biki-waxing (and a guy just doesn't want to go there), queen, vagina, ovulation, coitus, estrogen, pregnancy, kinaalda (if you're Navajo), fallopian tubes, vulvas, labia's, lesbianism, dresses, corsets, stays, fashion, misogyny, white-lies, mastectomy, whores, nymphomaniacs, matriarchy, sexism, Aphrodite, aphrodisiacs, erogenous zones, Skene's and Bartholin's glands, G-spots, cunnilingus, penetratee, teats and nipples – nipples and teats, I'm getting silly but you get the point and the silly list goes on. And on.

Why the hell did Adam get lonely? Or did God get even? "OK Adam, I hear ya. You'll get a mate but at a price and you'll have to learn a new language too." If the truth were known, it was only a man's world for a day and one-half plus the sleeping time God put

Adam under while he created Eve. And creating Eve wasn't easy. God first gave Eve one breast (not enough) then three breasts (so that Adam could never get enough), put them in back then front, shoulders finally chest. Should one call them hooters, knockers, melons, titties, ta-tas, or breasts and then there's the size thing: knobs, mountains, or maybe one of each? The placement of the beaver, bush, the pink-part, vulva, pint-taco, cooter, coochy (WWII), "thing" was a problem too. Really. God even thought of combining those things, the naughty bits. This was all before the butt considerations. Adam was probably asleep a lot longer then he realized. Did you notice He rested after that (and never created anything thereafter)?

As for the dinosaurs, there's no mystery. As soon as Eve got to her feet she said to God, "I'm sorry but they've got to go." She didn't even include, "Lord," "God," or "Your Worthiness." So he did, and they went – all, and he woke up Adam (and fled) before she said another word. End of story.

Did I mention shoes and perfumes in my list? It had to be a lot easier being a cowboy out on the range. And horses can be great and faithful (non-judgmental, non-talking) companions.

I'm sure you noted the "I hear ya" from God? Well don't forget God created Texas. He felt a little guilty taking away the Garden so he made TX and just waited for man to find it. Guilty? Sure, He can feel that, whom do you think created that too - guilt. Oh, for the record, after he created Texas he did a little improvement tweaking and came up with Tennessee. God, what an artist!

So I'm not closer to Melungeons or the lost State of Franklin. Without a trusty old archives like I used to have at the last job, I may not fine out whether they exist or how. How does one casually fit either thing into one's conversations? Not that any pride holds me back…no, never. Maybe my lost Austin Texas Editor set me up or liked riddles for those who rejected his job offers.

I just "have to run them to ground." I'm not sure of the derivation of that old saying but when I use it I, at least in my mind, give honor to Charles Lutwidge Dodgson (1832-1898). You probably more likely to recognize him form his famous work and pen name, *Through the Looking-Glass*, Lewis Carroll.

When I talked about the MEETING OF THE WATERS, I mentioned goofy-bumps. The misleading "goose bumps," resembling the bumps on the skin of a plucked goose and called "hen bumps" in France, Spain and China, can only occur in mammals. The British call them "goose flesh." The Hawaiians call them "chicken skin. Other names for cutis anserina (in medicine) are chili bumps and goose pimples. In Tennessee they're called "mini-knobs" (just kidding). But the all-pervasive "goofy-bumps" are not (usually) caused by (mere) cold but by a personal, surprising event with the effect of bumps on the inside of the skin as well as outside. It's reminiscent of the very first time and feeling, as a kid, one lays eyes on the true Walt Disney's Goofy.

One thing that had bothered me even before coming to the Ben was how I was hired over the phone by Lance. This festered just so long and then I had to ask him even before I was able to really get to know him well. Actually he asked me well before the end of my first month, "Mark, you're work is good, as expected, you seem happy. Is there anything special on your mind?"

"Well, yes boss there is – one thing. How is it that you hired me over the phone from Texas before meeting me, before interviewing me, and before I even had the chance to give you my resume?" By the way, I did pass the later on to Liz that first day after returning to the office with C.

"Good question Mark but it's not very complicated. I went to school with your old boss and have kept up the relationship seeing him often at the conventions as well as sharing a monthly phone call or two. He had known you were moving on, I can't remember now whether you had told him or he intuitively knew it but he had called me about you, told me you especially liked small towns, had recommended you and had even sent me several samples of your work. So you were good enough for me, sight unseen and if the truth were known, I had called you but you were traveling and weren't home to answer and I was just waiting to call you when you returned when you called me from somewhere. Was it Texas then? Isn't life fun? "

That's a thirty, (-30-), end of story – that's how us news guys sign off on a project or story.

I'm now wondering if goofy-bumps and girls might be related – at least where I'm concerned. Naw, I'm not going to go there.

Speaking of wondering, I found my Franklin State and Melungeons. I found them but in curious ways. Maybe life is.

Having hit it off right from the start, C and I started pal-ing around together, at least for work. I assume you know but maybe I should state that everything in a small town's reporter's life isn't glamorous meaning (just) reporting. One picks up or sells an ad from one of our many advertisers, brings in the morning donuts for the coffee-clutch, takes a few classifieds when the two class-designated gals' phones get backed up (we call them our Classics), run errands and even (occasionally) see to the distribution thing (when one of the vans breaks down or there was an important late breaking, time delaying, story that pushed things back, makes the office-coffee, helps old women across the streets, and more. You get the idea I'm sure.

C, not pretentious for a guy with an enviable journalistic education, didn't mind this (other) side of the business as either did I, having done it on the last job and knowing it was necessary - comes with the territory (however small). So we found ourselves writing ad copy together, pitching in for one another, covering stories together (we silently called them "MC Ben approved" – Mark and C, Master of Ceremonies, never mind – it's an insider), and with mutual respect (and different perspectives), we typically ran our work by each other for editorial-approval. After all, it was better to get another's slant on things, opinions, and any corrections before our boss, Lance, used his infamous, damn, red pencil, the dreaded re-write instrument of massive-destruction.

C and I, mostly at my behest, started (or tried to start) the end-of-the-week news drinking thing – to seal and review the past week (put it to press sort of) initiate the weekend, and brainstorm possible article-subjects for the next edition. It was a tradition back in the V. I even remember my old friends and colleagues back there (and I) coming up with a few outstanding ideas that would surely make for syndication – I just couldn't remember the details (the next morning) but it was a great feeling of camaraderie.

Here, the Ben, we had a little trouble determining our proper ambiance (drinking place). After the naked mermaids in the Alcove Lounge criteria that I may have boasted about too often to back off of, it was hard settling in to just any old place.

We first tried the Irish pub right in the center of old town on Main Street. They have the greatest fish and chips plate, good for an olé Catholic's Friday and memories of childhood rules. They also had Guinness on draft, large pints – what a way to start the weekend. They poured the dark brew with reverence, into a properly chilled glass mug, complete with foam head, and they topped it off with an impressed image on the foam-head, a shamrock I think. Classy. And delicious but I'm not sure if this was more English then Irish. I'll have to ask C.

I know I said "old town," something that would place me in the "obviously-an-outsider" category and something the prideful natives wouldn't say about their "historic town," which meant the same little area – not the whole forty-one square miles. But I said it (only) here and wouldn't be dumb enough to use it in conversation, an article, or even with my new but native friend C.

We next tried the swank (for a small town) bar and restaurant that was up the street (in old town – ha-ha) on the opposite corner. It was a possible but busy with tourists place and the bar area was an intricate part of the place, restaurant, as opposite to a separated spot. Never mind about this – I'll get back to you when we pick one. We were next going to try the Running Horse over the Harpeth and just up the hill. In front of the Factory, you know.

Meanwhile C and I were discussing favorite things and people in our lives one Friday nite (over fish-chips and Guinness's) when I got to tell him about my West-Virginia-ridge-runner Nana. Into my story I talked (OK, bragged) about knowing that WV wasn't a state at first, like all the others. Fortunately I was only into my second mug and not on a bar stool, which I would have slipped from, when he countered, "Kind' a like our Lost State of Franklin."

"YES, yes – tell me about this…and the melons." The last was a little slurred but my friend didn't point this out, rather this youthful fountain of Tennessee information simply said, "You mean the Melungeons. Well, they were going to be a part of the Lost State."

"I'll be damn. I guess that olé Austin codger (read editor) had something after all!" I exclaimed, more to myself, and quickly adding to the enquiry on C's face, "It doesn't matter. Later. Please go on."

Here's the long and the short of it (even if I don't think I'll ever be able to use it anywhere in an article). The Melungeons are a special Appalachian breed, C called it the "tri-racial isolate group" even if I had to have him write it down the following Monday morning (after coffee)(and a donut). This refers to a mixture of Indian, African, and European ancestry within the group that pretty much keep to themselves (not unusual in mountainous, rural areas). And, not that I would ever meet one, C added that they didn't like the "isolate-group" term. Maybe he's met a couple – to know this. That puts them in (our) East Tennessee (Appalachian) area.

Melungeons basically are distinguished by their slightly different looks I gather. So the title is more of an epithet, seemingly used in similar fashion with evidenced Tennessean (and Kentucky) history to the same era, which produced the terms "redbone," "moor," "brass ankle," and others. He was now talking over my head but from rote so I knew I could ask him to repeat it later if I needed or wanted him to. He felt pretty sure that they still existed but mentioned this was mostly "ancient" history, meaning a hundred of more years ago.

It's this East Tennessee area that also accounts for our Lost State and without any apparent connection to our town with the same name. The State of Franklin goes right back to our American beginnings and soon after the end of the American Revolution, circa 1786. It seems there were eight counties, now in Tennessee (I'm just not sure if their names are the same), that banned together to form an autonomous, secessionist territory between the Allegheny Mountains and the Mississippi River and who applied to the (new) federal Congress for statehood. The area, according to C, was filled with the Watauga people hence the Fort Watauga Tennessee State Park but I didn't interrupt to question whether the Wataugans were Indians or another peoples like the Melungeons and, for that matter, weren't the Melons there too (with the Wataugans)?

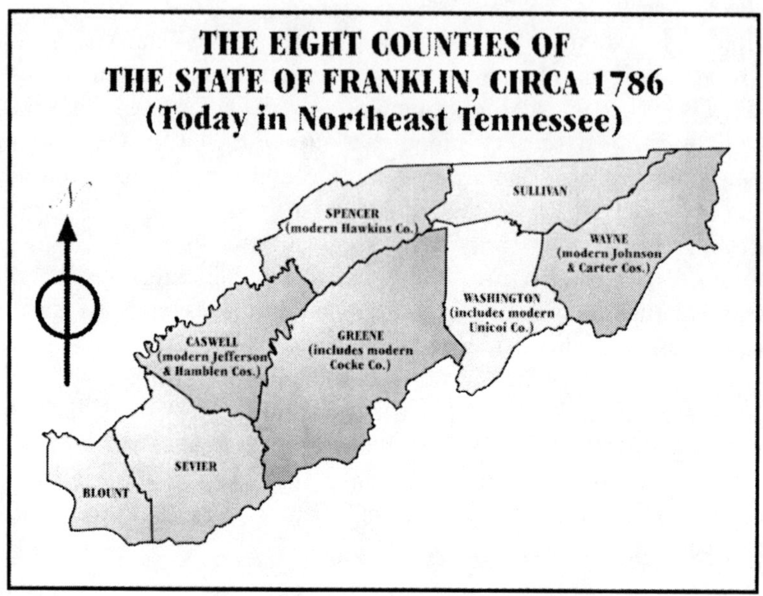

Continuing: seven states voted to admit the tiny-to-be-state under the proposed name of Frankland but if you know the process, this was short of the needed two-thirds majority. Creatively, the leaders (of the movement) changed the name to "Franklin" to win favor and gain statehood. They even tried to rally Ben himself for support but for whatever reason (and humility is not one of them) he politely refused. Franklin State set up state legislatures et al but by 1790 the idea collapsed and was soon to become part of Tennessee.

Mystery solved, actually two. See how beneficial a news guy's drinking night is? Then again, C's next comment didn't help, "You possibly know that there was the Lost County of Tennessee that had our Capital for a day?" I was about to leave it alone – what's a state without a couple mysteries – but C jumped in and solved that one for me immediately and with few words.

There was a ninety-six county, called James County, just east of Chattanooga (of *Chattanooga Choo Choo* fame, 1941 RCA Victor's Bluebird label). Its county seat was Ooltewah (and that's not why it became lost – no one could pronounce the seat). Actually in 1807 the Tennessee Legislature met at Kingston, James County, to fulfill a "technicality" of their Cherokee's Land agreement, which said that the Indians agreed to relinquished the land so that the Tennessee State Capitol could be built there. But the county went bankrupt before this all happened so the legislature made their Capitol-for-the-day and adjourned to Knoxville and James was absorbed into Hamilton county. The Cherokee's forgot to have a "30 days or null-and-void" or similar proviso. Now aren't I good to remember all this after drinking? And note, the Choo Choo info was my own, thanks to my parents fascination, nay - obsession, with that song.

On the drinking note, I have to add that youthful C didn't last the nights like my old compradors. Soon after eating and a second drink, he would excuse himself to do whatever. Maybe this was a needed excuse for the parents that he still lived with, "Yes, I'll be home late – having a drink with a colleague after work." I don't know nor do I know what he did following our new weekly get-togethers. Maybe he went home but I doubt it. All's that I know is that I'll have to plan on co-opting several more news guys if this tradition was to be firmly established here in the Ben (and not just a Lost State of Affairs).

Yes, there are other news-guys here even if I haven't mentioned our competition, the TRA, *The Review Appeal*. It was bought back in 1963 by a capable news guy, James H. Armistead, who might prove to be an even better businessman. They're over on Second Avenue. It's a good little paper with a different philosophy than the *Chronicle*. I'll try to phrase this as an observation rather than a criticism (you know, "different strokes for different...") and I assume that it works very well for them (from the amount of ads they carry). Their "news" is virtually the front page. I'm talking about "news worthy events." The rest of their pages are classifieds, weddings, man-boy-student-of the week, obs (obituaries), "The Summer of '72," "A Day with a Witch," court-reports, etc. So who knows; maybe their philosophy will work better in the long run. I'm still too new to have an opinion as to what will work here.

Wait, I take the "witch" thing back, I liked that and will plagiarize err; embellish the idea, some time in the future. But you get the idea; news per se is one page – not much room for more than one good reporter or two (of the other kind).

I'll have to find out how many TRA news-guys they have. I know, one has to be careful with fraternizing but deep down we are all one fraternity, one institution of members whose real competition is not each other or each new event but the next word, their own, and the next.

When you want to know about the "Kill 'Em All Club," "Franklin's Hanging Tree," or "Who Was Marcellus Cuppet – Slave or Soldier?" then don't put your dime down for the TRA. I just wish they didn't (also) publish on our Thursdays.

Other feelings about the TRA you ask? Well, I have good feelings. One in particular is rather good. In fact I really owe them a big one (that fortunately they don't know about).

It's the TRA that gave me a keen insight into the local culture, the seemingly, indigenous (more by adoption), southern culture. It amounts to this. Franklin has never been on the cutting edge of anything (yet) and while outstripping small town in America growth rates recently, it was conveniently close to and it was mentally comfortable to adopt the sophisticated, charming and endearing idea of grand plantation Southern Living. "Things are pleasant here and always have been."

But the true mind set of the local community and its idea of history only extends to the length of one's life here (not any deep set principles, laws, rules or ideals). And life is always advancing with the next generation and the next. Consequently, and for example, the prejudicial slavery, seeming anti-black roots in the deep south fostered only by a manufactured idea of "they must be inferior so we have to keep them in their place" rationalization (probably economic for the most part), only extents to what these people themselves have seen here, witnessed in their own life time. It's not a dyed in the wool ideal, it eases with the passing of time, and has been easing as progress is and has been made.

The same thing applies to what must surely look like an invasion of outsiders. It's big but not so overwhelming to radically change things so it's just "accepted" as also "pleasant." The knobs probably help – one doesn't see all the new developments being laid out like the infamous New Jersey (landfill – my opinion) project called Levittown after WWII. And there are a lot of knobs to hide everything – making it more "pleasant."

Does this make sense to you? I don't have any real insight into the real, deeper south and I got the impression from my brief foray into Texas that they're not the "South" per se but I had to try and understand why the Ben's architecture, furniture selection and trimmings, language inflection, culture, hobbies, social activities, et al didn't really correspond to the ubiquitous Private White in the Square. He's still (only) facing southeast even if the trains stopped coming a long time ago. I can tell you this for sure, even after my last Friday's weekend drinking night, mostly by myself because I checked this out. Yep, he's still there. I even saluted him. The Confederates did salute...didn't they? And who knows, maybe over time, it'll become a comfortable direction for him despite the interurbans (trains) demise. "Pleasant, yes?"

Onward!

Speaking of outlaws, we, the Ben, have our infamous, bootlegger, Willy York, still alive today. Of course if it wasn't for Willy being named in a couple of songs (including *Chelsea Hotel* by Leonard Cohen and the hit song, *Willie's Drunk and Nellie's Dyin* by the Ben's own, Johnny Sea), then Willy's appearance in *LIFE* magazine (plus one film documentary of the Netherlands – of all places) it might have been missed in the history pages.
I'm not exactly sure how this bootlegger, convicted bootlegger, criminal, killer, got so famous, the sequence of events that led up to

his international reputation since it was just before me getting here but it seems the *LIFE* magazine people's visit here and/or the Ben's very popular country singer, Johnny Sea's song, might have been the catalyst. I know I said, "the Ben's own Johnny Sea" twice – so? I wonder if anyone has ever captured the phrase, Tennessee-Proud?

I guess I should start from the beginning so I pick up one of the many copies of *LIFE* dated July 17th, 1970, the Willy issue, that you see all over town, in the barber shops, breakfast and coffee places – you get the point. The one I picked up is one of the three in our lobby. Not that the *Chronicle* has a real lobby, I just call the receptionist area by the front door, the one with Lady Godiva sitting at her desk there with a nearby small table with several magazines piled on it, including the three I mentioned, that a visitor could pick up to read while waiting for whatever, even if there wasn't a chair for him/her to sit down. If any of the many magazines that pass through our office end up on the little table then you know that everyone's done with them. They get tossed every so often but not to worry about this *LIFE* issue being lost to the trash, I'm sure boss Lance has his own copy somewhere in his office stacks and he (but not anyone else) will know exactly where to put his hands on it.

I take Willy back to my desk, mostly cleared including a place to put my feet up (when I dare) but not to worry now since the *LIFE* is so big that I'll have to make a little more space to turn the pages. Maybe you've seen this issue, it's the one with the Camelot Crew on the front, you know, a couple of the Kennedys. I guess it's Rose's 80th birthday as our 50¢ *LIFE* continues to try and elevate them to the America's Royalty status. I mean, is the news so lame that a birthday, anyone's, makes the front cover? OK, so I'd approve if it were Lady Godiva's birthday (suit). Sorry.

The six-page article that starts on page 53 is, "Willie York from Big East Fork." Some editor at LIFE feels he's clever – I can just tell from that headline. I also know it wasn't an underling reporter that suggested it – it wouldn't be there now – it had to be a higher-up's idea.

They meant the river, East Fork, west of town over by the stepchild town of Fairview in the county's Section #1, the more notorious part of the county. It's close by but had been without a direct road connection for many years before the new 96 West and it didn't help that it was long distance to call since they used to have Nashville numbers. It's notorious in that every "revenue man" used to claim that there was a still in every other hollow there, not that the rest of the area didn't have their share. It had been hard to get there even for the law and left alone to there own "devices," the leanings toward the disreputable ways won out in the area.

This goes back a few years but it seems Tennessee went prohibition ten years before the country did, which gave the "volunteers" of this fine place a good start on the bootlegging practice. It helped that it was a regular "practice" before anyone's prohibition anyway. It's always been a case of one's right to make their own stuff and do with it what they wanted without interference or taxes. They just had a head start on improving the practice of hiding their "factories" and inventing new ways of transporting Mr. Moonshine.

I'm not sure but it seems to me that his "leg-up" put Tennessee Moonshine on the top of the reputation list for the best in the country even if Alabama or Mississippi might argue. Anyone in the know just "knows" that it's still a viable practice in the Appalachians to this day – and all the days to come. That's just their way of life. God bless.

I just love this topic. I had researched the bootlegging thing back in the V and found that the main bootlegging road between Cleveland and Cincinnati went right through the V with many a story of cops, tax-revenue-men, and those-outside-the-law having high speed chases (for those times) going right through the middle of town in the middle of the night. It was great and here I am again in just a different state.

I had mentioned this to one of the cooks on break in town were I like to eat breakfast and she, who lived as a child over in the Fairview area said that it was the same there, that the road between Fairview and Nashville, the closest moonshine market, had two hills, Whippoorwill Hill, which was good for going down and getting speed, and Break Neck Hill, which slowed all the moonshine vehicles down trying to make it up and over to get to the Music City giving the police a place to sit and wait with a chance to "get'm easy."

I couldn't leave this alone so I said, "Tell me more." She said, "Well we, as a family, used to hear a truck skirt our farm at night, going back into the woods but as a kid didn't think anything about it since the parents simply said to one another, 'must be tak'n another load of sugar over to Lou's factory.' It sounded innocent. I didn't know about the need for sugar and moonshine and I didn't know the neighbors, Lou was the father, owned a factory but thought he was just a farmer like dad.

"One day, mom, sis and I went looking for one of our cows that had walked away. We were traipsing through the woods, thickets and all, following the little cow path when momma in the lead, froze. She looked all around and quickly turned to us, shushing us to be very quiet. I thought she had just come across a snake and was wondering why she didn't just kill the thing."

"Were there poisonous snakes there at that time?" I interrupted, asking.

Her answer first came with the roll of her eyes so I knew but she added, "Copperheads and rattlers! And they're still there.

"Anyways, mom then said, 'Run fer your lives' pointing the direction from which we came. So we did, all the way back to the edge of the woods. There, and all of us was out of breath, I asked her, 'What was that fer?' She said, that there ther must of been Lou's factory they came across! And I knew she meant a moonshine still. Guess she was worried that if anyone was there and spotted movement, us'ns, that shouldn't of been there, that they'd start a shooting.

"That night sis and I heard her tell pa, who said that he better go tell Lou he knows about it and that Lou better move it er else he'd feel obligated to tell the police in the not too distant future."

I had to ask and did, "Well did you ever get the cow back?"
"Not for two more days and dad had to go all the way around the woods to retrieve 'em."

I almost thought the stories were over at this point but, as a good investigative reporter, I said, "Is there more?" And thank god I did because she added the near present day one.

"Well, my granddad was a good lawman, a deputy with the Sheriff's department until he and his partner, another deputy, found a still over there, in a hollow in the woods near Fairview a few years back." She paused long enough that I said, "Well?" And she continued, "Well he reported it. It was raided and dismantled but soon word got back to him who owned it so he quit."

"Why'd he do that?"

"Because it was the Sheriff's personal still. Of course since then, they're harder to hide with the spotter planes, sniffin dogs, helicopters, and all."
Big as life, Willy's sitting comfortably on his uneven, unpainted, clapboard porch, in his debris strewn yard, with harmonica in his right hand, left one perched casually on his left knee, Walter Winchell news hat, small brim up, setting slightly back on his head,

dusty and worn work shoes, white short sleeves and collar out shirt, rough hewn farming overhauls, looking at no one or where in particular except maybe into the past, while wife Nellie, frail and haggard in a make shift, small checkered gingham dress probably hand-sewn some time ago, slightly behind and looking at Willy's back, leans against the porch support holding up the roof that one wonders might fail at any moment even with her slight weight.

Meanwhile two little'uns sitting to Willy's left, playing with a fur ball of some small animal dead or alive, young muskrat, dog, cat, squirrel, or rat, on top of a makeshift table made from an inverted galvanized wash tub that serves as an occasional bath tub, elevated by two inverted, used bushel baskets. The kids are obviously mesmerized by the character with the harmonica or the sounds coming forth, even ignoring the fur ball thing.

Thus, and pictorially, Willy is introduced to the world on the first page of the *LIFE* article. The ideal picture of what some will assume is white trash and others will see as a typical down-trodden family wanting to do better as life has knocked them down at every turn, so common but neatly shelved into and relegated to obscurity in all the dark nooks, crannies, and recesses all over America but brought out in *LIFE* to prove the rational of such practices and the righteousness of life on the other side. Johnny Seay, his real name, pronounced sea, had it right in his Willie song and *LIFE* missed the point in their journalistic crusade writing for the masses.

The *LIFE* article by David Snell, doesn't fully portray Willie, as a down and out man that may or may not be related to the other famous Tennessean York, Alvin C., Sergeant York (1887-1964) who is reputed to be the "greatest American hero of WWI," at least the most decorated, played by Gary Cooper in the 1941 movie and also consigned to that "hillbilly" genre as is Willie. Willie is not portrayed as a man who has done his "time" just a different type of time then Alvin's.

Author Snell doesn't impress one as truly understanding Willie, his trials, his fierce independence, the roads he trekked, or as one who knows the true makeup of such a man. But it is a very powerful article, one that can't be put down easily. It tells well the relational aspect of the two men from the Ben, Willie and Johnny Seay, it ties in how Willie's name got to be in another song with Ray Kid Marley and a touching forgiveness pub scene of one Charles Reed, son of Clarence Reed, the constable murdered by Willie and his brother back in 1941. It is a slice of Willie's life, just not a big one.

But I read with anticipation to see if one of the most interesting Willie stories, well known locally, showed up. It didn't and here it is: when Willie was sent to prison, Nellie married another. Then when Willie had served his fourteen years time and came back home, Nellie left her new husband to hook up again with "her" Willie. God, don't you just love hillbilly love and the small towns, where even the big boys don't learn all the stories.

The Franklin Rod & Gun Club

Yes, I didn't forget the few items I mentioned before with any intention of leaving you hanging – not a good thing for an ace reporter, book writer, etc. So here goes:

The Kill 'Em All Club is/was a real thing here in the Ben, just not connected with the criminal elements we've been talking about. Therefore you can quickly conclude it wasn't a lynching bunch, para-police organization or anything radical. It's also old history, circa 1913 but I'll tell you in a few words and possibly you've already guessed. The Kill Club was just a hunting club formed by a bunch of regular guys complete with by-laws, rules and regulations, seven in all. Reportedly the members, by oath, never thought of "transgressing" any of their seven, self-imposed directives. By 1947 there were only three members left in the Ben and they were lucky to go fishing let alone trek through the woods any more. There was a younger version of the Kill Club, kind of like what the Jaycees are to the Chamber of Commerce, called the Franklin Rod & Gun Club. There were also a county Fox Hunters Association and a Coon Hunters club in years past. So except for the Kill 'Em All Club name, I guess there's not much news there.

There's more news regarding Franklin's Hanging Tree but even that goes back a bit too and probably has more to do with the morbid fascination of one seeing the hanging-deed than any justice aspect. On June 9th 1863 one Colonel Orton and a Major Dunlap of the Union Army were hung on a "wild cherry tree, which stood on a knoll near the railroad and near Liberty Pike behind the old Darnell place." Yea, I caught the knoll part, maybe that's a small bluff that is a small knob – whatever.

It seems our two victims were reportedly confederate spies and considered successful until that point. The point being that one happened to be carrying a confederate officer's sword marked "CSA" on his side. (CSA is the typical marking for the Confederate States Army). They even had official papers from the War Department at Washington and claimed to be Inspectors General of the United States Army on an expedition inspecting the outposts and defenses.

But the story almost immediately revolved around the importance of "which tree" did the deed. Controversy after controversy after controversy lasted weeks, months, even years later. Really! There were many contradicting "eyewitness" testimonies proffered, Army investigations and reports, plus numerous local debates as to whether it was truly a cherry, an Elm on Mr. Figuers' mother's property (surely he would know since he was there), the white oak with the large horizontal limb projecting southeast, still standing not over 25 or 30 feet from Bill Wright's property or whether it was the one, you know, that was cut down and now not a vestige of it remains but had been standing just off a dirt road that ran from that low bridge over the Harpeth and went to the pike across Truett's land, or yet another, etc., etc. Maybe the night marauding, souvenir collectors whittled the thing into oblivion. It wouldn't be surprising if it comes up again on the annual Battle of Franklin reenactment coming up this November 30th.

Finally, the mystery of, "Who Was Marcellus Cuppet?" This was another CW dilemma that has lasted for over a hundred years and only just recently solved. It seems that there is one grave out at the McGavock Confederate Cemetery at the 1815 Carnton Plantation just south of downtown and the infamous Union/Federal breastworks/fortifications line. The grave was found along the fence line of the cemetery and the plantation grounds but (obviously) not one of the many confederate graves all in neat rows with markers attesting to their name, rank, regiment and anything else that was known. The second, to location, curious thing about this grave is that besides the name there is an engraved hand with the finger pointing upwards, one of a kind in the whole cemetery of almost 1,500 graves.

Local legend had it that Marc was one of the several slaves of the McGavock's who had died suddenly while helping with the two-acre cemetery layout and the fifteen-hundred holes that were needed. Following the Battle of Franklin, and as was the custom; bodies were buried where the soldiers had died. But within two years, John McGavock, who had given over his beloved two-story Carnton house to serve as an observation post during the fight and as a hospital after, saw that the graves were deteriorating.

It was down right unnerving for John and Carrie to trod into town past the fields and fields of sewn confederate (and Federal) soldiers knowing the previous purpose of these now sacred lands was farming (and would probably return to it). Besides, normalcy was needed, a new priority to obscure the devastation and slaughter that had happened here. Therefore he, and his wife Carrie Winder McGavock, decided to collect and re-bury the bodies of all the Confederates in a dignified cemetery laid out according to the states that the soldiers had served.

No one knows when the idea was first decided to be put into action but it may have been spurred on when the Federals sent the 111th United States Colored Troops to exhume, collect, and transport all the dead Federal troops to a final and dignified resting place at Stones River National Cemetery in nearby Murfreesboro. Note that the US government had no intention of transferring the Southern dead. This was a missed opportunity in my mind that could have helped the healing process – but then I wasn't there and maybe it would have been felt as sacrilegious or something by the southernly-inclined.

It was this very point and the irony - if one would use slave help in exhuming the confederates - that gave suspicions to a local historian and thus helped the research that solved the Marcellus Cuppett mystery. He felt it was unlikely that John McGavock would have used (hopefully – now former) slaves to do this work therefore it made sense that Marc was not a slave but something else.

Here's the story, just 100+ years later. Marcellus wasn't a slave, or even a soldier. Marcellus was the younger brother, only in his twenties, of the man McGavock (and probably the other nearby land owners) chose to do the deed, one George W. Cuppett, a former Confederate attached to Terry's Texas Rangers. Possibly a disease he picked up from opening the graves and transferring the bodies, i.e., doing the work, Marcellus became violently ill and soon died (before the completion of the project). He was laid to rest near the fence and near the men he had been working hard to identify and dignify. No, I don't know why the hand/finger pointing. I'm pretty sure it was the index finger and probably to identify the sentiment, especially to his family, that he was now upstairs.

I'm now an official landowner. But I'm not sure if that's one word or two. It doesn't really matter because I got enough land to officially be called a Squire or maybe that title automatically came with the precious land. Jealous? It all came about from my news-debriefing-myself-drinking-nights, one in particular, after C had left and I had no one to talk to but the (pretty) bartender. He (I'm just kidding, it was a she) – she said, "I see you like Jack and Coke." Fortunately she didn't add, "a lot."

"Yea, I really do," and either to impress her or myself, I added, "I even found that the Japanese like it a lot."

"So, have you been there?" picking up on my lead-in, pretty and smart. Good.

"Yes, a few months ago. They say that Texas is the biggest market for the Jack with Japan a close second."

She didn't pick up on that one with the expected, "So, you've been there recently too?" But what she did say was great: "Well you probably know that you can write to JDD, telling them how much you like it and they'll deed you some property there on the distillery ground."

I proceeded to blow it, because I didn't know it, or the details and didn't take the time to reconnoiter. And I learned long ago that reconnoitering is important in all conversations with that sex, women, but I had momentarily forgot. Mistake – I admit it. So I said, "Really!" That's a "Really" stunned deer with light in the eyes, blow your cool, show your ignorance, lose control of the conversation "Really" one.

"Yea, now it's only one square inch but it's true," She added without saying. "I won. You're a dork. Next?"

So I did. I wrote and promptly received my official certification, deeded lot number and the title, Tennessee Squire. Now I have to learn if everyone else has already done it already. Meanwhile JD, black label, tastes even better.

Jealous? Don't be, you can be one too, a Squire landowner, just write to Jack Daniel's Distillery just down the road in Lynchburg, TN for your official one inch square. Just ask to be a "friend of Jack's." Who knows, maybe we'll be neighbors.

I think I mentioned my Nana and her ferns. I know I did. What I didn't tell you was that cats, dogs, and FERNS SHED, So growing up, someone had to do the deed, pick up after my dog-pet and my mother's Nana-fern-pet. Have you ever heard the axiom, "Give the job to a busy boy and you'll surely get it done?" Well, no wonder, it was unique to my family, circa mother, and I was the one with the biggest Chore List (and not my sisters. I think I've already mentioned this somewhere but probably in my last book).

Fortunately, I didn't have to do the housework. And for where I'm going you have to understand that I hate the sound of any vacuum whether it's the dentist drills and home vacuuming machines et al - they drive me crazy. I just wipe the dishes that big sis washed for my inside stuff job plus pick up after the dog and the fallen fern-do.

If the dog had a dropping, it was a do-do and fortunately they were rare. In any event, one day I really wanted to get outside and play with the guys in our special swamp and didn't want to be called back in (to do anything I hadn't done) so I decided to kill several days of fern-do work by quickly taking out the vacuum and picking up the stuff on the floor but also running it over the plant for all the loose stuff that was going to fall off soon anyways.

Question: Have you ever since a bald fern plant? Do you think anyone would notice one? I'm not sure mom would have the plant from dad's mom if it weren't for him anyways. I remember when I didn't keep up with the dog combing for a couple of weeks and we had to take Lucky to the vets to get him shaved (the only out for entanglement. Excuse the pun). That dog was mad, really, really mad and wouldn't look at the driver-mom or the handler me for a whole week, wouldn't eat, and howled a couple of nights. He did look strange, shaved, but I wouldn't have ever guessed that a dog could feel embarrassed or ashamed of it's own looks. Lucky did. Trust me. He even did some dog do-do's – in protest.

Now for question #2: do ferns have a sensitive size too? Did I in essence kill the sedate, innocent, dopey, standing still and contributing nothing, dropping fern-do fern? Mom thought so. Dad just grinned.

Dad was a serious bloke with an impish twinge. Bloke was his English side; the word was borrowed from the Celtic "ploc" meaning, "a large and stubborn man." He was more "large" in my adolescence eyes and more average in height and build to the general public and me when I grew older.

Impish stands for his secret side, more mischievous than seriously threatening and this side only came out on giddy occasions like fern vacuuming. The "giddy" is not the "feeling unsteady" definition but the "giddy up" one; when one finds oneself on a high horse and wants to show off for the hell of it and for no other reason, in other words - no good excuse then because one's "up" there.

The best example I can think of immediately to tell you was the occasion when we had just moved into the G's Bread and Breakfast that the parents quickly took off the market (the B & B part) and the celebratory dinner that the parents had set up with my uncle Buzz and his wife, the unresponsive-sparing-partner. They were there since it was uncle Doc's money that had secretly backed dad's purchase of his new business. It was the only time they had ever (or would ever) come to one of our dinners and this was before we (at least I) knew of my uncle's other side.

No, I knew he was a professional wrestler before becoming a doctor and had the cauliflower ears to prove it. But we all didn't know and I'm pretty sure that this included mom and dad, that uncle had a drinking problem after which he went home to beat up my aunt providing he could find her. If we had lived in that small town for any time, we would have known. One of the advantages of the smallness was you know everything about everyone unless you happened to be in a cell in one of the many wards up on the hill at the north end of town, the ubiquitous State Hospital Funny Farm.

It seems it was most of the times that Unc Bart did fine her, his wife, since she wasn't resourceful in finding hiding places in their modest home and didn't have the initiative to leave let alone the obvious - shoot the bastard, which would have had the effect of curing both their problems. It was only after college that I learned at my first job as a reporter that there was such a thing as a victim-syndrome for battered women: they seem to always "forgive and stay" versus any alternative to the abuse they take, That is something that I, to this day, don't understand.

His name is Uncle Bart Barney, MD. I called him Buzz for his hobby, getting buzzed therefore the BBB. I don't know if anyone else called him that, picking up on my sarcasm, but I did freely just not to his face but always with a great deal of disrespect.

The meal, a dad prepared lobster tail feast served on the good china that was only brought out for the most auspicious occasions, went fine with only wine. I said that not to rhyme but to point out the lack of mind-altering booze present, the stuff that ignites the Unc's buzz-brain (or maybe numbs it).

The feeling was euphoric. Older sis and Nana were also at the huge heirloom dinning room table, Nana's co-opted formal dining room table, now ours when we bought/moved into her house back in the B. The two younger siblings, young sis and brother, had been feed earlier and off somewhere, either upstairs or down, doing whatever young kids do.

The meal was complete, mom's infamous (two) lemon meringue pies had been mostly devastated and the conversation had turned to "who's going to clean up?" This was one year sooner than when we would purchase that newly invented dish-washer contraption and sis and I knew better than to move a muscle, even look down, since up to this very day it had always been our duty to wash (hers) and dry (mine) all the dirty dinner dishes ever created in our households, three so far (in our very young lives).

The women, the three older women, were in the process of posturing about "women's work," tedium and boredom," and "there must be a different ending to a great meal;" the expected social, polite diatribe common from women after such meals at that time. Even as I, a mere youngster, had heard often.

But dad summarily stopped the conversation with the insertion, "I know what will solve the problem, the men are going to show you women how to quickly dispense with this simple chore and in the most efficient manner. Now you women – be sure and pay attention." It was one of those rare signals like a curtain was about to go up and we were about to witness a "play" most likely the "slap-stick" kind.

Not provoking enough comments to his satisfaction, he added, "After all, men can bring a lot more efficiency to household work." And of course that did it, all the women chirped in at once making points, defending roles, and trying to meet the challenge just thrown down.

I had looked over at Unc since I knew dad's comment about the "men doing it" didn't include me. By the shocked surprise on his formerly-in-the-ring, mostly poker faced, showing a no-emotion-exterior trained demeanor, I figured that this hadn't been preplanned and he was about to learn another side of his much admired business man, dad, for the first time. Tit for tat. We'd soon learn about his other side too. Of course this was a new prank/gig that we were going to learn.

Everyone helped to clear the dining room table, carrying things to the kitchen, stacking everything on the kitchen table after dumping the disposable excesses into the tall outside trash can on the way that dad had retrieved from just outside the back door. And when we all retreated, the large kitchen table was surprisingly full of the glass and ceramic dinner remnants.

Dad put on one of moms full-front (and green – like everything she chose) aprons and shooed everyone out, suggesting we go to the (two color green) living room (with the green gun and drapes) but knowing that his curious audience wasn't about to go too far from whatever spectacle he had created in his imagination and was about to play out.

We didn't have long to wait because he started filling the sink with (too much) dish soap obviously not being use to doing this. And the sink was bubbling - a lot and was sure to bubble over. As the sink was filling, he stationed Unc next to Nana's table in our (light green) dinning room. Remembering the best (only) china was stored in the dining room hutch. It was now obvious that Unc would be stacking the dishes and stemware coming his way on the dinning room table until the project was finished or there was a lull to be able to transfer everything to the hutch.

Dad proceeded to empty the drying towels drawer, taking all of them out (and we had a lot, mostly green – enough for three houses in any direction). Dad neatly placed them, one by one, end to end, from Unc's feet in the dinning room back through the doorway and up to his command center, the kitchen sink that already you couldn't see because of the mountain of bubbles. This visibly upset mom - the towels and bubbles. Mom tried to restrain herself in front of company and at the same time to be a "trooper" in the face of dad's play acting.

Personally I loved it – he was destroying my chore tools. Mom only did the laundry on certain days and I wasn't going to have any drying towels for three more. Sis was just going to have to stack the dishes and let them air dry. Yes! Go for it dad – I'm with ya. Do you have any "efficient" ideas on doing the lawn faster too?

Next he arranged the dishes by size loading the biggest, serving plates first, into the mound of bubbles up to his elbows, nay arm pits (and his business white shirt that he had only rolled up to his forearms). Not that he cared, it was more important to wet-wipe down the plates, one at a time, rinse quickly and throwing it (through the air) to my Unc in the other room who was suppose to catch it, dry it with one of the three (green) towels on the table, by his side that dad had stacked (they were the last three).

Well the throw wasn't the best. Unc caught it between his knees. Noting the wet seeping into his pants and with the poor throw, Nana shocked everyone and yelled, "Ball One!" Everyone stopped to laugh even dad who was about to toss the next one. Then he did and Unc had to one hand it since his other hand was still full. It reminded me of some of the dish throwing and juggling circus acts I had seen as a kid "under the big-top."

After the second smashed dinner plate and the first shattered coffee cup, mom and us bystanders went into the green living room. It was more to console mom than lose interest. I just loved to see the adults mess up, any one of them let alone two. Looks like dad's play idea was better in his mind that the one he was still carrying out. I tried to invoke a quick betting thing with sis on the "number that they would smash" but it didn't go over – was simply erased by the look mom gave me.

In the living room mom said, "I guess I was tired of those old dishes anyway." This may have been because what little color they had inside their gold plated rims, was blue not green, her favorite.

And the upshot of it was that the "men" stopped their playacting after one more broken whatever, I think it was one of the crystal stemware. Seems the thickness of a drying towel on the floor wasn't nearly enough cushion to prevent breakage. Unc joined dad in the kitchen to finish things and when they finally joined us in the living room, Dad came in announcing to mom (and all) that it was time for one of our NYC trips where she could pick out a new, full set of china as well as seeing the one or two plays we usually did on such treks. And I just knew that the new set would somehow be green.

I didn't stick around to see if his "apology" was going to work since I was curious to see the state of the kitchen, which wasn't as bad ad I had expected but not as good as sis and I were required to leave it. But I could tell it wasn't over, the floor was still wet in places and dad (or Unc) had used the towels that had been on the floor to try and dry it.

That wasn't the bad part that mom was sure to pick upon. It was that they, the two men, must have used their feet on those towels to try to do the drying job rather then bend over on their knees since several in the laundry stack had their soiled foot prints visible on the towels destined for a future wash. Future I hoped but now suspected that it might be moved up to tomorrow under the circumstances. I knew mom was about to do a late night wash. Damn.

Yes we went to The City, window shopped for china. Yes, we shopped for china a lot, saw two plays including the risqué *Fanny* but never came home with any china nor was any scheduled to be shipped our way. I think it was a case that we/dad were about to make a lot more money but we didn't have it yet so she couldn't see spending it too soon. Her new green china would have to wait.

Secondly, dad never gave a repeat dish-washer performance even though it made pretty good coffee-clutch conversation for the parents in the years to come. And I can tell you, since I had to look last trip home, the old china, what's left, is still in the hutch. In fact I can't think of another occasion that it was ever taken out again, that is what's left of it.

I said *Fanny* was risqué and it was, at least for those times maybe still. My observation of Hollywood, Broadway and TV to some is that they're always pushing the envelop as a limp device to get people's interest/attention/monies. It seems (to them) to be easier than work on really well written stories, interesting and new plots, intelligent dialogue, and the like.

Fanny, the musical, was based on a book by S. Behrman and J. Logan. I never (bothered) to read the book. It's supposedly a love story based in and around the mostly disreputable, old port of Marseilles (France) therefore the authors could purport that it wasn't America and would be "educational" about some far off place even though the actors, actresses and language was more the Twenty-Eighth to Thirty-Sixth streets Brooklyn docks of NYC. The plot focuses on a young teen whose childhood love, Marius, goes to sea but not before impregnating Marius. Her mother forces her to marry an older man who is so happy about this that he doesn't mind the two-for-one package. The predictable complications come with her sailor returns and old fires are rekindled, etc.

Divorce, pre-marriage sex, and the like weren't even discussed let alone recognized (at least in our family) up to that point. Remember mom was (still) cutting up the risqué parts of *Life* magazines. But somehow dad had heard that this was "the" play to see and had gotten tickets unfortunately with a premium from some well connected guy at the hotel. (A least he didn't but the Brooklyn Bridge too). Whether it was a bellman or the concierge I don't know or at least remember. In dad's defense, maybe it was the talented and popular Italian bass, Ezio Pinza starring in the lead that prompted dad to buy the tickets. We had seen him in Rodgers and Hammerstein's *South Pacific* and had sung *Some Enchanted Evening* in the car all the way back home for that trip.

To top things off, we had box seats, a first, and had arrived late missing the opening; too much china shopping. Maybe box seats (the private booths on the walls) holders were expected to be eccentric (arriving late) so no one stirred in the general audience below us as we settled in doffing the winter coats et al. At other times, we had seen the doors closed with the ushers admitting no one once the play had started. Maybe box-perks?

I had noted that dad had given a bigger tip to the usher to seat us but maybe this also was expected of box holders. All I could think about was the distance from the box to the stage and whether John Wilkes Booth had a similar distance to jump for his retreat in the infamous Ford's Theatre in Washington.

I don't know what it had to do with the plot but soon there was a topless, grass skirted, bare feet native gyrating nubile young girl on the stage probably inserted as a temptation to our nomad sailor visiting some distant island in his travels. It didn't make me feel sorry for him and I started considering sailoring as a possible profession. To my amazement (and enjoyment) her some-things were gyrating more than some of her other-things.

The fact that our awesome petite beauty was doing her dancing behind a thin net curtain was probably a moral concession to the more puritan of us at that time. They probably referred to is as a "necessary transition" device. Dumb me, rather than sitting back and enjoying what I knew to be a mistake (or at least a lifetime chance of someone so *young - me*), I was on the edge of the seat probably drooling. In good conscience (and also dumb) I said to my parents, "Should we be here?" They looked at one another, probably counting the money thus spent on this enterprise and said in unison, "Yes. It's OK." Without thinking I innocently responded, "Well then, can I have the opera glasses?"

Mom had gotten the mini-binoculars as a Christmas present last year and I knew she had them in her purse. Both parents just "tittered" and didn't budge but I really meant it. Seeing that I wasn't going to get them and already wasting a lot of precious time, I turned back my apt attention to the stage.

The next scene made clear the plot was "over the edge" as they, the parents-chaperones, said this to one another. I think they were talking about moral dilemmas but even older sis was now uneasy. So the eccentric box holders that we were and having paid for the privilege, left, with Enzio wafting some aria in the background. I just wish I had paid more attention; to remember what island that was where the young nubile women went bare feet. OK, so topless too!

"Dear Ezio, I would like to ask you about a certain island where the bare footed and nubile young virgins…

"My dear friend Ezio, As a devoted fan and special admirer of your work…

"Dear Sir, I assume this letter will never reach our Italian hero, Ezio, so I wish to enquire of the person opening this fan mail…"

Never mind. It won't work. He died in 1957. It must have been something he picked up at one of the many exotic Islands that he frequented.

Some say men like Willie York
Are just plain no good,
But let me tell you, Mister, Willies
Done the best he could

\- *Johnny Seay*

Campbell's Soup

The decade may rightfully be said to belong to Andy. That's Andy Warhol, world-renowned artist, avant-garde filmmaker, public figure extraordinaire, sought after socialite, intellectual bohemian, and many more titles. It's easy to build up a dead icon with many flamboyant titles and stories but it's a rare talent for anyone to have succinct analytical insights into the culture of the (any) times and this is the real key talent of our very alive Andy. Andy's second talent is to act upon the periphery of what he sees/knows about us, the who, what, and where we are as an American culture. On this platform Andy artfully captures the essences for us and even (and ably) pushes our cultural envelope. To have such talents in one person is called genius.

Andy, Pittsburg born, Andrew Warhola, spelled Varchola in Europe, from his NYC studio that he calls The Factory produces art as a "machine" (would) and with an insightful vengeance. The many notable figures, the in-crowd and the wantabes including Mick Jagger, Liza Minnelli, John Lennon, Diana Ross, Brigitte Bardot, and Michael Jackson that are attracted to this phenomena and visit/party/socialize with Andy, helps to propel him and his works to the forefront of the mainstream and the press.

He was born August 6th, 1928 and moved to the Apple (NYC) in 1949 giving him a good two decades to sort out our way of life and move to its helm. Maybe he was even knighted by the Queen if not by himself. But the most apt and socially credited (and accepted for now) iconic label for our subject is that Andy is a Pop Artist or Poperist if you prefer and currently at the top of his game. I prefer my own iconic label for Andy: The 70's Culture King. I very much doubt that he will be replaced from this crown as we continue our journey up the 70's.

Not everyone alive today, especially critics, are going to agree with me. But all's it would take is for Andy to have a tragic death and history will not let go of him for another one hundred years.

I point out Andy for perspective. Our decade is flowering with new ideas that historians will write about such as the sexual revolution (maybe exacerbated by the now available contraceptive pills), the feminist movement, gay rights, the continuation of the hippie culture, globalization, the carryover (from the 60's) of the green revolution, and probably many more that I can't see from here. Here being a small corner of the newspaper game and I point this out because you won't necessary see any of the above including Andy on the streets of small town America or in our small town newspapers.

Small towns aren't completely insular and will be impacted but only long after such movements and revolutions roll over the big and bigger cities as well as our culture in general. Our small town people know who Andy and/or President Nixon (who is humored to be considering resigning) but these people, cultural events, and items are of secondary importance here. And here in Tennessee it is arguably Dolly's Decade, that's Dolly Parton who has been cranking out bestseller songs regularly.

Maybe our competitive newspaper, the TRA, has it right – you can put our news on one page. Some cultural phases don't ever touch us at all including the reported new, New Journalism movement as signified by a book of that title bringing pieces from the currently New York Times Best Seller notables: Truman Capote, Hunter Thompson, Norman Mailer and several others. Here in small town America, it isn't even worthy of mention. I might not even know it except I'm in the right business.

What is important here is peace, a definite, identifiable, good feeling of peacefulness that comes from living in an American small town. I know, my (only) three don't make a hard and fast canon but it's evident in the people, not just me. Try waving or saying "Howdy" to everyone in the Apple (read NYC). You're likely to be arrested, even at Peace on earth, good will - Christmas Time. But hey – it's official: the Franklin Kiwanis Club declared the Ben The Handsomest Town in Tennessee (circa the 1920's). In other words, it's always been like this. Same can be very, very good.

It's not just a slower pace, or the lack of big city problems, it's a feeling of well being that you can put your arms around, that you are a respected, accepted someone who can hide or participate to whatever degree you wish, depending on your choices. Maybe the word,

contentment, would be better. And it's always been this way. I saw a picture of a bunch of guys sitting in the Ben's courthouse yard many years ago, circa1900 I think. Why are there sitting there? Why not? If I could share that with you I would ask, "When have you ever seen a bunch of more contented guys?" Maybe if you haven't experienced this it will not make sense. Hopefully you'll find it, have it, one day. "Come on down to our contentment!"

There are four pillars to the Ben and Masons all. I use that term, pillars, as some identifiable, recognizable personages that make us truly unique and raise the small-town-bar of which we are compared by outsiders. Yes, we have founders, first settlers, lots of celebrities, kind and genteel people, and more. You'll find Edgar Allen Poe in our history, the infamous bootlegger Willy York made famous in song by Johnny Sea as I've said, Matthew Fountaine Maury the Pathfinder of the Seas, and even Dolly Parton (of the 1970's *Mule Skinner Blues* fame) too. But I'm referring to four foundational American personalities that any town or city would be proud to build on.

I use the Mason reference as an observation, not as a requirement to the Pillar titular title. They happen to be. It's not a reference or endorsement but more of a surprising commonality. My two favorite uncles, dad's brothers, were Masons so I'm familiar with the pedigree bestowed on a lot of good men (and maybe some bad ones – I just don't know any. Maybe an interesting book in the future – *The Men Who Masons Should Disown*, or something. I'll have to work on it – a lot and yes, first find out who they are!?!).

The Ben's four pillars, not in any particular order are: Ben Franklin (of course) (1706-1790) St. John's Masonic Lodge Philadelphia PA, Andrew Jackson (1767–1845) the seventh President of the United States (1829–1837) Cumberland Lodge No. 8, Samuel Houston (1793–1863) American statesman, politician and soldier, joining Jackson's Masonic lodge, Cumberland Lodge No. 8, and Colonel David Crockett (1786–1836) American folk hero, frontiersman, soldier, Mason, politician and "*King of the Wild Frontier,*" who preferred to be called Davy. They're ours because we claim them.

Back in Ohio, in the V, they had Johnny Chapman Appleseed and Daniel Decatur Emmett. OK, they had the man that invented chewing gum, their own Civil War hero nurse Mary Ann Ball Bickerdyke and if you wanted to stretch it a little, Paul Newman (not exactly a pillar but a great actor). The Ben is awesome by comparison.

Yes, they're interrelated here in the Ben, our pillars, in what was once the (not so wild) frontier and I don't mind telling you how. I personally found out about the inter-relationships because of a pair of eyes. They were proud eyes, confident, with the right one seemingly much larger than the left or at least the way the owner usually used them. They came to my attention because of a little research on my part, looking for the answer to the simple question, "What's Franklin all about?" Admittedly that's not too esoteric for an accomplished, first class (if only a small town) news guy. Oh, and book writer – I've just forgot to call my publisher again.

The occasion was apparently the 150-year-old anniversary of the town back in the late 40's and the eyes appear on the first page of a well-written article by Louise Davis of the Tennessean (the later, fellow newspaper, is a name we don't mention around the office too often). Louise wrote about the founder of Franklin and it was Abram's eyes in the picture accompanying her article that caught my attention, even before the article's title, which I might have missed otherwise. And for the informed, I think the picture was from a daguerreotype (or a photogravure of an original painting but I'm not about to ask the Tennessean - since the photography thing came a good twenty years later).

So we can start with our true founder, one Abraham (Abram) Maury (1766-1825) to get to our pillars. With do respect, Abram was quite a man but more the underpinning of our pillars, the foundation for all good things to come. And I'll give you the postscript now: I just don't know if Abram was a Mason (or who to ask to find out).

Abram was an accomplished civil engineer, pillar of his own family and something more. He was a charismatic seeker, who to pursue his deep-seated dream and on the occasion of his mother's recent widowhood left comfortable Virginia in search of a new home.

Abram's new home ideal only existed in his mind, dreams and imagination. That explains the "seeker" part and it was the charismatic talents that explain his entourage, which consisted of wife, two daughters, his widowed mother, four sisters and his younger brother Philip.

In 1797 Abram Poindexter Maury Sr. happened upon a man, Major Sharp at Fort Nashborough who happened to be in need of a master surveyor. Abram said, "That's me," hence the die was cast and Abram and company set out to survey the owner's 3,840 acres of land (six square miles) due south with the promise of acreage to be paid for the surveying fee.

Abram found a well-traveled, Indian-cut path through the canebrake (high vegetation such as overgrown cane) about seventeen miles south of Fort Nashborough that ended at a well-flowing spring that was also a part of the land he was to survey. It was the place of Abrams dreams and he set up camp to start his task for Major Anthony Sharp, a veteran of McCroy's Company, Ninth N.C. Regiment, who had received his enormous American Revolutionary War Bounty (to the "any and all" military personnel) Land Grant based on his achieved rank in that conflict. The practice was an inducement for enlisting in the military forces and had been a long-standing practice in the British Empire in North America. After all, land was a commodity in generous supply, and governments seized upon its availability for accomplishing their goals.

Fortunately for the Maury times, Indian relations were at a peaceful ebb in this area, not so to the far east and south of Tennessee. Abram and his group set about building a log cabin home on top of the nearby hill (bluff really) that he figured was going to be a part of his stake. Abram wasn't a possessive type and freely shared the lands and springs with his new Indian neighbors. At the time, there were an incredible number of buffaloes, bears, deer, panthers, wolves, foxes, raccoons, and opossum let alone pheasants, grouse and other fowl so Abram's little clan didn't seem much of an incursion to the indigenous people, the Mississippians, inhabitants of this area for thousands of years.

In 1799 Abram negotiated the purchased of his 640 acres with the Major in settlement of his surveying fees and christened it Tree Lawn. Abram almost immediately set out 109 acres in the far eastern quadrant of his new land along and in the crook of the Harpeth. This area was for the new town of Marthasville, named after his wife. He formally filed his plat on April 3, 1800 only three weeks shy of the deadline imposed by the Tennessee General Assembly. The plat was strategic to the river, which was questionable for navigation purposes but the usual site for similar towns. This entrepreneurial and enterprising investment-move was to set Abram and descendents as key political personage for the distant future as well as a wealthy family for those times. He sold the 192 lots of the town for $10 each and gave the land for the town square plus a lot for a church with no charge.

Martha was an interesting person, reportedly only the second white woman to enter the area (providing she was ahead of her daughters, sisters and mother-in-law as she entered). Unfortunately she was ailing in her first years here and became known as the Pale Face Who Can Not Leave Her Bed. This was attested to by hordes of curious, friendly Indians who trooped into her log house (that they called her "long house") to see her – in bed. They never tried to harm her, just came in, single file, lining the walls of her room to stare blankly at her - in her bed. This may have been the timidity-key to Martha pleading with Abram, despite his nice gesture, to not name the town after her (and I have it on good authority it was not because he chose the name Marthasville and not Palefacewhocannotleaveherbed name).

In the Tennessee Third General Assembly at the (then) capital of Knoxville, the legislators created Williamson County, named after Dr. Hugh Williamson, one of the original signers of the Declaration of Independence. At the same session, the assembly voted to establish a town within Williamson by the name of Franklin, named after Ben, a good friend of Doc Williamson. This had been Abram's second choice also and the official date was October 26, 1799.

A thirty-year-old Scotsman, Ewen Cameron, and like Abram – also from Virginia, build a two-story, double-pin, log home in 1798, the Ben's first house and home, on Cameron Street what is today Second Avenue South, just across the street from the (to be built in 1823) Masonic Hall. The hall was built from the proceeds of the first legal lottery in Tennessee. Ewen lived across from it continuously for forty-eight years and his son, Duncan, was the first white child born here. Ewen and his second wife, Mary, are buried in the Old City Cemetery of the Ben.

Abram's land and city-plat deal did wonders to start his political career and the name-dropping thing didn't hurt any. You see his uncle, Rev. James Maury, back in Virginia was an eminent Episcopalian minister and educator whose students included Thomas Jefferson, and James Madison (Presidents) and Light Horse Harry Lee, the renowned Revolutionary War hero and father of Robert E. Lee. Abram was easily appointed as one of the Franklin Commissioners and was therefore very visible when the county selected his town as the county seat. Abram soon found himself serving in both the Tennessee House of Representatives as well as the Senate.

And this was just the start, various members married into other influential families (and Abram's family didn't stop growing - his Virginia two children were soon joined by six more). Grown, one daughter married a local lawyer and military aide-de-camp to General Andrew Jackson at the Battle of New Orleans and who co-wrote an early Jackson biography. It was the son of this marriage who had Edgar Allan Poe as a roommate at West Point.

Another daughter, Martha's husband was Secretary of War and then the Commissioner of Indian Affairs in President Jackson's administration. Abram Jr. was a member of the US House of Representatives and married a niece of the Mississippi Territory Governor. A cousin and playmate to the Abram's children, Matthew Fontaine Maury, a hydrographer became known for two titles, Father of Modern Oceanography and The Pathfinder of the Seas. His work set off feverish Arctic exploration with many stories to tell. And the examples go on. So it's easy to see how the influential attracted the influential (pillars) especially in these early beginnings.

But before we leave prolific Martha I have to tell you another interesting facet of her character. She had "second-sight" (and maybe this was a quality the Indians picked up on). For example, one night she had a dream about her old, left long ago, Virginia home. She saw her father dying there and upon waking up the next morning, Martha started wearing black mourning clothes and was not at all surprised when three weeks later word came that her father had died – the very night of her dream.

Now let's bring in AJ who went to Tennessee in 1787, age 20 with already a career behind him. He, the youngest of three fatherless brothers (his father died within weeks of AJ's birth) had joined a local regiment during the American Revolutionary War at the ripe old age of 13, during which he and his brother Robert were taken prisoners. When Andrew wouldn't polish the boots of a British officer, the redcoat slashed him, head and left hand. While in prison, both boys contracted smallpox. AJ's mother was successful in getting them both released but Robert died within days and his mother had died before Andrew's 16th birthday. Quite a life, all before the old age of 20 when he came to Tennessee.

Enterprising, self-taught, self-reliant, and now a Tennessean, AJ saw the need for lawyering in this, the frontier. Although he could barely read he figured he could have an opinion on the right and wrongs of things, especially the many land-claim disputes and assault/battery cases so he put out his shingle and was thus a Nashville lawyer. It was one of those land disputes that brought Maury and Jackson in to periphery contact but it wasn't until AJ was elected as Tennessee's first Congressman that they became closer.

Andrew became a US Senator in 1797 but of course the irascible AJ only lasted one year and returned to Tennessee and was appointed judge on the Tennessee Supreme Court. This too didn't last and he became a Colonel in the Tennessee Militia in 1801. This was to his liking and he lasted right through the War of 1812 including the Battle of Horseshoe Bend where a Sam Houston and David Crockett served under him. The Battle of New Orleans was significant where the British lost over 2,000 to Jackson's 13 killed (and only 58 wounded or missing). That's what the history book says – of course based on AJ's reports (nothing inferred). After the war Old Hickory, AJ, was nominated by the Tennessee legislature to be President in 1822 (and also made him a US Senator again when he lost that first election).

Let me insert a small detail about Andrew that will tie in to Sam Houston later. Jackson fought 103 duels in his life, mostly over the honor of his wife. Jackson was wounded so many times that they said that "he rattled like a bag of marbles" at times.

Lieutenant Sam Houston was asked by Jackson to help dislodge a group of Red Sticks, Creek Indians, during the War of 1812 now known as the Battle of Horseshoe Bend where 800 Red Sticks were killed. It was here that Sam was first wounded by an arrow but rejoined the fight only to receive a bullet through his arm and shoulder. His recovery period brought him into closer contact with AJ working at the command center. He even joined Jackson's Masonic lodge and following his recovery he was assigned as an Indian Agent to the Cherokees.

Sam left the army in 1818 and opened a legal practice in Lebanon, Tennessee (50 miles from Franklin and only 32 from Nashville) succeeding to become an attorney general of the Nashville district (bringing him to the Ben) with a command in the state militia as well. Only four years after leaving the army he was elected to the House of Representatives and was considered to be Jackson's political protégé. In 1827 he decided not to run again but ran for governor and won, defeating the former but infamous, Willie Blount. He planned to stand for re-election in 1828 but resigned after a shotgun marriage to eighteen-year old Eliza Allen only to separate from her after the marriage. Then Sam left the environs.

There has been speculation over the years that Houston went to Texas at the behest of President Andrew Jackson to seek the annexation of the territory for the United States but if true or not it served his immediate purposes. There he spent much time among the Cherokee, marrying a Cherokee widow reportedly drinking heavily at the time.

Remember the 100 plus duels in his wife's honor-Jackson? Well this wife-abandonment, Sam's drinking, and his ineffectual-gaining-Texas for AJ caused a major rift between the two. Eventually he became a leader of the Texas Revolution supporting annexation by the US possibly wining back some favor with his mentor.

There is further speculation that AJ send Davy Crockett to check up on Sam's Texas annexation activity but Davy went into the Texas territory too far, Alamo too far.

Davy Crockett, originally David De Crocketagne, was born of John and Rebecca Hawkins Crockett in Green County, Tennessee near the Nolichucky River. DC was descended from the French Huguenots who had settled in Cork, Ireland. His grandparents were the ones who immigrated to America. Legend has it that his father was actually born at sea on the way.

Davy was the fifth of nine children and named after his paternal grandfather. His namesake was killed at his own home in Rogersville, Tennessee by Indians. Davy's father John was one of the original Overmountain Men who fought valiantly in the American Revolutionary War and distinguished themselves in the southern campaign, especially at the Battle of Kings Mountain where they overwhelmed the loyalists. Regarding this particular battle, Theodore Roosevelt wrote, "This brilliant victory marked the turning point of the American Revolution."

Crockett (1786-1836) was engaged to marry Margaret Elder, but the marriage never took place, even as the marriage contract is still preserved at the Dandridge, Tennessee courthouse to this day. Crockett's bride-to-be, Margaret, changed her mind (and soon married someone else, more elder).

In 1806 Crockett married a Polly Finley. They had two boys, John Wesley and William and a daughter, Margaret. Unfortunately, Polly died. DC remarried in 1816 to a widow named Elizabeth Patton and produced three more children, Robert, Rebeckah (sometimes spelled Rebecca), and Matilda.

In 1813 he enlisted in the Second Regiment of Tennessee Volunteer Mounted Riflemen for ninety days and served in the Creek War along with Andrew Jackson (and with Sam Houston at the Battle of Horseshoe Bend if you recall our earlier discussions). He was discharged from service in 1815 but was elected lieutenant colonel of the Fifty-seventh Regiment of Tennessee Militia in 1818.

No stranger to our Franklin, a middle Tennessee hub of political activity, in 1828 Crockett was elected to the US House of Representatives, an opponent of wasteful government. He is remembered for one particular speech, the "Not Yours to Give" speech. Actually it was his opposition to President Andrew Jackson's Indian Removal Act that caused his defeat when he ran for re-election in 1830 but he won again when he ran in 1832.

In 1834 he published his autobiography and spend a lot of time promoting the book, maybe too much time because he was defeated for re-election. A man of few words, he said (publicly), "I told the people of my district that I would serve them as faithfully as I had done, but if not…you may all go to hell, and I will go to Texas." This he did at Pres AJ's urging or in spite.

In Texas, Davy, 49, signed on with the Provisional Government of Texas for the promise of 4600 acres of land and the rest you know. The only Alamo Texan survivors were a woman, a slave, and a child. DC was killed in the final minutes, having fallen back to the Alamo's redoubt position in the long barracks. He had survived the initial onslaught and was found with a dozen bodies or so of the commander's, William Travis, men.

Because of the popularity of Fort Worth, Texas born Fess Elisha Parker, Jr., the actor who played Davy Crockett and also Daniel Boone during the late 50's and 60's, Fess' picture is more recognizable and associated with Davy then David's own. Davy's last home in Tennessee, still preserved, is in Gibson County, Rutherford Tennessee about 160 miles west of the Ben.

Regarding the Indian Removal Act of President Jackson, mentioned above, more than 45,000 Indians were relocated to the West during AJ's administration. 100 million acres of land were purchased from them (for about $50 million). AJ was a slave-owner but not an Indian-owner.

And in August of 1830, guess where President Jackson met with five of the "civilized" Indian nations of the Southeast in a "council," titled by historians The Chickasaw council, to convince the Chiefs of the Chickasaw nation to sign the treaty (that removed them and sent them on a trip to Oklahoma. Remember the Trail of Tears?). Well your answer is that AJ, "Sharpe Knife," as the Indians called him, came to the Ben and met with them in the Masonic Temple, Hiram Lodge No. 7 built just across the street from Ewen's log house on Second Avenue.

Also it was about this time that AJ had an unsuccessful assassination attack on himself by one Richard Lawrence. Davy Crockett happened to be at his side and helped to restrain Lawrence. That's why you can see a statue of AJ in the Capitol Rotunda at the doorway in which the attack took place. I, myself, think they should (at least) keep a coonskin hat on the work (or was that Daniel Boone? Darn that Fess for playing both).

Jackson was over six feet, tall for men in those times. His hair was stark red until he became President at 61. He was sickly, suffering from chronic headaches, abdominal pains, a hacking cough, dropsy, and, after his retirement, tuberculosis and heart failure but not before gaining eight more years after retiring. He died in 1845 at 78, at his beloved Hermitage that you can visit in Nashville.

AJ disliked paper money so it's interesting that his bust appears on the very popular twenty-dollar bill. For the trivia lovers, it also appeared on the Confederate $1,000 bill.

At Jackson's funeral, his pet parrot had to be removed from earshot because of its swearing. AJ was the first president to have been born in a log cabin (sorry Abe) and was the first to ride a railroad (while in office). His administration was remembered for being the first (and last) as debt-free.

During his 1828 election, his opponents referred to him as "Jack-Ass" but he liked it so much he started using it as his symbol. Later this same symbol became the Democratic Party's.

Jackson was the first President to be given a baby to kiss but this was not to his liking. AJ promptly handed it over to his good friend and Mason from Tennessee, Secretary of War, John H. Eaton to do the deed.

By the way, there is a 69-foot statue of Sam Houston in Huntsville, Texas. It's possibly the tallest statue of a statesman in the world. Reportedly it's so tall, dwarfing over the trees so that Sam can look back east and see AJ's Hermitage here in Tennessee.

So those are the Ben's pillars, extraordinary men all and that we all can look up to. It's not that they were born here (none were) or that they spent many years here (they all were men of movement, constantly on the go, even international for Ben Franklin) but the

Ben continuously played a key role in their lives therefore we chose them for ours.

So much for avoidance, I just know that as you are reading this, about a guy in his thirties who has mentioned girls and women more than once - so far. I just know that you're beginning to wonder about what is the role of girls in my life.

Note: I said girls as opposed to women since I feel very young but more importantly, I'm at the beginning of this boy-girl entanglement possibility (versus a mature relationship, older thing). So here's the "skinny" (and that's not an expression that we journalists can write but typically use in trade-talk within the office. And in reference to girls when we can be so clever. Excuse the pun).

Yes I date, have dated and it's now accumulated to many dozen over the last years as I assume you have, do (or would under similar circumstances). But what I've come to find out is that dating, pretty girls or plain, it's just another "function" that happens in one's (my) life. It's like going to church, which I try to keep up, washing one's clothes even at the Laundromats of this world, setting the alarm for work in the morning before going to sleep-function, and the myriad of other, necessary things we engage in – in this thing called life. They offer (me) something and are a part of life but like church, I'm just not sure of the "what."

I don't mean this in any derogatory sense. It's kind of like brushing one's teeth. Yes, we all do it, daily – at least one hopes, but it's not exceptional by any means, just routine and forgetful. What I'm saying is that one doesn't bring it (teeth-brushing) up in conversation even to your best of friends. Does one? When was the last time you thought about your teeth this side of a dentist's appointment?

Think about it, when is the last time you told anyone about your last (or any) teeth-brushing experience? I could have used "shaving" but that probably applies to just the males (and I hope I have a wider audience than that). On further thinking, maybe shaving applies…never mind. On to the tooth-thing.

Some of my dates were more engaging then others – take that however you want; I'm not going there. But conversations over lunch or at the water cooler at work are engaging too.

Then – and just maybe there happens to be one memorable teeth-cleaning time in my life. It happened back at The 612, my place for the last decade, the apartment-home above the exotic dancers; their home, back in the V, Mt. Vernon, Ohio. I guess I can't remember telling you this even in my last book. You know the 612 about the Sixties, my sundry living experiences, life in another small town called the V, a very nice small town at that. Should I charge myself for an ad?

Anyway, it was with the advent of the new invention of the water-pik and maybe that's a trade name and not just an appliance description (similar to the Kleenex and tissue intermingling non-distinction). I'm sure you know the water squirting, pulsating teeth cleaning devise-thing with different settings (for the water pressure), electrical device with a snap on the top water-reservoir holding device and with the snap on tips (for different users).

I'm sold on the things since a friend (and not my former college best friend that introduced me to the V – the one with the bad breath) introduced me to the thing by having me brush my teeth three times in the normal way, convincing me that any and all particles would/should be surely gone and then having me use his water-pik to prove his point – how good that this new invention is.

Now don't worry, the device comes with several tips as I've said, he had saved a couple, unused ones, so that one doesn't have to "share" (friend or not). And speaking about dating, I can't ever image being close to a soul of the opposite gender when I would be comfortable sharing hers or my toothbrush. I know it's done but God forbid. And there is a horror story back at college about a colleague's breakup with his off-campus, live-in, steady girlfriend of two years (for her best friend) and where she stuck his toothbrush before exiting his apartment leaving said appliance behind. Pun.

It had been steak that I ate before the test but I didn't neglect the diligent cleaning/brushing one, two, or the third time since I didn't want his point to be true and that I would therefore have to spend ten, twenty or thirty dollars, whatever they cost, as the wise thing to do. But without boring you or disclosing gory details, suffice it to say that I was duly impressed how even a conscientious soft-to-medium hard brusher like me could miss the particles that appeared in the sink while water-picking - items one just knew would contribute to eventual tooth decay let alone the immediate, anathema, bad breath.

So of course I owned one shortly thereafter (and ever since) and it was a Saturday morning simple, non-descript, water-picking function at my 612 (something one can do on Saturdays when one doesn't have to hurry off to the office before or right after breakfast) that my memorable "incident" happened. Now mind you, the Victorian 612 was a clean place and my apartment up in back was a clean-place, kept up by one who had learned the neatness-need in college, a strange turn of events for a messy teenager while at home. Therefore what I'm about to tell you and the possible circumstances leading up to it is most unusual.

I was merely following my (now routine) water-picking motions after breakfast and before going out to do the mowing, clipping, sweeping chores (part of my rent-agreement). Mindlessly, as this task becomes, I'm thinking about the possibilities for things I could do for the rest of my free day. That's when I happened to glance down at the sink, again, something one neglects to do after the first couple water-picking bouts. It's expected to get residue particles washed out and that's not something one has to witness since it might even interfere with one's digesting breakfast – another Saturday free-day benefit.

What I saw were some very thin, elongated dark strings that would occasional wash out in the water-picking process. Naturally I started wondering if the thing, water-pik, was starting to fall apart. Then I went back, going over what I had to eat that would be masticated into this form let alone lodged into one's mouth or between one's teeth, that could possibly bypass the brushing thing and only now was being flushed out of my face-orifice by my new water toy. As I was having this "play-back" I suddenly noted that the few objects mixed with the water, going on their way toward the drain and infamy (or where ever), were hard and twitching, like frog legs thrown into a frying pan.

At first this was fascinating. I'm an open, curious guy and what one could have done to a meal of any kind to have these results in the "clean-up," the "what" that I was now witnessing in my own sink, was mesmerizing. Compelling yes, until I realized that they were mini legs and I was parting with something recently alive and in my mouth – a thing that shouldn't have been there under the worst of circumstances.

So I did the only sensible thing, I panicked. Unfortunately I panicked first in my mind trying desperately to remember whether I had done the Cheerios, Frosted Flakes, and/or Grape Nuts with the cutup bananas for breakfast (versus snails, crickets and/or bugs): any of which could have been compromised by a multi-legged intruder while on the shelf or even in the cupboard. All this precious time, I should have been panicking with my hands, shutting the damn thing off, or panicking with my internal-nausea-puking-device (whatever it's called) in order to rid any traces of this intrusive, uninvited, hostile invader that had attacked me. I knew it was going to be days or maybe weeks of scouring my mouth, maybe even Listerine or at least hydrogen peroxide, before it would ever feel clean again.

The upshot of the situation and my circuitous investigation was that somehow a very small, friendly, innocent long legged house centipede (that thought he was a millipede) probably looking for a drink, had climbed up into the handle of my water-pik and either became lodged or comfortable and was in there when I snapped on the personal, green "tip." For what it is worth, I now keep my blue tip snapped in at all times (and always will).

Do you see my point? Except for this one untypical exception of the thousands of teeth-cleanings, dating is similar – unmemorable in the long run of life. That is until the grocery-shopping thing that just happened to me yesterday and that I'm at a lost to explain (lost in reasoning let alone lost for words, something not good or expected for a journalist. A star journalist. An international writer star journalist. An internat…aah, never mind).

I know about "star-struck" and "not being able to keep one's eyes off (someone)" feelings and I probably will never forget the experience of kissing in the moonlight, late, after a fun, high school prom while walking a senior (older girl) home back in The G but I'm talking about something different.

Let me explain it this way. It was just a regular shopping for groceries trip (kind 'a like shaving, teeth cleaning, and dating…Ha ha). I had parked my car, picked up a cart at the grocery store door and had entered, the produce area to be exact. If I thought the name of the store was important, I'd tell you.

After bananas, potatoes, cherry tomatoes, a head of lettuce, and some asparagus (which I know is not to everyone's taste but a dutiful cleaner-outer) I was cruising into the cheese and pre-made potato-egg-salad and macaroni-salad area when I looked up to see a very good, very-very good looking gal just ahead of my cart, say 10 feet. She was glancing at me too and in a split second there was this overwhelming pull between us. I swear, the testosterone, which some have accused mine of leaking anyway, was on overload and flying through the air as was her estrogen.

Really. I was ready to leap over tall buildings, stop locomotives, move to Tahiti, start tithing at church, give up all worldly possessions (not that I had that many) and commit the rest of my life to serving, holding, loving the enchanting slightly shorter than I, female, medium length brown hair, burnt orange halter top mostly filled, matching but plaid Bermuda shorts revealing nicely developed tan legs leading to an attractive small waist with positively beautiful, silk skin (I just knew). It was an Eros lighting strike to my id-viscera.

Instantly I could tell she was passionate, about the same age give a year or two, and, as I, wanting to share our lives together for all eternity. God, what did I have for that breakfast yesterday?

It was simply unreal. Totally out of the blue, never happened before or since. And I hear you asking, "So what did you do?" Well the answer, even if I couldn't collect myself at the time, was, "I picked up a nearby package of pomegranates!" Can you believe? Not even Passion Fruit (not that they had any). So it became a Pomegranate Moment I guess. Da!

Now pomegranates may be your favorite food but I don't know what the hell they are anyways. I'm pretty sure that I've never had them, or don't think mom, back home in The G at my parents the 515, had ever prepared them. I know for certain that my favorite-person-in-all-the-world-Nana never canned them, or if anyone was so inclined, whether one could can/preserve the things in a Mason Bell jar. I wouldn't have even known what they were accept that I glanced at the sign as I was depositing the package of stuff in to my cart.

Did you notice I abbreviate the towns and homes I've been in and then neatly categorize the decade they fall in? Some people give their homes, rooms, cars, boats, and etc. names. Most people don't do anything let alone remember them once they've moved on. (I'm trying to get off the subject).

The naming thing wasn't planned, it just worked out that I spent the fifties in Gowanda, NY at 515 Buffalo Street, and the sixties in Mount Vernon, Ohio at 612 High Street. It just has worked out that way. Why would I lie? Gee, does that mean I'll be due for a move at the end of this decade?

OK, grocery: the feeling/pull was real and momentary. I immediately noticed a young boy, maybe 11 or 12 that approached to ask her a question. I automatically thought he was her son, his demeanor and all. She was paying attention to his question and giving an answer all the while sneaking glances in my direction. Was this flirting? Panic? Scared? Interested? A put-down (like, "look all you want little man but I'm too much woman for you to even think about")? Whatever!

With son in tow, I figured it was an impossible situation, a road I didn't wish to travel even if my four wheels were in the derby lane at the top of the hill starting to let gravitation take over. I turned left, headed for the canned veggies and decided to shop quickly (even if I found myself looking down aisles for another glimpse let alone a possible second-encounter). Maybe she immediately left the store assuming me a potential-stalker. Maybe she was so ditsy and insecure that she thought the worst – whatever. I guess I'm saying that a lot lately. Sorry. I bet she left her cart in the produce isle and ran out thinking it was a hot-flash (or one of the many other, unexplainable ailments of women).

No, nothing more happened nor did I ever lay eyes on her again (to this day). No, that's not why I moved. No, I still don't know what happened, where it came from, what it was and/or how to prevent it in the future. No I don't know if my interpretation of her possible reactions/feelings were completely skewered. No, I purposely avoid shopping on that daytime even if I thought about doing so. No I don't even know the color of her eyes let alone her name, (or her son's, or her nephew, or a neighbor's boy), etc. At best, and while very pleasant, it was indeed a most unsettling "incident" for me. And finally, no, I was too proud to put my surprise package of pomegranates back or on the magazine rack (before checking out). By the way, you couldn't possibly want a package of pomegranates would you? For free? I'll ship them at my expense. I wonder what the shelf life is on those things. Maybe I could use them to throw at any errant, howling cats sitting on the back fence in the middle of the night. No, I don't have such a fence outback and I've don't remember ever seeing any cats in the Ben so far and they never made it past two weeks. Did I at least spell them correctly?

Did it ever happen to you? If so, write me, I'm (really) interested. Thanks. (Our kind has to stick together – right?).

There was this guy in college. A great guy by the name of Steve. I and everyone that met him took an immediate interest and like to him. He was a little on the short side of manhood-height, reddish hair, trim little body that didn't reveal whether or not he was into athletics but you suspected he might be. Not that it mattered - any of that. He was chipper, didn't seem to have a problem with school work; just a happy, regular guy that one just wanted to get to know, to call a friend.

I got to know Steve and of course liked him from the get-go (where ever that cliché comes from). Maybe you've noticed too that there invariably are surprises, big or small, that surface when one gets to know another well. Steve, a guy I fantasized being my best man someday, business partner, surrogate-brother was from Bangor, Maine. Bangor became a friendly place and mission for me, a place I would have to visit or at least one day cross over into the state in order to experience more of Steve and to say I have.

My Steve's surprise was that he brought his personally cherished "morgue" from home to school with him from day one even if it was really the beginning of the second year that I met him. I met him as a friend of my new roommate. Yes, first year roommate

Charlie never returned nor has anyone ever heard neither hide nor hair from him to this day.

Like me, Steve worked as a waiter at the school but in a better waitering position – in the cafeteria, with the same money but lesser hours, and lesser hassle (especially since I was re-assigned for the second year in a row to one of the animal's table, the football players. Maybe all the fellow waiters threatened to resign before me or management saw that I was still alive after the first year – whatever).

Steve's morgue was his dating collection. At school his prized vault became this top dresser drawer when space of all kinds was at a dear premium to fellow dormers. It took several weeks before he even confessed to it and several months before he pulled the thing open to show me. Understand secrets of any kind are hard to keep in a small, closed community such as our college class, virtually all on campus (versus off-campus students). So Steve's secret was of the "first order" since I hadn't heard about it thus far into the second let alone the first year.

My first glance into his morgue-drawer, at least half full, of mostly wallet sized bust pictures of girls – the kind one routinely trades in high school, circa school picture package ones, was indeed impressive because my quick but vigorous scan could reveal no shabby entrants there. As time went by and we became closer (and his secret didn't get back to him via a new friend/confident – me) he even let me handle a couple of these starlets to see for myself. My first impressions were definitely confirmed; these former dates were prime-stock, dozens and dozens of them. It was only then that I began to question in my mind how a shorter guy in a state known not to have the biggest female population could have collected this treasured cache. So, finally, I had to ask (not the bit about being short, really – remember that I'm becoming "educated").

It was a family thing! "What?" I said. My two older brothers have been doing it for years so I started, maybe a little younger than they.

"So how does this work?"

He answered, "Well, you start dating a girl with the intent of somehow getting her picture. Some are easier than others and some take some doing to get there. You've got to work on it."

Somehow I started to silently wonder if his OLDER brothers were playing the game the same way, for the same goal and hadn't giving younger brother the full scoop, you know – substituting "her picture" for her panties or such. But I continued, "And then what happens?"

"The day or night you get their picture, you come home, throw it in the morgue (drawer), shouting, 'For Maine and for Manhood" and never see, call or talk to her again."

I was stunned silent and thought the older brother taught "For Manhood" thing, probably convinced me of my earlier impressions. So was it a Maine thing to do? A big brother not spilling the beans (at least on little brother) thing? A short guy program (I forgot to ask if his older brothers were)?

Maybe the rest of college or college and a few more years would teach me the "right" thing to say to this but I merely said, "Nice." "NICE?" Is that anything to say to anything? Girl: "Do you like my new hairdo?" Answer; "Nice." Wrong… "It very becoming." Right…

Oh well, friend Steve accepted it as an understanding-thing and we went on to other things, I just don't remember what they were for now. And on the principle of things, mine, I never asked to look into his morgue again – to see if it was still growing (or if there were addresses on the backs).

Girls - and we seem to be on that subject: There was this girl in high school that caused me an intimate, endearing moment that caused me to ask her out later (but soon-later). It happened at the school swimming pool, an almost Olympic sized pool (by half). Up until that point I hadn't really noticed her, she was on the short size and that was a "turn-off" to me. The guys and gals had dressed into suits in their separate rooms and entered the pool when ready. Us guys knew the water was on the cold side, administration cost savings, so we were in no hurry to get to swimming lessons and had entered the pool area, en masse, later than the girls who were mostly already in the water. You do know that women have a double layer of outer skin – an insulating thing.

Our, us guys', second delaying tactic was to stand at the pool edge, one end, as if we were going to enter but after we finished our present (long) conversation. You know, standing there swinging ones arms for warmth as well as effect, toes over the edge, sucking one's stomach in, looking good (for the opposite sex who pretended not to notice anything but themselves). The conversation? Well, I assume you guessed, "Never-ending" if we were to have our way – or at least until the swim-period ended. Topic? It didn't matter (we weren't really paying attention to what we were saying or what was being said – a guy thing. It was more important to be "lookin good").

So along swims this little lassie (I almost said hussy – but after what she did I didn't think of her that way). She stops at my feet, and definitely looks better in a swimsuit (than street clothes – but then maybe all women do. I'll have to check that out somehow. Of course in college that would become, "All women look good naked"). Uninvited, she took a hold of my big toe, slightly turning her hand as she caressed it. Freud would have a field day with that, I know.

Up until that point, I didn't really know I had a big toe let alone two, just on different feet. Well maybe on the occasion of an errant ingrown toenail but in my wildest guy dreams I never thought that either one was possibly a caress-able object. I was more concerned about them working properly, boosting my jump shots for basketball or enabling my quick stops in tennis or not getting (any more) of the dreaded fungi that marketing pundits couldn't resist calling athletes foot even though most people had two (feet) and as if to be an athlete one needed their concoction.

She said, sweetly, well doing this, "Come on in. The water's fine" as she smiles and merrily swims away back toward the talkative, gangly girl-gang along but in the water other side. Girls don't do this sort of thing. They don't even (usually) go to the bathroom by themselves. What gives?

I can't say I speak for all guys or even a much, much smaller number of them, but I hate the uncontrollable things that happen to a guy when the "sex-card" is suddenly dealt to you. Actually it's more like shoved down your throat (or wrapped around your toe). And that's an appropriate comment since it's the throat that immediately contracts – a first signal (a red flag). "Hey! You're getting the sex-card. You're getting the sex-card and you don't have control and you can't do anything about it. Ha, ha and ha, ha."

Sex-card? It's kind of the puberty and beyond, dreaded Old Maid loser card of adolescence fame.

Another defining moment, for me, was the first time I kissed my first blond, Slovakian to boot. Tall, willowy, not-to-be-missed in any bikini, girl-type. I like tall and I was sure her legs went all the way up to... Sorry.

It was in the parking lot on the first casual date near her car as we were parting ways. I meant it to be one of those tender, "Had fun. You're special. Hope we might do it again some time but maybe not. Have a good life," kinds of kisses but on the lips not just on the forehead (that I feel would be a definite turnoff to me if I was a woman).

I'm not one to parse women's anything so I certainly can't speak for her but, and I was up against the car, it was early evening with no one else around. She placed her hands against each side of my face and planted, aggressively (meaning with some pressure), a very big kiss all over my lips. But the "defining" moment was not that but what her right leg did. Her right leg started ascending my outer left leg in a certain embrace (of it's own). And I swear, a warm embrace too. I could instantly feel the extended warmth through my pant legs.

Damn! My throat contracted, my gonads started coming to attention, my heart said, "This damsel is worthy of fighting a dragon or two. And this ain't over by a long shot!" Oh, yes – then my usually silent heart added, "WOW." The later was in case I hadn't been paying attention to it.

It ended just as quickly as it begun. I couldn't detect anything different in her quick departing, "Bye" and didn't know that maybe she treated all her (first) dates to this, whether this was a Slovakian custom (knowing I would just have to look into that culture of which I literally knew nothing – up until now). She sure seemed Hungrier to me. (Sorry, I meant Hungarian knowing you would get the play on words).

Do you think I'm just a sucker for this type of outlandish male-female contact? I better dig up Steve's phone number and ask the expert. Maybe all women have an arsenal of these types of "contacts." I know - I'll look up Steve's number in the *Guinness World Book of Records* under Dating-Morgues. He's just got to be there and at the top by now. He was the type of younger brother that would out-do his older ones. I wonder if some of those pictures appeared in all the brother's morgues.

To sum up, let me use Johnny Seay's words, *My Babe Walks all over Me.*

It wasn't until I was fifteen that I learned about the game, Marco Polo, the blindfolded "it" person who had to locate others by the sound of their voices' the "it" shouting "Marco" with the roving others responding, "Polo." It's great in a swimming hole with the "it" shutting one's eyes in place of a blindfold (and even more fun having "it" use one's bathing suit. No…it was only guys – what are you thinking?).

Admittedly I had heard different groups of kids playing the game at the kids' end of the public pool back in the B but since I was usually there on my own, and one doesn't mingle with an established group of other kids too easily in a big city, or I was there with a friend in the deep end, I didn't pay particular attention or know what exactly they were doing. With a name such as I have, it seemed, at fifteen, to take a long time to pay it any mark (pun intended). I was always alert to the Mark Anthony's, Mark Twain's, Mark's Gospel, Mark of the Beast, the German mark, Trade marks, Mark of Cornwall, beauty marks, President Mark Washington, our first…never mind – I was just checking to see if you were reading.

The game was adolescent or at least too simple in my mind to give it any real attention until I started thinking of the global "Polo's" that had been calling out to the adventurous, Venetian, Marco and what would take one from the epitome of culture and civilization at the turn of the thirteen century. They were his sirens and beckoned him no less. I had to know more.

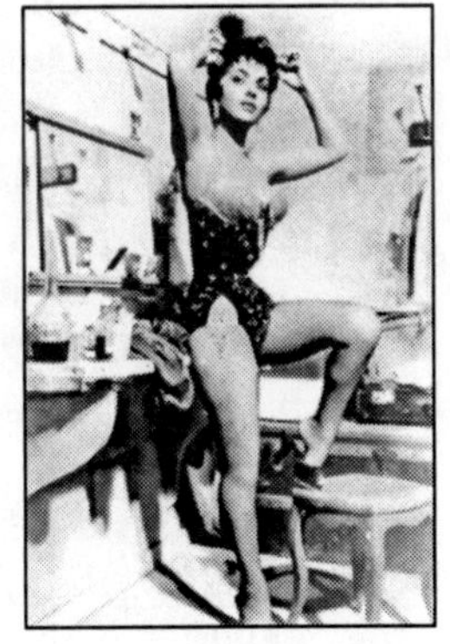

It didn't hurt that the Italian language fell like musical lyrics on my ears or that Italian meant nothing without the corresponding and many hand gestures. All right, in the spirit of full disclosure, Gina Lollobrigida didn't hurt. What…do you think that I am blind? Gina brought me puberty early. I didn't even mind if her real name was Luigina in fact I used to refer to her as Luigi with the guys when a girl or two walked by interrupting our guys-talk. And no…I can't spell her last name to this day but who cares…there will only ever be one "Gina." Personally that's a "Polo" that would inspire one to swim the Atlantic Ocean and the Mediterranean Sea to mark.

Did you know that there is a statue of Marco in Hangzhou, China? It's near the West Lake. There are over eight hundred lakes in China but the fresh water lake in central Hangzhou, West Lake, is probably the most famous with it's "Ten Scenes of West Lake" epithets, a Chinese thing, and the major attraction of Three Pools Mirroring the Moon Island (with corresponding epithet that I don't know).

Now that statue has secretly become a personal polo for me that I must see and it is probably fitting just as Marco might have felt, that I have no clue as to the how or when that I might "Mark" it.

Bet you can't guess my new assignment regarding a two hundred year old instigated by a telegram to our local County Judge, Wilburn Kelley. Dramatics aside, our county, with its seat, Franklin in a pivotal position, has been designated as an official Bicentennial Community by the American Revolution Bicentennial Commission for it's planned programs to celebrate the upcoming 1976 Bicentennial of our nation. This, if handled properly (by an ace-reporter), could be front-page stuff for months to come since there'll be pageants, expositions, tours, and even films will be in the offering. Of course the pageants will include a beauty contest. Remind me to take a couple photographers to that. This coincides with the 177th county's birthday but I'm at a lost to make too much of it. Many restoration projects are planned including our Fort Granger with many more to be added regarding our famous 1864 battle once the Civil War groups get into the swing of things.

Timely as it is, we've just had the unveiling of a replica, numbered, limited edition, *Liberty Bell* (3/8ths scale) given to the Ben by an anonymous donor (and friend of Mayor Ed Woodard). I didn't get that assignment but was interested to read in the front-page article that it was made by the same bell manufacturer as the original bell now in Philadelphia.

Of course the article didn't mention if it was a replica of the first, second or third *Liberty Bell* since the first, ordered from the Whitechapel Bell Foundry in London, cracked on it's first ringing in March of 1753, the second, re-cast, by John Pass and John Stow of Philadelphia had a weird tone and was rejected, and the third, also cast by Pass and Stow, was the one hung in the steeple of the State House in June 1753. This, the third, was rung to announce the opening of the First Continental Congress in 1774 and after the Battle of Lexington and Concord in 1775. Yes, it too (eventually) cracked and was removed from the steeple in 1852 to be put on display in the Declaration Chamber of Independence Hall with a replacement, the *Centennial Bell*, placed in the steeple.

The *Liberty Bell* was known as the *Independence Bell* until 1837 when the American Anti-slavery Society adopted it as the fitting symbol of abolition. But then all reporters aren't "aces." Of course maybe this article was written by another ace but had all the above edited out. I guess I'll meander over to City Hall to see if our mini has a crack.

I'm beginning to think that maybe small towns have a lot in common and similar things happen wherever they are, even in different states. Two news items in as many weeks that just happened here in the Ben brings this to mind, deer and dead fish.

Back in my last small town, we had the Banking Deer, a real, live young one. I think I recall it was a doe. It visited one of the main street located banks in the heart of the V. The wild animal was on an errant visit into town, ran through the lobby of the bank when the security person happened to open the front door to see what the commotion out front was all about. A surprised patron provided the deer's exit out a side door when she was trying to use the same. I can't imagine what would have happened if the frightened, hyper deer had been bottled up in there without an escape-exit. And yes, it made a deposit before leaving, just not with any of the three tellers but in the middle of the lobby floor.

Before that, back in my adolescent home, the G, it was not unusual to see deer especially early morning roaming through the apple/cherry orchard on the hill behind our house, The 515. What was unusual was when one of them happened to meander into town like the one that tried to do grocery shopping at the little mom and pa grocery located on the corner next to the town's fire station in the middle of town. It didn't help that the store hadn't opened for the day or that the two firemen who has seen the creature coming down the street decided to test the fire engine's siren so early in the morning. To their credit, the engine was already stationed on the station's drive-up apron ready to have it's weekly washing once the town and the other firemen woke up. Of course it served as a good resting place for the backs of their chairs to rest against in the cool fall, breaking morning while they had their first cups of coffee, talking idly, and watching the deer's progress coming down the street into town.

The deer, probably confused by all these strange forest structures (houses, telephone poles, a few parked cars and such) might not have understood the image of the sleeping red giant fire engine anyway but when one of our playful guys hit the siren button to see what the deer would do, the deer, rather then turn around retreating back up the street and hill to the outside of town and its wooded sanctuary, took two leaps left, the second up the three small entrance steps of Ragona's Grocery store going head first through the glass entrance door that was not only closed but still locked so early in the morning.

It was the siren that alerted all their fellow, sleeping comrades in the upstairs' chambers of the station and who were now falling over themselves to get ready for what they thought was a new fire emergency. Yes there was a brass pole down to the main floor but one thought twice about using it before one was truly awake and for the most part they weren't.

But it was the combination of the breaking glass and siren that alerted the Mister and Missus storeowners sleeping in their upstairs, over the store apartment/home. The commotion also disturbed their very pretty, sleepy-eyed teenage Italian daughter getting some more (unneeded) beauty sleep. Regina was one of my school classmates, a very popular one.

Maybe the deer, a six point young buck, liked his new gym or was challenged by all the grocery aisle hurtles he decided to master but this deer, the one who didn't just turn around out front, didn't just turn around and exit the way he came in either. For the next fifteen minutes you can't imagine the noise, commotion or the destruction caused by a rampaging buck in a little corner grocery store. I'm pretty sure he didn't come across any venison in the meat display that might have upset him, the display that now had a hoof-hole through it's front.

Soon the entire entourage of firemen were downstairs in various forms of dress (or undress) realizing the trouble their early rising, playful colleagues were in. They were also joined by several of the street's neighbors wearing bathrobes and such. And soon all were joined by the night duty policeman who office-ed behind the fire station in the town's police department and who had contacted the Chief even before venturing out to see what was happening in this usually quiet little berg. It was the same cop that had already been raked over the coals by our police chief for disturbing his much needed rest with only a sketchy report of what was happening and was now on assignment - about the business of learning if it was truly a police matter with the proviso that when he found out, he was suppose to call back the Chief with the particulars.

The Ragonas noticing the building audience out front of their store were now at one of their front windows calling out, asking what was going on. And if it wasn't for the Mrs.' long Italian dark hair rolled up in a dozen or so two inch curlers covered with a pink net scarf tied under her chin that one could hardly see because of her oversized paisley terry cloth robe with a huge collar that surrounded the mass on top or maybe it was the mister, minus his regular toupee in his dark navy blue silk robe showing a good quantity of black chest hair, enough to be seen from the street (and nothing more since he slept in the nude) complete with a loaded two-barrel shot gun in his one hand but protruding out the window or maybe it was the two vying for the same small window opening, that got the crowd to laughing. In any event, the grocers weren't getting any good information as to what calamity was happening below in their noisy store. "Deer me."

No, she didn't appear at any of the other windows, but the dark eyed, dark flowing long hair teenage beauty who at first glance could have easily passed for an Italian movie star, would have had a calming effect, at least on the firemen of all ages, gathered in the street below. Too bad.

Not to keep you in suspense and while the less than brave policeman had retreated to make his follow-up phone call to his irate boss, the industrious firemen decided to take action into their own hands and unraveled one of their hundred fifty feet hoses with two volunteers taking the nozzle lead. They used the brass nozzle to breakout more of the glass font door to enter since there wasn't a simple turn-lock to reach through and open the door. Their intent was to confront the grocery marauder who seemed determined to undue the neat, well stacked everything and the men's presence wasn't enough to turn the beast back out or if attacked, they had arranged a signal for their comrades to start the water which would surely control the deer and force it back out the door from which it entered.

Unfortunately, the best laid plans, or the worst…they forgot to tell the deer who was now beginning to tire or who had run out of cans of things to splay or pierce with his hoofs and was about the business of tearing up and seemingly eating the kitchen paper rolls of Scott Towels in aisle number three. Maybe he didn't like the packaging. Anyway, when the brave firemen entered and faced the monster, all three, deer and men, acted like deer at night caught in a car's headlights. Stupefied, they just starred at one another. The deer was first to act and as it was about to jump over and clear aisle number two, when one of the panicky two firemen called for the water.

Now to relate the next scene, I was told you have to imagine yourself out in front, south of the store closer to the fire station, looking up the street from which the deer had first appeared. Now imagine the surprised crowd when the huge plate glass store front display window complete with the hand painted store signs of this week's specials pasted on the inside and a small stack of some brand of spinach cans piled in a small pyramid suddenly burst out into the street.

Glass, signs, cans, frame and all followed by one re-energized, terrorized deer burst out. And then there followed a gigantic torrent of high-pressure fine city water that would have easily removed the window if the deer hadn't already. The high-pressure stream easily cleared the entire street, and even emitted a slight rainbow by the accompanying mist in the early morning sunrise and was now battering the unsuspecting wood paneled Ford station wagon parked carefully on this out of the way side street since it was the owners intent to keep it mostly parked until it reached the 16 years mark that would distinguish it as a "historical" vehicle. Unfortunately, the forceful water was now removing some of the wood paneling on the driver's side but that wasn't the worst. The worst was that the owner had left the driver's side window open in order to air out the insides from the Charlie's Super-Garlic Cheese and Pepperoni pizza that he had brought home in the same car last night from the little shop across town on the other side of the bridge.

To answer your question: no the retreating deer never got wet since it sanely took an immediate right turn when it landed in the street. And, for reasons unknown to me (lack of insurance for this type of vandalism, such a scary situation, getting an insurance payment with the opportunity to move on, settlement or lack of one with the town, or whatever) the store never reopened. The threesome Ragonas moved to a different town. Damn.

And while the locals mourned the loss of the convenient little store, especially known for it's particularly fine meats and masterful butcher-owner, I mourned the lost of one of those ideal girls you definitely wanted to met when you finally grew up. Double damn.

I'm sure it wasn't the same deer or even the same deer family since this is hundreds of miles away. But our local incidence, front-page story, was a deer that rampaged through a local house. Really. One just can't make this stuff up – and why should one since it happens in real life. Maybe I'll just quote my competitor's story here so you'll believe me. They did give more space and details of the event than we did in our paper anyways. Here goes:

Oh Dear! A deer did all that that? (No, I don't understand the quaint headline either)

A deer...in downtown Franklin...running through a house??? Believe it or not, such was the case Sunday afternoon."

Eyewitness Reese Potts details the freak occurrence: "I was driving toward Five Points along Fifth Avenue South about 4 p.m. when suddenly a small deer bounded from between two houses on Fifth Avenue at my right, raced across the street and crashed through the narrow glass panel to the left of the front door of a four-unit apartment house owned by Horace Edgmon. The animal came within ten feet of Miss Irene Bizwell on the sidewalk and was also seen by another nearby resident.

"I stopped and then heard glass breaking. I did not see the apparently terrified animal leave the house through a screen storm door at the back of the hall. Those who gathered could trace the path of the apparently terrified animal, although we found a small amount of blood on the premises.

"The animal broke a large mirror in the hall en route out the back door." The deer was small with no anthers and probably weighed about 70-80 pounds, although Potts laughed; "It was really moving on" and hard for him to judge the size.

A small deer reportedly has been sighted in downton Franklin on several other occasions recently. Dr. Jack Hall said he and his family were driving on Fifth Avenue North when son, Mike, calmly said there was a deer going into a house. Dr. and Mrs. Hall did not challenge the youngster since he frequently watched deer on their farm on Summers Road but Dr. Hall did turn the corner to Evans Street to go behind the house and found that the deer had already gone through the screen door.

He did ask a neighbor who was sitting in the yard about the animal and the reply was just as nonchalant as Mike's unimpressed remark in the beginning of the incident. Apparently the dazed animal had sped away along a neighboring fence. *(30) (That means the end of the article – in case you forgot our newspaper stuff).*

OK, so I purposely left their "downton" (competitor-mistake) in since that's not a local colloquialism. Is that mean?
Dead fish? And maybe bridges too.

If you read my first book (hint, hint) you'll recall the fish-killing (and maybe some weaker residents) stench of the world's largest glue factory's (and neighboring tannery's) effluents emptied into and running down the raging Cattaraugus Creek through the middle of town, the G, the stuff that even took the paint off the nearby homes. Well guess what.

We just had our own fish-kill in our own Harpeth River running through the Ben. And since the Harpeth isn't as wide (or as raging) as the Cattaraugus, I think it would be better named a creek or tributary. That reminds me, some optimistic (or humorous) resident put a sign up on our "river" bank that said, "Do Not Dredge Here" as if it was the likes of the Erie Canal or the navigable Cumberland that the Harpeth empties into. Lately, one would be hard put to use a canoe let alone a dredge in it.

The kill occurred in an approximate six-hundred foot stretch between the Franklin treatment plant and the next bridge with the closeness to the raw sewerage treatment plant being a dead give away to the reason (excuse the pun). A breakdown with one of the three pumps coupled with the recent lack of rain "depleted the oxygen level," so stated the state inspectors called in to investigate. I guess raw sewerage is more adapt at sucking up water's oxygen then fish. This just couldn't mean "survival of the fittest," could it?

That's two out of three. As for the bridge: do you recall the 153 foot, 1889 iron-steel Gaton Bridge build over the G's creek in the middle of town that the firemen blew holes through? You see, fire hoses have many uses besides putting out fires – routing deer, blowing holes in bridges, contests, celebrations, serious water fights, entertaining children, etc. Well it looks like the same company, Gaton, build one of the Harpeth bridges but I'm having a little trouble "running that to ground." Gee I really miss the old archives like the office had back in the V. I think every newspaper or at least every community should have one. Otherwise one never knows how much is lost to history.

News flash: our veteran Opry star, Sam McGee, 81 born 1894, was just fatally injured in a tractor accident last Thursday. 81, appearing every Sunday night on the Grand Ole Opry stage and still working his land – that's enviable.

In the issue was an interesting article regarding our just released flood plain report compiled by the Nashville District Corps of Engineers. Of course the 1972 flood was a while ago and people tend to become complacent as evidenced by the mere forty in attendance, including me (so count 39). The study seemed very comprehensive and complete. Someone or ones put a lot of time and engineering know-how into the pages. But the idea that most future flood damages could be minimized, practically eliminated, and/or the scare that our previous flood (1972) was by no mean the biggest we could expect in the future didn't raise too many eyebrows was my personal observation. Fortunately Editor Lance agreed to run it on the front page so I feel we did our part for now. How can one care more that the person/people affected? Hope that Sam is buried on high ground.

There are strange things done in the midnight sun
By the men who moil for gold;
The Arctic trails have their secret tales
That would make your blood run cold;
The Northern Lights have seen queer sights,
But the queerest they ever did see
Was that night on the marge of Lake Lebarge
I cremated Sam McGee…*The Cremation Poem*
(This is about another Tennessean named Sam McGee)
- by Robert W. Service

Another first-page-burner: Our county is officially the fastest growing state county since the beginning of this decade, 1970 (or should that be 1971 – Oh well, I'll look up the correct timeline distinction before the end of this millennium – and probably not before). Yes, it's big news even if the entire county only lists slightly more than 43,000 persons. Maybe you have to live here to appreciate this.

So much for driving around our town. I just found something I didn't want to find.

Remember the Ben's founder that I had introduced with the words "our true founder," one Abraham (Abram) Maury that was so influential in his time that the named another Tennessee county in his honor, Maury County, 26 miles to our south and a little to the west. Well the (very active) historical society is in charge of his family's burial place, a little cemetery in a small development appropriately called Founders Pointe just west of town off of the New 96 West (that our town fathers or the planning commission doesn't seem able to come up with a good name other than the Route).

I drove out, on my own time, to see it. It's there, Abram and clan are there, at least their names on the various assortment of stone edifices in different states of (slightly needed) repair but I decided to drive the few roads, all with residential houses, to see if I could find the original spring well and the little well-house that Abram built, the spring he continued to share with the Indians at the time.

Up on a small bluff a couple of streets over but within the complex, there's an obvious couple of lots with a gigantic, beautiful, well formed tree in the middle that is conspicuously absent of any houses when most all other lots were filled. There was a tiny black sign half way up the hill that caught my attention so, my newsman's curiosity got the best of me, I stopped the Blue Tail and walked up to the sign to see what it said. That's when I found what I didn't want to find and it wasn't anything to do with the spring-well.

Our founder, who I wanted to heroize, had slaves and this was their designated final resting place. I was shocked. Maybe this had a lot to do as to where I was born and brought up. Culture and one's immediate environment has a lot to do with who we are.

But it wasn't bad enough that he had "owned" them during life but it didn't seem that his ownership was lifted at their death since the sign clearly read, "Abram Maury Slave Cemetery." He didn't call it The Workers Cemetery or the Tree Lawn Cemetery. Did he really think of "them" as chattel? Wonder what he thought of his wife and/or children in terms of ownership or superiority. Did (some) men count the number of slaves like we read the wild west gun slingers carved notches in their gun handles to prove they were whatever?

Another surprise was the location, on a small hill toward the back of the development that one would assume would be a prime location for Maury's home overlooking the rest of his Tree Lawn land, cattle and crops. Maybe it was too far from the spring or there were other circumstances - but it wasn't obvious, at least to me.

OK, I know, from history, that Andrew Jackson had slaves. I don't want to know if Samuel Houston or Colonel David Crockett let alone our Ben Franklin had them too. I wonder if the Historical Society knows their names, these people buried here, some of those human beings that history had turned against.

Maury's family place was like a stone garden where his slave garden was just a field. Both cemeteries had little red flags that I assumed where placed by the Historical Society for maintenance or whatever. There weren't many red flags on the slave bluff so maybe no one knew who or how many were really entombed there. At least it seemed to be treated as sacred ground and that's more respect than the Indian's cairns were given. And no, I never found the spring or Maury's well house.

Here's a story you're not going to see in the big city papers: Nineteen of our area farms join another six-hundred plus farms across Tennessee as ones that have been cultivated by the same family for at least one-hundred years. The Family Land Heritage Century Farm program tracks such statistics and reported that this means more than fifty-eight percent of Tennessee land is still committed to farms. I'm impressed – aren't you?

And since we're pointing out some of the differences in big city vs. small town newspaper reporting, the national elections results, (Headline: "Carter landslides as Reagan tops Ford here") took a second place finish to our Ben's planned Independence Day activities and was on par with our local county upcoming elections. Do you begin to see/feel the difference?

In Cupid's
Little bag
Of tricks,
There's one
That clicks
With all
The chicks
- *Burma Shave*

Funny? No - Just Life

Love the Appalachian mountains. In the colonial times, the major Indian pathway through the Appalachian area, called the Great Valley at that time, was known as the Great Indian Warpath and would later become the colonies' The National Road. In the early 19th century, Washington Irving of *Rip van Winkle* and *The Legend of Sleepy Hollow* fame proposed renaming the United States of America to Appalachia.

As a kid we (the family) used to vacation at Beaver River Flow in the Adirondacks portion of Appalachia. It was back in New York State just a few hours East of the B, about as far one way as the grandparents in the G were the other. But with due respect, I tingled all the way to the Flow whereas I played Zit, counting the cows or station wagons, with whoever would play with me, even a sister, going to the G.

You might know Zit by another name. With the cows, you would get one point for every one you saw (and say Zit to – first) with (totally) black cows counting as five. Station wagons were similar with the red ones getting the more points. Variations included that the cows had to be on your side of the car (driver or passenger), and if you passed a cemetery (on your side – that your opponent saw and Zitted) you lost all your points and had to re-start. The game could go to 10, 21, etc. but on the trips to the G we'd pick 100 only after driving the parents crazy with the infamous song, "100 Bottles of Beer on the Wall" (the one you count down to 0) and they would finally command (like after the third time), "That's enough. Why don't you play Zit or the Alphabet games?"

OK, the Alphabet was simple, you watched for any sign (outside of the car so candy wrappers et al didn't count). You started with an "A" sign, then B. You could Zit them or only count the ones on your side of the car, etc. Yes, X's and Z's were the hardest but surprisingly I's and J's weren't easy even if this was the era of the billboards.

We had a little log cabin on the lake at the Flow. Yes, there were real beavers and their conspicuous dams were there too. It was there that I saw my first possums and yes, hanging by their tails on a tree branch.

It was here, during the night, after bedtime, that I saw my first raccoons. Sis and I, having been waken several nights, were very, very curious as to what these masked creatures looked like; the smart ones that were always invading our covered, galvanized garbage cans out back and making lots of noise in the process, begged the parents to let us see these nocturnal varmints. Sis' help was good even though quite unexpected since I was the "nature boy" and she only got "nature" out of her many books. If she would only do more of this, we could even be "partners." You know, like saddle-buddies in the cowboy genre.

Dad finally relented to help us after much begging. With dad in the lead and with the flashlight (he always referred to as the "torch" for some unknown reason – other than the obvious) we snuck out the front (only) door in the dark, holding on to some piece of clothing of the one in front (well, at least sis and I did). We noiselessly rounded the house to where the trashcans were, between the house and the toilet (read: one-holler out-house). Dad turned on the light, shining it toward the clamor. Low and behold three little marauding, masked bandits were rifling the garbage having undone the roped tops and having removed the rather large snap-on lids. At first they reared their heads giving us a great view of them, then one scurried off in a hurry while the other two, quite un-afraid, seemed to sense no real danger/threat and continued rummaging, more intent on finishing their mission, almost thankful for the added light.

We'd go practically every year to the Flow and I have a lot of great memories including another one – the time we had a visit from a bear. I think it was brown, I'm pretty sure but never actually saw it – even if it was only a few feet from me – thank heavens for trapdoors.

Fortunately we were all sleeping in the loft (with a closed floor-door one came through after ascending from the downstairs). My bed was across from the floor or trapdoor entrance to the loft that stayed open during the day to air out the windowless loft. The head of my bed was against the slanted (due to the roof pitch) loft and the foot of my bed faced the trapdoor.

I'll never forget waking up early in the morning, still dark, to the silhouette of my dad standing on the trapdoor, slightly jumping up and down or at least seeming to. Mom came out of their side room through the cloth-curtained door with a lit kerosene lamp that made the scene more graphic, graphically scary.

Now I could see my two frightened sisters huddled, holding one another in their far corner and about to scream. For some reason that I didn't understand, dad clearly was bouncing up and down on the door not of his own volition one that I wasn't sure was going to hold his weight.

My first thought was that somehow the door got locked from the other side and his activity was to try and loosen the lock or at worst, break the door so we could exit. But then I saw his eyes, wide eyes, mostly black and scared. And maybe even scarier, dad was bare footed wearing only white boxer shorts and his favorite kind of sleeveless tank tee shirts that I hated. I always saw those tank tee shirts on the older men sitting on porches drinking beer, or walking the sweltering neighborhoods of the lesser boroughs of New York City in the late, hot summer. Air-conditioning was yet to come.

Besides, we never saw dad like this, not our "proper" father. This was just before he shouted a loud whisper at mom, "Douse the light! We don't want him to be attracted to the light." Not that he really raised his voice at mom, but this is the only time I ever saw anything approaching it.

So, OK, I'm the fifth scared member of this entourage (baby brother would come several years later and after such vacations). Images of big-bad him-robbers came immediately into my mind from dad's comments. Burly, black ski-masked bad guys intent upon stealing the jewels we didn't have.

Actually dad's small ups and downs were caused by the bear, who having finished checking out the kitchen and downstairs, tried to visit us upstairs and was pushing-pounding on the other side of the floor trapdoor.

Yes, bears can climb loft-ladders (da, even trees). Now new respect came for my father, our savior (hopefully) for two reasons: the door was holding with his weight seeming to be enough to keep the bad bear at bay and secondly for what he had done with all of our food, every evening after supper.

The food thing made me think at first that dad was "over-the-top" with what he did with it - he insisted on placing all our food in a roped shut, canvas bag draped between two trees and roped high off the ground thanks to a pulley system he had jerry-rigged. Yes the bears, raccoons, and other food-seeking, night-marauding varmints could climb trees but couldn't navigate the ropes or the thick walls of the rope-tied-canvas bag. But was this in lieu of a really secure front door, cabin structure? Did the parents leave the door unlocked or open for the cool night breezes with only the screen as our protection (against "lions, tigers, and bears…Oh my")?

As I pointed out, we had the real, outdoor, one-holler, out-house, plumbingless thing as our toilet. No, you can't flush it. We did have the luxury of using the real carried-in, regular toilet paper as opposed to the ubiquitous Sear and Roebuck catalogue (pages) that the parents reminded us of bringing up the good olé times (that weren't as good) but probably more for trying to defend their choice of cabins with out-door vs. in-door plumbing. Then maybe such facilities weren't available at or near the Flow. I don't really know – it was only the late forties and early fifties. Besides, we were on the relatively poor side of life, I just didn't know the difference at the time but was constantly reassured by the parents that fortunately, "we lived on the right side of the tracks." This comment was to bother me later in life as I constantly traversed many-a-track to see for myself never quite making out the distinction. I know; I can be too literal at times.

One year, dad brought his brand new outboard motor, mom's Xmas present to him. It caught on fire and he had to dump it in the lake off the back end of the boat. He had only ventured out a little way from our cabin shoreline so I could see everything happening. My older sis was in the front of the boat. But he had roped the Evinrude (or was it a Johnson. Maybe a Mercury…whatever) to the boat (he was obviously big on rope – trees, boats, etc.) and therefore was able to retrieve it once dowsed. Unfortunately it never worked again but became one of those, "I can fix it when I get the time. Meanwhile I'll just put it in the basement for now" things. As I said, it never worked again.

You're probably asking, what was my bookworm, older sister doing in the front of the boat and me, the true fisherman, doing on shore, sulking I might add. Well I had done a "bad," not unusual for me within any three hour period in my younger life and was being "punished." As it turns out – so was sis. The last place (maybe on earth) she wanted to be was in a boat (vs. ship) on an unknown lake, with a can of slimy night crawlers at her feet, with the prospects of seeing, smelly fish caught and hauled into this rocking wooden, questionable seaworthy container that housed her and was now with a engine on fire in the back. She was holding one of her many books for security's sake.

She would have traded with me but it suited her earlier purposes (on shore before leaving) that it was clear she would be taking "my" place as dad mentioned to mom, "It might be good to expand (sis's) horizons by taking her out in the boat for the (dad's) evening fishing trip, especially since Markey wasn't going." This was sis who couldn't swim, didn't want to learn, and had never been in a boat, raft, canoe, skiff, schooner, barge, yacht, or ship of any kind at this point, which mother dutifully pointed out to dad. He responded, "She'll be alright since I have a smaller life jacket that will fit her just fine." She merely nodded approval while keeping her little nose in the air for my benefit.

And now I had visions of my extra wood model airplanes that us guys (from the neighborhood) used to dogfight with - ending with the looser being ignited in the tail and thrown out one of our second story windows. Crash and burn! For the record, the German and Japanese models didn't due so well (during the dogfights) and will usually end up as ash in the yards. As they should! After all, the American's had many, many air-aces. OK, a better reason – we won (and therefore we write the history). Wow that smelly airplane glue and balsa wood burns fast. Wheeeeeeow-crrash!

I just realized that the following year, on our bi-annual trip to the City (NYC) sis never made a fuss when it was suggested that we, as a family, took the Circle Line boat tour around Manhattan. Previously we couldn't afford such things; we hadn't even been to the top of the Empire State building, which I assumed required a fee for the elevator. I (now) figured that our trips to The City were mainly the room and board and that's why we did tons of "window shopping" and walking buying an occasional Easter Hat for mom. One time we ate in one of the eight plush dinning rooms of the infamous Mamma Leona's Italian restaurant. Maybe dad got a bonus of some sort that year.

The Circle Line had been there forever and I'm sure still exists. It seems they use ancient Roman or Grecian ships or at least leftover World War II stuff - they seemed quite dated to me. As I recall, the tickets were a huge four-dollars for the adults and two for the kids. I believe they had the long trip, the one we were on – all around the Island, and a shorter one that just circled the Statue of Liberty.

I can't be sure but I think it was required that us kids wore life jackets during the trip, which added to our discomfort to the point that when we finally reached The Lady, sis and I were into one of our "quip" things and weren't appreciated by the parents who were also seeing the Statue for the first time and especially after the "sacrifices" (I assumed money) that it took to get us here, on this auspicious occasion.

Trust me, once you've seen docks and shorelines and docks and shorelines, you've seen them all. Hey, it wasn't like white sandy beaches and azure blue water. Oh yes, the beaches had hundreds of bathing beauties – all young. Maybe thousands and all women, all in bikinis of every conceivable color and lessening design even if they were banned from the Miss World contest in 1951. OK so I didn't see the 1957 *And God Created Woman* with Brigitte Bardot's bikini but I saw a poster. Wow.

The "quip thing" you ask? A kid's thing and she started it, err mom did. Sis and I didn't have playing cards, puzzles, or the like, had already used the standard "we're bored" excuses, had visited the loo (called a "head" on boats and ships), couldn't (hardly) play Zit or the Alphabet games on board this thing, were hot despite a small breeze from the sound as the boat proceeded, didn't even have string to play the Cat's Cradle (called the scratch-cradle, or manger cradle to some. Anyways, the ties on the life jackets were too short) so we had to reach into our vivid, young imaginations for something.

Remember how unusual it was for Sis and I to be thrown together in seeming fond, mutually playful (or common) anything. Oh, other sis? Dad's favorite? She was either in his arms or being led by the hand, mother's hand, but not part of our poop-party (read either pooped out or bored – take your pick. A freebie).

As we neared the Lady and some Ellis thing that the parents were intent on burning into our memories, mom said, "Kids, get over here (to the railing)." We dutifully, resigned our fate and complied sulking with every step, intent on beating the other with the sulking bit.

At the railing and before the expected parental lecture that we both knew would be forthcoming on a subject/object important to them, Sis said to me, quietly but not in a whisper as to completely hide her boredom (I respected her for these valiant acts targeted at the parents – something I was not inclined to do), "You would think she should be holding an umbrella in case of rain since it's not light out." I instantly caught on to the quip-game and added, "When do you think she washed her toga last? It sure looks moldy to me."

"I understand her book is titled, 'How to speak and write English.'"

My turn: "Is that her bare feet I smell?"

Meanwhile the parents were playing their own – ignoring the kids game on us.

"It might be her under arms. At least the sculptor had the sense to crown her, a woman."

"Yea, she's a woman, you can see the air holes where there are suppose to be brains." Oops, as I was saying this I knew, just knew that I was about to lose my companion of late.

"Well you don't think they could have put a man up there without a beer bottle or him scratching himself!" This was delivered with a little more voice than the foregoing, more for everyone's benefit than just mine. Some fellow tourists on the rail walked away.

Fortunately I wasn't the only shocked member of this family. Previously stoic mother was actually stunned and starting to fume and it didn't help that smirking dad was trying to hide behind the sweet little sis bundle he held in his arms who had no clue as to what was happening. Ah, youth.

Neither parent, let alone me, had guessed older sis had reached that level of maturity to know, let alone, put forth such diatribe. In (virtual) public no less! In front of The Lady! I got' a start reading them books!

Mom? Well she was in a parental quandary, not just the first. She said, "Enough of that!" Addressing our game, Quip, more than the substance of what sis said. But somehow, if I could ever close my mouth or not think of this when I ever when to scratch myself, not remembering that I had ever done it in front of sis (or would ever again), I figured this wasn't going to be the last we heard of this. Maybe the stuff that was in sis' books was edifying after all. Do you think this was one of the seeds of my journalism? The need to "report" things? Like the bikini evolution? Little did I know that thongs were just over the horizon or is that "between two horizons?"

Most of my life I have gathered info on log homes and hope to build my own one day in fact East TN, our Appalachians in this state, is only about three hours away. Fortunately, they have many, many lakes just none called Flows.

I always thought this idea of a log home in the Appalachians was something that I had successfully held close to my own heart and not necessarily shared it with many but the guys back at the V surprised me with a very touching going away present that told me that they knew. Maybe it was the drinking parties we held back at the Alcove Library Lounge (with the naked mermaids behind the bar – in stain glass). Come to think of it, we didn't really care if one another knew our darkest secrets because we all adhered to the "journalistic code" and knew nothing would ever exit our party (and certainly would never appear in print). I wonder if that means book print – mine?

The gift? Unbeknown to me, someone started publishing a great book twice a year (in 1968), just before I departed, called *Whole Earth Catalog*. The guys gave me a couple of them and a relatively new magazine called the *Foxfire* magazine. The WEC's are great but I noted in the magazine that they, Foxfire, were going to publish a collection of their articles in a book (in 1972) that would be their attempt to document the lifestyle, culture, crafts, skills, oral history, and daily lives of people in Appalachia. It was going to be a mixture of how-to information written, mostly, in first person narrative. This is something I will stand in line for, even camp out for, and I bet they will include detailed descriptions on how to build a "real" log cabin. I can't wait.

If I were ever to get married, I'd take my new bride on a honeymoon to the Pocono's. And I would discuss this way in advance because if she objected in any way – NEXT! Once in the blood, it's the *Appalachian Way or the Highway*. Gee, is there a song there? I wonder how much one of those new keyboards cost. Or should I go with the traditional Music City guitar. On our streets cowboy boots, and a guitar slung over the shoulder of one walking around doesn't raise an eyebrow, except for the tourist who strain to see if that's someone special that they should know. Did I mention the third prerequisite – long hair? Well, then, funky (clean) clothes help. And if you visit and want to get recognized at least by the tourists while you're taking in the Ben's sight, that's a recipe.

It's time to do some landowner site inspecting so I gassed up the Blue Tail and headed an hour and one-half south to Lynchburg and the Jack Daniel's Distillery, mellowing spirits since 1866. Now I know, because I've been there just after they opened, that there's a special Jack Daniels Saloon in the Opryland Hotel/Resort up in Nashville just off the Briley Parkway but the idea of toasting my little chunk of Tennessee soil from the distillery on the same land had great appeal.

Hopefully they'll have an end-of-tour gathering place (bar) where they'll let you taste the Jack like I hear they do at some of the beer places, breweries, like Stroh's in Detroit that more than one colleague has mentioned. Life is good and a little drink makes it better – journalistic license.

The tour was great, educational, folksy with lots of stories tucked in by an amiable tour guide and the place wasn't hard to find, very popular. They'll take your picture, you'll meet the Master Distiller, you can go and see Miss Mary Bobo's Boarding House Restaurant, you'll hear that JD is made with cool, pure, iron-free cave spring water right there in the hollow you'll see, et al. And yes, they have a gathering place at the end that I was more and more anxious to get to having seen the process and hundred's and hundred's of aging barrels of the stuff.

No, it didn't smell so I don't know what the Ben's Womack brothers' problem was – Jack didn't teach them that. I tell you more about the brothers in a minute.

But low and behold – they asked me if I would like some orange juice. Now I had never had JD with orange juice but I really liked the idea, maybe one should start one's day that way. Might help. So I said, "Yes, thanks." And I didn't say, "You can just call me Squire if you will."

I got the juice in a little three-ounce paper cup. Drank it (of course) expecting to taste the JD but no. No, there wasn't a distinctive JD taste. Is orange juices that dominate? I asked for another, and another saying I was really thirsty climbing those hills and all, expecting them to refuse soon since one doesn't drink and drive responsibly – at least us Squires don't. And now you've probably guessed, Lynchburg is in a dry county. I'd do better at Opryland. Maybe on the way home.

Conley got convicted if you were wondering, my first case/reporting job. Conley had shot the six-month on the job, Deputy Sheriff Heithcock. Conley had twelve male peers that dropped the verdict on him. I didn't attend the trial or write the follow up. I was on to other news, news that effects one's life here in the Ben but would never get a mention anywhere else. But that's the nice thing, it's personal to our residents whereas the national and international stuff hardly hits home, here in the Ben. Now the down side is that a reporter in this situation can't really expect to win a Pulitzer – ever. Maybe that's why I write other things, books.

There's a personal thing about book-writing, especially when you do it just for fun versus not having to impress, sell, or target a particular audience as I would have to do if I spent my time doing magazine articles and the like – just look at the *New Yorker*; even their cartoons are very specifically targeted (with the unique *New Yorker* genre).

To this end, a different type of writing, I bought a computer. No there are (still) only a few at work and it'll be a challenge to learn – even how to turn it on. But the worst part is that I can't think of how to get it over or next to my Thinking Tub. Not an original name (yet) but I'm working on it and no "TT" is not a viable possibility. Just hang in there.

Yea, "genius takes time." Those were the first words I typed into what they call a document. I wonder if they have a news-guy's computer where it would be called a "yellow?" Damn, now how do I save my prophetic words? Files, Formats, Tools, Preferences, and Help (that doesn't help) – this contraption reminds me of my dad's extensive tool room when I first saw it as a kid – awesome and I knew I wanted to be there but completely un-understandable. Oops, the machine-editor didn't like that non-word. Maybe I should give this thing a name. Maybe I should get a parrot since I think I'm going to end of talking to something.

Now I've assigned me three tasks. Do you think everyone complicates life for one's self? Maybe I should call the tub the Tub Without (a computer) or the computer The Tub. Maybe I need a JD (coke optional). Yea, "genius takes time" even if I never did find out how to save the damn thing. Task #3.

Oh yea, the Ben's news. Well there's a lot more of the stepchild-town, Fairview, Section #1 stuff. From a reporter's perspective, it's a hot bed of activity. I've got to get a local-contact to keep me informed (since I do not want to spend the time going there or elsewhere either). And there's a lot more murders that what I was use to – thanks in no small part to, you guessed it, Section #1. Speaking of dividing up one's counties, I never heard of that before.

Remember what I said about "outside" news that doesn't effect us and therefore not covered in the small town papers per se? Well the exception, of course, is when one of our own participates in that news, good, bad, or tragic. And it was the tragic that was covered here this fall.

It started this summer when a simple article, that we could all be proud of, appeared in one of the July issues of both TRA's papers and ours. It had to do with a great, young local who had been a star in our high school basketball scene. He was destined to be a factor in college and maybe more but an unfortunate automobile accident interfered. Not dissuaded, our Dale Wiley of the Ben, started competing from his (necessary) wheelchair.

Training hard and succeeding, Dale went to the Pan-American games in Jamaica last year and qualified for the nationals in the May regional meets in Florida. He earned his spot on the Olympic team in the National Track and Field Events that were held this June in New York.

Dale, a remarkable young man by any body's standards, will compete in the Olympics shot put for which he currently holds the world's record, as well as competing in the 100-meter dash, the slalom, and basketball. It's the Summer Games of the XX Olympiad held in Munich. Since no other Olympics have been held in German since the 1936 Summer Olympics in Berlin, these are the games to present the new, democratic and optimistic Germany to the world.

For the occasion, Germany has created the Olympics first mascot, Waldi, a dachshund representing the tenacity, agility and persistence needed for an Olympiad to succeed. The Germans, having beat out Detroit, Madrid and Montreal for the honor, have designed their "Happy Games" logo as the blue solar "Bright Sun."

The games are from late August until September 11th. The Ben's Rotary Club sponsors Dale's trip. Dale will be going on to Amsterdam and Sweden for exhibition games before returning to the Ben. Dale has been a draftsman for the state for eight years (and even designed his own house).

Yes, Mark Spitz, an American swimmer, set a world record when he won his seventh gold medal there. Yes, the petite Russian gymnast, Olga Korbut, set her team competition sport spinning with her fantastic performance and athletic abilities. Yes the United States basketball team got screwed by referees for the entire world to see. Yes, if you're inclined to feel a proud nationalistic spirit, you could be embarrassed by the two black American runners who acted up on the winners stand, getting banned from the Olympics for life, a pseudo repeat of the 1968 Summer Olympics that could have put you down another earlier peg. And yes, all this is newsworthy if you're curious about the world, man in general, and athletic events but other than knowing these things to be able to talk about them over coffee with someone else so inclined, how else would this actually effect your day in this small town or any?

But put one of your own there, a fine, outstanding, upstanding athlete from the Ben, an exceptional person by anyone's standards, one who just left on a worthy cause, who went to one of your high schools, with family ties and relatives that you're apt to see around town daily and then hear the news that a group of eight deranged, well armed Palestine terrorists broke into the Olympic Village and took some of the attending athletes as hostages for some political reason that affects another, completely different, unknown part of the world - and the heart of the Ben goes "stop."

The question on everybody's mind here goes, "Is Dale safe? Is he one of those taken?" And the reoccurring unspoken thought is, "There certainly are some crazies out there. Hopefully they'll never visit here."

When Indian mounds were mentioned in another article, I knew I had to look into it. My experience back in the V was that the mounds offered up a plethora of archaeological evidence to the indigenous inhabitants, those before the first white settlers. Because the Indians routinely choose prominent sites on top of hills or summits, it was also some of the most sought after sites for burial by the more prominent of the town with no consideration that those mounds were already burial sites from long ago. In the article they were referred to as cairns versus earthen mounds. I guess when there is a significant amount of stones placed over the mound one can use either name whereas cairn usually refers to an artificial pile of stones like markers. Maybe the most famous cairns are the Chilean Easter Island moai, the coastal stone statues sentries.

Most states have passed some form of American Indian Grave Protection law (ref.: Natural Resources Conservation Service under order number 40-3A75-7-102). But to date, this does not include Tennessee. Nashville lists one cairn/mound that is also considered an Historic Place by the National Register. It is the Brick Church Mound and Village site.

Cairns in this area are usually represent work done by the Mississippian civilizations and/or the Stonegrave Indians (probably associated with the Mississippi Civilization). They can be u-shaped, oval, conical, square or rectangular and are usually found in conjunction with native stonewall complexes, temples as well as early dwellings. More recent Indians can be found mounted on top of the original builders.

Cairns generally occur in groupings ranging from tens to hundreds. But the more I look into this, because it's interesting, I can see it could only form "background" for any possible articles since the material is too dry as we say in the trade. Maybe I should say dead. Well at least old. (Did you get the one about looking into it? I wonder if funeral directors say that. Sorry).

Speaking of the burial any things, I found it strange that the Ben wasn't better known because of the ivory tusks and bones of a huge-elephant like Mastodon was found here. Further it was analysized that the beast had been killed and eaten by humans.

"*Dear Marky*," (it's my mother and I never hear from her. I've tried to change her thinking to just "Dear Mark" but whatever).

"I hope you are well and doing fine. Everything here is OK. I'm writing you this letter and enclosing what I have because it only occurred to me recently that you're not the first family member to visit Franklin." I have no idea what this is all about.

"Years and years ago I saw these well printed cursive pages in your dad's box." She's talking about his so-called "treasure box" that followed him from his youth and was in the attic when he died, now several years ago. I kind' a followed suit and have my own, my first jewelry box I received as a new teenager and never really used for anything else. It has a marble from my father's first house that my aunt found on a nostalgic trip into her past and gave to me as a souvenir after my father died. I'm not big on any jewelry, even the last watch I wore was lost in Lake Erie when I was about sixteen but that's another story you can read elsewhere. So this (former) jewelry box is still useful (to me).

"When you said you were moving to Franklin Tennessee, something struck me and has bothered me all this time until I remember the name had to do what was in your father's box. Then it was a spell before I got up into the attic to go through your father's box. Here are those pages that were in there. They're not signed but I'm pretty sure I remember the story. Your great, great grandfather was in the Civil War and wrote these pages in a letter he sent back from Nashville after a big battle there. I don't know how interesting they are for you but they weren't doing anyone any good upstairs. I hope you can read the old style cursive printing and without the proper punctuation. I'm sorry I'm not able to visit you there and I'll be happy to see you on your next visit.

"Love, Mom.

"PS: did you ever get a washing machine?"
(That's mom. I think she left out at least one "great." And here is what she sent).

It happened at the Franklin,
Somewhere in Tennessee

It started as a whisper
I almost paid no heed

Amazing grace is what I heard
Maybe tricks played on my mind

It grew like gentle breezes
Put chills upon my spine

It happened at the Franklin,
Somewhere in Tennessee

The sound was so familiar
What could this really mean?

The sounds came out the ground
At least or so it seems

It happened at the Franklin,
Somewhere in Tennessee

It came from the hills around
T'was a haunting sound

I shoveled, shoveled and listened
Trying hard to build my mound

Was it them across the way?
No other souls were here

I feared it was the angels
My time was coming near

Dig deep and then dig deeper
Built mounds and forts today

I feared to stop my digging
They'd be a comin right our way

It happened at the Franklin,
One November day

Johnny Rebs were coming
But here we mean to stay

We all could hear that sound
Something strange but sweet

It weren't no battle cry I heard
But the Johnnies on their feet

Bitter cold and bitter lonely
Each man fer himself

Flintlock, shovel and vittles
They were our only pelf

God bless the men that make it
To see tomorrow's light

God bless me mom and homeland

And help us with this fight

The battle raged in to the night
And lasted five hours long

Gen Hood lost eight thousand men
And six Generals he'd had were gone

We are Schofield's undefeated
But had never fought a song

It happened at the Franklin,
And maybe it was wrong

I heard a ground swell of voices
Soldiers mostly teens

It happened at the Franklin,
Somewhere in Tennessee

A twenty thousand Rebel choir
Coming at us strong

We knew their men would/could die
But never, not that song

Weren't this here a battlefield?
Weren't soldiers over there?

What hellish plot was this?
Being played upon our lair

Goose bumps unfamiliar
In battle or the cold

Now raked my arms and fingers
Then seeped into my bones

As a boy I've heard it
Amazing Grace I'm sure

Pap said fer what er ails ya
It's always one's best cure

It happened at the Franklin,
Somewhere in Tennessee

We're first attacked by rabbits,
More scared then maybe we

They came flushed by the rebels,
Running fast as legs can be

It happened at the Franklin,
Somewhere in Tennessee

They sang and sang for a thousand yards

And then - they charged and charged

The bold brave brothers of the south
Into our ranks they barged

They rush'd n stormed our breastworks
Cowards not a one

They were our rebel brothers
Soldiers every one

T'was just last night we'd slipped them
Coming up the Pike

God and man be thankful
It'd been a deep dark night

It happened at the Franklin,
Upon a moonless night

They came on heels of vengeance
We fought with all our might

It happened at the Franklin,
This cold and wintry night

I saw my comrades killed
Both left and on the right

A burning fog of smoke
Every gun was hot

Screaming, yelling, guns roaring
The grounds a sacred lot

It now all seems so futile
Scores and scores left there

Many a graves to dig
No joy left anywhere

It happened at the Franklin,
Somewhere in Tennessee

It was about the midnight
That sound began again

It came from over yonder
Just a whisper now and then

Once when I was lost...
But now I'm found again...

It's that amazing grace
How very sweet the sound

T'was the dead that sang?
I will never know

It covered us like babies
Our first new fallen snow

Words were softly carried
Hummings so it seemed

It was at the Franklin,
Where mortal lives were ceased.

It happened at the Franklin,
Somewhere...in Tennessee.

The Durango Boot Company, who makes 10,000 pairs a day, has just purchased twelve acres in our new Century Industrial Park for their new 138,000 square foot office and distribution center expected to house 135 new employees. And not to be outdone, Santa Claus will arrive "in style" Friday night, November 28th this year distributing candy and prize-contained snowballs (since with our 72 degree F, mean, annual temperature – there's no guarantee you'll be able to make your own over one of our winters). And if Santa's smart, he arrive in a new pair of the Durango West #11650.

Just think, I could have bought my cowboy boots right here. Admittedly I don't wear the (only) pair I own very much. Maybe I would if I saw another pair on our streets or maybe if I was here longer, being my "own" man. Of course I would probably end up having to research the subject more. You think I'm kidding? In the Durango announcement, he, the senior executive vice-president, Leo Le Roy (and if not talent, that Texas name probably propelled him to the top) discusses his new line coming out next year. See if you can follow this: two new boots, one "is a men's 12 inch. show-time boot featuring all over buffed-off burnt apple leather, puffed vamp and shaft in self stitching." And the second; "is a men's 13 inch double dip boot featuring puff-stitching with color-changing thread and all over burnt beech leather with brushed off highlights. Both boots feature a leather sole with reduced shank, slacked leather walking heel and folded and slotted pull straps."

Now I don't know about you – but I never knew all that stuff went into a pair of cowboy boots. It makes me want to buy a pair just to study it – any size will do. I wonder when you buy a pair if you have sign a "don't disrespect the boot" affidavit promising not to placing them upside down on fence posts, like that do in Texas, when you've worn them out.

Oh, and he will not be arriving by air this year, Santa, or in the foreseeable future. The proposed airport we don't have yet on the Hugh Dallas farm between Lewisburg Pike and Columbia Pike and the proposal to build one seems to have melted even before it reached our political grounds. Like many small towns the politicians learned long ago that in lieu of making a decision you can legitimately commission-study and research-groups ad nauseam. As for a Ben's airport, I would suggest that most large and medium sized cities would have spaceports before we get one.

The Ben is graced with many stately ante-bellum plantations and historic homes, many more than I have seen anywhere else (with the proviso that I don't consider myself a particularly well-traveled individual). These residences seem to follow either an Italian Renaissance or Greek Revival genre according to most of the write-ups I read. Not being a student of architecture but as an observant outsider, I think it has more to do with the new elegant-grand American Style architecture that the country has struggled with since it's inception, one that has yet to have clear delineation let alone a recognizable definition.

The Historical Society routinely sponsors an annual "historical home tour" of many of these lovely homes, which is quite special. One common denomination of these homes, maybe predictable, is the proliferation of priceless antiques gracing their rooms. But I think it's the bicentennial fever that seems to be catching on and one such home, with the charming name Magnolia Hall built in 1840 by a Franklin banker and just a short distance west of downtown, has been declared, "opened to the public." With the surprising number of tourists coming to the Ben at all times of the year and seemingly increasing every year, this will be a special treat. Hopefully this will set an example for others to join for out big, festivities-marked next year.

Damn it – I've got to get an Ah-ooh-gah horn for the Blue Tail. Just any olé horn including its factory installed one – won't do. It's something I saw once growing up as a kid. It was on a Senior's 1951 two tone brown Ford. After all, if I was in Texas I would have to consider a long horn on the hood. Won't I? Sorry, I'm just talking to myself out loud.

Did I mention that we had a dolphin performing in the town square? Things are never quiet or ever the same here per se and in most small towns that I'm familiar. No it's not a permanent fixture but just a "traveling" dolphin for performances for our annual Trade Appreciation Days. He, Splash, is reputed to be the world's most traveled dolphin (I just wonder if he had anything to say about it).

That reminds me, our competitor (supposedly) reacted to our recent coverage on the many and increasing visitors to our town with their own article headlined on the first page, "120 visitors here from 'all over'." I didn't read it so I don't know what day they were talking about but I hope they keep it up – in the same vein – that way we have a chance of "walking all over them." Sorry. Competition's good. They might win. There's lots of room here. Onward…

Something I don't quite understand here. There's the obvious devotion to Country music, and the root of Country, Bluegrass, which is gaining on me, but there seems to be a visible, goodly amount of Jazz enthusiasts here too. I have never run into one let alone three such musical genres in any town (except Nashville and Austin) of at least that they made a difference.

Now of the three, I suggest the jazz is the lesser. Some of the old timers don't quite accept it yet, like the comment I had in the barbershop when I, bored and waiting, brought up the subject. The (usually quiet guy) in the far chair curtly chimed in suddenly with, "Jazz ain't for Middle Tennessee and that's that." Except for chuckling to myself for the next twenty minutes, I felt there was nothing more to say on the subject.

Here all three have their annual festivals and the crowds are big enough to close Main Street, set up several stages and bring out all the arts, crafts, and food booths. Don't misunderstand me, I like fun and think that's it's great – I would just like to understand it. On second thought, before coming here one could have heard the classics right next to my country western music in my apartments and cars. Actually that should be apartment (1 previous) and one car that was unhitchable to make the trip here.

Yes I said that Bluegrass is growing in me and I'll be at the next Bluegrass On The Harpeth. As a kid and on the WSM broadcast over The Tower I use to hear a Bill Monroe, reported to be the Father of Bluegrass, right along side of George Jones. And then you know I have an affinity to Appalachian anything, part of my ancestral roots. Well the story goes that Bluegrass came from the Scots-Irish immigrants that settled in Appalachia that Bill help develop into a legitimate genre during the mid-1940's.

Since I'm in the contrite/confession mood (must be a Catholic leaning), it wasn't until I saw an old photograph of Grand Ole Opry's founder, George Hay that showed him in front of a microphone with the letters WSM that I put the two together (chicken-egg-chicken). Now I know that it started as the WSM Barn Dance. If I liked any clichés, which I don't, I would spout "Better late…" Sorry, but now at least you know.

Yes, I heard teenage Elvis Presley's 1954 first performance with the polite but muted audience response. I also saw him on the Ed Sullivan show.

Not one to leave things alone, one doesn't think of the Opry without thinking of Minne Pearl, at least I can't. Are you ready for this (no she's not from the Ben but) her husband is. I just knew there was something (actually a lot) special about her.

So our paths have (kind 'a) crossed. Someone more knowledgeable than I can write me but somehow I never remember her singing anything yet she was regularly on that stage. And while you're at it, tell me (if you know) whether all those products that they pitched were real? I could never tell (nor saw them in any store my mother dragged us too for grocery shopping).

Franklin is strewn with festivals, parades, and happenings thanks a lot to its Heritage Foundation. I can't remember all of them. Maybe (as a news guy) I should make a list during the year. Here again I miss the olé archives. But some of them are the different music ones I've already mentioned and then there is the huge Main Street Festival, the Pumpkin Festival, the local favorite Dickens of Christmas Street festival at Christmas time and many more. It's not grown to the extent of one a week but it seems we're well on the way.

As a self-proclaimed punster, I was looking up the subject of Chautauqua, one of those reoccurring similarities I've so far found in my hometowns, I came across the pun of puns. It's in one of those important journals of the Heritage Foundation retelling a local man's experiences including his retelling his many visits to the Ben's Repath Chautauqua. He, a judge, was a "season's ticket" holder for the annual seven or five day performances. He tells about one man on stage that relates the following story of a couple of gentlemen at the Cheshire Cheese (as if it was a place in the Ben or a well know place somewhere – I'm just not familiar with it other than that it is a famous, one of the oldest, dense, crumbly cheese type from Cheshire England. But I'm sure the judge said "at" and not "over"). Anyways, the judge goes on, "He said that one of the, I

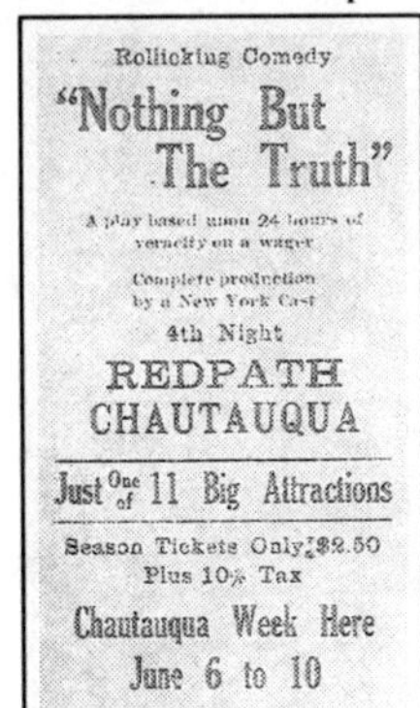

forget (which man), was the greatest punster that ever punst. Another man asked him one time to make him a pun, so he did, he said 'U-pun what subject.' The man who made the request was a little dense and didn't catch it so he said 'Make it on the subject of the king.' And he answered, 'I can't. The king is not a subject." Isn't that great?

Yes, the Ben has had their Chautauquas, until the 1930's, specifically some of the touring Repath Chautauqua groups also called the Circuit Chautauquas or colloquially, the Tent Chautauquas. They claimed to have appeared in over 10,000 communities to audiences that added up to some forty-five million at their peak in the '20's.

The Repath name (I'm pretty sure) referred to man, possibly one of the organizers of the early adult educational touring groups called the Lyceum Movement that promoted the Chautauquas. I don't pretend to know the exact connection and the research here is fuzzy on both but I do remember from high school that Abraham Lincoln, as a young man, gave a speech (or speeches) at his Springfield, Illinois Lyceum and later, the writers Ralph Waldo Emerson and Henry David Thoreau used the podiums to promote Transcendentalism. I don't think they were founders of either, Lyceum or Transcendentalism, but were just advocates and both were promoting a pet project for some reason. You can write me if you know. Thanks.

The Ben had its Opera too, on the town square, two hundred and fifty seats. It burned down around 1890. Minstrel shows and Blind Tom reportedly appeared there.

Of course I wanted to know if the born to the V's world famous and father of the minstrel shows, Daniel Decatur "Dan" Emmett appeared here. Since Dan was the author of *Dixie*, it would have been appropriate. Dan also authored the popular songs, *Polly Wolly 'Doodle*, *Old Dan Tucker*, *Turkey in the Straw, Walk Along John*, and many more.

Dan is remembered, in his retirement in the V, for his almost daily appearances on the porch of his little house that still exists and you can visit, I have (many times). He used to enjoy just sitting in a hard back chair watching the world go by and many neighbors that he would always acknowledge with a slight wave of his musically talented hands. Dan used to walk the streets of my olé V, down the middle (only – and they let him). He's buried there just up at the north end of Main Street in the only cemetery of the V that I remember. Ironically it's just a stone's throw from the Civil War soldiers' area. I've often wondered how many of them heard Dan's *Dixie* as the last thing they did on earth.

His last performance, an honorary thing for the people of the V, was at the still standing on Main Street, Woodward Opera house. He filled the Woodward to overflowing and to the point that the police, owners and storekeepers below (who had stayed open with longer, evening hours for the special occasion) were fearful of the structure. The theatre was two stories complete with balcony but situated on the second and third floors. The storeowners immediately below said they couldn't close their doors if they wanted too because of the frame's "buckling." Reportedly the audience's warm welcome and responses to everything Dan did was thunderous in applause and foot stomping. Some of the overflow observers filling the street below that couldn't get in said they witnessed the building swaying to Dan's simple music.

Of course I don't think the erotic pictures of my two landlords graced the stage to either side when Dan performed. Those distracting monuments came many years later with the first attempted restoration of the then closed facility (but that's another story).

Speaking of cemeteries as I just did regarding Dan, I understand there is something worthwhile looking up here in the Ben, at one of the several cemeteries located around the town and not the famous Confederate one out at the Carnton Plantation even if it has to do with a full sized horse statue as I understand it. I said I visited Dan burial spot out of tribute to a special small town character and I did that is until I came across a very said statue there, just over the hill from Dan's plot. It was a statue of a kneeling, prayerful, mournful mother presiding over her five young dead kids. I couldn't take it, as I assume she couldn't either as she was buried there under her statue. I haven't been back since.

But hopefully the horse doesn't have such a sad tale to tell me. I'll just warm up the Blue Tail and point it in the direction of our … I guess I'll have to remember which one before I do any warming up or pointing.

Oh, Blind Tom - Thomas Wiggins (1840 – 1908). He was an autistic savant and musical child prodigy that even performed, by invitation, for the musically interested President James Buchanan and the President's family in reportedly one of the most amazing performances held at the White House during this era. Because a couple local musicians in attendance were skeptical, thinking Tom's talents were mere trickery, they challenged him to repeat two new compositions they had prepared. He did.

Tom was born on a Georgia plantation. He was sold along with his slave parents, Charity and Mingo Wiggins to a Georgian lawyer named Colonel James Bethune who gave the one-year old boy a new name that has been recorded two ways, Thomas Greene Bethune and Thomas Wiggins Bethune. Being blind Tom did not work but wandered around the plantation paying particular interest to the music played by the Colonel's daughters. He learned to play tunes before he learned to speak and at the age of five, had composed one of his own, *The Rain Storm*. This brought him to Bethune's attention who tested his talents by hiring professional musicians whose tunes Tom replicated on the Colonel's piano easily.

Tom gave his first concert in 1857 and went on tour, extending to the major cities of the world and most cities, even a lot of towns, in the US. Tom was an extreme introvert only using a vocabulary of about a hundred words even though he developed more than five thousand pieces of music, mostly classical, in his repertoire. Mark Twain was one of his regular audience members.

I can't ascertain that Blind Tom, who basically retired in 1883, appeared on the Ben's Opera stage since the Opera dates I have for now are 1885 with it burning down in 1890 but many here report that family members saw him perform here (probably in the 1860's, maybe at the Masonic).

Locals also report that the Wild West Shows came to town in 1905 or 06. If you've read anything, you just know I'm not going to let this go easily. I've only heard of one, the Buffalo Bill's Wild West show starting the American soldier, bison hunter and showman, William Frederick "Buffalo Bill" Cody (1846-1917).

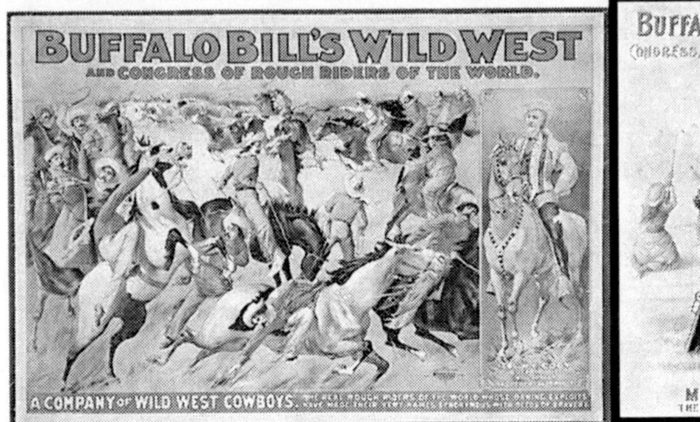

I guess there was an Annie Oakley (Phoebe Ann Mosey Ohio born, 1860-1926) in there somewhere – maybe with Bill's show. Yes – it/she was.

Talking about things out of the past, you're not going to believe this (but it's the truth), I was just in conversation with a neighbor, meeting for only the second or third time. Such conversations here inevitably turn to, "Where're you from?" since so many of us are new to the area. I purposely avoided the word "transients" because someone might consider me such. Anyway, upon questioning (read, nothing else to talk about) we got back into our respective genealogies at which time she said, "Reaching back into history, we have a murderess in our family. She's even in the Louve somehow."

This was probably for effect. I have one, not as effective, "My grandparents on my mother's side came from Prussia." See?

Anyway I had to ask for more. It seems before her ancestors left France for Ireland (which sounds more like an escape or fleeing to me – who would do that with any choices?) and many years ago, that this girl stabbed a guy in his own bathtub.

Do you get the connection? Do you remember me talking about my Thinking Tub? No, I haven't got a proper name for it yet – that's not the point. In that conversation I referred to one of my favorite painter's works The Death of Marat by David? Jean-Paul Marat was the writer of the radical French newspaper *L'Ami du peuple* (*The Friend of the People*) and prominently associated with the Jacobin faction during the Reign of Terror.

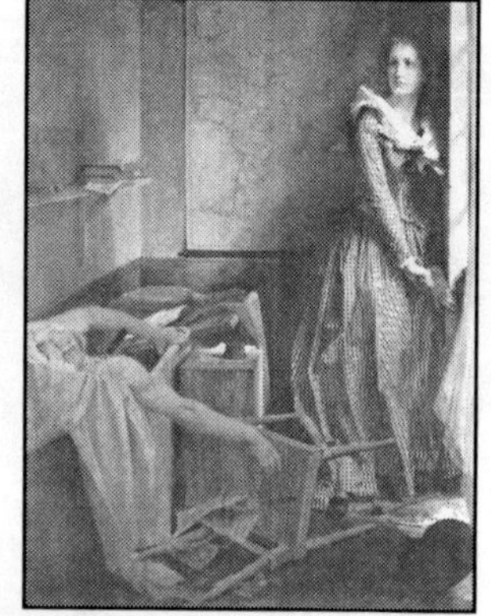

Yes, that one. Jean-Paul was assassinated by a woman, Charlotte Corday, in 1773 and in his own bath. He thought he suffered from something he had picked up while hiding in the sewers of Paris and needed frequent cold baths to stem the itching/irritation. Honestly.

Maybe you caught the more recent article maybe the New York Times that it was more likely (thanks to modern medicine and thinking) that Jean-Paul was suffering an allergic reaction to gluten, the stuff commonly found in wheat (and maybe other places, I don't know). Charlotte, originally from Normandy (France) and convent educated (I remember) felt she was on a mission to save France by killing this "radical." She was successful but the tide turned against her, he became a hero-martyr and she was beheaded rather than sainted. It's worst, the incident virtually started the thing she wanted to prevent and France bathed in a cold Reign of Terror for about ten months.

So I punsted a little. So what?

Next: Oh, yea, our heroine if only in her own mind, was defended by the same guy that had defended Marie Antoinette, Claude François Chauveau-Lagarde (it's easier to write than trying to pronounce). Ironically Marie met the same fate, the guillotine. Not a good record for Mr. Unpronounceable.

Charlotte was (kind 'a) immortalized in her own painting, similar to David's, by someone who understood her actions, Paul Jacques Aimé Baudry, showing her at her pinnacle moment of her brief, political career. And I know Marie was painted too. I wonder if both paintings hang in the Louvre.

And one last thing (that you'll probably not believe either) it was rumored that the Bonaparte family received the Charlotte (head) remains and that one Napoleon (born Napoleone Buonaparte) carried it around with him on all his campaigns. What's with all the people that don't go by their birth names?

If God were on our side, you would think he'd plan his floods in consideration of Thursday's publishing day and not the night before.

Maybe he gets complacent knowing "all things" anyways. But here, and trying to make a living, we have deadlines to meet. Well He didn't seem to take this into consideration (or even say "Oops") for our Wednesday night flood, that the Nashville Sunday paper billed as the worst since the 1948 one. This one exceeded $5 million in estimated damages. By the following Thursday publishing date, when "it" was completely gone, we couldn't even headline that there were six inches in the well known (and visited) J. C. Anderson Franklin Laundry. Even the 2 pm on Sunday funeral for the five year old swept down stream had passed.

I saunter over, in the rain, to the Historical Heritage Foundation to return a couple of those great journals I've mentioned and said as much to the new guy, Rick Warwick. Rick, I predict, will be the Town Historian one day since he has set for himself the goal of reading and capturing every single recorded detail of everything that has happened in Franklin since its onset. And from one of two visits, I don't think he'll need a computer or quill (for the old stuff) to write anything down if he doesn't want to. His memory about what he has already absorbed and even in his short time here, is awesome. I know because you can ask him anything and he can tell you.

The thing that amazes me is that neither he nor his wife are originally from here. Rick came to the Ben about the same time I did, maybe beating me by a few months and right now he teaches school with the Franklin history as his own personal passion. He even knew Willy York's story and I think taught some of the family in his classes.

Rick introduced me to the venerable Journal Volume #1. Its publish date is 1970. Looks like it just beat Rick and I. It differs from the more recent ones being published about one per year. The first was started with articles from members, reminiscences and such. Don't misunderstand, they're valuable, just (maybe) not as complete for all the Ben's happenings that the later issues are. It would be nice if all small American towns took this project upon themselves.

But the fifth article in this Volume #1 made me stop since it was a subject I had never heard, *The Order of Pale Faces*, by Virginia Gooch Watson. My first thought was "Indians" and having had real Indians in my life, having gone to school with them, lived and worked (apprenticed) with them, and having been told by Nana that we had Cherokee in our family blood lines, and having been called a pale face myself, I wasn't going to let this go. I couldn't.

As it turns out, The Order of Pale Faces had nothing to do with Indians per se and I have to tell you about it or be negligent because of its history-role in the Ben. But thanks to my incessant page turning twitch I have (maybe it's even a compunction), the next article does mention Indians. The article is titled *The Franklin Treaty of 1830* by Stephen S. Lawrence.

First, The Order of Pale Faces: You already know that I'm not an historian and don't purport to be and am simply a newspaper guy that likes to research things. Well it didn't take too much research to see a probable misconception about the formation of the Ku Klux Klan and therefore an alleged association of The Order of Pale Faces. Since the (white) KKK (there was a black KKK), originally founded just down the road in Pulaski, has done some dastardly deeds since it's founding it gets a very bad rap without the full understanding of the causes/reasons for its inception. Overlooked are the inhuman, unjust and unlawful acts that gave people the incentive to protect themselves. Unfortunately and in an environment of lawlessness, the formation of self-protecting paramilitary forces can quickly and easily lead to "hate." Hate is a great motivator. Give a person or group of people a reason to hate and stand back out of the way!

The Klan's materialization was in 1866 and if you remember your history, this was immediately following the Civil War. As with virtually any war, the victors seem to think that once won, their job is over (and go home). With the Civil War, lasting several years, the focus and efforts were on the winning of battles with little if any consideration as to the vacuums created by the disruption of the law in the conquered communities, their infrastructure, jobs, schools, lack of resources or money to rebuild, and all that makes up a society into which comes lawlessness, opportunists, and a myriad of evil.

Now don't make the intellectually lame leap that you think I'm going to attempt the justification of the KKK and their actions, I'm not. My approach is from a newsmen's simple curiosity as to why they ever existed at all and I've found that were there is an action or reaction as big as what we're talking about, to motive tens of thousands, there's usually some reason(s) behind it.

Here's one account of the war's aftermath environment here in middle Tennessee. "Federal troops (the ones that weren't lucky enough to go home) roamed the streets, robbing and murdering the citizenry with almost complete impunity. Rape and molestation were everyday occurrences. Law and order as we know it today was practically nonexistent…the carpetbaggers (northerners who moved to the South) and the scallywags (Southern Unionist whites) gained control of the key public offices. The Federal government had passed the 15th Amendment and Gov. Brownlow had disfranchised the confederate veteran and the confederate sympathizer (making them powerless, helpless non-entities)."

"In retaliation of these chaotic and oppressive conditions there emerged many different kinds of organizations each with stated aims and objectives, but all of them seeming to have the common underlying creed, 'For the betterment of our race.' Some of these organizations were secret, some not so secret, some were violent and some were nonviolent. One of the nonviolent organizations that sprang from these hectic conditions was the World Order of Pale Faces. The Pale Faces stressed its principles to be 'not for individual profit or gain, but for the relief of the destitute, for the elevation of our race…and their motto to be 'Truth, Justice, Right and Charity."

"The aims and objectives of this particular organization matched the mood and the deep feelings of insecurity of many of those people who felt they were being discriminated against. In the first 10 months of its existence, 35 camps were started throughout the State with a total of 10,000 members. Perhaps the riot in Franklin six months before between the Union Leaguers and the Southern Radicals may have given impetus to the rapid growth, but, in any event, steady growth and an ambitious desire to be recognized as a world-wide order resulted in a charter being granted by the Secretary of State, Charles N. Gibbs, on February 14, 1876, and stating the name of the organization as Most Excellent Supreme Camp of the World Order of Pale Faces."

But once the KKK violence started, it was more sensational to write about those acts then the reasons behind the movement especially to motivate the powers to be to eliminate such organized "lawlessness." It was also easier to group all other organizations that started up into the same "pot" rather than try and distinguish the differences. The Pale faces were thrown into the pot as early as 1868 despite their clearly stated non-violent platform but because they also stated "...of our race" which was narrowly interpreted by some to be the same as the white KKK's.

Second, the Indians, The Franklin Treaty of 1830, and Andy's another visit to the Ben but first a little background perspective since what happened in Franklin that day, had more to do with the overall single focus and strong determination of the invading immigrant population going back to the very first landing on the shores of "their" New World. There was no room for attempting respect to or for the civilization that had occupied the new land for centuries and it served their purposes to categorize these strangers as "savages" which would justify their actions to eliminate them from their single minded quest. This rationalization continued as the hordes of additional immigrants came and with the "frontiers" continuing to expand even with the Indians who had succumbed to the "white man's ways" learning the new language, living in houses, taking up farming, sending their kids to school, (some) attending church, starting commerce, and even accepting the new, white man's concept of land-ownership.

"The westward advance by the Anglo-European immigrants along the American frontier displayed a universally single-minded attitude toward the American Indian. The germ of their European civilization had me the frontier of the new land, and the white settlers were experiencing a freedom that had not been enjoyed for centuries. The movement was aggressive and uncompromising, with no regard for the Indian. To the western man who made the penetration into the wilderness came the task of destroying the Indian who stood in his path."

Five (Indian) nations, the Choctaws, Chickasaws, Cherokees, Creeks, and Seminoles numbering roughly 60,000 were lumped together with the titular title of the "southern woodland Indians." These "red-men" occupied the land south of the Ohio River, east of the Mississippi and west of the Appalachians. And it was these tribes that resented and resisted the white westward movement and the continual encroachment into their ancestral lands.

"After the Creek Wars of 1813, the military power of the southern Indians had been appreciably broken. The Cherokee and Creek in Georgia and the Choctaw and Chickasaw in Mississippi and Alabama had given their word to bury the tomahawk. They had become peaceful and were developing the traits of civilized people. Many tribal customs such as the use of vermillion paints on their bodies and pagan religious practices were forsaken. Now they were beginning to live in houses, to practice farming, and to raise livestock. Some tribes had begun holding their own courts and used peace officers. However, crimes were rare, and much less trouble was experienced than among the frontier whites. The peaceful development of the southern Indians had started to attract national attention. The easterners and missionary groups encouraged these peaceful pursuits. At the same time, the whites of Georgia, Alabama, and Mississippi who were alarmed at the success of the Indians, feared the Indian would take permanent possession of the land.

"After a bitter battle in Congress, the Indian Removal Bill was passed on May 28, 1830. Most active opposition came from the Northeast for that section had been most ardent in the missionary efforts. The Indian Removal bill was significant in the fact that at last the nation had adopted a policy favorable to Indian removal. It placed in the hands of the president, Andrew Jackson, the means to initiate steps to exchange lands with any tribe for lands west of the Mississippi. Terms of the act also allowed certain annuities to be paid the removing Indians.

"Four days after the enactment of the Indian Removal Bill, President Jackson sent word to his confidential agent, D. W. Haley, that he and the Secretary of War, John Eaton, would like to confer with delegates of the four major southern Indian tribes. At last, the Union would get down to the serious business of the Indian removal problem (and Jackson would soon set up office in the Franklin's Masonic)."

That last sentence was key in giving a formal, backed by law-status to what had been in the collective minds and hearts of virtually all the immigrants to this land, would continue as the frontiers pushed ever westward and without regȧrd to whether the red-man could (eventually) swim. It was interesting to note that the leading advocate, the strongly defiant, fiercely independent, Andrew Jackson, the boy and man who refused to clean any other man's boots, leaped on his role to quickly carry out the intent of this "enacted law." Of course it never occurred to him or anyone else to call upon the "delegates" of the major tribes to appear before, to argue, or plead their case in Congress as the bill was being made into (the white man's) law.

Oh, you probably didn't know (because no one formally mentioned it) but gold had been discovered on the Cherokee land. This got them the "Trail of Tears." And the shocking thing to me is that of the six routes carved out to move the Indians to Oklahoma, two passed close by. The Benge Route passed through Mt. Pleasant in Maury county just 43 miles to our south. But the Northern Route passed closer, only 15 miles to our north through the Athens of the South, Nashville, This route passed through the center of the Nash right across Hermitage Avenue just a few miles from Andy's home (The Hermitage).

As it turned out, nearly seventy Indian "treaties" were ratified during Andy's presidency. This number was a record for any administration. Finally, the Southern Woodland Indians tribes, after their removal west, would be referred to as the Five Civilized Tribes because of their recognized adoption of the colonists' customs.

Yes, I don't like games but, confidentially, I play a few with myself and you probably want a "for instance." Well I have this old thesaurus that went to college with me and since I don't like to use the same word twice (and still working on that) I use it a lot. When I use it, I note the page, keeping a bookmark for every page on which there's a word I use - going toward the front and page 1, and another bookmark to the back. I figure that when my bookmarks are on the first and last page, I've mastered it (well, sort of).

This probably has a lot to do with my dad. First Nana but then mom (on several "encouraging" occasions) told be that dad, who I now know did graduate from high school, read the dictionary from cover to cover (presumably as a "self-taught" man). Unfortunately I was too young to ask whether it was an abridged version or not. Maybe it's just as well, since that question won't have gone over too well. As of today my *Roget's International Thesaurus* (I don't like the more modern editions or the competitors') is at Page 2.3 and 925.13, front/back respectively (and counting).

I miss dad. If you discount the first few years of my life that I can't even remember, I've already lived more years without him then with him. Then if you discount all the times he was away working, it was a lifetime ago.

Because of his untimely death, I have a deep simmering resentment toward the tobacco industry and it didn't help to learn that one of the county's biggest crops was tobacco. This caught me by surprise because for the many drives around the county now, I've yet to see the special tobacco drying barns with the side panels that open for air to pass through. Maybe it's ancient history but I often wonder how many of those deadly leaves went into making my father's unfiltered Camels (not that that marketing gimmick – filters, made any difference).

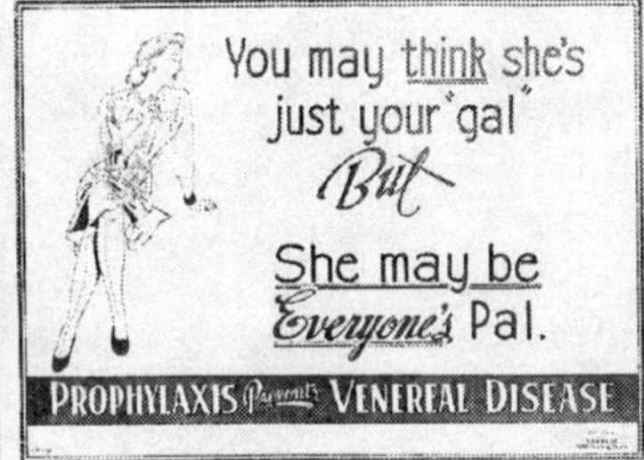

I cringe with I see their lies called advertisement even in our own paper. There are unsubstantiated rumors that the tobacco companies know their lies. Here and because of our own ad-revenues, we can't put anything "not substantiated" in any article, even innuendoes.

It probably didn't help Dad's health (or maybe any of our family's) that nutrition was not yet invented or discovered at that time. I had cut out one bogus ad years ago on "lard" to discuss with mom because, and even as a kid, it didn't set well with me. She pooh-poohed it and continued to use it saving the bacon grease in a tin can she kept under the kitchen sink, which happened to be next to the garbage pail that was one of my chores to empty so I saw them both often. Both were disgusting and when mom started a second can – somehow the first would just disappeared (the health fairy).

Remember this was before plastic and the leaky garbage was only contained in the leftover brown paper grocery bags that if, once filled, they weren't taken out often, would end up on the kitchen floor since the soggy bottoms would fall out. Guess who would be responsible for cleaning up those messes. Everyone else didn't seem to appreciate this since it became "my problem" once they had dutifully deposited their whatever's into the bag under the sink. I always figured the tin grease-can had missed its real place, the garbage, by just a few inches.

Oh, the lard ad? It's in page 925.13. Roget is taking care of it for me. Then (in the vain of full disclosure) in the middle of the book, between the pages of "Excitement" and "Inexcitability," there is another cut-out-ad that I would never discuss with mom (or dad) (or Nana) but I wanted to discuss with my uncles, the warring ones, but haven't come close to getting up the courage. Nay, I never will. But I'll keep the ad since it's legitimate. Yes, "prophylaxis" (while unpronounceable) is in Roget's (687.18). If you want a laugh: 687 is "THERAPY." (And ".18" is "methods." What a life).

This calls for some Chess Pie and The Ben has the best. "Say what?" you ask. Well before you start asking all around middle Tennessee what that delicious desert is, what's it made of, and especially where did it get that name, let me tell you since I've already done all that. The simple answer is that the name is derived from people asking about it and being told, "It's jes pie." And it's good enough to have been around here for a long, long time. As for the ingredients, well; come see for yourself.

⇐ Lynchburg – Franklin ⇒

They Came - 10,000 Strong - and Again

They came and came. It wasn't a Presidential visit, we have already had several, and it wasn't the turn of the century that was thirty-one days away (and technically one year and thirty-one days but we Americans can't seem to understand that the new century doesn't start until the end of the 00-year). They came to what had been Tennessee's third wealthiest county but now only half of that. 10,000 came to the county seat with its population of only 2,000.

They flooded downtown Franklin, the old and very old, the youth, the residents, Nashvillians, Atlantans, even the from-far-away Richmonds (Virginia) and others from parts unrecorded. They came on foot, horseback, carriages, and many on the several trains. They all showed up the morning of November 30, 1899. They came because of the UDC project, the United Daughters of the Confederacy who wanted to make the 35th Anniversary special, to honor the most significant event that had ever happened in Williamson County, the Battle of Franklin. They came to see the dedication of the anonymous, ubiquitous confederate infantryman alight a thirty-seven foot plus marble scepter, ubiquitous in the clutches all their living hearts, standing among their heroes in gray.

A third of the one million confederate soldiers were still alive. The Union with their two million did slightly better. 625,000 total lost their lives. One of the first battles and the war's bloodiest, Shiloh, saw 24,000 casualties. Chickamauga saw 36,600. Franklin scored 10,000 and Nashville 16,000. These were just four of the 3,000 encounters, forty plus recorded "battles" that happened all in Tennessee. TN was formerly the breadbasket of the south, the state Lincoln called, "the keystone of the Southern arch," but now was the virtual graveyard of the brothers war.

If ever you want an electrifying answer when venturing into a new place, and you have the time to listen, just ask an assumed to be knowledgeable native, "What is the most provocative event in the history of this area?" Then stand back as your questionee thinks and braces for his own word deluge.

If you want to learn something interesting, look into the details of whatever it is that is "reported" to you. For example, the above dedication was such a solemn occasion it was going to go forth no matter what, act of God (and I'm thinking rain, snow, etc.), train wreck, bank robbery with hostage taking on the same square – you get the idea. Well the few days building up to the dedication of Private White saw a horse and buggy being driven by a confederate veteran, Joseph A. Lockhart, becoming entangled in the support ropes hoisting the statue with the resulting whack – the statue had with the shaft. It broke off part of Mr. White's svelte hat giving our infantryman a slightly, "disheveled" look. It has never been fixed. We call that "tweaking." It somehow looks even more authentic, at least quiet appropriate.

And there's more: technically our statuesque hero is facing southeast (not sympathetically toward the south or defiantly toward the north). It's your turn to speculate why – and I bet it'll be a long time before you choose their reason Their reason is so that the (many) people getting off the trains coming into Franklin would see Mr. White head on. Honest, this is the reason. This is the truth and I guess about the only thing one can say in its defense is that like the southerly inclined during that period, which Private White represents, they faced things head-on.

Speaking about details and any interest in the Civil War, the War of the Rebellion, The War of Northern Aggression, The War for Southern Independence, Mr. Lincoln's War, the War of Secession, the War in Defense of Virginia (Richmond was the capital of the Confederacy), the War of the Insurrection, Slaveholders War, War for Abolition, War of Southern Reaction, and/or the War Between the States (and I could go on – and you don't believe me: War to Prevent Southern Independence, Second War of American Succession, The Late Unpleasantness – and there's more left for you to discover. Anyways) one has to be careful of the details such as the names of the battles (e.g., our Battle of Chattanooga III included the Battle of Lookout Mountain and the Battle of Missionary Ridge, which after two others of Chattanooga, sound much more quixotic).

The same point stands for our Battle of Franklin. There was a first, April 10, 1863 with a total 137 casualties. This pales in comparison to our second, in importance and casualties, and therefore the titular title, The Battle of Franklin is given to number two. Then there are the listings of casualties that needs the details of what is included (or not) such as "actually" killed, wounded, captured, missing and/or all the foregoing (also killed by disease et al). I'm sure you get the point. Have fun and plan, once hooked, to spend a few years absorbed in what has to be America's most "provocative event." Remember the numbers of losses and our other conflicts, police actions (Korea), and even world wars, annual death rates (by auto, guns, disease, etc.) pale by comparison.

And I assume you know that our Civil War is clearly the fault of the British. Seriously, remember 1642, 1648 and then 1649? The first was the first pitched battle of the First English Civil War between the Royalists and the Parliamentarians fought to an inconclusive result near Edge Hill (we would say, Edge Knob) and Kineton in southern Warwickshire. The other two dates are the start of their Second and their Third; all before our 1863. Therefore it's *plainly* in the English tradition.

Someone said they thought I needed glasses!?! Now that's disturbing. Why – I can see OK, I think? Oh no, do you think they would make a difference – in the dating thing? Here in my thirties and already falling apart, without a marriage partner, kids, or the like. I just know that if I ever attended one of the olé high school reunion things, they're probably already have grandkids. Yuck!

I just know that going down the dating-marriage-path I'd be changing everything and feeling pressure. It's obvious that women have this nesting thing and the biological clock thing and it seems to me that they get those things by manipulations/enticement/finagling – I'm searching for the good word (luring, baiting, entitlement, ensnare, decoy, alluring…). Hey – can you help me out? I know that whatever I say is going to be construed against me. For that matter, since (I guess) I feel that way, why bother with that "aisle" anyway.

For example (I guess I can't leave it alone), how many would put up with my apartment and crazy tub. They have to work for the home and picket fence, then the kids, dogs, and lots of yard work. This is before the "security" of a nest-egg for retirement (and leaving one's inheritance to the kids). Did I mention the "mean-whiles?" (They include the "monthly" thing, menopause, postpartum depressions, hours and hours of makeup-getting ready thing, and the needed collection of shoes and I'm not talking the practical one pair of black and one pair of brown).

But I like my apartment – really like it. I'm happy, content, even with the years of Laundromats – I find those to be quiet times, even (occasionally) interesting if you get a good conversationalist doing theirs at the same time. Besides, how many women would put up with washing the darks and the lights together? Seriously - I can hear the screams. But it works, they're fine – and I have years to prove it. And forget the softeners, additives, and all that other nonsense (crap, really). Basic Tide powder, as long as it hasn't lumped on you, does everything just fine but never ever tell a date you do things that way – they become mothers, or Mother Superiors, and the night is shot. Trust me on this - bachelors.

Glasses? Do you think it's an aging thing? Just the other day I noticed that my left hand tried to take over the chores I was don't for my right. Did this ever happen to you? Do you know what I even mean?

It was a simple task of putting the clean silverware back in the drawer. Yes I wash (not lick) them clean after a single use.

I was using both hands although I tend to be left handed for most things. With my left I was putting spoons away, there's more of those, and the forks with my right when I saw my left stop what it was doing and then it took a fork out of my right hand as if to say, "No, no. You're doing that all wrong. It goes in the drawer this way. See?" Gee, is this my feminine side coming out in my left hand?

I kid you not. Mother or Miss Lefty just took over before getting back to it's own chore and, disturbing as it was, it proceeded to do the same thing with the ice tea spoons, which were clearly relegated to the Right's Task List for the right side. What the hell is going on? I swear this has never happened before. Maybe I should see a doctor. See a specialist, one on aging or right and left stuff. Are there such? Are family doctors trained in these sorts of things?

Witches, I'm partial to witches and they're on my list just under ghosts and it seems like a good subject for changing another. I was particularly fond of a ghost back in the V that lived upstairs at the Alcove Restaurant, where I had my first job after college and before I muscle-wrote my way in to the local paper. I just, as a friend, wrote up a few business articles for several of the local establishments including the Alcove. My writing was liked when I submitted it (or it was given to the paper by the establishments I wrote about) and the local Editor thought it could be developed into something significant for his paper so…

Her name was/is Emily, the ghost not the editor, and she likes to dance. Emily waltzes, she loves the one-two-three steps. It's appropriate in the Alcove's upstairs Victorian chandeliered ballroom that sees the bi-monthly meetings of the Lions Club, the Rotary, the local union, big guest parties, and such.

There is a second big room across the way. Its motif is black and white, kind of the Roaring Twenties art deco style. Emily does the Flapper/Charleston dances there. She keeps mostly to herself, seems quite happy, maybe giddy. She's youthful, a wee bit solemn but I don't know anyone who actually knows her age. She's in her own world, never uttering a word, and not bothering customers or the help.

Emily always wears dainty, shiny, black paten leather, single strap shoes with short sheer white stockings topped with ruffles or white hose – better for dancing. Her dresses are an assortment of contrasting crinolines or chiffons in striking, flowing but muted pastels. She also always wears a matching ribbon crowning her head. I especially like that – classy.

None of the employees talk about Emily. Some locals think she's a witch. I think this upsets her some. Not everyone sees her. I think she's a nocturnal person/ghost for the most part. I don't know whether she's connected to or a relative of the owner or any of the previous owners. There have been a few. I asked around and checked the archives at the paper but found no missing person-Emily or a murder etc. And she's still there even though I'm gone, at least as a waiter, lounge patron, local news guy, Friday-night-news-guy-lounge-drinker.

This, Emily, had/has been my only real encounter with a "spirit." Of course one lives with many reported sightings, rumors, gossiping, and the like - growing up. These (other) stories just never interested or concerned me. Emily was special.

But as special and personal as Emily was, her reality pales in comparison to what I have run into here in the Ben. It started because of my interest in The Battle, and who wouldn't be interested in something like it especially if one found one's self sleeping on such hollowed grounds.

I guess it would be like an adventurous person putting down a sleeping bag for the night at the century's long-forgotten Machu Picchu, atop the 8,000 foot Peruvian mountain. This pre-Columbian "Lost City of the Incas" holding untold spiritual significance with its numerous temples and ritual structures build by artisans the likes of the stonemasons of the pyramids offers no clue how a people could have hoisted the tens of thousands polished blocks to these inhospitable heights to construct such perfectly designed edifices complete with water fountains, an irrigation system, et al, without mortar, a lost technique called ashlar. I just have to do it in my lifetime, sleep on those hollowed grounds. If you want to also – join me. But be open to what may happen. It has to be the closest-to-heaven city.

And this is what I did, the "open" part. And I didn't need a passport, ten hour flight with the needed connections, tour guide, physically-fit test by the local government in order to receive a "pass" just to trek the two-day Inca Trail. I merely took a thermos of black coffee and a thin wool blanket big enough to sit on and at the same time to put over my shoulders when the cooler, fall twilight came and went out to Carton Plantation late afternoon taking seat at one of the several trees, not there at the time of the Battle, facing the Union breastworks to the north, sitting, waiting, sipping, listening.

It's one of the most moving experiences I shall ever encounter and probably not for the faint-hearted. It came before the muted sounds of ten's of thousands shoes and bare feet tramping in the areas knee high grasses moving forward, moving into the face of death.

Schofield's undefeated Division was before them, "The Army of the Cumberland."

The tones and sounds seemed to emanate from the ground, not mouths, or maybe it came from hearts. It built and built until the sweet sounds of John Newton's *Amazing Grace* spilled over the land and flowed over me however so softly. I was transformed. It gave an eerie message as if the words, "Thro' many dangers, toils and snares, I have already come...The Lord has promis'd good to me..." were replaced with "Well men, if we must die then let us die like southern men."

Amazing grace, how sweet the sound... Damn, I even dropped my half full thermos that spilled into the ground reminiscent of the blood spilled there many, many years ago. But looking down in the approaching evening dark, I saw blood and imagined the river of such that would soon flow into these fields on that fateful November night long, long ago.

I got the impression from mom's letter that the first wave to hit the Union breastworks were a surge of displaced rabbits that the twenty thousand Johnny Rebels had flushed in their forward march. No I didn't come to see rabbits; maybe they're all gone too. I never saw a one. But I had done something similar in Japan, visited and sat in quiet meditation at the edge of their little 30 meters east-west by 10 meters north-south infamous Zen sand/rock garden at the Ryoan-ji in Kyoto and I

remember the strange but pleasant feeling that came over me in just a short time. And I said to myself, we don't have rock and sand-raked aesthetic gardens but we have acres upon acres of sacred grounds. And they're here. Here in the Ben.

I haven't bothered to research it and haven't read it many places but it's reported by some and believed my most, that maybe the most humane thing General Hood did for his men on the frightful day where he lost a good eight thousand men in just five hours including six of his generals, possibly the best the south had, was to have his band play that tune before the ensuing battle, before he sent his men into the teeth of hell.

No, I heard no band, merely a ground swell of men's voices, mostly young. It was so moving I know I'll do it again, just not every year or often – the heart can withstand only so much, even a northern one.

Speaking of spirits, and maybe I have been, do you remember that I said the TRA talked about (ran an article) about a resident witch, Miss Jean, 2001 years old. Well I couldn't leave this alone and found three more in the Ben, two of which were very upset that they weren't approached for the article (nor approached since for their own article). The third said that she, "Paid it no attention. It was bad for business anyways." Must be referring to the Witching Business whatever that is.

"Now I'm not going to spend a lot of time on this," I told myself from the start and have mostly stuck to this self-rule. So here's the story:

I went to see Miss Jean, Witch. Actually I went to visit her place, the Bell Book and Candle, which sounded interesting and would give me "the lay of the land," an idea of the subject matter that I virtually knew nothing about. And a visit should provide an occasion for a face-to-face interview, a starting point for my article. You ask, "Why - since she was covered by the TRA?" Well, why not? I wasn't going to go over old ground. It was just a starting point. After all, a good fisherman can go into a well-fished stream and catch the limit – just watch my Nana. Well, if you had the chance you would have seen this happen when she was alive.

My second reason was that I had seen Alfred Hitchcock's 1958 movie by the came name, *Bell Book and Candle* starring Jimmy Stewart and Kim Novak. I remember because as a teen I fell head over heels for Kim's poster picture and wanted to fall in love with her but her acting or at least her role was so weird that I said, "Forget it." AH's *Vertigo* wasn't much better (where Jim and Kim starred together again).

Miss Jean was very accommodating, liking the possibility of being mentioned in another paper. One of the first questions I asked was, "Are there any more witches here in Franklin?" I was a little surprised at her answer since my competitor hadn't mentioned anything of the kind. She said, "Why yes, three more." And she said this without the burden of competition like an answer you might get from the same question posed to a retail toy store or pharmacy owner.

"Who are they and why wasn't this mentioned in your article?" The first part came out naturally as a follow up and the second question was directed at the wrong person, I knew after I had said it – it was a question for the competition that I could never ask them. But she answered both with, "They never asked but if you like, I'll give you their names and addresses." And she did.

When she gave me the three names she said something odd, "We're missing one."

"What? Why?"

"Well our area is obviously in formation, you know, the pentagram, so we need another."

It was nice she assumed that I knew what she was talking about but I didn't have a clue so – into the hopper I went with an honest, "Can you explain that to me?"

"Sure. You'll notice the points on a map of my colleagues' addresses. It's haphazard but it happens. They start to form a pattern. When five legitimate witches are established in a territory, whether it's a state, a town or a city block, the area is empowered and becomes their coven, a pentagram coven."

"A what?" (I'll have her spell it for me).

"A coven, c-o-v-e-n, their gathering-place. Kind of a district or franchise in the broad sense but one that happens versus one that's chosen by one of us."

"What if it's a state and another witch moves in to it?"
"That's how it works, the established area is sacred but then separates from the new area started with the advent of a new arrival. The new area can be completed only with the addition of four more."

I had looked up the definitions of witchcraft, wicca, wizard, sorcerer and warlock before coming but now I was getting into the meat and bones of the craft and I wasn't sure that I wanted to go there or that I needed all that information. It was kind 'a like learning a little more than one's comfortable about the funeral director duties and I was always on that edge with my former back door neighbor and good funeral director friend back in the V.

Of course I came across the pentagrm in my quick research and found it fascinating, curious, that the symbol was used by the Greeks, Babylonians, Christians (representing the five wounds of Jesus) but also the Freemasonry. What a small world.

Then, as curious as I am, I couldn't quite leave this alone so I asked the question, "When has it ever happened as a city block?"

"All the time but maybe one of the best examples is Lily Dale."

Bells were starting to go off. Life is becoming too much of a coincidence. "You don't mean in upper New York state do you?"

"Yes, that's exactly what I mean. Do you know it?"

"Do I know it? Are you serious – do I know it?" I didn't say as I tried to measure my facial expressions that I was sure were telling. And she confirmed this with, "Yes, I see that you do."

I used to pass by the front gate of Lily Dale near Cassadaga, NY every time the family or I went to Lake Chautauqua of to the Chautauqua Institution from the G. And one time, after hearing about it, older sis insisted, well goaded me, into driving through the place in the off-season when we had a better chance of not running into anybody.

Lily Dale is a reputed spiritualist community of "free thinkers" and heralds itself as the "Largest Spiritualist Center" in the World or at least the deteriorating sign at the entrance said, the sign that bothered sis enough that we had to see for ourselves. Of course we had given the place, bigger than a trailer park but smaller than a village, about as much respect as the loony bin up on the G's north hill and relegated the Lily place to gypsies, palm readers, witches, and weirdoes. In our defense, this was appropriate for two teenage, born-in-to-the-faith Catholics. I don't know if or how it's connected but sis and I saw that there was even a Lily Dale Pet Cemetery there.

Off season you ask – well we weren't about to fork over the $3 per person (or $5 per car) that the sign said was the fee for admission into the closed off area. It's probably higher now especially since Miss Jean confirms that it is still in business and popular enough to be mentioned far enough away as Tennessee. And if you know anything about it you're probably wondering if we saw the two swans, Lily and Dale. Your answer is we saw only one and I couldn't answer you as to which it was. My gender deduction thing doesn't work on cats, running squirrels, beetles, bits and bytes, yin and yang, or swans. Sorry. That's assuming that one of each for the fowl - with names like that. Maybe they had mated and she ate him – like the preying mantis types.

OK, so I'm trying to be erudite since mantis is derived from the Greek word mantis - meaning prophet or fortuneteller. Sorry. Again. But there sure were a lot of them, fortunetellers and tarot readers at the Dale or at least shingles outside of the dozens of tinny tiny cottages that lined the many streets with their white picket fences and little manicured lawns that carried at lease one to five statutes, gnomes, leprechauns, trolls, orges, ferries, or whatever they were lining (or warning) the walk up to the tiny front doors. There was probably a reason for the place's name, other than the swans, but that was a turn-off for me anyway so I never pursued it.

After our drive through, sis and I never hesitated to point it out to any guests we might have going by on our way to the lake, only a half hour more. After all, this was a leap forward for the kids that use to play Zit on long car rides.

Over time sis and I learned that the likes of Susan B. Anthony, Frederick Douglas, Madame Sofia Andreyevna Behrs Tolstoy (wife of Leo), Mohawk Chief Oskennonton (born May 27, 1886 to the Bear Clan of the Canadian Mohawks, recorded for Columbia Records and appeared in the Broadway musical, *Toot-Toot*, he died 1955), as well as Mae West were visitors/patrons there.

It was one of my weekly (end of) drinking soirées and the consequential trip to the men's room that brought this about. And it was a wakeup call that it was time to either go home, walking, or to start on coffee (read espresso strong and only black). Expecting to see one of the three wall urinals that I've visited on a weekly, Friday night basis, I was surprised to see a squat toilet in place of #1.

Now I don't know what they call them in Japan, but I had a similar shocked surprised coming across the first one there and was no less surprised to see them on the long distant trains. Fortunately, all the hotels that my trading agent had booked me into had our regular, American Standard types in the room but I started to wonder if all the hotels were as "modern." I know, I know, that's a cultural prejudice and I know they're the "modern" thing in China (at least the ceramic ones) and maybe most of Asia but nothing had prepared me for this encounter.

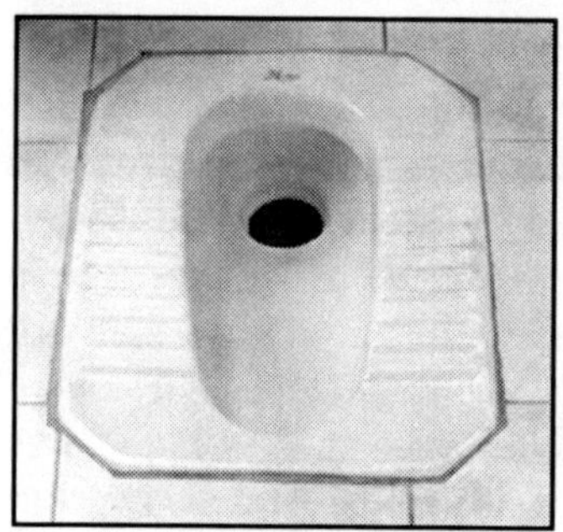

No, it wasn't there, it was a just a large floor drain that happened to be surrounded by slightly off-colored title that seemed to define what I saw. The later became apparent with the succeeding eye blinking that I went through as I unzipped, zipped and unzipped, then zipped my pants again in shock and indecision. I'm sure it was for easy mopping/cleaning but was so real that the whole of my Japan trip flashed through my mind, something I hadn't thought of in a long time. Maybe it wasn't the eye-blinking but the thought that I had again neglected to call my publisher that sobered me up.

Yes, it was a good, worthwhile trip that I would recommend for anyone providing you had a guide of some sort. Well, on second thought I think it was great for men but I'm not so sure it would be the same for women. From little experience, I think the world hasn't caught up with us on the equal rights for women issues. My observation was that men ruled in Nippon (and I liked it. Sorry – but I kind 'a did).

My greatest moment during the trip happened with I least expected it, when I talked to three angels.

It was during a lull in my hectic Japan trip, when I had a moment to spend by myself. I did the tourist thing and visited their little 30 meters east-west by 10 meters north-south sand/rock garden at the Ryoan-ji in Kyoto that I mentioned earlier. It's the same place that you can see/visit the Golden Temple.

"When in Rome..." so I decided to pretend, to be monk-like and do the meditation thing at the edge of the garden by sitting quietly, empting my mind, focusing on a distant rock and letting things (whatever) come to me. I was succeeding pretty well, off to I-don't-know-where, despite the milling tourists when suddenly three little Japanese Cherubim girl-doll angels popped down at my right side with one, the closest to the garden saying, "Excuse me please."

They were kindergarten or first grade equivalents of our USA school system; I'm not familiar with theirs. They were dressed in the school uniform outfits that I was getting used to seeing from my various early morning buses and train rides and were obviously on a field trip.

"Our teacher," started the same one, obviously the "spokes person" for the threesome, maybe one that excelled in English or was the more extroverted. "Our teacher said we could introduce ourselves to visitors and ask for a coin (as a souvenir). Is that OK?"

"Sure," I responded mostly from my stupor. Then my hesitation, being mesmerized by their beautiful, enchanting faces, confused them. I really did feel I was in the presence of beautiful little angels in the guise of Japanese schoolgirls.

They probably had memorized the "approach" and thought their request was clear. But not getting the intended results, they quickly huddled their heads and a lot of Japanese was exchanged with the result that the spokes person started to repeat her request but stopped when I started to reach into my pocket to display my foreign coins for the three's education.

There was no question they knew I was American (versus the Swedish, Australian, or the many other countries present in the tourist mix that is typical at all the tourist spots in this fascinating country). Maybe (and probably) it's the clothes but it could be our walk, or the manner we carry ourselves – I don't know but it seems obvious that most Japanese seems to sense one's country of origin. I had already decided that if I was ever to come back here that I would bring a white Stetson, large belt and flashy buckle, and cowboy boots.

I knew what was in my pocket but proceeded anyway as their little heads drew closer to the spot that they felt would be a good viewing position for my proffered hand of foreign coins. Because I knew my hand held only a variety of Japanese coins, I slowly (for effect) opened it in front of their eyes.

There was a moment of silence and then all three jumped back in amazement, giggling, at seeing their own, familiar coinage in this foreigner's hand. It was a precious, unforgettable moment that I hope to never lose. I continued, "I don't have any of my own country's coins but I can give you one of these…" as I reached for my wallet, pulling out a good olé US of A, one George Washington dollar bill causing an instant commotion before the little spokesperson said, "Our teacher wouldn't like us to take that much for a souvenir."

I insisted with some authority saying, "I insist – it's OK. You can tell your teacher that you didn't ask but I wanted to give it to you so that you three can show your class." It worked and they started the "thank you sir's," bowing, and backing away. All this time I wondered how many of our US angels would be able to speak in Japanese to any such visitors they came across.

And now - the reason I went to visit America's first squat-toilet (at least this side of the Mississippi). It was because of the slight commotion I had started back in the bar, in this near-neighbor, pseudo-suburb of Music City, USA. So I was bored! And the talk had turned to famous Masons, a topic that just isn't appropriate for a Friday night, end-of-week, fun sortie even if the immediate area was/is infested with them, them/there masons.

OK, so it wasn't the bar/bar talk but the nearby table talk of likeable Masonic members that had just joined us (us meaning the "bar-regulars") after some sort of secret meeting at the lodge that evening. The "secret" part was a soft-dig since the masons are routinely accused of secret-rituals, secret-conspiracies or whatever and who cares "what goes on behind closed doors." Was that a song or just another one of those damnable clichés? And having been around for hundreds of years – for the masons-them - I've never found anyone who is/was affected by their alleged "secretness-es." Damn, listening to myself I sure was in need of that black coffee. Make that a double-expresso.

Anyway – famous masons – and if you've heard this conversation once, you probably recognize the familiar litany that ends with Masonic Ben himself, at least in this town. And I've heard it a time or two, maybe one too many for this night.

So I turned around, glass in hand (I just can't remember what was in it, if anything at that point) and boldly interrupted, "You've left out one of the most famous! Shame on you!" No, I don't know where that last part came from – maybe leftover mothering or something. Come to (try) to think of it, I can't even remember what kind of glass it was. Could it have been a "long-neck" with me about to reminisce about my (one and only) trip to Texas?

"WHO?" was the more loud then necessary response from my table audience behind me that I didn't expect, which meant "commitment" if not "challenge." Commitment to finish what I started – OK, maybe you knew that.

So I said, raising my glass, "Hank, of course!" And I turned back around starting to build the shit-eating grin that routinely starts at one ear, my right, and eventually ends up at the other without recourse especially when I'm in such a state as this – with few resources to stop it.

I had purposely led them with just a teaser; a partial answer and I did receive the expected, confused, all-kinds-of questions response going on behind me. Many of their words were directed at each other in trying to verify and test the correct answer to my question (if indeed there was one). And after some discussion amongst themselves they, in unison, turned to me (my back) and chimed in together, "You mean Hank Williams?" Damn, it sounded like a chorus – a very respectful choral group. Maybe the secret meeting they had just come from was for forming the first Masonic Barbershop quartet.

When one says Hank, or Hank Williams, there is only one and it's not the new (fine) upstart Junior but his dad, Senior. Slowly I turned noting the spreading silence emanating from my position. Again I slowly raised my glass savoring the moment being the only one that knew that I did have an answer so that the next step wouldn't be an unpleasant moment of one being punished or castigated for speaking tom-foolery, or sacrilege about arguably one of Country Western's most famous singers/character/martyrs.

"HELL Yes!" I answered. (Pause) "Did you know? (Now slowly) He was even named after our beloved local lodge, Masonic Temple, Hiram Lodge No. 7...Gentlemen, (another pause for dramatic effect) Hank's full name is HIRAM 'Hank' King Williams." And slowly I turned back to my bar and admiring friends (hopefully) as the new information was slowly digested (and tested) by the four lodge brothers at the table to my backside, all the while thinking to myself that my head of trivia was bound to get me in trouble (again).

No, I don't know if the lodge just up the street is referred to as "our beloved local lodge," nor do I know if the proper terminology for members is "lodge brothers" or some secret title/name they have amongst themselves. But those things weren't the items that were making me so uncomfortable here in the men's bathroom. The one thing that made me think of a necessary, immediate, quick detour to here was the fact that I had no idea if Hank was a mason at all even if his first (real) name was Hiram. Did I drive here? If I did – where the hell did I park the Blue Tail? There just has to be a back-way out of here. I think I remember one – if it's still there. Yea, things will probably cool down and maybe even be forgotten by next Friday. Amen to trivia.

The list of similarities between my new home and my other ones continues to amaze me, and yes, this includes my own Friday nights. But I wasn't looking for this one; I just happened across it by accident while looking for some other happenings in this little town, specifically, the history of our Williamson County Fairs. If I hadn't turned the page, I would have missed it but now I just can't leave it alone. I swear that as long as I have been here, that not one person or one word of this spectacular event has been spoken to me. It is the Third Civil War Battle of Franklin and in some ways this one far exceeded our infamous Battle itself.

Eerily The Third lasted about the same five hours and it too had everything to do with what happened here on that bitter cold day of November 30, 1864 when Franklin had been completely engulfed and overrun by non-residents and huge events they didn't invite and couldn't control. It totally happened again just fifty-nine years later than the big one and, fortunately, minus the barrels of blood and thousands of deaths. It, the Third, and its memories, just seems to have been more successfully buried than the Battle itself.

In contrast to what happened in those hot, mournful days in November, the Third took place in the hot, rather muggy days of September 1923. No the South didn't rise again, well not exactly, and it was Hollywood that was totally to blame.

The occasion was the visit of the well know and dashing director, producer, and former leading man Allen Holubar of Metro-Pictures (now known as Metro-Goldwyn-Mayer), his dozens of assistants-entourage and three filled to capacity baggage train cars loaded with his cameras, gear, props, and all that is necessary to stage a gigantic battle scene of thousands. Holubar, who had directed the 1916, 20,000 *Leagues Under the Sea* (remade in 1954 starring Kirk Douglas, James Mason and Peter Lorre), was rarely seen without his expected director's garb, whipcord riding breeches, high-laced dressage boots, multicolored silk paisley sport shirt, expensive cherry-wood pipe, jaunty fixed brimmed panama hat (really made in Ecuador, not Panama) and his favorite "bat," riding crop.

His director's outfit was, more or less, the expected wear of the more influential or successful directors at that time. Holubar, the man who had already launched Rudolph Valentino on his quest for stardom, just elevated it to a new level. And maybe more importantly to the public, Allen was married to the vivacious actress Dorothy Phillips.

The idea that one might see Dorothy on the streets of the Ben spread like wildfire for one hundred miles around. With due respect…Allen.

Now, Holubar wished to stage the original Battle on the original battle site for the climactic scene of his next movie, *The Human Mill*, a version of the late John Trotwood Moore's novel, *The Bishop of Cottonwood.*

John Moore (1858-1929), who with his wife and a small group of their friends was present for the filming, had written other good Tennessee books including the one of the early history, *Tennessee, the Volunteer State* and another on the songs and stories of old Tennessee. John happened to live in Maury County just over the way and now has a Middle School named after him in Nashville. Our own Moore's Lane in the Ben may be named in his honor but I'll have to check that.

But when I enquiry about John at the library here, it isn't John's books as much as his one poem that he composed for the *Confederate Veteran Magazine* in 1893 that he's remembered here, at least in the Special Sections department. It's a very moving, poignant poem titled, *Cleburne's Banner*. If we haven't already talked about it, Major General Patrick Ronayne (Pat)("If we're going to die, let us die like men") Cleburne, was one of the six confederate generals killed at the Battle of Franklin. I'll give you the first stanza of Moore's poem (and encourage you to look it up – to read the rest):

Folded now is Cleburne's banner,

Furled the flag that kissed the stars,
Gone the dreams that dropped like manna
From its skies of bonny bars.
Nameless they who fell before it,
Dust the hearts that died in vain,
Dead the hero-hands that bore it
Through the blight of battle's rain…

As I continue to relate this event, The Third, I must give credit to the well written story, *Second Hour of Glory* by Marshall Morgan that I found in the very informative *Journals* of the Williamson County Historical Society, journals that do well to capture the many events and stories of a town's past, something I would like to see in all small towns. MM's article was the one I found turning the "next" page.

Beside the needed directing talent, many of the better-known directors had a PR gift, a "flare for the dramatic" that they used successfully when dealing with the public. Holubar had more than his share.

Soon after Holubar's arrival, he announced the leading male and female actors of two of Hollywood's finest. This served to stir the gathering small army of news people who were starting to clog the telegraph lines with their early reports.

Holublar had chosen and now announced that Henry B. Walthall Jr. who was still riding his popularity crest from his role as the little Colonel in the epic, *The Birth of the Nation* was going to be the male lead and Blanche Sweet was to be Walthall's star counterpart. That he wasn't going to use his wife, Dorothy, was a disappointment to some but it was like the difference of having to choose between a hot fudge sundae heaping with whip cream and maraschino cherries on top or a banana split with six flavors of ice cream instead of only three.

It was what followed that stirred the town into a frenzy, which was starting to overflow with the curious, movie aspirants, Confederate veterans, politicians wishing to be seen with famous, and those many others so inclined to be drawn into such events similar to moths to a flame. Holubar proceeded to say that his stars weren't about to be part of the battle and therefore he needed "doubles." Word spread fast throughout the state and its adjacent neighbors and faster than a strong wind whipped wild fire in one of Tennessee's draught stricken, dry-tinder national forests. The first Tennessee Hollywood Idol Contest was born.

Not one to leave a good PR thing alone once he saw it, Holublar stirred the pot with the added innuendo that of course this should mean (for the doubles picked) a probably future stardom in Hollywood - causing a near-stampede. Then putting gasoline on the fire, Allen announced that at least four thousand men-extras would be needed to populate the battle scene, a figure far exceeding the entire population of Franklin including all men, women, and children, even all humans in all the immediate towns around. Maybe recognizing the political feelings, he added, "That his battle would not be complete without the presence of real Confederate soldiers in the gray-line."

The volunteer response from hundreds of miles around was overwhelming as if they were invited to the apocalyptic Second Coming. World War I veterans, National guard troops, Spanish War veterans, members of any American Legions posts and any other veteran organizations, Confederate every-bodies started arriving by the rail-car full, even schools volunteered their young men while virtually all surrounding businesses declared a "Battle Holiday" in order to relinquish any males in their employ to populate the undertaking.

A crew of forty workmen and builders spent ten to twelve hours a day for a week to prepare the surrogate battlefield that happened to be near the original. The battle's chosen location was the many acres of sweeping fields on the J. W. Yowell farm some half mile west off the Columbia highway south of the Ben adjacent to Winstead Hill, the very spot that General Hood had used as his headquarters during the original battle and a place one can still visit today.

A number of "prop" houses and barns were build along with dozens of dummy structures that were designated to be burned during the filming. Hundreds of trenches were dug, old-fashion split wood rail fences were strung across the field, a stone fence "made of appropriately weathered rock" was built, broken-down caissons were hauled in to place, hundreds of explosive mines were buried throughout, and every field gun-cannon in the state was sought.

"By twilight of the eve of the battle, Franklin was packed to the gutters. Crowds of strangers pushed through the town's inadequate Main Street and depleted its restaurants. Mays Hotel, the one hostelry, bulged with five and six occupants to the room. A Kiwanis plea for extra housing swung open the doors of numerous townspeople; but squads of shelterless individuals, nevertheless, roamed the streets all night. The evening was gaspingly hot, anyway; so those who sought sleep on the church lawns perhaps had the best of it, after all.

"The great day came hot and fair, with a velvety blue-sky and mail order puffs of clouds. At his 6 o'clock breakfast Holubar declared: 'Gentlemen, it's perfect movie weather."

“Captain Koch, the costumer, was a thick-gutturalled, red-faced veteran of Germany’s world War army. His troubles began while the senior director was still breakfasting. The Masonic Hall one of Franklin’s oldest landmarks, had been selected as the armory and supply depot for the occasion; and before Captain Koch could open its ancient doors on the thousands of blue and gray uniforms stored inside, he was besieged by a mob of early-bird, would-be soldiers.”

(Two hours later). “Holubar, whacking at his thighs with a bright green megaphone, appeared on the battlefield at 8:15 o’clock. He mounted a camera stand and studied the positions through binoculars.”

“…the Columbia highway (was) almost impassible under its burden of automobiles, buggies, wagons, bicycles, baby carriages, and plodding hundreds of pedestrians. Twenty special deputies had been sworn in to augment the everyday forces of law and order; and as fast as the movie-spellbound throngs (3000+) arrived on the scene they were herded into a roped off hillside area…the traffic inched forward in squeaks, jolts, and frenzied horn-blattings. Thousands more were coming…The crowd of spectators had swollen to 6,000 persons by 9:30 o’clock. Four thousand more managed to scramble to vantage points in the next half hour, at the expense of every fence and corn field in the vicinity.”

“At a few minutes before noon, Holubar turned to McDermott (Vincent McDermott, assistant director). ‘Shoot the works, Mac,’ he said. And the Third battle began.

“A land mine in the middle distance went up in a roaring black geyser of earth; the signal for the battle to start.

“What happened during the ensuing 40 minutes can best be described, perhaps, as an ear-splitting inferno of thunder, flame, smoke, and stumbling, falling men. Individual participants, swallowed up in the billowing smoke, blinded by rifle flashes and borne to earth under cascading tons of dirt, remember only shreds of their own experiences. The immediate and first general reaction among the troops was the shocked realization that the thing was terrific-far more realistic and hazardous than anyone had foreseen. One astonished Confederate soldier, struggling to his knees under a deluge of dirt, expressed the overall reaction of the combatants when he shouted to the companion lying beside him: 'My god, I didn't know it was going to be like this!'

"Hundreds of the attacking Confederates ran forward to kneel, fire, and advance again; others crouching low, fired from the hip. Dashing wildly through the melee came riderless horses, whipped into the scene from the sidelines. Federal gunners, stripped to the waist, sweated and cursed at their flaming field pieces; Federal infantrymen loaded and fired and loaded again, deafened by their own musketry, choking under the rolling clouds of smoke.

"Casualties had been designated in advance and played their parts well. Some pitched headlong to lie still; others staggered forward, or crawled in simulated agony.

"Jack Pierce, the leading extra, suddenly rode into the vortex at full gallop. He was bareheaded, and his familiar black beard streamed in the wind. At a point squarely in front of a camera he flung his arms wide, grimaced, and sailed magnificently earthward in a bread-neck stunt fall.

"The dummy houses, now flaming, added their glare and smoke to the lurid pandemonium. By the time the uproar had become so incessant that shouts had become only meaningless mouthings.

"Holubar, his megaphone at his lips, bellowed into the ears of his cameramen:

> "Catch the action on the left.
> "Sweep toward the right flank –
> "Pick up on Gun Crew Number One!"

"Coldly, mechanically, the camera eyes followed the struggle.

“The first charge broke, and fell back. But a moment later, waved on by officer-extras, the yelling and firing Confederates surged forward again.

“Hernandez, master of the mine fields, played at his switchboard as though he were a harpist. Here he sent up a hurtling mushroom of earth in the face of an advancing platoon; there, neatly he bracketed an entire company. The fact that unexpected results were taking place did not deter him. Oddly enough, it seemed that at certain key points some one had forgotten to sift the dirt over the buried mines, or had been so negligent as to overcharge the explosives. Chunks of sod as big as footballs, accompanied by swarms of rock fragments, soared skyward.

“Hand-to-hand fighting developed on the Federal left flank, and quickly became more real than simulated. A 50-yard segment of rail fence became a focus of struggle as Confederates, swarming over, tried to wrest an American Flag from the hands of their foemen. Opposing troops emptied their rifles, then grappled in desperate wrestling matches; rifle butts were swung. Locked figures fell headlong from atop the fence. Holubar, taking advantage of this unforeseen development, quickly brought one of his cameras to bear.

“The clash of battle was too much for one Confederate guest of honor. Behind the restraining ropes he scuffled feebly with a beefy, placating deputy.

“Let me at ’em, boy!” shouted, ‘I fit ‘em in ’64, and I ain’t afeard to fight ‘em now!”

“One participant remembers that at the height of the struggle a terrified dove came veering across the battlefield. Suddenly a mine was touched off directly beneath the speeding bird; and an instant later two tiny gray wings whirled earthward.

“A Federal sniper was one of the key extras. This sharpshooter, in real life, Dr. T. P. Ballou, of Nashville, wore a curly blond wig; he plied his seemingly deadly trade from behind the stone fence in the immediate forefront of the battle scene. At a designated moment he fell, face downward, and remained motionless during the rest of the battle.

“Another close-up extra, at that time a boy of fifteen, recalls the unpleasant consequences of falling face upward. ‘I had been instructed to stagger, clutch my head, and fall face upward,’ this participant said. ‘No sooner had I fallen as directed, however, when a mine was set off about 25 feet in front of where I lay. It must have been overcharged; for one of the protective bags of sawdust arched upward in a beautiful curve, then started downward squarely toward my upturned face. Horrified, I watched this flight through half-closed lids. I remember now that ludicrous, almost insane threat that Holubar yelled; ‘I’ll kill and dead man who moves?’ Luckily, the bag broke wide open while it was still 20 feet or so above my face, and all I suffered was a solid inch covering of sawdust. If the bag hadn’t shattered exactly when it did, you can bet I would have rolled clear of that baby-and the hell with Hollywood.

“When 500 feet of the battle scenes had been filmed, Holubar stopped the camera. He leaped down from his stand, exultant. ‘That was a great battle scene, boys.’ He exclaimed. ‘Let the buglers sound ‘Cease Firing.’…”

“Miraculously, no one had been killed. Indeed there had been astonishingly few casualties of any kind…The Kiwanis club, outdoing itself, immediately served a mammoth barbecue luncheon for all the sweat and smoke-begrimed participants.

“Franklin had known its second hour of glory, in its second greatest day.”

However, Holubar missed one very important, I think crucial, part of the Battle. The original didn’t begin until after *Amazing Grace* had been sung. But this wasn't why you, or anyone else, have not seen his epic film. You see John died shortly after leaving Middle Tennessee and returning to Hollywood, never to complete his movie. He may in fact have caught his case of typhoid fever while visiting the Ben. Despite the pure spring water system used here at the time, there were still a few cases reported in the county. The unfortunate upshot of these events proved disastrous and the original footage has since been lost due to the Hollywood brokers not being able to imagine anyone else capable enough to take over, finish, and edit this famous director's work.

Interestingly, the several films about Tennessee, prior to this endeavor, were mostly not filmed in the state. One of the most famous, John Huston's classic *Red Badge of Courage* (1951) about the Tennessee battle of Shiloh based on Stephen Crane's novel was shot in California. The dramatic story about Tennessee's *Sergeant York* (1941) starring Gary Cooper wasn't shot in the state either.

Unfortunately, to many Tennesseans, the *I Walk the Line* (1968) starring Gregory Peck and Tuesday Weld, a film that the locals feels was too sordid and deals only with the less admirable "stereotypical" types associated with the state, was shot in our counties of Smith, Overton, Fentress, Jackson, and Putnam. The feelings are that this film should have never been released. I don't pretend to know about you but that brief introduction is enough for me to put it on my "must see" list.

Many of our historic Tennessee figures, including our three Ben's pillars, Davy Crockett, Andrew Jackson, and Sam Houston have been portrayed in numerous films. Of special note is Stanley Kramer's *Inherit the Wind* (1961) that recreates the legendary Scopes Trial, often referred to as the Scopes Monkey Trial that pitted lawyer Williams Jennings Bryan against lawyer Clarence Darrow.

The similarity I spoke of before telling you about the Ben's Third Battle was the Hollywood films of the V, Mt. Vernon, Ohio, my former hometown. “After the Big One, WWII, our government wanted to impress the USSR with ‘real’ life in the USA so they picked a ‘typical’ town in the US, made some documentary films about this ‘All American’ place, The V, and strongly encouraged Hollywood to make movies with their special choice-city as the backdrop. Out of the tens of thousands of cities and towns across the US that they could have picked, they picked The V. The V starred in many celluloids shown in Moscow shortly after WWII. Fascinating? Well it’s true!”

And the County Fair information that I had set out to research was important because someone remembered that Andrew Jackson had been invited to be the main speaker at one of the early fairs and I wanted to run that to ground, Andy being a pillar and all. And he was invited, did speak. In July of 1869 John McGavock, President of the Williamson County Agricultural & Mechanical Society wrote our Honorable Andrew Johnson cordially inviting him to the October Fair as guest speaker delivering the annual agricultural address at our Third Annual Fair.

Speaking of the upcoming Fair, I will be attending this year since one program note in the livestock area caught my attention with yet another similarity to my previous home, the V. It was the mention of the presence of Charolais, white cows, at the Fair.

My former Knox County had jumped on the bandwagon early in the century and had become a leader in growing the completely white cows back in the ‘60’s. It was even considered the national center thanks to the *Charolais Way,* a newspaper with national readership published there.

Competition caught us off guard with a front-page article that got my attention while probably not appealing to everyone. It was about the archaeological dig northwest of the Ben, just before the next county, Davidson, border. I love the name assigned by the guy responsible, Malcolm Parker who is responsible for the Parthenon. He found the Owl Creek People, circa 3660BC.

Wait a minute, I said the Parthenon but wasn't referring to the famous Greek Athena temple or it's older sister (on the same site) destroyed by the Persian invasion of 480 BC. I was referring to our own, just up the street in Nashville. Really. Our Parthenon, in pristine shape (no dig intended) and built in 1897, is a full-scale replica that was built as part of the Tennessee Centennial Expo, a.k.a., World's Fair. The year just about coincided with Tennessee's one-hundredth birthday and saw almost two million additional visitors to our own Athens.

In the effort of full disclosure, our original Parthenon was built of plaster, wood and brick but was rebuilt in the 1920's out of concrete. So it's kind 'a like the other one, also a "second, rebuilt" one. I'm not sure the Greeks have the original (or any) statue of Athena that their structure originally housed but the word is that Nashville expects to erect one in theirs, gold gilded et al. We'll see.

On the occasion of the World's Fair, many Tennessee cities built huge edifices, buildings, and exhibit halls on the Exposition grounds including Memphis's pyramid. Today, our Parthenon is an art museum and is responsible for the titular title of Nashville, "The Athens of the South."

OK, so maybe it was the other way around (they build the Parthenon because of their moniker – research fodder). And I'll have to research the Negro Pavilion and especially the Egyptian Pavilion, which has nothing to do with its belly dancers. Sure.

Anyways, that's where you can usually find Malcolm (when he's not digging). Meanwhile he hit the mother lode at the confluence of our Owl Creek and Mill Creek. First the owners, Mr. and Mrs. H. Rodes Hart OK-ed his intrusion, even monetarily contributing to his efforts, and then, over two years, he uncovered seven types of burials totaling over six hundred graves with several dating back to 3660 BC as validated by the carbon 14 readings at the geochronology laboratory, University of Georgia. Hundreds of bone tools, clay pots, whetstones, arrowheads, knife blades, pestles of limestone, thousands of mussel shells, marine and terrestrial snail shells, and the mandibles of many kind of wild game were found. The mussel shells and marine snail shells makes one wonder if this wasn't an ocean site as well or at least closer to one then what we are now.

He also found something that I'll have to look up: an eye-catching, conglomerate, spherical, "chungke" stone that looks like a bowling ball. This striking stone was made and put together with sand, clay, brown chert and other heterogeneous materials from the area. And the look-up wasn't hard – one just has to look to the well informed. OK, confession time; check the *World Sports Encyclopedia* to start.

It seems there were two (basic) types of chungke games depending upon the stone. One was like bowling into a square area – closest one wins (guess they didn't think about pins). Then there was a discoidal (disk-shaped) stone, maybe warrior games, of the same name. On the later game-note, one variation was where the disk-shaped could be "hand-hurled" (I assume like our discus). Another was when the disk-shaped stone was rolled out and participants were to spear the disk-opening (first one to do so – wins). The later was continued by our North American Indians like the

Mississippians, as Chungke or Tchung-kee with the disk being thrown afar and the two participants threw spears to see who would succeed in getting the closest, proving that "close" counts for horseshoes, grenades and chungke. Sorry, I'll re-try to be good.

It's another historical marker-plaque I happened across on a side street while I was looking for the cemetery with the horse statue. Thanks to the info, I have some idea as to what our Hard Bargain is. Unfortunately it creates a few more questions too. Let me relate what it says:

"In 1873, W. S. McLemore subdivided 15 acres, which he called 'Hard Bargain' because of a difficult land deal struck in 1866. Hard Bargain became a stable community, largely African-American. The Harvey McLemore house on this lot, built in 1880, was the home of a successful ex-slave and his descendants for 117 years. To the north stands the Franklin Primitive Baptist Church, organized in 1867, and Mt. Hope Cemetery, begun in 1875. On the east stood St. John's Episcopal Church, the church's Negro mission, and a tobacco warehouse. Due south was the 1910 subdivision of Franklin banker E. E. Green and the Green Street Church of God. On the west stood Polk Town, a row of shotgun houses, now a playground."

Wow. I guess my main question was whom did he bargain for the fifteen acres. It's close, about a mile, away from the original Maury place. Was the Hard a town? Since it is (now) clearly in Franklin, are we just talking about a neighborhood? Is this the same for Polk Town? And what are "shotgun houses?"

Finally, how nice is it to own a bank so one can afford one's own church? One has to wonder whom their deity was/is.

I have to be careful, there are 105 churches listed on one list and yes, I'm talking for the Ben. And yes, I think Green's is still in there someplace, it's just too cumbersome to sort them all out: we have Alliance, Anglican, Apostolic, and Assemblies. We have Baptist (galore), Bible, and (only) a couple Catholic. We have Charismatic, Christian, a good share of Church Of Christ, Messianic Jewish, Lutheran, and Methodist. Nazarene, Non-Denominational (can't make up their mind I guess – sorry), Penecostal, Presbyterian, Vineyard, and the list goes on. But we don't have the Salvation Army, the Unities, Westleyan, Missionary, Quakers (Friends), Full Gospel, Evangelical or the Brethren. And what's a community to do without at least one, Foursquare Gospel? (It's interesting that the Masonic is not listed. I wonder if they're incensed? Maybe it would be inappropriate – who knows?)

I just love that name, "shotgun houses." It so conjures up a covey of images. One might hit a slew of them nestled together - with the right buckshot. And like churches, there's a lot of "denominations" for houses too. Really. Have you ever heard of the Backsplit, the Sidesplit, the Mews, or the Triple Decker? I first lived in a Bungalow (and not a Chalet bungalow). There are Faux Chateaus, Lustron houses, Igloos, log cabins, the (inflated) McMansions, Queenslanders, Mudhif, and Patio homes. We have the Prefab, Saltbox, Sears houses, Stilt houses, and the Snout. We even have the Pole houses, the Octagon and the Patios. There's the popular Tudor, the Mock Tudor, the Unit, Vernacular, the Victorian and the Villa. Of course not all types are found in the Ben. But one hasn't lived until one has had a Foursquare house (or maybe those that do belong to the Foursquare Gospel church afterwards coming home to a foursquare meal. Sorry. Sorry. And sorry again.).

Besides the Hard Bargain and Polk Town, there's mention of a Belltown too. It's on another one of the Historical markers found all over the Ben. Some have numbers too, I guess that's for a tour, maybe walking but as long as the Blue Tail is running, I'm a driver first.

The marker happens to be just over the hill, knob (excuse me), from the Hard. It marks the site of the Toussaint L'Ouverture Cemetery that sits smack-dap behind the white one (Mt. Hope Cemetery).

Toussaint-L'Ouverture (1743 - 1803) (also François-Dominique Toussaint Louverture and Toussaint Bréda) was a Catholic slave from Plaine du Nord and became the leader of the Haïtian Revolution (1791-1804). He was the first indigenous leader of a free Haiti. He organized the majority of blacks and led them to victory over the whites and free coloreds and established his control over the colony calling himself the dictator of a free, black republic, Haiti.

Toussaint expelled the French, freed the slaves and wrote a constitution. Next he successfully invaded the Spanish slave colony of Santo Domingo doing the same for them. At the beginning of the nineteenth century, he tried to reestablish commercial contacts with the United States and Great Britain and rebuild the collapsed economy. Unfortunately he was deceived by Napoleon, kidnapped to France and there met an early death, but he had given the colony a taste of what freedom was. And freedom, once given, seems to be a cache that cannot be retracted.

L'Ouverture was not from the Ben and probably never heard of it. My guess is that in the naming of their cemetery, our African-Americans felt that symbolically at least, once one of them had arrived there that they were truly free (at last). I also figure that they got the name and spelling right.

Some assignments are duty, others are just fun. I was asked to cover the newest movie, advertised as epic, to open at the Franklin Cinema, Cecil B. DeMille's, *The Ten Commandments*. Hey, someone has to do it. But it's not just the movie that makes this one great. The Franklin Cin is very unique. Where else can you sit at a table, order a pizza and watch the movie too? I've never seen anything like it but this is true.

I never went to a movie in the V and the classic Hollywood Theatre in the G was something one would never expect to see this side of Broadway, something Cecil would have been proud of (in it's day, organ and all).

Now don't misunderstand, it is a 1956 movie but for whatever reason, never shown in the Ben until now. And the fact I had happened to see it years ago makes the pizza very important. So it wasn't a big assignment, maybe a publicity favor to the Franklin Cinema but I figured that I could check if Charlton Heston, Yul Brynner and Yvonne De Carlo were still in it. (Just kidding).

Thank heavens I didn't get the annual Franklin Marathon assignment. I would have probably tried to participate. No, I'm not a runner per se and it would not have looked good for a Chronicle ace reporter to be found slumped on the side of the road at the two-mile marker. But one does get better interviews if one participates. OK, so it's only a 5 and 10 K (and not a marathon like in the Nash) but both exceed the/my "wall" (the dastardly two mile marker).

Persistency is a virtue of your average ace reporter. I never say this in public (because it fails me on a regular basis but) "I never give up!" Now thanks to a fellow news guy and native of the Ben who even has his own regular column, my friend Hudson solved the bridge question for me.

It turns out it wasn't the same builder as the one the firemen blew holes in back in the G and the bridge didn't last as long as the G's structure but it too buckled under the weight of a truck and get this: about the same year as the G's. But this is a much bigger story with a headline you would never guess if you started now and worked for ten hours a day for thirty years. Good guy that I am, I'll save you the trouble: THE CHICKENS DID IT.

Our story, really three, begins in the wee-morning, on a cold December 6th about 4:30 back in 1956, not a good year for bridges. I know that you heard about "the chicken that crossed the road..." Question: how much does a chicken weight? OK, now it stands to reason that if a chicken is stirred and flighty (flapping its wings), that she should weight less. Right?

Question #2: including all the crating necessary to contain them, how much does five thousand, seven hundred, and fifty-four chickens weight more or less in a early morning stupor not cognizant of their intended, fatal destination, the Dixie Poultry company on the Ben's Second Avenue and South Margin Street? Yes, the "chickens at rest" weight is more appropriate since they are packed rather tightly together, like sardines so to speak, but definitely over their consternation of having been rousted from an expected good-night's sleep and packed this way for the 167-mile trip. I can't speak for all the chickens but it seems that the majority of these usually amenable, adaptable plump and well-feed fowl had succumbed to their unknown fate.

I used the pronoun "she" since all were hens except twenty-three, eleven years old (or close) males. Actually that's not absolutely correct since that number included ten capons (the unfortunate, previously doomed, castrated roosters), which (I guess) can't really be considered males. Can they?

Further, an unfortunate five had succumbed during the trip to cannibalism, which happens in close quartered chickens that strive for a continuous source of protein, or maybe they, the culprits, were high on the pecking order and were just frustrated. Interrogating chickens is a yet to be developed science.

Question #3: can you add to your "crated for delivery" weight answer from question number two and add one slightly plumb, sleepy-eyed forty-two year old driver, Issac Rob of Gallatin, TN plus the truck to see if you exceed the imposed 10,000 pound load limit on the Murfreesboro Road, 60 year old bridge originally constructed by the G & N Construction Company out of McMinneille, TN who gives their address as the Brown Hotel - the bridge primarily build for foot and horse and buggy traffic?

Maybe someone with due diligence would have calculated this imposing difference and foreseeable dilemma in advance of testing the same.

Maybe an astute calculator assumed that the load-limit was conservatively published against the true breaking point of this senior structure.

Maybe such a theoretician had plugged in a rolling-speed-truck factor that would have (theoretically) lessen the weight-impact, a necessary speed that hadn't been conveyed to the un-scientific Isaac.

Maybe our enterprising mathematician hadn't taken into consideration the less than well-oiled and maintained truck engine laboring under its load and unable to attain this theoretical speed even in a fourteen percent downgrade and irrespective of the much lower legal city speed limits.

Maybe the chicken owners, anxious to make a deal, had ignored all the above including the possible outcome to their truck and sale let alone the biblically named driver and had arranged to send this doomed cargo in the wee hours to avoid a possible confrontation with the law or such details as load limits. After all, didn't the moonshiners do similar things all the time – with impunity?

Whatever the answers or assumptions to the preceding; at 4:45AM the town's first iron bridge, which crossed the Harpeth, completely collapsed into a tangled mess of iron, truck, a few thousand crated but mangled dead chickens, and one miraculously surviving Isaac who started to rethink his life and the possibility that his scared naming might have had something to do with his obvious good fortune of survival. His thoughts still hadn't taken the leap of faith to his possible legal quandaries and applicable fines as the (ultimately) responsible driver at the time of the arrival of the investigating officers, some of our finest from the Tennessee Highway Patrol.

Fortunately (for Isaac) but unfortunately for the nearby community, thousands of terrified, pissed-off and miffed but freed chickens had taken to the air, the river, and the immediate surrounds spreading out in incessant cackling, a disturbing protest to their fate and new community. Granted chickens (Gallus gallus) aren't our most intelligent species, domesticated or otherwise, despite having achieved the dubious distinction of being the most numerous bird in the entire world primarily do to their two food sources, meat and eggs (and not because of any handsome features or chores they do/can perform other then to flock or to "be").

Maybe they should have celebrated in quiet because their noisy exodus of the accident, into the nearby neighborhoods stirred the populous no less than the April 18th 1775 infamous midnight ride of Paul Reeve. This was not good for hundreds and hundreds of chickens but was very good for the residents that did rise to investigate the unexpected intrusion to the quiet nights of the Ben, something that had grown to be indigenous since after the un-pleasantries of 1864. I should say the stirred, enterprising, but deft Ben-ites who saw opportunity (or free groceries) running across their lawns with the resultant chicken-fest for the next couple weeks to come.

The dogs, cats, foxes and the few coyotes in our area did well, as well. And for the next couple of months one had to be careful where one was to step due to the errant nests of eggs or, in one occasion, two pullets, off the beaten paths due to the more enterprising, surviving, and stealthy hens.

Oh yes, somehow three sticking together hens, actually made it, wattling their wattles, right up to the very back doorstep of their intended home, the Dixie Poultry, just four days late. Don't laugh, within the week, one was found in our biggest downtown dry cleaners, two in City Hall and one, seemingly un-catch-able, in our Franklin Cinema (must have been the aspiring Hollywood acting type).

The excited kids could hardly contain themselves with the events and the coming Christmas celebrations. The Dixie, thinking of erasing any tainting of the bridge-loss and hoping to recoup some of their lost, thought of proposing to the Chamber an Annual Chicken Day for every December 6th. They even toyed on the rationalization that it would help overcome the stigma of Pearl Harbor Day (the 7th). But it never got out of the poultry shop.

On the later point about our Boston hero, Paul, I hate to be a ball-buster but I assume you know that there were actually three riders despite the reliance of Longfellow's (fictional) poem as historical evidence, which created substantial misconceptions but warmed the hearts, spirits, and cockles of the colonial hearts. Not that my writing compares but it would be like my version of happenings in the Ben becoming gospel in the years ahead. Gee – I like that – a lot!

Sorry about the cockles thing – I just always wanted to use it somewhere and you have no idea how hard that is. I know; it's just a phrase that technically refers to the ventricles or something. Sorry.

Wait – the big story's not done. Guess what happened just four months later, just when the last of the Ben's Free-Range chickens had disappeared. Yes, unbelievable but true, on the afternoon of April 11th, 1957 a second bridge, this one on Old Hillsboro Road (opposite side of town) collapsed into the fifty-foot ravine under the (excessive) weight of a load of concrete blocks (on another truck) owned by the Franklin Concrete Block Company. Chickens and concrete were taking their toll on our bridges. But wait again! You've heard (some) things happen in threes? Well you're not going to believe this but it certainly lends credence to that olé wives tale…it happened again. This time frame could have very correctly called the Period of Fallen Bridges. The God of Bridges had declared war on the Ben, maybe having felt "being taken for granted."

Chickens, concrete and college kids spelled death and destruction to our aging bridges in our Period of Fallen Bridges. Yes, our beloved Cotton Bridge (one of our only named bridges) on Berry's Chapel Road yielded to two young college commuters' car that happened to strike the structure just three weeks later then the Old Hillsboro bridge collapse. Jovial attendees at the barbershop started musing about the Madison TN lads with: "Yes sir, those cavorting college commuters done picked the Cotton clean."

And that's the end of the story except: #1 somehow and thankfully (to the God of Bridges) there were no fatalities or serious injuries to the drivers, sightseers, repairman/re-builders, (and we can't begin to accurately count the chickens). Secondly, I forgot to ask if there happened to be a run on boats for our local marina for the same period, the Fallen Bridges one. Thirdly, I also forgot to check the possible declining meat sales in our local groceries and especially the Kentucky Fried Chicken. Poor Colonel Harland David Sanders – fate. Meanwhile, anyone have any drumsticks left in the freezer?

Washington Irving, the 19th Century author of The Legend of Sleepy Hollow and Rip van Winkle fame mentioned earlier, lived in Tarrytown, NY. Older sis went to a college in Tarrytown. Wash and his wife, lived in Sunnyside, the name of his homey estate. Sis lived in the dorms. Wash and James Fennimore Cooper (The Last of the Mohicans and more than two dozen other novels) were the first American authors to gain fame in Europe. Wash is buried in Sleepy Hollow Cemetery in Sleepy Hollow, NY next to Rip van Winkle. (I'm just kidding about Rip but the rest is true).

Evans Strickler, 23 and an apprentice pharmacist in Latrobe Pennsylvania, invented the banana-based, triple ice cream sundae split in 1904. Back in my G, it was called The Pig's Dinner at the dairy just down the street from my (parents) home. It was heaping proportions served in a wooden trough and one received a wearable button but only if one completed the entire thing.

Part the Waters - Please

The first official national flag of the Confederacy was the Stars and Bars. A general misconception is that the more popular battle flag, 48 inches square for the infantry, 36 inches for the artillery, and 30 inches for the cavalry – not that size matters (ask any woman), was the official and only flag or that the Confederate Navy Jack flag, probably the most popular, is the Confederate Flag. Not true.

Actually the battle flag, Stars and Bars, caused much confusion with its counterpart, the Stars and Stripes, at the First Battle of Bull Run because at a distance they (reportedly) were hard to tell apart. Following the battle, General Pierre Gustave Toutant de Beauregard pleaded to have a different flag but was rejected. I wonder if he felt his name might have been an impediment?

1st: Stars and Bars **Battle Flag** **Confederate Naval Jack (Rebel Flag)**

One story no reporter wants to cover, the next town disaster. Of course it must be done even if is so big and obvious that everyone in

town knows it. At this point the reporter's role is to put it in perspective and add the little sundry, aside stories that make a bigger whole. Such is the case for 1975 and our Act of God.
Flooding wasn't a stranger to our Harpeth River and the "bottomland" since any man or record would remember. Spring floods were especially unkind and often fatal.

March gave us days and days or hard, soaking rain so that the Harpeth was already high but it was the tenth day of such rain that the Harpeth burst its banks on the 13th the likes the Ben hadn't seen since the flooding in 1948 deemed, maybe prematurely, "The Flood of The Century."

By late afternoon, all major roads into town with only the exception of the Franklin Pike were closed. Nothing was sacred and safe from the water, even our city cemetery. HQ for a disaster relief effort was set up in City Hall on West Main. Over five dozen families required immediate evacuation with significant damage to their homes, valuables, and property. The people involved were safe for now. Others were not so lucky, for example the five-year old Jan Martin, swept from her mother's arm when mom abandoned the stalled car she had attempted to drive through the floodwaters where it stalled. Jan's body was found two days later.

The three-year-old son of Mary Joe Rodger's was luckier when his driver-mother and another passenger-friend, were swept off the road in the family's Volkswagen and carried for more than a mile, bouncing off bridge abutments, trees, and whatever that was in their path until they were miraculously pulled to safety from the torrents of Flat Creek.

Our county jail was flooded. One bit of good news was that the Coronada Shopping Center didn't flood even though the floodplain waters were its intended home. The numerous disputes and disagreements had delayed its construction up until now.

Our mayor, Democrat Ed Woodard was beside himself having almost completed a good, almost uneventful (at least in these terms) third two-year term in times that were politically changing in favor of the Republican venue. Ed and the other Democrats were bracing for a probable backlash in this years elections later this year. Interesting, the new Republicans didn't change their registry, as Democrats, but were all voting Republican, almost a straight ticket.

Speaking of Republican leanings, we saw the startup of a new, local, weekly, newspaper, the *Williamson Leader* last year by Bailey Leopard. But that's OK, competition is good, will sharpen us and frankly, will sell more of our papers.

The Harpeth – who would name a thing like that? Actually in 1768 the first British to surveying the Cumberland River, engineer Thomas Hutchins, came across the Harpeth and gave it another name, it's first recorded name, Fish Creek. I'm sure the Indians had their own name that would predate all of this but that name is lost to history.

It's the two names, Little Harpeth (a branch) and Big Harpeth that engenders one of our local folk stories, our Bonnie and Clyde type, the early American criminals genre. Their names were really the Harpes but that was close enough for the locals just before the turn of the 19th Century.

Micajah "Big" Harpe, (1768-1799) and Wiley "Little" Harpe (1770-1804) were brothers and were our notorious Tennessee outlaws. Their highway robbery and indiscriminate, numerous murders, mostly in the eastern sector, have been assigned to the Blood-Lust Chapter in Tennessee's history. Initially the two farmed peacefully but soon began plundering neighbors' hogs, sheep, and horses. Soon thereafter the Harpe brothers distinguished themselves with murdering a man named Johnson. The reason was lost due to the means Big and Little used to cover up their crime. They cut open Johnson and filled him with stones before throwing him into the Holston River.

There were reports the two Harpes even killed their own children before leaving for less populated areas, namely the Tennessee and Kentucky border where they continued their murderous ways. Several books addressing their exploits extended their reputation. They were called American's first serial killers and even appeared as offensive characters in the Disney Davy Crockett television series. And even though the Little and Big Harpeth rivers received their names before, if one calls up the Tennessee State Parks Department, you might receive an affirmative to the brothers being the reason for the names - but then maybe there is a good, marketing reason for that.

One Harpeth related story that I can tell you that is the truth is that Tom T. Hall, songwriter of the Ben, who wrote the 1968, Jeannie C. Riley, pop and country charts' hit, *Harper Valley PTA*, did have the Harpeth in mind (i.e., the Harpeth Valley Elementary School in Bellevue, Tennessee, 17 miles from the Ben). Personally I'm glad he shortened the name.

My own personal belief, if a relatively new outsider can have one, is that the Harpeth was named not by one of the hordes of "commoners" or any of the bureaucrats around at the time but was graced so by an erudite gentlemen who was fascinated by the enchanting story of Hilpa and her lover Harpath (who perished in a river). It's a story of Joseph Addison's fame.

Personally, I remember Joe for his infamous and timeless quote, "The great essentials for happiness in this life are something to do, something to love, and something to hope for." Joe, a Whig Kit-Cat Club member had a Kit-Cat portrait of himself done, which is where he first came to my attention. Joseph Addison (1672-1719) is buried in the North Aisle of Henry VII's Chapel in Westminster Abbey,

London. You can visit him there. And the Kit-Cat story is for someone else to tell.

Have I mentioned what I've learned about the newspaper business that is in direct conflict with what is the public's perception of our primary "service?" We, big city or small town newspapers, don't print all the truth, the whole truth, and/or the double/triple sourced truth. Maybe you knew this, and as an educated, reading public; you probably did – even taking it for granted. But I didn't. Call me naïve but I looked forward to printing the truth, putting it all out there for public consumption, being an instrument of "disclosure/exposure/truth." But my own truth, of this, came very slowly, over time, and in small nuances while doing my day-to-day job.

Our words are skewered and filtered many times by many, many factors, not just (but including) our editors. I suspect this holds true for all of our politicians' words too and maybe most things in life – it's too early for me to tell. I'm still young and still learning. But it has never been said, even when you purposely choose the higher education for this industry at a considerable investment. There is no such course, "The Truth of Newspapers #101" trust me.

I'm not sure it would have made a difference, my choosing this line of work. It's mentally challenging, fun, to build something out of words that must attract the public's attention (or your days are numbered). And it's satisfying when you succeed even if you aren't going to get rich doing it.

I knew an Economics major in college that I just happened to run into on the streets of Memphis while attending a weekend newspaper workshop conference. We were talking about our Alma Mater and got to talking about how school did and didn't prepare us for your respected vocations. He commented on the fact that his biggest scarcity of education had to do with the politics involved in his profession, something that was never ever addressed at our college or even in his subsequent MBA training.

Maybe Jesus' words were meant by God to be the only "bare-bones-truth" and Lord knows that they've been filtered a wee too many times for healthy digestion, at least mine. This isn't to disparage Mohammad, Buda, Moses, and/or any of the religious leaders or anyone's religiosity. I truly wonder if the full context and meanings of such leaders revelations have come down the history-pike unfiltered as such.

Second revelation: it's always been that way, at least in this country, just ask our Ben. It drove our Mr. Franklin bonkers even as a young man of seventeen. The early eighteenth century newspapers were published "by authority." That meant that the owners and editors were filtering anything that might be offensive to the "authorities." For authorities you can read "government" since (at that time) the government printing contacts made the difference between survival or having to choose another profession. Now think of our own "advertisers," the local "authorities" that could make things intolerable for a going-business, the "rich developers" who have an economic impact on any area, etc. The list goes on. So many people one depends upon to get at the "truth" let alone how you interpret it, print it - since you happen to live in the came community.

Ben's Boston's two to four page newspapers, even his brother James' the *New England Courant*, which became the fourth Boston paper, and one at which Ben apprenticed, became dull and innocuous trying to avoid controversy and to remain politically neutral. Ben even (and surreptitiously) submitted his infamous Mrs. Silence Dogood essays to his brother's paper lampooning this practice. I have to wonder if we have seriously contributed to the public's cynicism over the years.

Having mentioning the Monkey Trial, I was reminded of not doing my homework before coming here, at least at boning up on what I had learned in high school about the state. I guess I didn't think about the "watershed" trial or put it with Tennessee necessarily. It was one of the state's defining moments but certainly not one during my high school days.

I remember that it was a big deal for the teacher. He was adamant about the event defining it as one of the defining moments in the history of man's freedoms. He intended that we knew and remembered every detail.

I know he spent more time, days, on this one thing than I'm sure his syllabus dictated. Maybe because it was obvious that he felt it was so important that I listened carefully at first. But I'm not sure if my overall take on the subject was due to my own insights and conclusions or that he presented and tainted it with his own prejudices.

In any case, I recall it had a lot to do with an enterprising Dayton businessman willing to foot the bill. He was also Christian I believe and felt he could put some attention into his community by convincing one of the local teachers to pretend to teach evolution/Darwinism in his classroom in defiance of a new Tennessee law banding such. I know it was Dayton because at the time I only knew about a Dayton, Ohio and had never heard of another in Tennessee.

The fracas promptly went to court and there two prominent lawyers took the stage for some period of time with each trying to upstage the other. I remember teach impressing us that the media from around the world were in attendance overcrowding the courtroom so that the judge took things outside despite the heat at the time. Somewhere the American Civil Liberties Union put their fingers in the pie, probably for the teacher.

But when teach told us that his colleague in Tennessee ultimately got off on a technicality even though he never testified at his own trial and that the Supreme Court merely clarified that the law was really meant to prevent the establishment of a state religion – my buddy and I, fortunately in the back of the classroom, tuned teach out and proceeded to try and out do each other with monkey cartoons. See no…hear no…etc. It was especially fun on the second day when the monkey heads started to resemble teach, the coach, our principle, and some of the kids in class.

Oh yea, the two lawyers were William Jennings Bryan and Clarence Darrow. I now remembered because I always try to switch Billy's name to William Bryan Jennings and C's to Clarabell (the Clown) Barrel. That's also how I remember who won (in my humble opinion) since I didn't take as much license with his name, Clarence.

You do remember mute Clarabell – of freckle-faced Howdy Doody fame? You do know that actor Bob Keeshan played Clarabell and later became Captain Kangaroo. Then there was the Canadian actor by the name of William Shatner who would show up as Ranger Bill but my favorite character was/is Princess Summerfall Winterspring (actress Judy Tyler who died in a car accident at the age of 23). Have I just aged my self? Now if I could just remember the big Hollywood movie about Scopes – I think it starred Gregory Peck. Oh well.

Speaking about not doing my homework on Tennessee and being one associated with horses in early life, I guess I should address the world famous Tennessee Walking Horse breed. I was fascinated with them as a kid. No, the too-proper English style of riding (To Hounds, To Fences, etc.) was too pompous for my cowboy tastes, the awesome Spanish Riding School of Vienna Lipizzan were too contrived, and the Budweiser Clydesdale were great but only good for show.

But the proud, special gated Tennessee Walking Horse caught my eye - probably as a very American thing. It helped that most of the riders I saw were older, slight men that looked like dapper businessmen complete with hats.

Of course and for this cowboy (at heart guy) it didn't hurt to learn over the course of adolescence that the Lone Ranger's horse, Silver was one and the crème de la crème was when I learned that Roy Roger's lighting fast Trigger was also. I'm pretty sure they didn't know the technique of speeding up the film for those early westerns. Did they?

Someone had mentioned "the Sun" as if I was supposed to know what that meant. It was like the proverbial slap across the back of the head thing and I'm sure my blank face was an immediate give-away to my lack of knowledge (remind me never to play Poker). So I looked into, being the astute news guy that I am (Ok, proud too).

The first thing I should have remembered was that the Tennessee Walking Horse is the states' official state horse. Now I remember asking kid-myself if every state had an official one and especially what was Texas'.

I should have guessed, the grand daddy of all the walking horses, Midnight Sun came from the Ben, and is buried on his farm, the Harlinsdale Farm just a little ways north of downtown (still in

Franklin city limits – remember "We Annex Everything We See" – watch out Memphis. Don't laugh Knoxville – you're probably next. Let the Franklin State rise again – we'll just not use *Dixie* again – it didn't work. We'll use *Stepping on Toes* – yet to be written).

According to the locals, the Harlins, even Bill himself, generously allowed all visitors to see this famous horse when he was alive, parading him out of his stall for them and there were hundreds, maybe thousands that did. I know that there is a National Walking Horse Association in Lexington, Kentucky and probably more associations since the breed has become an international favorite.

Midnight Sun was twenty five when he died having achieved the status of being the first stallion to become a World Champion Walking Horse that was in 1945 and repeated in 1946 at the Tennessee Walking Horse National Celebration in Shelbyville, forty-three miles to our south and a little east of here. After those victories, his owner put him "out to breed," successfully since he grand-sired the supreme winner five times, sired seven grand champions, and even great-grandsired nearly every year's champion since that time. Now that's one hell of a Franklin stud! With due respect Sun.

I guess I have danced around the subject too much, at least in my mind. Dating, girls, sex, marriage, family et al, it's like an invisible node attached to the cerebellum or on it's neighbor the medulla oblongata at the top of and a seemingly extension of the spinal cord thus explaining why those thoughts seem to constantly be bombarding the entire corpus, at least mine, at least lately. Then maybe it's a male thing and is a parasitic microbe attached to the prostate where as the women's nesting, biological clock, etc. thing is attached to their ovaries; the ovaries we don't have. I know the male thing is not the same as the female thing, any observant anyone over the age of seven can know this for themselves.

I've done the expected newspaper-guy research thing and have not found any satisfactory answers. I've see the studies/reports that say they're significant differences that exist in brain areas of males and females manifesting each of their intelligences although there are essentially no disparities in general intelligence between the sexes. Did you know that women have more white matter and men more gray matter, that no single neuro-anatomical structure determines general intelligence and that different types of brain designs are capable of producing equivalent intellectual performance. It's true but just doesn't get me any closer.

I've gone so far as to see comparisons such in our dolphin counterparts but without success. The brain of an adult bottlenose dolphin measures over 1,600 cc (versus the average adult human brain of about 1,450 cc). But you don't what to see one, trust me (I have – at least a picture). Dolphin brains have complex languages, social structures and (voluminous) memory areas. They store their history, culture, and knowledge passed down verbally from generation to generation. Eventually they, our scientific community might even ask my question – what's the male/female (dolphin) difference.

Hey, don't laugh, we, as humans, learn a lot about ourselves from other species. My favorite that I try to emulate is the ant life. Ant's think winter all summer long and build up stores of whatever to make it through the winter. There's also my tree thought, life-emulating imperative that I try to follow: Question: How high do trees grow? Answer: they grow as high as they can. I call it the "Be all you can" philosophy.

So this male/female thing throws me. I don't like something that impedes, imparts, and penetrates one's life so compellingly. I compare it to how the devils seem to work, even in a good person. Thoughts and things seem to pop into one's head from nowhere, seemingly not the urging or original intention of the person. When you cover the news beat, human nature, long enough – it's apparent. But this is an observation that I (also) can't quantify. Try it for yourself; ask anyone in religion, science, the smartest person or anyone you know or even come across on the street: "How does the devil work?" Of course everyone thinks they know even to the point you'll be considered crazy for asking the obvious – but they don't and can't explain (well) what they think they know.

I think women are cleverer than man. Maybe it's starting from the second position (like the new Avis advertising, "We try harder") but never be foolish enough to say that to them. As a whole, women are created beautiful, yes – as distinct objects. They instinctively know this but you take your life in your hands by saying this to them. How many statues of David would the public bother to look at compared to all the Venus statues that portents an insatiable curiosity of men (and women).

Women use these, beauty and manipulative clevernesses, with an accompanying arsenal of nuisances derived from these weapons, against us men. I bravely put it to a test one time asking a very intelligent woman mostly on the serious side of things whom I had befriended long enough to gain her trust. I asked her, "Knowing what you now know, if you had your wish to come into this world as a man or women, which would it be." This, conveniently, had been prefaced by the ubiquitous "It's a man's world" conversation so I thought I knew her answer. I like to ask questions when I already know the answers.

Wrong. After a thoughtful pause, she (most sincerely and without a hint of sarcasm) said, "A woman."

This opened up a mental chasm in me and topped my (personal, not China's) Great Wall. Not because I had guessed wrong, but because I then knew it was truly a woman's world that they had the power to possess and control via men. Nothing else made sense. One would only answer that way from a secure position – whether we/I recognized it or not.

Maybe the jokes about God being a woman weren't so funny any more. Secondly, and in deference to my intelligent friend, I knew the only thing holding back this movement was that all women (thankfully) didn't grasp (or at least utilize) this power. Thirdly, how could I possibly (figuratively – for now) get into bed with an entity that I truly didn't understand?

It's obvious and intolerable that millions and millions of men and women are thrown together populating the world by these unknowns. Biology (or lust – the drives) must truly be awesome. God must truly want Billions; I'm just not convinced he wants quality too.

Free will? Not really, we (all) have forces and forces driving us (to whatever) that we truly don't understand let alone recognize. We are more cultural-products than anything.

It's no wonder that divorce is rising so rapidly in this country. Maybe the unhappiness, incompatibilities, the rivalries, and disparities have always been there but only now are more freely manifesting themselves.

One of the most amazing stories I have ever heard in my life was one about marriage that I, as a mere youngster, overheard my father telling someone (I don't remember who, probably a business colleague) about one of the town characters who had just died. I'll call him Fred because I don't remember his name and it went something like this: "Yes, Fred was quite a character. He used to drink quite a bit in his younger days even met his wife in one of our local bars one Friday night only to marry her the very next day. The story goes that as Fred was walking down the steps from the Justice's office he pulled out their license right in front of her and said, 'Guess I better read your name to know who I just married.' That was forty-three years ago, happy ones I'm told, even by Fred himself."

These thoughts come flooding into the forefront when I mentally approach dating or get kicked in the psychic butt to approach a good-looking gal that I think I might like to date. I'm not blind and they do look better on Friday nights when I'm imbibing. Fortunately men are much more comfortable to be around. And the best are the ones that keep their word.

I'm talking friendship, understanding, camaraderie and never homosexuality. I know it exists but that's an outlet not a natural order in my mind. No I'll never preach it – I'm not anyone's moral compass but my own but in my defense, look at the overall design of nature and tell yourself what you see. If you could pick one function of the male/female difference – what would it be?

OK, so maybe men's conversations and surrounding one's self with men is for an insular effect because drink does lower ones inhibitions, at least mine. Of course the surrounding men don't always inhibit the "approach," when girls (for what ever reason) make the first gesture. But for the most part I observe that they, the opposite sex, "position" themselves rather then "approach" making a males approach more amenable, letting their weapons work to reel in the prospective male even as sport, for vanity, a look-see, or for a possible relationship. I don't know which sex takes "rejection" better but it's definitely part of the male life that doesn't seem to get much better with the myriads of necessary piercings of dismissal.

Blind dates are pathetic. They are the worst. Friendships can be completely destroyed by these togetherings. The absolute worst are the ones arranged, subtlety or blatantly by women for men whether it's a friend's wife that puts your male business colleague or friend up to it or a business female colleague who is on a mission for her dear, lovely friend. Lovely in that case can mean a pretty face (and nothing more). Women seem to think that this, a pretty face, is paramount (the first prime-directive) and everything else doesn't or shouldn't matter to a male. In a lot of cases the pretty faces of the world let everything else go. If a women friend sees that her friend has this pretty face she feels it's totally acceptable and nothing else should matter to the unsuspecting male. Blind dates are a springboard for disaster.

Speaking of "positioning," it looks like coincidence – until it gets too obvious but it seems "a woman on the hunt" is not to be deterred easily. It started at the 5 Points Starbucks, at least for me. It's a routine, three times a week and on the way to work, so obvious to anyone who wants to know.

I'm a morning coffee connoisseur with maybe a couple more at the office, we call them joes – it helps one to focus on writing, at least me. And then a good stiff one after a formal or good dinner (not pizza or a sandwich) but that's it. Anything more seems to interfere with the seven to eight hours necessary sleep.

Maybe she had been there many times before. I tend not to notice too much before the coffee goes down. I hate the apt description but dirty blond hair sitting at a table, nicely dressed, not extravagant, showy or kinky, actually tailored, cute beret hat titled to the left, my side from my vantage point, which is standing in the coffee-line. Acceptable legs and so much for a quick glance, Oh, she was reading, a good sign (versus talking incessantly to a friend). And not much more since she was sitting down and in a lightweight coat. OK, so she had a pretty face (that I could see – still to be critiqued as symmetrical or beautiful, etc.).

Women seem to have a sense that someone, men, are looking at them. Or maybe it's when they want that to happen that they keep looking your way until they catch you looking – I don't know. Anyways, I got caught, she saw me looking as brief and fleeting as it was, instantly smiled even behind the plastic coffee cup at her lips, smiled corresponding with her eyes, and in an instant looked back to reading. Now I noticed it was a newspaper – good sign but I hate that, being caught. How could she smile so fast? What does she know? What does she see? I'm pretty sure I have never seen her before let alone know her? Is she such a risk-taker?

I didn't have a chance of fully appraising her let alone summing her up as worthy of a smile-back. How do they do that? Is that a sport,

"Hi Sally, I've got a record five smile—backs already this morning. How you doing?"

Damn, there's a slight smile on my face. How did that get there? Really, where did that come from? I swear it had to be an instinctual response but I don't like being NOT in control. Is that part of their arsenal? Are they that much in control?

Did I just send a signal? "I'm OK, you're OK?" Did Tommy cover this in his book? (Thomas Harris, *I'm OK – You're OK*, 1967. It's a good book).

I didn't look again trust me. I don't like those feelings of uneasiness especially if someone else brings them on. But she was there again, two days later, in the same seat, drinking coffee, but with a different outfit. I guess that's good, a different outfit. Maybe self-sufficient hopefully a professional and not one of the many girls trolling for someone to "take care of them." No, not that "professional" type – where's your mind. Maybe those things exist in a small town but to my knowledge, they're not apparent (like in the big cities).

I spotted her from the back coming in before she spotted me. I had parked in the back lot – yes, also routine.

I wasn't going to look this time but I was curious what newspaper she was reading, was it ours? Was it the same one she was reading two days ago? With our next coming out tomorrow, it's now old news? Was she reading some of my work? Did she know? Was it our competitor's, their damn Tuesday edition that we still don't have?

Double damn, she did it again – caught me. I was really trying to look at the newspaper but she caught me again. I'm in trouble now. Twice caught and with the damn smile on my face again. What does that mean? Or better, what does that mean to her?

This is silly I feel I'm in high school again, playing the puberty games. But from experience I know it possibly never stops. Dad's been dead for years and on my last trip home to see mother I was asked to be "available" for her as it seems an ancient school chum from her old high school that maybe she had a crush on or the reverse, was in town to attend her 100th or 40th (whatever) high school reunion and wanted to drop by beforehand to see her. Understand, my sisters had several times said to mother, 'Maybe you should date or even re-marry. Dad would've wanted you to be happy." Her regular, curt response was, "I AM happy." (I never went there).

So I made my self "available" in the foyer when he and his friends, a couple he was staying with while in town, appeared at mom's door. I, fully grown son, felt embarrassed standing there having only said, "Hi, pleasure to meet you," while my own mother blushing as a high-school girl went through the social pleasantries-motions.

I knew she would adamantly deny it later and fortunately it only lasted for an exhausting twenty minutes when they left so I would never confront her with what I saw. But I did, actually in both her and the old school chum. It had to be obvious to the other couple as well, maybe matchmakers. In those twenty minutes the air was cleared as to the "openness" (maybe I should say – availableness) of each (without other commitments, persons in one's life, etc.) but it was childish at best. Sorry, coming from an old bachelor that I may become. But it was her priceless comment to me once they left that engraved the all that had happened in my memory. She, this nice old lady who happened to be my own mother, summarily dismissed the whole visit with, "He's old."

What? "Look in the mirror, mom," I didn't say. Maybe she was setting herself up for possible rejection if nothing ever went to second base. But – gees? She did attend the reunion that night and nothing ever – repeat ever – was said again.
But now I'm having those high-school moments-feelings. Right then I knew I was going to skip the Friday – day-after-publication-

before-the-Friday-night-out-morning-Starbuck-coffee. A third "happening" would have been devastating – it would have been an anti-coffee moment and I couldn't take the chance.

But it's not over. Guess who was at the Friday night men's bar-jam session. So she was off at a table with two other girl friends/colleagues or whatever and not looking our/my way but she was there. I had no way of knowing whether she was at the coffee shop that morning – that I had purposely missed. I had no one to ask whether she was maybe always there, every morning or even out Friday nights as a usual thing (that I was just now aware of). I wasn't even going to ask anyone her name or anything about her but there she was again, big as life.

Coincidence? Not on your life – not when it comes to women. If a guy, that a gal was after, published his likes in perfume – she would have it on. Ditto for dress code, and everything. And God help the guy when a gal puts on her hunting outfit, you know, the revealing, tight everything every thing that brings out all her "assets" that a guy wouldn't want her to wear after their marriage but that heightens all his senses to get her down the proverbial aisle. Son-of-a-gun, we really are transparent, easy prey – aren't we?

It's my observation that they, women, are chameleons too, perfectly adaptable (until they get what they want). I've had dozens and dozens of guy-friends see a complete change in the girl that they married. Maybe not necessarily the Jekyll and Hyde change but subtler. Of course one of those J & H examples does comes to mind come to think of it.

That Saturday and Sunday I had to cover the Polo event. Yes, right here in the Ben and yes the Ben has a (little) high-society thing here. It's not quite the "class' system or haughty that you see in the more prominent big cities. It's more "old school" here, as begot from the "traditional" monies.

How many people do you know that attend (or even know) about a Polo event happening in their circles? Well, it's not a big deal (to me) and an interesting challenge to cover/write. Thank God I would never have to cover the pomp and ceremonious English steeple-chasing or the infamous, annual thoroughbred Royal Ascot horse race-meeting. Those are off the my-chart.

Yes, she was there too. Two coffee smiles, one Friday night unaware-of-me-but-there, and now here. But how would she know? Do I have an informant or matchmaker in my mist? It's not that I would ever be voted "the most eligible Ben's bachelor."

Women observation #457 from my (mental) diary: Women are fascinated with what they can't have (or think they can't). Most never pursue but some get a mission. No, I don't flatter myself at this point thinking it's the case here but I mentally prepare, steel, myself for this possibility.

So I did, once, take buddy C's incessant promptings, went to a single's meeting here in the Ben some time ago. But that was an unpleasant experience to say the least – and right from the front door registration/sign-up thing. C, while still single, went with me and was signing up first. Fortunately they weren't asking for the full pedigree, just name, address, age, and occupation. Uncomfortable as this (much) was, I figured they needed something for starters, conversation breakers if you will.

So when C was signing himself up I looked around and spotted a good looking gal in the center of the small room, an ante-room that I assume would go into a larger room complete with soft music, hors d'oeuvres, drinks (if they're smart) and few chairs (tables and chairs are not good for getting/keeping a crowd mingling). I figured she was single – something we were likely to have in common so I gave a warm, knowing smile. She welcomed it, returning the same, almost blushing.

When C was finished and knowing that it might take a minute of two for me (they seemed to lack space and/or pens and a small line was forming behind me) C said, “I’ll meet you at the bar” and walked away. No problem. I set about paying my entrance fee and deciding what questions I was going to and not going to answer thinking my fee gave me the privilege to do so.

When I was finished (without answering all) I was sheepishly given my name tag by the overweight (probably single) receptionist who I just knew wanted to hand back my registration card with the “Please fill in the rest” but didn’t, probably thanks to the growing line behind me. I proceeded to cross the room, giving another smile adding a “hello” to the gal fixtured in the middle of the room that I thought might be waiting for someone. I wasn’t sure and had the more pressing matter at hand of attaching my name tag (that, I’ll give credit, fatty had written in a very impressive cursive. Seems everyone is at least good at something).

I succeeded with the nametag and was just about to leave the little alcove as C met me at the doorway, the entrance to the next room. He was a welcome sight especially since he had a drink in both hands, one for me. We said the expected “cheers” before starting to sip when a slight commotion had started behind me. The gal that I had given (only) two smiles, OK, plus a passing, “hello,” had broken out into tears. Two other gals had seemingly appeared out of nowhere and were already at her side counseling her. I guess she expected more from my first smile – proposal/marriage or whatever. Of course I looked around but at the wrong time as teary-eyed Jane (I don’t know her name) said something to them and all three suddenly looked in our direction with arrows, three quivers full.

Defensively, C immediate said, “What did you do to her?” Fortunately I could see the growing smile on his face as he finished. Unfortunately, I was more interested in catching up to him and his half filled paper, spiked-punch cup so he said it before I could. Looking back at his amused face but only after I gulped my entire drink, I said, “C, it’s a nice thought to bring me here but I have to get the hell out of here – this is much too much for me." In the background: tears and ladies attending-in-waiting.

Testing me, "Leave now?"

"Yes C, I'll refund your fee or you can stay but I'm out of here. Is there a back door?" Smart and a friend that he is, he, wiping off the smile, said, "Sure, this way – we won't even take the time for another punch." And we left out the back.

Fourth: this is your test, to tell me truthfully whether this is coincidence? After changing my Monday, Wednesday, Friday Starbucks to Tuesday, Thursday, and Saturday's and not seeing you-know-who for last week, guess who's seating at Sunday mass in the next section, toward the front so as not to see me but always-in-the-back-me can see her (da). The scary thing is that she may not even be Catholic. I have to observe if she knows the calisthenics' of our ritual, you know: the ups and downs (keel, stand, sit, kneels, etc. The Sunday Morning Exercises Church – others call us). I'll be able to spot whether she's just following the crowd of knows this stuff, whether she's mouthing the words (Credo, etc.).

Damn, damn – to the fourth power. She looked over her shoulder and spotted me. Worst, she smiled. Now she just knows she owns me. What's a guy to do? Leave now (and ruin my good attendance record or my chances of gaining the afterlife or whatever)?

At least she's tall. I don't like a girl I can't dance with. What am I saying, I don't go dancing.

So she's on the attractive side, all over, but I still don't know if she's a serial killer or not. What's a guy to do? I feel I am about to be the hapless victim of one caught under a landslide of pomegranates. In one sense I feel like sticking out my tongue at her if she looks again. That would surely confuse her.

Wait, I'm confusing myself? Who is this nitwitted imbecile talking to me? How can anyone have such an affect on another – worse: someone you don't even know?

She's 5'7" or 8" 36-24-32. She's from Colorado educated in Marine Science with specialization in ocean biology at the University of Miami with a passion for clogging, soaring (the glider kind), and looking for a man that would be willing to re-locate to nearby one of the Sea Worlds, an oceanic research facility preferably in the United States, a world class aquarium and/or a private company but an academic or government facility (in that order) would do. Maybe she thinks that news guys, the likes of me, can go with virtually any paper anywhere.

She, a natural brunette, medium length (more convenient for swimming) partially dyes her hair (not convenient for ocean water swimming), doesn't pierce her ears (or anything), wears light makeup, tans easily (all over), cooks lightly, likes a "bikini cut," likes to eat Italian, and while she doesn't like beer she drinks sociably, usually daiquiris. She tried the "protest" thing in her college years (once) but found it "inconclusive" to effectiveness and turned to studies in earnest in stead. She almost tried a rose tattoo on her upper right back after one less-then-memorable college party and was thankful she didn't. She played indoor intramural volleyball, swimming, and declined to pledge to two sororities that she was invited.

Her parents come from a Scottish and Ukraine background, father, mother respectively. Her mother, is a non-practicing minister comes from the (English) unpronounceable Kyiv Capital and met her father at the infamous San Francisco fish market, the Anchor Oyster Bar to be exact. Her father is a US military defense consultant for a Colorado, Boulder-based private firm and has been with them for the better part of twenty years. She has one older sister, even prettier then she if you were to read her mind, and two younger brothers, both in college.

She, single, never married but having lived with a guy (Cuban) for six months in college, happens to be spending the summer with rich relatives on one of the bigger farms here in Franklin. They are from her mother's side, having made it big in the hospital healthcare industry in Nashville after migrating just after her mother many years ago.
Not that any of the above is true; I've yet to meet her, it's just the stuff you need to know before you ask anyone out. Sorry.

Conclusion: Life is very, very complicated. Dating is a bitch.

I know you're going to ask me about her, Miss No-name, so I might as well get it of my chest:

The events bothered me the rest of the day, and the next. I was loosing (some) sleep and my work was even (slightly) affected to the point that friend, C, asked me, "Is anything wrong?"

So I faced the music, faced things square-on. Bright and early Wednesday morning I walked into Starbuck wondering if they had missed me. Yes, she was there, did the smiley-face when I was in line. After I put three times the sugar, stirred and put a to-go-top on (in case I needed it), I walked up to her table and when she glanced up I said, "We've got to stop meeting this way."

Well, what do you expect from an un-practiced pick-up artist. Give me a break; it's the best I could do.

She said, "Excuse me?" And thank God for her answer. I paused for a retraction but none came along with a non-smiling face so I fumbled with the coffee and my words saying, "Sorry, wrong person" promptly retreating, out the back door, to my trusty Blue Tail and to work (out of her life).

I don't care if she was stalking me or had done voluminous research on me but news guys don't like "cute." Didn't she know we strive for "truth," even if we might have to temper it a little in the telling.

“Actions are the fruit of all truth, it is by your words you may be heard, but by your actions you will be judged.” Sorry, I don’t know who originally said that but you could probably tell that it was too sanctimonious for me to have made up.

She let me off the hook. I was (again) free. And I really meant the “wrong person” part. She dug her own grave and would never ever be a problem (to me) again. Even naked. Even naked and panting. Don’t ask: naked, panting and riding a white horse. Whatever.

Put a grave marker on that one. If I had her picture I would start my own drawer-morgue.
I never saw her again – really, and I went back to my normal routine. In deference, maybe her later research turned up something she didn’t like about me. Maybe she hooked up with someone else at church, maybe a water-treatment man or the horse stable guy at her relative’s farm. (Oops, that would have been my imagined person). Maybe it was all very innocent. Have you ever been stalked? Well, it just felt like it. What’s the next subject (please)?

There are two things going on at once that have been bothering me all year, going back to just before Christmas. The first is being blamed for a blown assignment.

This I know I should get over. I know it wasn’t a big thing nor was the office-kidding that resulted. The later was just good fun and lets face it, most people are in a (more) jovial mood around the Christmas holiday. I know this. I do and I can’t dwell on it or I’ll have three. So on to the second.

Our friendly competitor, TRA, somehow gets the Bens official governors proclamation first. This is not a “biggie” either, I know. But this year, actually just before the start of it, I was given the assignment to get it at the same time as they did because this was going to be the third year in a row that they were going to usurp us.

I guess I'm talking/writing as if you too lived here and knew what I'm talking about. It's the State of Tennessee's Proclamation by the Governor making January 17th Franklin's official Benjamin Franklin Day. Hear ye, hear ye...Whereas...and Whereas...and all that sort of stuff. Somehow The Review and Appeal seems to get their copy just in time for their Thursday publication date whereas we somehow get it on our Thursday publication date – too late except for next week's edition and that makes for old news.

Of course we're to be treated equally and were if you dare ask anyone at the governor's office. But two years running and this might be the third, therefore, "Perry Lance White, head of the Daily Planet Chronicle, the Metropolis' biggest and best paper, calls in ace reporter Clark Mark Kent..." or was is Lois Lane, star journalist, he called in? I would have (called her). Anyway, boss Lance, gave this ace the chance to square things.

I took pride in being called in to clean up "another debacle, avoiding all kryptonite, leaping tall building in a single bound, stopping locomotives..." Sorry.

One would think it was a simple call or visit to the governor's office to rectify this thing but any ace would assume that this had already been tried for the second year by whoever had the assignment before and especially since something was amiss for the first year that this happened. Therefore I figured it required some thought and planning to be able to report "mission accomplished Sir."

Naturally I started in my clawfoot thinking-tub that very night. Forget the clever naming – it's been too long now. Alone – in the tub, I might add if you discount the bottle of Pinot Grigio, Italian white (dry) wine and a 3 X 3 (three inches diameter, three inches tall) lit almond scented candle.

Pinot G comes from the Veneto region, northern Italy and helps the thinking, the light thinking.

When I have to think deeply I have to go to the Bardolinos or Valpolicellas, also from the Veneto. And since I'm on the subject, Merlot (technically French) is comfortable for just a mild euphoria, no thinking (but then drinking for non-thinking is a French secret).

Yes, I remember that I had mentioned Sherry a while back but I tried it and it burned the stomach (a little) – maybe when you hadn't eaten anything with it. Anyways it wasn't conducive to (my) kind of problem-solving-thinking. Probably OK with a good cheese.

Wet, lounging, remembering that I had forgot to start any thinking-music, there trying to think if I had locked the front door, and trying not to think of Marat, I realized that something bothered me about last's years governor's proclamation. My first urge was to get up/out of the tub and look for last year's paper. It's good to resist such impulses such as in this case since I was naked, I knew I wouldn't have saved any of those ancient issues, the office was closed and it was never good to be seen there afterwards, especially after the break-in at the TRA. Thirdly, the library, the next paper collection, was also closed and even if it wasn't, I wasn't going to get much thinking done on my feet, running around. Fourthly, did I mention I was naked (and not necessarily a pretty sight)?

Fortunately the Franklin - Ben Franklin Celebration Day date sprung into my mind, January 17th, his purported birthday. Things like that just happen, the popping in, when one lingers with a good wine. Trust me. Better – try it.

Yes, it was the "purported" birthday that has been bothering me and may be the key to solving our paper's "one-upmanship." Now I had a key, to be pursued in the morning with Plan B to investigate the "evidence chain," (who gets the proc and when – down to the TRA), and Plan C to spread my charm at the gov's office for first preference treatment. Now to more Pinot. Maybe I should invest in bubbles. Do they make them for men? Damn, did I really lock that door tight?

"Good morning, hope you slept well (too)." I remember from journalism classes, the engraving into one's mind, the need to clearly and factually establish one's facts with any "date" being on the order of the prime directive. The prof had used the well know fact of William Shakespeare's and Miguel de Cervantes' (you know, the Spanish novelist, poet of Don Quixote fame) death dates being the same. Many theories and yarns had been spun from this purported fact over the ages. Well he stunned everyone (at least me) by announcing that, "Despite the whiskers on that assumed fact, it wasn't true. Miguel had actually died ten days before."

It all has to do with how time is measured and in what place/country. We currently use the Gregorian calendar to tell our time but that wasn't always the case, as in the time of the colonies. Like many European countries (and their colonies) the Julian calendar was in use. This has caused untold consternation and reporting problems until someone started the "Old Style" (OS) and "New Style" (NS) system. For a period of 170 years, 1582 until 1752 both dating systems were in concurrent use and had to be distinguished for accuracy. Thomas Jefferson lived during the time that England finally converted to the Gregorian calendar and left death-instructions to have both (old style and new) marked on his gravestone (despite or because of the eleven days difference).

Now guess what, Ben F. was born in the Old Style and died in the New (January 1706 – April 1790). Therefore his birthday is January 6th (and not the TRA's 17th). OK, so I know I'd be climbing the North Face of Mount Everest even without the means to get to Tibet, to try and change things. Yes, it's a mute point but maybe will have to be my Plan D as a news article if all else (read A-C) fails.

Ever have something stuck in your crawl? Like that saying? Remember what I said before this whole thing started, that "There are two things going on at once that have been bothering me all year?" Well, this is the second one. Where (in hell) did that phrase come from, the "stuck in your crawl."

Yes, I've seen (and re-seen) Maxwell Smart, Don Adams, a.k.a. Agent 86 or Get Smart fame (TV 1965-1970) meeting one of his arch-villains, the Chinese Claw, the one with a magnet for a hand, with the scene:

Maxwell: "Well, well, if it isn't my old friend the Craw."

Claw: "Not the Craw," exasperated but continuing in a distinctive Chinese accent, "*The Craw*!"

I've searched the famous quotation books when I happened to be at the library, even Lance's two in his sacred, personal library in his office. Yes, I asked the reference librarian, at least one of them. All with no results and over time the "stuck" thing has been slowing growing like tooth decay. Growing until I went to the repeat showing of one of the greatest movies I had ever seen. I'll tell you if you promise not to make me decide between it and *Gone With the Wind* as number one.

It was The Big *Country* (1958) starring Gregory Peck playing the part with the beautifully characteristic and unassuming name of James McKay. So now I can tell you since I rushed home and took notes.

During one critical poignant scene, actor Burl Ives, as Rufus Hannassey, says to his counterpart, "I've seen every kind of critter God ever made, and I ain't never seen a more meaner, lower, pitiful, yellow, stinking hypocrite than you! Now you can swallow up a lot of folks and make them like it, but you ain't swallowing me, I'm stuck in your crawl, Major Terrill, and you can't spit me out!"

Cogitate mediate, ruminate, focus, concentrate, concern, focal point, cudgel the brains, hammer away, puzzle over, ponder study, deliberate, brood, mull, but things just (still) weren't right. Even the insufferable song, "The worms crawl in, the worms crawl out" penetrated my psyche. Hey, that's better then "It's a small world after all," or "A thousand bottles of beer on the wall." And yes I know it started as a hundred bottles but if you travel that route – it grows.

Claw, Craw Crawl – and then it struck, even with out a really good Bardolino. Crop, a pouch…yes…it was Nana. It's now many (many) years ago but I remember. My hunting buddy bent down in her full hunting regalia after first unloading her 412 and placing it aside, even pointed it away from us as a secondary precaution. Her attention was the partridge I had shot at but she had, waiting her turn, shot, that I was now keeling before. She, without fanfare and without looking, produced a very sharp hunting knife usually scabbarded in back on her belt. She sharpened her own knives just like she cleaned her own guns before and after each use/hunting trip.

"Let me show you what this bird eats. It's important to know since if you know what they eat you'll be able to look for their food sources and be a better hunter. Do you see this part of their throat called the gullet? Well this bird has been eating recently and a lot." She proceeded to open that part with one deft swipe, as neatly as any surgeon I could imagine. Her knife was razor sharp. I expected blood and guts spilling out like the many fish she had taught me to gut/prepare but it wasn't anything like that. It was like opening a tiny grocery bag that carried seeds, twigs, etc., the stuff these colorful, fast, and beautiful birds dieted on, at least in that immediate area where we were hunting.
But I also saw a stone. "Did he pick that up by mistake thinking it was a big insect meal or something Nana?"

"No. That's how fowl help to digest their food but it's usually sand or pebbles they ingest. They take those into their stomach to help grind up their feed but every once in a while they swallow some that are too big and it gets stuck in their craw. If you want to see something very, very interesting you should see the unusual things cows pick up and are found in their stomachs. Even barbwire. You do know they have four compartments to their stomachs? Farmers have them swallow magnets so some of the bad stuff doesn't go through their system tearing up everything."

Wow. Stuck in the craw, the crop, pouch, gullet, the pre-stomach of fowl, the throat; when things don't go down the shoot, throat, esophagus, when one can't shake or digest something. Hunting is good. And I miss my Nana.

Yea, I never went the cow route. Unfortunately, of fortunately, I learned (before going there) that the ruminating mostly color blind cows are proficient methane gas emitters, the fast majority through burping (and how should I say this nicely) flatulence. (Sorry, I couldn't find *fart* in the olé Thesaurus). These simple, tip-able farm animals have even been sited as culprits by the greenhouse gas peoples. But I have (safely) read about the myriad of weird things found in their rumen, reticulum, omasum and abomasums, the four compartments, i.e., stomach(s).

It was the politics! The Proclamation is officially entertained to and by the governor's office from the Mayor's office (not the paper, TRA, directly). But I learned this too late into my mission and after having spent much time wooing the governor's lassies. So much for charm (and non-reimbursed trips up to the Nash. And it was TRA's supposed better connection there at the Mayor's that things were happening the way they were – and did for the third year in a row, my year. To add insult to ace-injury, Lance didn't want the Ben's Correct Birth Date article I had prepared in advance but as a condolence said that thanks to my investigation, he would approach the Mayor's office and suggest (threaten) that if it happened again that this inappropriate unfairness would be the subject of a next year's article. That's it – the ace investigative, cleared craw reporter is signing off.

Burl "Rufus" Ives is awesome and not just as a scene-stealer. He's a fabulous singer. I bought his *Rudolph the Red-Nosed Reindeer* (1967, Decca) when it first came out. I start playing it right after Thanksgiving (and sometimes during the year when the Merlot doesn't work). He's got mounds of other albums and someday I hope to be able to afford the entire collection. Someday.

I mentioned the unfortunate break-in at our competition. Their office was burglarized by professionals needing specific merchandise or someone in the know as to where certain, expensive, equipment happened to be located. I DIDN' DO IT! Besides, what do I need cameras for – I would have went for their crib notes or to copy off their "Future Assignments" blackboard I heard they have in their editors office.

AND if I did, I would have noted one particular, upcoming, front-page article, and the TRA wouldn't have upstaged us – again - as they did. Thanks to a Dr. R. H. Hutchenson of Franklin who happens to be our State Health Commissioner, an office I didn't visit on my sojourn to the State Capitol, the TRA ran an article complete with documentation, House Journal 1827, #670, about a little know fact. Franklin, the Ben, had been considered as being the Tennessee State Capital back in 1827. Really. I felt like sending a copy to one erudite editor in Austin that I encounter way back when. It seems one of our friendly representatives from nearby Rutherford County proposed that Franklin would be the site for holding the legislative sessions, which would qualify it as the capital. Kind of like a "Capitol for a Day." Unfortunately the proposal didn't pass. The later constitution required a permanent site be chosen (1843) and, Nashville a.k.a. Fort Nashborough, a.k.a., Music City, won.

I hate apologies, especially for the truth.

- Harvey 'Big Daddy' Pollitt, Burl Ives
Cat on a Hot Tin Roof
1958 film based on the Tennessee Williams play

The cool wind blew in my face and all at once I felt as if I had shed dullness from myself.
Before me lay a long gray line with a black mark down the center.
The birds were singing. It was spring.
- Burl Ives

It Is What It Is

The town historian, when asked, "What makes Franklin a *southern* town - still - to this day?" started his conversation with, "Well there's a confederate soldier standing guard in the square downtown for one thing." And after more brain searching and mutual questioning, he shook his head yes when I tried to summarize, "So basically and today our cosmopolitan little Franklin is comfortable to continue to be a southern town because it's a romantic, endearing theme that hasn't been challenged or replaced by another;" With his head continuing to shake yes for encouragement and being on a roll, I continued, "It might be considered similar to our '50's and '60's Diner in Cool Springs that has chosen the Oldies and Goodies to set itself aside from the many, competitive restaurants and uses this theme to attract and entertain patronage." And I stopped but hoping for a final yes.

"I'll have to agree Mark, it's hard to find a native-born Franklin let alone Tennessean these days of fantastic growth but I won't write that in your paper. Some things are best enjoyed and not parsed."

After I left from what I found was a gift, a profound truth to understand my (new) home even if it wasn't going to be an article or headline, I happened to think that if I would have taken that Texas job I would probably be writing about the Alamo, Jalapeno peppers, cowboy chaps, and rodeos, Honey Mesquite, Peyotes, and/or roaming salsola (tumbleweed). Life is surely an interesting experience. And, I might add, especially in small towns.

"Hold on just a dern-minute! It jes occurred to me that this here is the home of Colonel and Congressman Davy Crockett who ended up at the Alamo. Now can ya beat that?" Davy's last Tennessee home, a log one (of course) still stands in the next county Rutherford.

Little by little I'm learning that the history of this area is keenly tied to the houses (and they were named before the historic events associated with them – so this doesn't solve the house-naming mystery). And it's not necessarily pivotal by the Battle of Franklin, their own personal Civil War. It was an atom bomb dropped here a hundred plus years ago and the resulting crater just hasn't been covered up with new history (or anything) yet. Maybe it never will.

One interesting example of a home tied to history here is the Homestead Manor, circa 1819 built by Virginia-born, Francis Giddens. It was the first in the area to brag foldaway beds and a closet in every upstairs bedroom. The Manor was situated along the infamous (Civil War) Columbia Pike just south of the Ben. At that time, Alice Thompson, the seventeen-year old daughter of Elijah Thompson (for whom the nearby Thompson Station, TN was named) lived there and the five-hour battle called the Battle of Thompson Station was fought in the yard and immediate surrounding grounds of the Manor.

Alice and friends were hiding in the cellar when yet another charge of the Razorbacks of the Third Arkansas tried to dislodge the dug in Union Federals around the Manor. Unfortunately the guidon bearer was "shot through" dropping the Rebel flag just outside Alice's cellar lookout window and just as the Razorbacks were beginning to fall back. Alice raced up the stairs and out the door, fetching the flag and furling it high overhead yelling all the while. Col. S. G. Earle saw this and also started yelling at his wavering regiment, 'LOOK BOYS, A WOMAN HAS YOUR FLAG!" They attacked with a vengeance, routing the Yankees.

There is a postscript to the Alice story. She died just six years later (23), the wife of a young Rebel soldier who had fought that very day - at Homestead Manor.

I came here because of my job. A job that I love because people are an inexhaustible source of news and fascination even in a small town – one just has to be more patient. And for that reason I was passionate about wanting to have attached to my work all the benefits of living in a small town. I did, actually worked hard on accomplishing these two things, job and small town, knowing that the first, the job, would probably be mundane by comparison to the happenings of most big cities therefore not lending itself to the highest accolades in my news-writing industry and might even be dictated, tainted, steered, and/or filtered through the cultural pressures of the small town I landed in.

Each small town seems to be a living, changing entity with an undercurrent of a personality unique to itself. The key to my job is truth and I've come to love it even if the reported small-town-truth is quite different for the aforementioned reasons.

I didn't come to the Ben to find out how it compared with all the other small towns, even if only two that I'm familiar (have lived in). But as time goes by and I happen across similarities, they strike me up the side of the head like the proverbial "something striking the side of a barn." And even if valuable to only me, I've come to love the comparisons just like I love a third thing, "coincidences."

I have just stumbled upon a humdinger of a comparison with coincidences galore, buried deep, deep-down in the relatively recent archives of the Ben but a story that they never wanted to happen, never could have happened in their peaceful town – but did. There's a story that they never wanted reported, and certainly once revealed - never to be talked about again.

It started coincidentally when I was looking into the possible impacts (if any) on a small town for the showing of one of the most provocative movies ever made to date. I put it that way since Hollywood can't help itself to continually push the envelope. The H can't stop going to the next level whether for violence, sex, tricks, kicks, stunts, action, etc. It's the nature of the movie-making beast called Hollywood.

To start the story it was only prudent that I check to see that the movie did in fact play here. The movie is *Peyton Place* and it played here as mentioned in the paper, our competitive TRA, in 1958. Peyton turned into a TV series running on the ABC network from 1964 to1969. Consequently many neighborhoods and small towns have been informally termed Peyton Places due to its use as a catch phase to describe any place known for its questionable or sordid goings-on. Another one of "those" of the provocative genre would be the 1955 racy, raunchy (naughty) Vladimir Nabokov, 1955 novel *Lolita* and the subsequent Stanley Kubrick, 1962 film starting James Mason but that didn't play here.

Our *Peyton* showing lagged well behind the premier's and big city showings as you would suspect but the controversies surrounding the film (1957) and the year earlier novel were already well known so I didn't have to check back into the old issues and the Franklin Cinema's ads to see when it was here. It popped out on the front page of the TRA Thursday edition, April 17, 1958. This was hectically unusual and probably was the first time ever that such a story, even if only a column-inch, ran about a local movie showing – I'm just not going to go back through the many years and hundreds of issues to establish this point for sure.

The story, front-page news, was offered in a "tainted by small town culture/living" way even on the front page. It was "buried" halfway down with smaller font size headlines, just under the smaller column-inch story, "Franklin Banks Close Wednesdays" and on the page where the top stories going across the top included, *Hospital Shows Monthly Profit, School Board Names '58 -'59 Teachers At Three City Schools, Three Shows At Rodeo Next Week*, etc. So it was there for all to see but painfully obfuscated as if one might happen to see a small piece of chewed gun carelessly deposited on the sidewalk that one happens to notice as one walks down our pristine and historic Main Street. Am I making sense to you? Do you see the nuance?

In other words, a town tends to build a façade that's comfortable and then they instinctively, ferociously defend it. And their papers wishing to gain favor get "in step" (taking the more traveled path in Robert Frost terms).

Not to belabor the point but even the little story carried the following, "…the movie made from one of the most talked about books in recent history…" To a news guy, that notation is like a herd of elephants rampaging through our many but fragile antique shops downtown. It could have been developed into an awesome, several page story – even an eye-catching titled book. Just not here.

OK, so immediately I knew what I was up against. It wasn't as big but had the same thrown out and buried stink of another subject I will have to pursue one day, "the colored question." Both were going to take some serious digging, extended trusts and interviews by this northern white guy, and in both cases, I would probably only end up with something my audience of one could use. But that's OK, because I wanted to know.

In the same paper there was (an objectively) other incongruence-story that also struck me. First it was out of place for obituaries. Secondly it was out of place for our "prominent people" death notices/stories. It was being handled "differently" and just begged to be read by my casually scrutinizing ace-eye. The headline said, "Funeral Services For Mrs. Betty Burge Held Here Sunday." It was several column inches but tucked back into the paper. It was at the top although well nestled by a couple oversized ads. So I read it.

I hit a really big coincidence and I haven't been back to my Peyton Effect on Small Towns story yet. Listen to the first sentence of the story, "Mrs. Betty Burge, 75 years of age, died Friday night of a heart condition in General Hospital in Nashville." OK, no problem, a local old woman kicks the bucket. So what's new? Of course Journalism 101 teaches that you lead with the most important part of the story – people are busy, even in a small town, and you grab them or lose them. So ordinarily I would assume that this was the story but then not all reporters write as they should so I read on.

Second sentence, also casual I might add, "Mrs. Burge was transferred from the State Prison March 26th, where she was serving a life term, to General Hospital." My (news) heart started palpitating. And my mind leaped back to my last small town, the V, and another Top Town Story I stumbled across when I just happened to proffer a simple question to a reference librarian on one of my first visits to their library. I asked, "What do you think was the biggest scandal or event in this town – ever?"

MISS MARINDA BRICKER

It turns out that the answer was the dastardly, brutal murder in the early Easter morning hours of a virginal maid as she innocently walked to work and it happened on the very grounds in plain sight of the house she was attempting to reach to begin her Sunday morning chores. The murder, still unsolved to this very day awe struck the community stone cold because it or anything like it was never suppose to happen and it devastated the very prominent family with the result of them moving out of the house and then the community eventually, as the family moved the family owned company's headquarters with the resultant lost of jobs, then literally plowing over one of the most historically significant homes (well cared for) in a community that treasured the same and the town re-zoning the area to permit some cookie cutter apartments or condos to cover up and bury the sacred ground and the town-tragedy once and for all.

I would mention the lady's name if I could recall. The story included bloodhounds, a shot sheriff, small riots, botched forensics, the "colored" question, scary indefinite community-times, false arrests, shoes, and a bunch of other things I'll have to dig it out when I have more time. But it too never produced another news story from me and I am well aware that my new *hot mission* might not either.

Now here's the Ben's Betty Burge story: 1949 started out the year like virtually every other year in the Ben. The only depressing news was on in inside page, 3-1/2 column inches of the year's first edition, about a young man who had died on Christmas Day, James David Bennett, 25, who was interned in Mt. Hope Cemetery. There was no mention as to why he died.

The front page carried the usual and sundry headlines: *First Tobacco Sale to be Held Mon. Jan. 10th*, *Post Office Hits Peak During '48*, *Circuit Court Selects Grand, Petit Jurors*, *Bank Statements Rendered Today*, and the lead story, *Real Estate Sales Approach $3,000,000 Mark In 1948 As December Is Best Month*. The later should have been improved.

Harpeth Motors, Inc. kicked off the year with, *Try The New "Ford Feel"* featuring a car the spitting image of my old news car if only the paper had

been in color and not black and white. Weather was reportedly mild for this time of the year.

The second edition was more of the same with two front-page headlines that caught my eye. The first was eerily prophetic as it turns out, *Got A funny Feeling Someone Doesn't Like You*. And the second, *Colored School Election Begins on April First*, surprised me until I remembered that segregation had only ended in 1964 with the Civil Rights Act.

The next edition, last of the month's featured *Despite "Spring Weather" Many Fatal Accidents Have Occurred in Williamson County During The Month Of January*, at the top and center nestled along with another 16 stories. Inside a picture of Bob Tour-the-World Hope caught my eye. It was part of a Lever Bros. ad that also ran a picture of Amos 'n' Andy featured on CBS Sunday evenings. And the two-column by six-inch regular feature, *Know Your Neighbor* ran as well. How prophetic.

The year continued with *92 Blood Donors Answer First Call of Bloodmobile*, *Truck Hits Boy Who Breaks Leg*, *92 Williams County Men Killed in WWII*, and *Percy Jennette Attacked by Hog*. A March headline made me take a double-take, "Slick Duck's Uncle Caught Stealing Chicks, but it was about local petty crime unless your "colored" I guess.

Studebaker joined the auto rivalry with their new Commander Landcruiser offerings. June finally got juicy with Amos Hollars, a simple-minded Linton Farmer was charged with killing his mother-in-law (51) and her son (32) in his yard where they had come to visit their kin, Mrs. Hollars. Amos wrote his own story with his own down-home quips including the headline, *"They Were Both Just More Aggravating Than I Could Stand So I Had To Kill Them."* I suppose his errant cows, chickens, and dogs received no less. Maybe his wife caught on and kept "in-line." Having done the deed, Amos promptly headed for the safety of the woods.

Once caught, his unabashed interview with a local reporter proved no less insightful to a simple mind when asked had he ever contemplated suicide. I suppose it was put into simpler terms because I assumed he had no earthly idea of what "contemplated' meant. In any case his answer was, "I sure did. I came back home the next day thinking I would find my wife there but she was gone and you see - a man can't kill himself if there's no one around to take care of the body." You do see?

After that, things resumed to their *regular-lethargic* and, if the news guys were anything like us, the staff assumed that they could pretty much rubber-stamp the rest of the years' stories and headlines. Even the town's visit in July by a "*Walking Goat Train Enroute To Chicago*" didn't warrant a follow up anything. That was until the last issue and our own version of *Peyton Place*. A five-ton meteorite striking our Private White in the town square would have been less earthshaking in the Ben.

Five columns, two and three-fourth inches headline, usually reserved for world wars, announces the Nashville Tennessean Tuesday Morning, December 13, 1949 edition: *Woman Found Slashed to Death Identified as Roaming Waitress From Indianapolis; Killer Hunted.* It was a down-on-your-luck story all around. It was just eleven shopping days to Christmas. It was a Franklin story but dominated the big city paper as well as our own and would command attention for weeks to come.

She arrived at the Franklin depot at 11:30 PM on the L & N, the Louisville and Nashville Railroad, pulled by the powerful Mountain 552 engine. Today she came from Portland, Tennessee via Nashville where there was the

unexpected but typical hour and one-half delay.

It was cold for the Ben even if only considered very chilly by more northern standards for a Sunday December night. She was Mary but also called Mary Margaret by her mother when she was in trouble or had done something wrong and her mother wished to make a point. But that was long, long ago.

More recently and here she was called Rose and/or Rosa by a few necessary people, mostly men. She had purposely chosen those pseudo-names to distance herself from those unhappy occasions although quite necessary for her survival at least economically in one of the oldest professions. Life seemed to often deal unhappy Mary unpleasant but necessary choices whereas down deep she always felt she deserved more.

Mary was always considered pretty by most even if in an impish sort of way. She was always considered pretty for most of her twenty-nine years and felt this was about to change for the worst as she entered older age. She had never ever liked her chin, nose, or smallish lips and wafted on her penetrating eyes framed by her naturally thick dark eyebrows and would have been called Mary Opinsky if she hadn't married. But that was also a long, long time ago.

It was raining most of the way here on the train ride and foggy too. The bumpy ride seemed to take forever because she was nervous and it was late. Dark, short haired, five-foot seven inches, Mary Margaret Opinsky Dean, native of Fayette County, Pennsylvania, often looked outside her window for distraction but couldn't see anything because of the trains inside lights' reflection on the panes. Besides, there wasn't much out there anyways, between here and Nashville, for the half hour ride.

The constant click-clack of the rails didn't lull her to sleep like the last time when she was on the same tracks going north as she departed here. She had left feeling on top of her world, empowered by having successfully accomplished a deed of her own design, with money she had collected, nay earned and in her pocketbook, suitcase on the overhead rack - quite the opposite of what she now felt. But that was during a sunny spring day seemingly a long, long time ago.

The train, while not toasty warm tonight, was pleasant but as she departed after the train pulled into Franklin and she descended the train's two steps, the cold made her button up her scruffy black second-hand coat and safety pined the collar around her pretty face since the appropriate button designed to do that job was long gone.

She longed for one of the several pretty hats she used to have but settled for the silk headscarf she had folded neatly in her left coat pocket since she didn't have a pocketbook. The scarf, a personal treasure, a mainly green but multicolored, patterned scarf had accompanied her on many of her travels, travels that had seen virtually all of her other worldly possessions littered here and there and someplace behind.

Mary was glad she didn't wear glasses with the rain that had slowed to a misty drizzle. But that could change with age.
She took shelter under the overhanging depot roof to slightly peak her headscarf over her forehead for protection and tucked the knot at her throat and the two left over scarf-tails into her coat's collar. Then she started out.

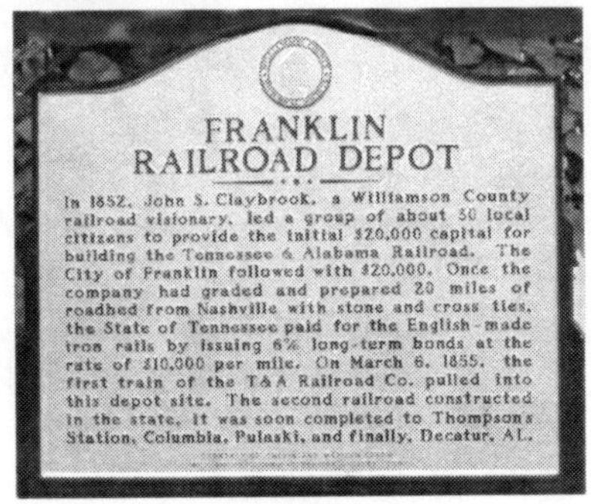

Down-in-her-luck Mary was the last one off the passenger railcar even if there was only one other couple, obviously but not newly married, that had departed the train first and were already a good block ahead of her on their own way going up to the main square about a quarter mile west. She knew where she wanted to go and knew the town well enough that she could cut over South Margin to get there faster. The streets were safe here and there too but she wanted the time to go over things so she lit out behind the couple toward the square.

Her shoes were worn, about to get soaked, and thankfully low heeled for walking. She was glad her coat was mid-calf length to help keep out the cold but more importantly so that no one would notice the several holes in her nylons, which, and at least, the seams were straight.

Without a suitcase someone would assume she was a late commuter coming in from Nashville from visiting or on an unfruitful shopping trip since she carried no bags of purchased goods. She walked determined and seemed to know where she was going even if a little slow for someone anxious to get there. One hand holding the coat at the neck to augment the pin and the other hand in her pocket, fiddling with what little money, change, she had in her life as if the fondling would make it grow or what little she had left would be better warm.

The scarf had occupied its pocket traveling place with a mostly crumpled pack of Chesterfields with only three left after she had smoked two in Nashville anxiously waiting for the train to get back on schedule. Now and then she could smell the tobacco from the scarf as the slight cold, drizzling breeze stirred it up. A slight craving started deep inside and was quickly depressed so as not to derail her from her mission.

She turned directly south at Private White's, the confederate soldier on his thirty some odd feet granite pedestal, the official Franklin greeter in our square posturing for all to know, "This here has been and still is a southern town." But then she didn't look up at him because of the rain and skirted the square with its circular drive around as she started south pass the courthouse then down Main

Street past the many sleeping retail outlets. The town was bare of people and lights but the sidewalks shone with the reflecting wet, she knew her way, and didn't care to be recognized anyway. It was late.

After the second block the nicotine craving kicked in again or was it the need for an excuse to abort what she had intended to do. In either case she took a brief left around the corner until she remembered she had no matches although she was sure there were still smokes left in her coat.

Back on her southbound, she headed toward the Ben's Five Points intent upon going down the infamous Columbia Pike to confront her enemy, the same road where an Union army had passed undetected by their own enemy south of town some time, long, long ago.

Passing The Historic Franklin Presbyterian Church to her left at Fifth and Main, she was about to enter the Pike. She temporarily got cold feet for her real cold feet and crossed the street perpendicular rather than going straight pass the Post Office. Mary had rationalized that maybe one of her old friends just up the street would take her in or at least have a match she could borrow. She hadn't eaten anything for most of the day and couldn't tell if her hunger outweighed her cigarette craving more.

After only half a block and even knowing which house she had been headed, she had been there before, she remembered his wife wasn't home when last time she was there. Mary soberly turned around, back on the one course, the only choice she seemingly had left in life and entered the Pike heading south toward the infamous 1830 build Carter House sitting atop of the rising land wave next to the Franklin High School, a rise well suited for the defending Unionist to build their breastworks that would dwarf and defeat the attacking Confederates trying to retake their land, long, long, ago.

Yes it was the bloodiest five hour battle in the War of Rebellion as the winners would call it and the Carter House was the site of some of the most intense, bloodiest fighting and also the death site of one of the most brave, Captain Theodoric Carter, C. S. A. Tod had traversed a mile and one half of devastating Union fire and horrendous odds of success six times, leading his men onward only to be mortally wounded in his own backyard and to die in his very own family house he had left for cause and for country, only three and one-half years ago. Tod was even younger than our Mary, he was twenty-four.

Now it was passed midnight, some say the bewitching hour. Mary didn't like walking this part of town even if she had done it safely many times months ago. She had had a driver's license many years ago but never owned a car of her own, never drove much, wasn't sure how much she could remember about the rules or driving skills and had come to expect that walking was the more normal means of (her) transportation.

Going over and over her firm resolve of the ploy she was about to deliver helped to distract her as she passed in front of the sundry goods store owned and operated by a nice but quaint couple who lived upstairs over the store. Soon the Franklin High School was in sight and Mary knew she would soon take a right to cut through Evans Alley that went over to Acton Street to a place she once called home.

The small community of working-class residents and shot-gun houses, mostly of African-American descent, was formed by two tiny alleyways squeezed between two of Franklin's major streets were the "big houses" were. The area was originally known as Scruggs Bottom after the Crutcher-Scruggs family. Alex Crutcher, a well-known and respected black, Franklin businessman with a store on the square in Franklin, bought three acres there a long time ago.

Evans Alley got it's name from the family of John Evans, a black lawyer who started practicing in Franklin back in 1870 and lived on the corner of this alley way. Locals, like Mary called it "The Alley" and everyone knew where that was.

Betty B. Burge, to be known as Number 43081 soon after the beginning of next year, had only finished seventh grade. Her gross, strong, rough neck son had only completed the third. Mary had graduated high school and in that way felt intellectually superior to them both.

Betty, 60 but only ever admitting to 57 of those years, a chunky, dowdy lady was many things but mostly a survivor. She was resourceful given the setbacks life had thrown her way including the death of her husband older by sixteen years, nine years ago. Betty was not to be underestimated mainly because of her finely honed street smarts. Son Sherman, 37, tall and medium built with a purposely cultivated Abe Lincoln beard, was just as he appeared, transparent, erring on the side of laziness, a man of few words mostly because he had never learn'd many, strong, defiant, but devoted to his mother mainly because she needed him, overlooked his many idiosyncrasies and gross bad habits, and mommy provided for him in kind. Besides, he had no ambition to provide for himself or his three children he had fathered somewhere along the way.

Betty's home was a two story cheap house of cinder block with more rooms, especially bedrooms, then was apparent from the outside, was well known for providing the area's bootlegging products whether drunk on premise or hauled away in any quantity one could afford. Her abode was well known and reported often to the police for the many and loud, rowdy parties and tonight was no exception but the report was drawer-ed by the half-asleep officer taking the call that night. It was a Sunday, rainy night in December with a skeleton crew of three officers on duty and no one wanted to venture out unless the mayor was shot or Jack Benny was seen climbing the square's sacred statue after an impromptu violin concert. Drawer-ed versus filed (or acted upon) meant "to be discarded in the morning" since the mere quantity of such complaints about this particular place surpassed all other addresses in the Ben.

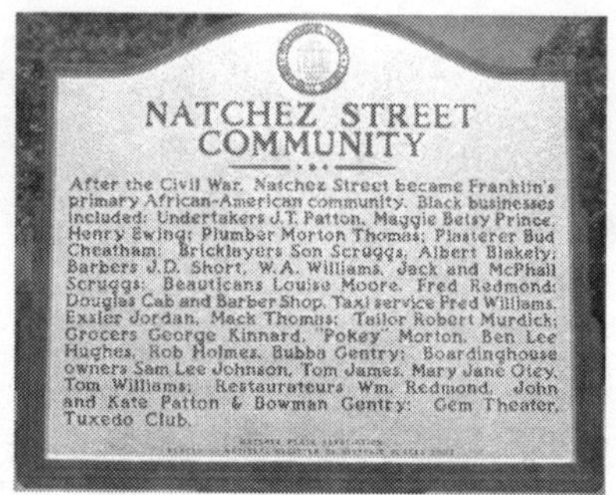

There were other reasons the called in complaint wasn't acted upon including the resentment of the soon to be retired, elderly officer taking the call who was resentful of his night duty tour that obviously ignored his many, many years of devoted duty. Another reason had to do with the same man and some underlining prejudices that his family of one hundred thirty years living here in the Franklin had developed about the colored situation. Betty's rowdy house, known speakeasy and bordello was smack in one of the few colored districts, Evans Alley. Teasley Town, Polk Town, Belltown, and Hard Bargain are the other ones I (think) I've (correctly) identified as such, small and as "hidden from sight" as they are.

The Alley was a part of a bigger community, the Natchez or Natchez Street area. The original Natchez Trace wasn't just one trail but had several coming together and one of the main ones bisected Franklin, the 5 Points and when through this area now relegated (by default) to Afro Americans or colored if you prefer.

And why not – have a name? The whites seem to cut out their own little "developments" with names like Founders Pointe (the original site of Abram Maury land and home on the west side of town). They were all over the Ben complete with formal homeowners associations, rules, fees, and such.

Betty didn't think of herself as a Madame any more than she thought of herself as a bootlegger. It was just a convenient source of income, easier than some others and she seemed to regularly have some willing female borders unable to afford the rent. Little did she know that some of the turnover of her female borders wasn't due to her regularly visiting cadre of men folk but was due to the aggression of her bad breath and unwashed son who regularly sought a "freebee." Betty maybe knew but just looked the other way thinking some other poor, homeless, helpless girl was already on the way.

Everyone knew that Monday was a slow day for activity at Betty B's so Sunday nights seemed logical to be the occasion of a "party." Since it had been/was raining, this Sunday night's happenings were lasting longer and louder into the wee hours of Monday morning. Too bad for the dutiful blue collar laborers nearby trying hard to get some sleep before starting their another-day, for another-week, for another-paycheck that would be too small to contribute to make ends meet let alone provide for an exodus from this noisy, rowdy neighborhood. The later was thanks to the only crazy and white woman in the vicinity, Crazy Betty B. Burge.

Mary could have found the place down the alley in the dead-black night of a lunar eclipse simply because of the noise coming from the place. She mentally tried to fortify herself again as she rounded the front of the house planning to knock on the front door as her next step. And she did.

Self-build fortifications, on this very land that had been reinforced by ten thousand blue troopers in order to face their own forthcoming onslaught by gray troopers, were necessary since she was approaching a door that she had been summarily usher out with the firm instructions, nay threat, "Never come back here again. Ya hear?"

Tonight, this morning, she faced the same door as a penniless, unwanted and uninvited intruder. She thought she could feel her every hair stand up on end, even the unshaven ones on her legs that felt like they all were now poking through her holey nylons.

The night hid the tattered, paint-pealing door also battered by the occasional police raid and/or errant customer trying to return to get what he claimed would be his money's worth whether in a lady's services, watered down drinks, swindled gambling, poor cards, picked pockets, forgotten eye glasses, coat, human company even if of the lower sort, or whatever. Most of the expelled, out of money clients were too drunk to put up a descent fuss and Betty knew they'd be back for more of the same when means provided them the opportunity. Bad habits seemingly just don't disappear and here again was one, our Mary. Knock, knock.

Unlike most speakeasies of earlier times (and some that sill existed here) the windowless, reinforced door she faced didn't have the lookout-slot nor even a common front door chain but had a regular car-towing chain stolen from the gas station over on Columbia when the owner wasn't looking and jerry-rigged by handyman Sherman on the inside from door post to door post with just enough room to open the door to view any newcomers.

No one had ever bothered to work out a knock-code for identification like some places. No one would come here except those who were hell-bent on doing so and had to come out of their way. Besides, who would remember from week to week - certainly not Sherman, so who cared?

Mary didn't have to knock a third time as she was prepared to do, forgetting that it was son's, B. Sherman Burge's post, to man the front door in order to keep the rift raft, uninvited, and the cops out if he could help it. Mary jumped as it opened, light and foul offending smells, and old memories spilling out as well as a pair of dark beady eyes that she knew were Sherman's and were now peering out at her.

"What the hell do you want?" He was loud enough to be heard over the loud music, familiar jazz as only the blacks can play, in the background. And before she could answer, "Didn't we tell you never to come back?" he continued. Then he interrupted himself again and said, "Wait here Bitch!" and slammed closed the door. Mary knew Sher, the slaughter-king, didn't do anything without checking with mommy. So she waited thinking that the worst-case greeting she had imagined hadn't happened.

She had never seen a gun when she lived here before. She preferred to think of it as only visiting. But rumors persisted about a shotgun type gun that Betty's old man had had and Sherman had squirreled away in the attic, behind a loose board, or somewhere. Rumor or not there was plenty else to fear there including one of Sher's only ambitious obsessions, irritating as it was, sharpening and re-sharpening the kitchen cutlery. Once sharpened, they all would cut paper like butter and anything else.

As she waited on the lightless stoop she removed her treasured but now wet scarf carefully folding it and placing it in her left coat pocket not thinking that the moisture might ruin what few smokes she had left in the same pocket. Her mind was on other things so she didn't notice the trickle of sweat that now ran down the small of her back.

Sherman had his nickname tag from his day-job, working over yonder at the Doyle Crunk Slaughter House on Carter Creek Pike. Maybe they called him that, the slaughter-king, at work, Mary didn't know. No one in the house called him that to his face or "Sher" either except his mom and then only when she wanted something because otherwise it was "Sherman do this…" and "Sherman do that…" – for emphasis. Sher was to have two other titular titles soon but two that Mary would never learn.

Mary was alerted to the distinctive noise of the chain being removed on the inside of the door. Mary steeled herself for whatever was to come hoping Sher didn't have enough time to retrieve the rumored gun.

The door opened inward and there was her nemesis and victim, Betty, just standing there, arms folded with a shit eating grin that

Mary couldn't quite discern, framed by the cacophony of stale familiar smells, lights, cigarette and cigar smoke, humans mingling in the background, and the old sounds that Mary thought she had escaped long ago but certainly not long enough.

As much as one plays a planned scenario over and over in one's mind whether for business, profit, or bad – it's not unusual for the unanticipated to interfere. And what Betty now said had that startling, unexpected effect on Mary. The one thing our visitor had never projected to herself to hear was, "Come in dear…" Uneasy Mary prophetically but unknowingly finished it to herself, "…said the spider to the fly."

Betty didn't move she just stood her ground. Mary hesitated but took a step over the sill, into Betty's lair. A tsunami of memories washed over her with the next step into the old, but too familiar.

Then slightly taller Betty put her arm around her in a seemingly welcome gesture saying, "You remember Carl over there…he missed ya. And Jesse too. There's Jimmy as always…Sherman, take her coat!" Sherman had relocked and chained the door.

At his momma's command he roughly reached for Mary's tattered coat starting to pull it off her arms. "Wait…" said Mary, reaching for the safety pin that was about to choke her. She no sooner got it unpinned and her coat came off behind her. Since Mary didn't have the time to re-pin it, she wondered if it, her safety pin, would be lost forever. These days she was more conscience of losing things forever even the little things. Fortunately she had palmed the almost empty pack of Chesterfields and now put them in her pants pocket knowing full well she could get lit-up in here.

A few of the dozen or so people there caught sight of Mary's Jodhpur riding pants when her coat was removed. These were her prized-pants where her Chesterfields and hand now went into one of the two main pockets. She didn't have the boots or lacy white blouse but it had the effect Mary wanted from people and she felt "higher classed" as they stared. It didn't occur to her that her red patterned dress ducked into the pants didn't do anything for the outfit, her increasingly matronly figure, and definitely wasn't "classy" by a long shot.

Jimmy had never looked up from his self-assigned position at the three-legged card table, the only card gambling site in this main downstairs room used for mingling and some impromptu dancing. But Jimmy acknowledged her presence with a lift of his dealing hand unfortunately showing the card he was about to deal himself, a ten of diamonds. No one of the other three at the table said a word, hoping to somehow capitalize on the new learnt knowledge for himself.

Long ago the fourth leg of the cheap card table was broken off in a scuffle that cost a cheater his left eye and forty stitches that he tried to refuse but conked out at the ER before being successful so they sewed him up unable to do anything about his punctured eye. He was still paying on that bill when they caught up with him and that was constant being one of the few lowlifes around town that wore an eye patch. He eventually paid return visits to Betty's place proud of contributing to another one of its legends and finally accepting the distinction of being the only one with a real black pirate's eye patch.

Since that night and with cheap Betty not wanting to replace the broken table, the players decided that who ever dealt had to cross his leg to support the fourth corner and if he wasn't adapt enough and anybody's drink spilled, well, the replaced drink became his bill (not theirs). Other, probably thirsty players use to down most of their drink and not pass their cards back or place their chips squarely in the middle so the dealer found himself in the dilemma of reaching out, probably spilling drinks and caulking up a bar bill that Betty was happy to keep track of. Soon it was evident that tall and lanky "Slim," a.k.a. Jimmy with the long arms, could cross his leg for table support and easily reach all three other corners without much effort so Jimmy became the unofficial, regular dealer from that point on. Of course a player or two would get around to some friendly kidding about, "Jes which of yer three legs is holding up this here three-legged table Slim?" Jimmy would just laugh and start his dealing saying, "Ya'll get me drunk enough and I'll tell's ya." The occasional tips from dealing all the time kept Jimmy in a lot of the games and the more serious gambling again became the norm versus the drink-chip-pranks.

Carl was white and Jimmy was black, not that color was a factor in this house. There was always a colorful mixture in and out of Betty's place. Race was not an issue – not because it wasn't apparent and it occasionally reared its ugly head when too much mountain dew whisky had left the glass Mason canning jars across a few palates with resultant "fisticuffs." It was economically sound for Betty to be here in this "low rent" area and nothing else mattered.

Mary didn't want to remember Carl. Carl always drank too much before asking for "his" girl the last thing he did before he left at night about every other month. Drunk and too limber to "perform" Carl always, always tried to pound out his frustrations wanting to perform but always, always left dissatisfied and ashamed from his lack of manly-hood.

Carl routinely chose Mary in the past and paid the expected going-rate but that wasn't Mary's reason or the fact he didn't believe in tipping. And it wasn't his insufferable paunch. Carl had a very, very bad habit of drooling when "performing" and both went on for an indeterminate time. It made Mary feel unclean more than the act itself and she found herself washing the sheets the next day as well as a full shampoo and bath, things she couldn't do before the next morning – too disturbing for the little quite time for the house dwellers after everyone had left.

Betty's place was hardly a bordello per se since it only had one or two "busy" girls at most, those poor souls down on their luck, in transit, or whatever. It wasn't a speakeasy as such because it was too well know for its illegal moonshine availability and small time "bootlegging" distribution so the real bootleggers might supply her but would never chance a potential run in with the law because of her being so well known to them. It certainly wasn't a club even in this neighborhood when the favorite past time was dancing (with drinking) and took place in private houses or in the little house-restaurants like Patton's on Natchez where the tables and chairs were quickly moved to the side after dinner or after hours and voilà – the dance floor appeared and yes, there was gambling upstairs if dancing was only one partners idea of a good time. It, Betty's, was strictly small time and, more than less, a hand to mouth operation and day to day. She was better off then a lot but not "in the money" by any means.

Mary's quandary continued as Betty poured her a Mason jar of white lighting. This was nothing like what Mary expected having left the last time with a wad of Betty's money she never expected for such a simple bribery scam. When she did it, she knew it worked or didn't and if the later, she was out and on her own with the little savings she had mustered, all from the "tips" that she had lied about not receiving since the house-rule was to split the same with Betty. Mary had picked her "tips-to-keep" carefully without getting greedy and caught. She had also picked her timing for approaching Betty, a time when Betty was flush with a good take on the night's activity and the moonshine sold. Mary had packed the night before and had secreted her suitcase outside hopeful that it would be there when she fled. And it worked - it worked.

But now, what was this pseudo-welcome all about. "Here Mar," that's what Betty called her, "Have another…mingle and take a load off your chest," Betty said. Mary had one, chest, unlike the other girl who used to be here last time Mary was - so what she said wasn't meant to hurt. But Mary was doubly nervous with Sher seeming to watch her every move and with a steamy evil stare. Sher had visited Mary a night or two but she felt it was just part of the price she had to pay for being where she was at.

Mary didn't have to wait too long cause Carl was talking to Betty and both were looking her way from across the room just before Betty meandered over to Mary's side. Mary just knew what was coming and pretended extra interest in the five-card-stud Jimmy was dealing at the three legs.

"Mar dear, Carl would like to bring back old times..." Betty was saying when Mary interrupted, "What about the new girl over there on Willy's lap for doing the deed with Drool?" Everyone in the house including Betty knew whom she meant.

"Just this time, Carl says he can do it now...for old times sake...he missed you...you can use my room and maybe we can make some arrangements for you to stay...You don't have any other plans do ya?" The last was a rhetorical question even if Mary knew without being able to call it that.

Mary thought it was good to get Betty away, and to her own bedroom that would be private enough to do what she came here to do. So she said, 'Maybe...let's go to your room and talk." Betty's room, unlike everyone else's, was on the main floor just in back. She wondered if Sher actually slept at the foot of Betty's bed when his room was needed for a client. But she didn't know. Maybe he never slept. It was funny that he combed his hair to match his beard. This with his high receding hairline really did make him look the part of Abe Lincoln, or at least the image Mary remembered from her school books. No one ever approached Sher with the subject or conjecture to Mary's knowledge. Sher was unpredictable and basically a dark uneducated man that even his few drinking buddies wouldn't really know.

Betty didn't respond immediately which gave Mary a chill but then she said, "Have another drink. It's on the house. Let me make my rounds and then we'll talk." Now Mary thought her welcome had somehow ended and that Betty wanted and was trying to get her drunk before anything else happened. Smart but not something Mary was going to let happen.

The Carl thing was probably just to make more money or a test or to get Mary back into the fold. Things weren't transpiring anything according to the way Mary had imagined but then neither did most things in her young life.

She spotted her coat of one of the far pegs on the wall and thought about fleeing even though it wouldn't be easy. She started watching the door for anyone to leave when Sher would have it unchained. She even started mentally retracing her steps back up town and to the station. Then she thought, "I have no place to go and no money to get there. Her Chesterfields roomed with just two pennies in her one pocket and there were only two more, a Buffalo nickel and a thin dime in her coat.

This will work. I can do it. They owe me. It worked before. I can do this." And she stayed taking the drink but sipping it slowly, just to relieve the chill going up and down her spine and not caused by the outside December cold trying to enter the drafty ill build house but defeated by the human activity pushing out its resultant smoke, body heat and sundry smells.

It was an hour later that Betty said, "Let's go to my room." Mary hadn't seen her approach and was slightly startled. Mary had never felt so uneasy nor as an outsider in a place she used to fit in quite well and even felt was hers too. She was still sipping on the now empty jar not having been offered another drink, and famished for something to eat. It had been almost twenty-four hours since she had had anything and the rye alcohol seems to have burnt a hole in her stomach. She had gotten used to and liked the corn stuff better but one never knew what was going to be available, at least here.

Walking behind Betty, she felt one of those recurring déjà vu moments so familiar in most of her adult life that fate was really in charge even leading her feet as she walked. She clutched the Mason jar to her chest as if it might be the only weapon she had. She wished she had been able to hold on to her little safety pin and took one look back to make sure Sher wasn't following them. He wasn't and was numbly at his doorpost sitting on a barstool probably stolen from some place long ago. He was talking or rather listening to Carl who seemed his usual drunk self and now ready to leave.

Betty let her enter, closed the bedroom door behind her and proceeded to lowered herself to the end of her bed probably the first and only time she let herself sit down for hours and hours tonight. Mary felt empowered looking slightly down into Betty's eyes and expressionless face chiseled free from any semblance of emotion by the life, seemingly all and only seamy for as long as she cared to remember. Mary said to herself, "I can do this. I did it before."

Outside it was turning much colder and the rain had completely stopped. Hard rain was always heard on Betty's tin roof. Mary, late at night, used to listen to it in her upstairs bedroom, the tacky pink and lime green one she had when staying here. Betty liked the décor, colors. Mary figured she was secretly colored blind or had gotten it free, probably having Sher steal whatever paint he could from one of the stores over on Columbia Pike.

It happened almost exactly five years to this day but kind of started with the death of Betty's husband, John W. nine years ago. John, sixteen years older then Betty, is in Mt. Hope cemetery with a tombstone that also has Betty's name on it but without a date for her demise. If the "his and hers" was suppose to keep them closer together, well… For clarification that you'll see is necessary in a minute, we'll call this John, Betty's husband – John #1.

Well maybe it was not different then the last years of their marriage according to another John, John Golden that we'll call John 2, Betty's paramour because he says that he had been her lover for the last ten years that old John 1 was alive. Now both Johns are the same age (and just about as poor) so whatever John 1 wasn't "doing" John 2 filled in the cracks so to speak. Besides, when the lights are out, it's not easy to tell the difference between Johns, especially old Johns, at least for Betty.

But this was the key; Betty was all about business and wasn't taken to romance, men folk, or the "doing" it when she always had a couple girls in house to provide that for her constantly changing, more indigent (than rich) clientele. So those "in-house" girls picked up on this pretty quickly. Soon it became their favorite subject of gossip especially after John 1 died and John 2 became a more-regular visitor even one of the over-night kind. This in itself was unusual for two reasons, Betty routinely shooed any and all of them (who ain't boarders) out, a Betty-House rule, unless of course they paid her a little extra. And secondly, it was Betty that was bending her own rules in the case of John 2. Soon the girl's gossip went to: what was the "little extra" Betty was getting.

John 2's wife, Sallie, was older then he – so I guess this made her on the order of "ancient." In any case and as time went by, John 2 wanted to trade her in for his true number 1, Betty. Betty wasn't necessarily big on the idea but felt it might be helpful to have a more-capable John to help run things. John 1 hadn't been very helpful, even bed ridden for the last of his life – another burden.

Johnny 2 didn't give up and after the typical Sunday night party and in the wee hours of Monday morning, November 27, 1944 Betty B and John G laid out a simple plot to "extricate" Sallie G from their scene. Since Sallie was going to completely disappear so that no one would know, it would be clear sailing for the two plotters (I just couldn't bring myself to say "love-birds"), the perfect crime a.k.a. murder. Now understand, they didn't think of it that way, murder, it was just the logical removal of an obstacle so that they could continue on with their own plans.

1945 was an interesting year. Five Navy planes mysteriously vanished on a routine flight off the Florida coast on a clear and sunny day. They were on a simple training mission over an area superstitiously referred to as the Bermuda Triangle. A new Gary Cooper movie appeared on the movie house marquees called *Along Came Jones*.

A fifteen-year old son shot his dad so that his mom could get it on with her next-door farmer, lover friend. "I just shot pa down like I would a hog." As it turned out the friend had promised the young man the gun to keep if he did the deed.

Prophetically another movie starting Shirley Temple, *Kiss and Tell* hit the big screens. Of course the year started out with a bang with the headlines, *Flattops Assault Japs* referring to Halsey's aircraft carriers pursuing the near-end of World War II to the China Coast.

Dinah Shore of *The Chevy* show and others ranked at the top of all TV popularity charts for *Gal Thrushes*. I guess that was the pop equivalent of Divas. I have no way of finding out now but I think reality played a wonderful joke on prejudice at the time because it wasn't known that she was black in a culture that was still grappling with the subject of race. Dinah was a generic name for an African-American slave woman. That should have been a clue and I know I said that to you already.

I was determined to buy a Chevrolet after that. "*See the USA in your Chevrolet, America's…*" I forget the rest.

And two personal items stood out in those papers, the fifteen-square block area in New York referred to as the Bowery made the following headlines in a back page: *Doctor, Lawyer, Merchant: Bowery Hides Forgotten Men on Dead End Streets*. The second item that was also tucked into the inside versus front-page: *A & P Chain Break-Up Petition Causes Nationwide Uproar*. It was the biggest food chain and had a lot to do with the idea monopolies and the adverse impact on American consumers (according to the politicians) but both articles referred to my dad in my mind, hence "personal." I guess you'd have to read my first book, *The 515* about another small town, the/my G, during the '50's. But it's not a really big deal – just personal.

And to add to 1945, at least in Franklin, comes the State vs. Golden murder trial. John and Betty had worked out the following plan, which to their credit – they carried out to a T. I know you can detect a "but" coming and in this case the "but" was nature – nature didn't quite cooperate to the successful conclusion of a perfect murder, their second.

It's amazing how one is empowered by success, even in murder. Oh, didn't I mention the suffocation of John 1 in the wee hours of a November night? Well no one else will either since it was recorded as "natural causes" for an old man that had been ailing and bedridden for sometime anyways. Beside, who cared? One of the many cellmates of John 2 didn't – really, but he passed it on to the authorities for what it was worth. And yes, they sat on it as jail-house gossip stories.

Likewise, who was to care about ancient Sallie, John's wife, the stay-at-home, and slightly ailing, ancient wife of another semi-recluse (except for John's very active socializing on Acton Street just down Evans Alley)? With only one John left, I'll drop the 1 and 2.

Unemployed John had good information that a farmer just out on Hillsboro Road on Del Rio Pike could use another hand and it would be to John and Sallie's benefit if he was to get that job. John convinced Sallie that the two of them would make a much better appearance showing up together at the farm then if he were to just stop in off the road by himself. Therefore Sallie was to walk up the road with John that Tuesday giving up one of her two regular daily naps. This was the plot BB and JG had laid out only hours before with the (not-so-subtle) coincidence of Betty happening to be walking along the same road, meeting up with them, and walking along together "for a spell."

Tuesday, a "job-hunt'n day," John and wife Sallie set out for Hillsboro Road. They didn't say much of anything to each other despite John's incessant convincing for Sallie to accompany him on this trek. With this exception, their conversations wouldn't have filled a child's book if every word over the last several years were included. Low and behold, guess whom they happened to run into.

Yes, Betty just happened to be out on her first Hillsboro stroll ever. Her lame excuse was that a farmer up the road, not the same one as John's, was willing to sell brown eggs at a good price to someone willing to buy in quantities. "Lord knows, I have enough mouths to feed," said Betty as if Sallie would know anything about her place. Together they turned off Hillsboro and entered Del Rio Pike walking until they were close to the Old Hillsboro Road (and the river).

Sallie was old, on the feeble side but not completely dumb and became suspicious. This sent the plot into high gear. John and Betty ended up "escorting" (one arm each) Sallie off the road, into a nearby field.

A walking stick that some say "cane" is mainly used as a support appliance but can be used as an instrument of punishment and/or defense. They originally started out as necessary tools for the shepherd and traveler long ago.

John Golden's was a knurled affair, a hickory walking cane measuring forty inches. It had six curls. The hickory and curls make it very rare indeed. He never went without it unless he was otherwise engaged in the occasional bath, game of cards, or beds whether his own or Betty's.

Specifically John's cane was Scrub Hickory, endemic to central Florida and John had started using it when he was kicked by a horse with the resultant limp at the age of forty. It cost a lot but he felt he deserved it with what had happened to him.

It was originally finished in a high luster but long tainted with nicks, scratches and wear. It had a shiny short round hame on top. The hame made it an effective defensive weapon that John would occasionally banish but never really ever had to use. The cane is sometimes supplied with a thin leather lanyard strap that one would place around the wrist when in use but John didn't have it nor did he know why the hole that would have supported such a thing existed at the top of his fine cane. He just ignored it. He also ignored that some cane users had names for their helpers, he thought that was damn silly. That was another thing he picked us after his accident, profanity.

For many the more popular and lighter walking stick is the Sassafras cane but it is softer, weaker, and brittle if used or misused for "other then" support. Scrub Hickory is extremely tough, heavier yet flexible. It is valued for tool handles, bows, wheel-spokes, durable carts, and even golf club shafts sometimes called hickory sticks. Richard Parente and Dick De La Cruz owned the Hickory Sticks golf manufacturing company in the 1940's. It was a good choice made long ago by John.

John was partial to hickory because it had routinely been used on him as a punitive tool in the few years of his adolescent schooling as well as in his family life. In fact his first and last act of rebellion, leaving home at an early age, had a lot to do with hickory. His only fond memories of Hickory-use were when the wood graced his father's smoke house for curing their meats, and especially the barbecue. He didn't like when a hickory switch was use on his adolescent backside.

John had his trusty hickory, knurled cane when he took Sallie's one arm to lead her into the field toward the river. Actually he had to switch sides with Betty to have a firmer hold but that wasn't a big problem with docile Sallie.

Then what happened wasn't pretty. Poor Sallie was thrown to the ground, face first and held down by Betty as John started "awack'n a way." As formidable as a hame crested hickory stick is; it takes time to completely annihilate a human being unless one's lucky. John wasn't and it's speculation if Betty took over when John tired – only the two knew despite the "he said versus she said" especially since she said she wasn't even there.

They unceremoniously dragged Sallie to the river, our Big Harpeth, one leg each and that's where nature stepped in. They assumed Sallie, overweight, over-aged and obvious dead weight (now), would sink. She didn't cooperate and an unsuspecting farmer, Joe Reese, found her floating down the icy river near his home off Del Rio Pike on Saturday, December 3rd.

Sheriff Earl Gatlin, not a man to be trifled with, soon had John in his office with Mr. Golden spilling his guts seemingly leaving out no detail. "I and Miss Betty hav been gettin it on for better then a dozen years. I done offered her a hundred dollar to help me with the promise of marrying up after the deed was done," John confessed. Earl didn't even have to press John at this point and John continued, "We done planned it when I stayed over Sunday nite last month..." Was that last Sunday, November 26th John?" the sheriff asked. "Sure it was that, Sheriff," confirmed John.

"We was to meet on Hillsboro Road there yonder and she was to help me. I got Miss Sallie to company me to a possible job and we was walkin there and met Miss Betty on the way, walking up Hillsboro. We turned into Del Rio and crossed a rock wall surrond'n a wheat field I said was a shorter way. It were nearer the river. But right away Miss Sallie got wonder'n and started out to run away. I can't so Miss Betty obliged and threw her to ther ground and I did the deed. Then it took both pulling a foot apiece to take her to the river, which we done. So be it Sheriff, that's all I gots to say. Except it seems she didn't sink like we was expecting. Right Sheriff? But that's neither here nor there – we left there goin our separate ways so that no one was about to take notice. I can take ya there if'n you want."

"Wait here John. I'll have to have this typed up," said Earl. John repeated that what he said was the truth and freely signed the confession as Sheriff lit out to arrest Miss Betty for first-degree murder.

"Well I declare Sheriff, I don't know what that crazy old man is a'talkin bout. We ain't getting it on and he's only been here once or twice some time ago. I was car'n for my ailing mom at the very time he's citing," claimed Betty. John didn't budge from his story despite that an upon-the-scene investigation by the Sheriff showed a shoe print that John said was her's, "She's wear'n the same ones now as then. Check 'em Sheriff!" And Earl did – perfect fit.

In all the many accounts of Betty's offenses, her name is spelled Bettie, Betty, and Bettye. The later is from her official prison record but not from this felony – she wasn't even brought to trial whereas John got sixty years.

John's testimony was "natural" and "very convincing" to the Sheriff who had no doubts including that John wasn't going to be able to drag a dog let alone Sallie across the field to the river by himself. But the jury didn't hear John tell all since his criminal past usurped the possibility of him saying the Betty-facts to the jury, so ruled the judge. A "she-said" trumps a "he-said" if the he has a record. Something anyone planning a murder should keep in mind.

When you get away with two, why not three. Mary Margaret Rose Rosa Opinsky Dean was standing before her on the wooden plank floor between the bed and the window in Betty's bedroom on the first floor of this infamous house on Acton and Evan's alleys. Betty was a little taller but not so as to tower over her. Mary had played her cards, the same one she had dealt before about knowing some incriminating, damning evidence that would implicate Betty once and for all with the Golden murder that Mary had picked up the last time she was staying here.

She had been meticulous gathering what information she could listening at walls unobserved, even going to the reported scene of the crime only to fall in the river, which made her end of at Doc Guffee's for a third time. The first two were related to her Burge House activities regarding something ill she may have picked up even after cauterizing "everything" by pouring moonshine over the privates after every deed. At first this hurt like hell but as she repeated the process she soon became use to it as just another necessary practice and this was for her, for her own protection.

She had been patient and bided her time for the right moment and it had worked, leaving with riches she hadn't known up to that point in her life. Now she tried not to think how they were so easily squandered, even the last dollars she had coming here paying a Nashville taxi driver to go fetch a jar of moonshine to fortify her resolve to stand here now. That was what she did on the nervous, unexpected hour and half delay/stopover at the Nashville station just hours before.

But now she didn't have the luxury of choosing a second time. She was backed up to the proverbial wall of her life without so much as a trap door. The door through which she and Betty had just come wasn't an option with Sher nearby. Betty's only bedroom window wasn't an option and Mary knew this. The window, and all the first floor windows that weren't boarded up, was barred for Betty's protection and a less easy entrance for any police raid if they were so inclined.

It was now or never and she steeled herself to stand up to Betty's killer looks momentarily forgetting what deeds had etched them so deep into her face. She dealt but then Betty raised the ante. In a bellowing voice that woke up a couple of the boarders upstairs including Robert “Bobbie” Woodard. Betty yelled, ”Sher…get yerself in here!”

Sher was a big man even if not the strongest. His mass intimidated most. He had longer arms than Jimmy Slim and one heck of a hairy chest that Mary preferred not to remember but since he liked to show it and picked shirts to do just that, it was difficult not to. But it was his dead eyes that put fear in most and Mary didn’t want to turn around now and see them again.

Mary involuntarily started to wet her pants, her precious, classy jodhpurs. She instinctively knew this was “serious-bad” as her long ago mother used to say back in Detroit where her coal-cutter father had moved them from western Pennsylvania to take a job in the booming “automotive industry.” Mary had seen that Sher was never without a knife, a shiv as he called it, whether it was from the kitchen or stolen from his work. It was on him somewhere. He used to wear them out by whittling on anything or sharpening them razor sharp again and again until they were worn to nothing or finally broke from being so thin.

What happens next is best described in poetry by one William Claude Yates and comparing his photograph in the last Yates book I mentioned compared to a pencil portrait in this little booklet I found nicely tucked away but dwarfed by bigger books in the Special Sections of the library, I’m pretty sure he is one and the same man.

He tells it well even if changing the names and I will be in touch with the estate or whoever to encourage them to publish another edition or to re-produce it here if they approve. It’s worth the effort and after all, when something’s this well done, why try to duplicate it. Here’s a sampling:

“Here I am, Ma. Whatta ya want?”
The Grizzly creature growled.
He sounded like a savage beast,

Roaring as he prowled.
"This dirty wretch is here again
Demanding that we pay,
Or else she threatens ill of us
'Bout going to have her say."

"Just when things have quieted down
And no one seems to care,
She comes to stir it up again
And make her mighty dare."

"She promised she would stay away
And tell no dirty soul.
And now she's here to tattle tale
On what she had been told."

"Whatta you wantin' me to do?"
The beastly creature roared.
"Slap her dirty little face,
Or beat her with a board?"

"More than that, the woman yelled,
As her face began to bloat.
"Grab her by her mangy hair,
And cut her stinking throat."

The big brute caught the tiny waif
And squeezed her like a vise,
Then yelled to the woman standing there,
"Gimme that pocket knife."

Without a thought or reasoned word
The inhuman brute obeyed
The prodding of his evil ma
And the order she relayed.

He held the wispy figure firm

And squeezed with all his might,
Her stringy muscles drawn and taut,
Unable to move or fight.

He jammed the knife into her throat
And split it ear to ear.
The blood gushed out and spread apart
On clothes and everywhere.

He dropped her on the bloody floor,
Looked at his ugly ma,
Then shouted like a maniac,
That's killing in the raw."

And it goes on but Mary's gone. However quick such a murder is, the clean up is horrendous. The body is mostly water I'm told, and an average of six quarts of blood but it seems more like ten come gushing out when that well is unexpectedly tapped in that matter. Blood flew in every direction for 180 degrees. Of course Mary started to fight after dropping her jar and received cuts on both hands to prove it but she was dead before her hands dropped to her side.

So the planning for (another) perfect murder finally kicks in as Betty starts to delegate, "Get rid of that corpse, Sherman!"

"But ma, how's I supposed to do that?"

"Well start by taken my counterpane and wrapping her up and then get some help but get her out of here, boy." Counterpane is a New England expression for the top covering on a bed and I have no idea where Betty picked it up unless she had some lineage from there in time.

"But where," Sherman continued, "We don't have time to dig! And the ground's hard as a rock." This seems true of all middle Tennessee. It's a limestone state with, if you're lucky, fourteen inches of soil on top and that thin top-covering can harden in the best of winters.

"Well, dummy, ain't there a incinerator at the school up the hill?" The juices were kicking in and Betty was on a roll. No body, no blood, no memories equals the perfect murder (and she's right).

"Yea, mom, there is but it's way up the hill, ma and she's still dripping."

"Well get Bobby down her to help wrap her up and ta help ya carry her out of here. I got to get rid the blood – it's everywhere, now go" said the house's matron. Bobby leaned on the side of "push-over" and it was a good choice.

Another choice that Betty had was yet another boarder upstairs, a skilled carpenter "that could whittle anything," Lewis Smith (47). Smith wouldn't have been a good choice because his second most hobby, drinking was the first, was slicing up people at any excuse or even without one. Lewis had already been convicted, sentenced and had served time for this once or twice or five times. But then Betty knew her house and knew Lou had lost a bit at Slim's three legged table and drank it off with the result that he was currently dead drunk to the world and upstairs in his own bed. She and Sher had put him there.

Bobby had already been awake when he heard the scream. Mrs. Mary Smith Ivy (35), in the next room was awakened by the raised voices just before the scream even if her "satisfied" extra-paying-for-overnight client didn't stir for any of this. Mary was already getting on her scarlet terrycloth robe that she wished was silk when the down-stairs blood curling but brief women's scream did come piercing the walls. Then came Sher's holler, "Bobbie, get down here, now." When that came Mary Ivy was still searching for her slippers in the dark.

Bobby, a forlorn, theatrical character that any movie plot would do well to include, will play an important role as we go forth so I'll briefly describe this unforgettable character that will be emphatically remembered by the fifteen thousand attendees at the Franklin Court House coming up, some with knitting, crossword puzzles, or scratch pads, some skipping school, lots playing hooky from work or other duties and coming from miles and miles around. But first Bobby:

Age 22, former soldier that didn't look military at all mainly do to his very hunched shoulders, Bobby was discharged from the service due to a case of rheumatic fever with the resultant heart damage. Bobby was a boarder at the Burge house, which sometimes went to14 residents in total. Robert, Bobby Woodard looked like what he was, a sick demoralized, man, very thin, who was leading a life thought to be brief so that one should run with it. This meant booze, women, gambling, et al, everything and anything one could do, or afford, for distraction and/or pleasure before it ended.

Bobby, not having changed out of his clothes was down the stairs pretty fast. However sick he had thought he was, he became green as fresh asparagus when he walked through Betty's bedroom door. Sherman was still walking back in as Betty was removing her counterpane, somewhat blood spattered as it was just like the curtains and a nearby faded gray plastic-covered slumber chair and footstool. Of course he saw the body and pool of blood seeping everywhere , the unbroken Mason jar but with spilled contents, then Bobbie noticed the blood on Betty and more on Sherman's overalls and hands. Damn, Sherman still held the knife, the bloody knife.

Sherman saw Bobby's aghast look and his left foot starting to back out the door so he grabbed Bobby's arm. "Where ya think you're going, soldier?"

"Yea, I killed her, Bobby. This here woman came demanding money of my ma here er else she was to go to the sheriff's about what she knew of John Golden's Sallie so I killed her. And now yer goin'a help me take her up the hill," spouted Sherman as he put the blood stained knife to Bobby's throat. Bobby started to protest but Sherman held the same knife to one side of his neck and said, "You're a helping me or getting the same. Now what'll it be?" Just then Mary Ivy in her scarlet terrycloth robe came to the door but quickly retreated back upstairs, shaking but without ever saying a word wondering if she would ever be able to sleep in this house again.

Bobby dutifully helped Sherman wrap the body but not without getting blood on his own hands, shirt and overalls similar to Sherman's. Meanwhile Betty had retrieved a small bag of clothes from the hall closet of things she had collected of Mary's once Mary had left before and now casually dropped the bag on top of Mary's body about to be wrapped up by the boys. This act of "cleaning out any memory of the bitch once and for all" by Betty, would serve another purpose that she didn't think of, evidence tying Mary to the house if the bag was found here. Of course Betty also didn't realize that the trinkets Mary left were of the "unwanted/discard" kind. Everything that Mary had wanted to take had been secreted outside in her suitcase before she made her leave.

In the early pre-dawn hours, Sherman and Bobbie carted their package down the alleyway and up the small hill to the Franklin High School incinerator set behind the gym, which was behind the school. The gym was a separate, after-thought building almost not erected back in 1926 when the school was built except for the insistence of the then graduating class

seniors and an additional $30,000 school bond that they were instrumental in getting passed to finance it. There reasoning was, "What's a school without a gym?"

It was probably less than the distance down a football field and if it weren't for the now freezing weather, the rain the day before, the slightly slippery muddy hill and the dead weight, it wouldn't have been too difficult of a job. Sherman made it a little more difficult for himself by trying to due both jobs with the help from his half pint of "better" Canadian Club whisky from the stash he had secreted away. Since it had a foreign name he thought it had to be special although he wished it was the more expensive Seagram's Royal Crown that he had tried once. But the mere fact that Al "Scarface" Capone used to drink CC made it awesome in his mind. It didn't really help like he thought it would but he kept taking a slug and then another when they unceremoniously rolled her up in the bed covering and were carting her up the hill. It never occurred to him to share.

Of course when one said the "Franklin High School" at that time, it was the same as the "white school." The "colored" high school was tucked in behind on lower Natchez Street, between Columbia and West Main Streets and now a nursing home.

It was Monday morning and the janitor's duties included getting there pre-dawn to stoke the furnaces especially in December, open up the doors, turn on lights, check things out, and un-padlock the separate gym, and the schools' incinerator in preparation for another day. But it was a cold Monday morning that the lead FHS janitor overslept and the incinerator was still padlocked.

Sherman knew he could saw off the lock or maybe even break it with a crowbar but only if there was time. Not owning a watch, he didn't know if he had any time left before the errant janitor, school kids, passer-byers, or even dawn showed up. Meanwhile Bobby was repeating and repeating, "What we goin'a due Sher?" Finally, after another slug of CC, Sherman said, "Shut up Bobbie, we goin'a puts her over there." Sherman knew he wasn't going to tell his ma this turn of events but would answer to her predictable question, "Did ya take care of it Sher?" knowing full well what she meant. "Yes ma, it's all taken care," was going to be his nebulous reply.

Sherman was smart enough not to leave his mother's bed covering thinking it might tie into their house down the alley. It was a mess, bloody yes but now muddy from when they laid Mary down the several times across the alley and up the hill, resting a spell or so. Now they simply pulled up the covering to let her roll out.

Neither paid any attention to the accompanying bag of stuff Betty had included nor did they notice the crumpled up article from the *Indianapolis Star* newspaper dated October 25th that mentioned a reward for information on six recent slayings in that city, the very thing that gave Mary the idea of monies to be gained by returning to Franklin.

They were both fascinated by her bobbing head almost off, as it turned over and over out of the counterpane. At one point Bobbie thought it was going to come off and had to look away as her body, thankfully, ended up face down on the hard icy mud and December grass surface not far from the drive going behind the school, near the sidewalk, and near a locust tree.

Sherman made Bobbie carry the pseudo body bag wrap back until they passed an oversized trash can of old lady Nellie's in the alley that she never used and Sherman had Bobbie stuff it in there covering it with some of the wet trash spilled around the container there. It was disgusting stuff but would probably serve the purpose of no one else checking things out.
Sherman knew if the wrap came back into the house that it would end up as his problem to get rid off it anyways so this was good. This side of trying to dig a hole in this frozen ground and with no

time to do it, he had no other idea for getting rid of it since the incinerator wasn't an option.

As Bobbie was doing as he was told, stuffing the trashcan, Sherman reached for his precious Canadian Club pint and realized it had been left behind, "Probably when they were unrolling the bitch," he thought to himself. This really pissed him off because it was still almost half full. He considered sending Bobbie back for it but thought he might be seen or caught with the morning coming on fast. His mother would never forgive him and Bobbie was a woozier, would talk the first time he got the chance and no one wanted that so it was best if he didn't get caught. "Yea," he thought, "I better make sure he understands things."

As they reached Betty's place, it again began to rain. It never occurred to either that they had left tracks on the hill. But not to worry, the rain was their cleansing agent and their tracks would not be found.

Pretty Peggy Williams was driven to school that morning by Paul Tucker who worked in a garage here in Franklin. Walking up the back sidewalk Peggy spotted what she thought was a practice football dummy somehow left out in the rain and cold. Drawn closer she gasped at the horrific sight and immediately went to tell the principal who was satisfied with Peggy's competence without seeing for himself and without delay called the Franklin Police.

The body was wet, muddy and presented a lower profile than one would expect. Because of the pants and short hair one had to come very close to see that it had been female, to see the delicate small hands and frail arms for instance. Mary's body seemingly was attempting to burrow itself into Mother Earth, a body's ultimate destination, or it was at least trying to become one with it. Wet on the surface, it had tried to turn to ice like the thin sheet of ice adhering to it on most sides. The flailing but suspended arms, the unusual pants, and one missing shoe, close by, make it look more pathetic especially when one noticed the numerous holes in her nylon on the shoeless foot.

Sheriff's Deputy Otto Frasier and Franklin's Chief, Oscar B. Garner, were the first on the scene. Dr. Harry Guffee arrived on their heels and was the first to say, "Doesn't she look familiar?"

"Let's turn her over to see what we got," said the Chief. "My God, is that Mary Ivys?" Chief asked no one in particular. "You might be right Chief," came the attentive deputy's reply with a confirming, "I think you might be right Chief," said doc. It wasn't easy turning her over and the head needing it's own coaxing since it didn't come with the beginning to be frozen body.

"God help us, I think it is. She's just down the alley there isn't she, at the Betty's place?" continued Oscar. They were thinking Mary, but not this Mary. They were thinking Mary Ivy who lived there, Betty's, for a good while. "Well I'm pretty sure she used to be there," said the correcting Otto. "Damn! We better go have ourselves a look-see," said Chief. And they started down the slight bluff together while leaving the scene in the capable hands of the medical examiner, coroner, the doctor and the few other officers that had arrived and were handily cordoning off the scene.

Set on what they thought they knew, they passed by the trash can containing the soiled, bloodstained bed cover, body wrap and were stridently on their way to Betty's with nary a thought of looking there or even later although Betty's four trash cans would be thoroughly searched and inventoried eventually. Sherman won that one. And Sherman had wisely unchained the front door, not in anticipation of their possible visit, the furthest thing from his or Betty's mind, but because that was the usual procedure during the day so as not to impede the in and out traffic by them or the boarders.

Very much alive but badly shaken Mary Ivy was, at that moment, in Bobbie's room talking about the last night's events. Mary and Bobbie were close as two forlorn people with little or no hope could be. It wasn't completely platonic but mostly. The times that it wasn't were to take care of a need by a feeling friend.

No one knows exactly how it started, some say weak and frail Bobbie came to her rescue when a client got out of hand. Fortunately that's all it took, Bobbie showing up for the rescue, and the client left, pants in hand. Their rooms were across the hall from one another and Bobbie could hear Mary's calls for help that he knew would not be forth coming from anyone else. Bobbie and Mary talked when one or the other couldn't sleep in the wee morning hours and were seen going, walking, talking together uptown occasionally.

The floor had been completely scrubbed in Betty's bedroom, she had changed the bed clothing and her bloodied dress, had the two boys take off their overhauls with instructions to "rid the blood," had taken down the one bloodied curtain to be washed hoping it would stand up in the cleaning cycle since it was so old and Betty couldn't remember ever washing any of them. She had Sher and Bobbie take the chair and footstool to the only vacant bedroom after cleaning off the blood and was feeling pretty good. And with a little imagination, no one would knew from what they saw that anything unusual would have happened there last night.

Mary Ivy came down at that point to take the pulse of things when the clamorous knocks on the door came. Betty grew as pale as her new bed sheets after jumping back grasping for breath. Betty just knew a policeman's knock versus any one else's.

Mary thought she was having a heart attack and was about to call out for Bobbie when Betty's worst fears were realized. She could hear Sher said louder than he had to, a signal to everyone in earshot,

"Why hello Sheriff." Betty asked Mary for her help in lying down on the bed.

Next day's newspapers: Coke was five cents. There was a new idea on the horizon called "Charga-Plate – Especially useful when shopping for Christmas." A woman's salon suit cost just $49.95. Short and/or long sleeve cotton dresses could be purchased at $2.98 each at the Cotton Shoppe on Fifth Ave. Christmas was only two weeks away with only 11 of those for shopping. And subjugating the "Airliner Plunges Into Potomac" story relegated to only one column, was the five column-three tiered heading that read:

Woman Found Slashed to Death,
Identified as Roaming Waitress,
From Indianapolis - Killer Hunted.

Things started to move very fast for such a case and in a small town that seemingly dropped everything else. Witnesses and wantabe witnesses were coming out of the "historic" woodwork. And the lethargic (by design) press came to life with all cylinders cooking. Lots of calls to the cops.

Usually shy officers of the Sheriff's, Franklin's and Highway Patrol lined up for pictures of anything, reenactments, important locations, interviews, updates, arrests or anything and with lots of locals as volunteer backgrounds. Press and reporters were coming out of the woodwork.

The next morning a waitress picked up on a deaf mute hitchhiker that had scrawled some things on a blank menu about the slaying, things that were in the paper, on the radio, and the talking-airwaves of Franklin. SUSPICION. Call to the cops.

Two students, Jimmy Smithson and Bobby Robinson, swore they saw such a woman walking in the vicinity of the High School Sunday night. Call to the cops (and newspaper). Got their picture on the front page.

A taxi driver said he saw her leave the Depot the night before. Call to the cops but he forgot the newspaper and only got "honorable" mention (no picture) in the paper.

A Nashville Tennessean reporter picked up on the scrawled man's name, even though misspelled and with only a street address (no city or state) on a piece of paper which was found beside the body. Call to the cops. And as improbable as that is, there has to be another story there.

Meanwhile Sheriff Oscar didn't feel right about things he had seen at the Betty's Place even if he didn't pick up on the shabby black coat still on the peg near the door that contained a scarf that Betty would eventually wear to her trial and even be photographed and appear in the paper. His gut feelings mainly based on his suspicious reception when there were beginning to tear at him and he wasn't about to leave it alone.

Sure he knew they had a lot to hide but didn't act right when the body didn't turn out to be Mary Ivy and they "Had no idea who else it could be." The strong smell of cleaning stuck in his nostrils. Never in any of the raids or visits previously had there ever been an attempt to clean anything. The place was dingy, ragged, and a disgrace to a neighborhood that already needed lots of help and didn't need this eyesore. Just from a sanitary point of view, they didn't even maintain (with lime or anything) their crapper, their two-holer out back.

"Hello? Is Sheriff Fasier there? Oh, Hi Ewine, it's Oscar here. I had a question for ya. Wasn't that knife wielding fanatic, what's his name, at the Betty's address – a boarder? Yea, Lewis Smith, the carpenter, that's him. We've picked him up on drunk, disorderly, and on several cuttings. I think he even spent some jail-time on cutting. Oh, one of yours – no wonder you remember him. Well I brought it up since it seems too coincidental for him to be there, right down the alley, so close to a corpse that had her throat slashed four times from ear to ear. No, let me call Inspector Jim over at Highway Patrol and see if he wants to pick him up for questioning. Thanks Ew, see ya. Yea, I'll be in touch with any developments here. Bye."

Oscar just knew the Inspector was good for a picture in the paper and that would have the effect of calming down the terrified town. In fact, he figured he'd suggest that a picture with Lewis would do the trick. And it happened Wednesday morning's *Tennessean* edition. This helped take some of the pressure off for a good and thorough investigation in an already Hollywood building atmosphere. Only two days in and the press was clamoring for a big name like The High School Mystery Slaying, or The Franklin Slasher, or worst, Franklin's Ripper, etc. Oscar thought they were incorrigible.

Incredibly, the Tennessean reporter who somehow seemed to recognize the misspelled name and the partial address scrolled in poor penmanship on wet, soggy paper found with the body at the FHS scene, somehow woke up the Beatty's in Portland, Tennessee, on the other side of Nashville, some sixty miles north of Franklin almost to the Kentucky boarder. This was Monday morning bright and early before anyone at the Beatty's household had a chance to go to work.

After some twenty minutes of conversation and with a story within a story, our reporter figured he had the first identity of the murder victim and called the cops plus his editor. The editor was ecstatic and reserved the lead story space for their Tuesday morning edition figuring the paper had a one-upmanship on the Franklin's local The Review Appeal that wouldn't be publishing until Thursday, their once-a-week regular date. This was especially good since the news was going to already be two days old. Therefore it never occurred to him to ask, "How did you get this?" And as far as I can tell, it's still a mystery today.

Our industrious newsman reported the following to the police and the Isaac Beatty's of Portland, Tennessee tentatively identified Mrs. Rosa Mary Dean, a native of Texas and/or maybe Pennsylvania with no living relatives and happened to stay at the Beatty's in Indianapolis, Indiana just before they moved back the two-hundred fifty plus miles to their home in Portland, Tennessee over the weekend. A Beatty nephew, Earl, found her wandering the streets of Indianapolis on his way home from work at a local glass shop on December 2nd and felt that his generous aunt and uncle would give her boarding for a night or two so that she could find a job like waitressing or something to get herself back on her feet. This she did and it was a waitress job she found on December 5th and 6th at the White House Drive-in.

The thirty-year old mostly deaf, dumb former bootblack, shoeshine employee, from Asheville, North Carolina just happened to be passing through Franklin Sunday night, hitchhiking to Nashville late at night. He had been left off just south of town and not being able to find any rides that late, walked up Columbia Pike into town therefore seen on foot. He figured the best he could do was to find a sleeping shelter in town and re-start his sojourn in the morning.

Unfortunately the town was such a buzz Monday morning that when he stopped in at a Commerce Street restaurant for coffee and a piece of toast, he heard lots of the goings on. His waitress was so interested in town' happenings, she got his order for wheat toast wrong and even left her pencil at his table when she went to sit his food down.

With nothing else to do, caught up in the excitement all around him, and no one to talk to, he started to doodle what he heard and on the menu left by the waitress. Returning to his table after he left and looking for a tip that wasn't there, she noted the scribing having to do with the murder and called the police.

He was found by the police on the edge of Nashville having successfully hitched a ride there. He became very confused as to why they were interested in him and especially since they showed up with sirens blaring and lights flashing as if he was somehow a murderer or something. Actually his thought processes didn't go that far and he was just plain olé scarred-out-of-his-wits (those few he had). Besides pissing his only good pants, his thoughts went in a completely different direction and he looked down to see if he was jaywalking or something to cause this commotion.

When interviewed our white, deafly mute with a distracting large blackish and hairy mold on his left jaw went spastic when he finally understood the reason for his detainment and was shown a picture of the slain woman taken at the morgue by a resourceful Tennessean photographer. "The man became extremely agitated and screamed bloody murder reported the investigators." Unfortunately this immediately spelled GUILT to some at the station. He was promptly returned to Franklin.

From the start Chief Oscar felt "they were barking up the wrong tree" with this suspect, one who didn't even have the wits to lie, but decided they couldn't afford to let him go. Oscar, long on experience, knew that the public's perception that the police had acted so fast and now having a suspect or two in custody would go a long way to have a calming effect on the town. Therefore holding him had a purpose for now.

They filed technical (bogus) charges of vagrancy and loitering that would keep the hitchhiker in their custody even if he had been picked up in Nashville. Oscar, feeling guilty about the sheer terror in our hitchhiker's wide eyes that he couldn't seem to close even for a moment finally convinced our visitor that it would be good for him to stay "in custody" with three-square and a good bed. Oscar ordered his clothes be changed and cleaned, especially his pants and had one of his boys call over to Goodwill to see if they had a newer pair of "walking" shoes in his size since the ones he was in were about to fall apart.

With concentrated due diligence to their investigation over the next twenty four hours, the police couldn't shake loose one person in Franklin that would admit to recognizing the FHS ground's victim. This, while not necessary unusual, was frustrating.

At the same time, our astute and resource reporter was at it again. First he had the police promise him first "dibs" on interviewing the Isaac Beatty's after they arrived in Franklin since the police agreed to drive over and get them. Plus, our ace reported wasn't about to let go of the Portland-starting-point or the fact that the Beatty's had first met our victim in Indianapolis. He was like a hungry morning shark after the first smells of blood in the water. He called the respective police departments of both cities and with dramatic results.

First, there was more to Mrs. Rosa Mary Dean than apparently any one person or police department knew. Indianapolis police said they had no record of a Rosa Mary Dean but had arrested a Mary Rose Dean with a similar description on several occasions for soliciting, prostitution, vagrancy, and loitering.

He was no sooner off the phones with dozens of calls when he received word that the Beatty's had arrived in town and the police, good to their word, were inviting him to the station to be a part of their interview process. Any doubt that the police had for this collaboration were dispelled when he related a few tidbits he had learned and told them there was more to come so to hold his place – he was on the way.

There's only one better type of ace reporter, it's an ardent ace. Here's the story our ardent ace reporter put together and passed on to his newspaper's ed and the police:

Mary, middle name Margaret, was born the second of ten children to an immigrant coal cutter, Frank Opinsky and his wife, Bertha Crawford, who he met at his first home and boarding house in Uniontown, Fayette County, Pennsylvania, after arriving from his native Austria-Hungary, in Central Europe. The marriage lasted twenty-five years until the stronger of the two, Bertha died in 1945. Frank died in 1947. A coal cutter is one who goes the furthest into a mind to deep cut the kerf in order to undermine a coal deposit to start the evacuation process. This is particularly common in long wall mining such as the Frick Coke Company where Frank worked.

By all accounts Mary was a typical child, attending church with her family and the local public schools but a little on the rebellious side. The seemingly rebellious nature reared its ugly head when she was nineteen and brought up on morals charges and jailed overnight by the police in the nearby town of Keisterville. Her companion was a thirty-one year old coal miner, Aaron Dean. Two weeks later the couple was married in the Fayette County courthouse.

In an effort to better his state in life, Aaron moved he and Mary to Detroit in 1944 to work in the automotive industry. The following year Mary's mother died and Mary's life's downward spiral started with a serious drinking problem, followed by separation from Aaron, and moving back to live with her family in Pennsylvania. In December of 1945 she was picked up for prostitution on East South Street in downtown Uniontown with many more arrests until her father's funeral after which she left, never to be heard from again.

Wandering, prostitution, hitchhiking, waitressing and picking oranges in Florida, peanuts in Alabama, cotton in Mississippi, Louisiana and Texas, loitering, and drinking, Mary was living day to day. She happened at Betty's twice about fourteen months apart having left the first time for "a planned trip to California, its beaches, and a look at Hollywood" but this was never realized. It was her second time at Betty's that she lucked into the extortion/blackmail thing and left after a few short weeks for Chicago with "Betty's wad," the money she had extorted.

Chicago was "big-time" and Mary went through what money she had rather quickly only to learn that the local girls had "assigned turf" by the pimps, and/or the criminal element controlling the seedier streets and her backup-prostitution money making plans didn't work there. She soon left for the quieter town of Indianapolis, not that the city allowed the engagement of the world's oldest institution but it was basically only the police a girl had to worry about (not any criminal element too).

Is that a cliché or just a fact, "The world's…?" Anyway, and by this time, our reporter was pretty sure of where young Earl Beatty stood as far as offering Mary the comfort of his aged aunt and uncle's place but didn't think it would add appreciably to his story so he let it go.

Uncle Isaac worked with horses and this was the tail end of his Indianapolis job so that by Friday, December 9th Willie Earl and Mary passed favors for the last time that included what little money Earl had on his person and Mary left their place Saturday afternoon in anticipation of their moving back to Tennessee. Earl said he had said his good-by to Mary in front of the Fisher's Garage on E. Washington St., where she asked for and wrote down his Portland address, "in case she would ever be passing through there." Earl thought she was still working at the White House, could get a place with her first paycheck and would be fine. But then those weren't necessarily the things of Mary that Earl was paying the most attention.

The Beatty's interview with the police added the following observations to the story. Mary told the Beatty's that she was hitchhiking to Missouri eventually going back to Texas as she left their place in Indianapolis, that Mary had no living relatives including her two sisters that had lived in a reformatory. Mary had been married to a man named Dean and had traveled everywhere and had seen everything with him but he had been killed in an automobile accident (maybe she meant he was lost to the automotive industry). Mary and her husband had twin babies but they were dead too. Our reporter tried to slice this into her 1944 Detroit stay to help explain the seemingly quick depression and change of life style but after several phone calls couldn't substantiate his suspicions with any birth certificates, hospital records, etc. He also tried to locate this Dean person but without success. Mrs. Beatty felt she would need a coat for her travels to cold Missouri thinking it was somewhere north near Canada and offered Mary a checkered coat she happened to have in the closet. But it didn't fit, too tight, so she generously gave Mary a second one, larger, darker and with a collar one could pull up around the face if it became especially cold but it had to be held by one's hands since the button was long gone.

Mary didn't quite understand the Beatty's moving schedule and after an all-nighter on the streets of the Indy, she figured she could talk her way back into their life in Tennessee and bought a ticket to Portland late Sunday morning. Meanwhile Isaac and Earl had taken a first load down to their Tennessee home on Sunday and had returned arriving at their Indianapolis place in the morning hours to pick up the Mrs. and the remainder of their stuff for their last trip on Monday. They had to vacate the rental by Monday and figured that could mean Monday morning. After a few hours sleep they packed up and left for Tennessee only to arrive with the phone ringing off the hook, an old expression from the previous generation of phones that were wooden, had a "hook" on the side for the listening receiver, separate from the speaking device.

Mary had just missed the two Beatty men when she arrived at their home in Portland on Sunday afternoon. Seeing that their place was vacant and obviously not being lived in, Mary started wandering around trying to figure what to do next assuming that she had been lied to again. Lies, lies, and more lies. It seems that her life had been one big one. This was nothing new for her and she now assumed that their story about being here over the weekend was to get rid of her. After all, this was the end of the weekend and she was here – and they were not.

Wandering Mary Margaret Rosa Rose Opinsky Dean soon became the attention of an observant policeman, Patrolman John Mullins of the Portland force. He approached Mary to question why she seemed to be wandering about his fair town. This, of necessity, cauterized Mary's thoughts when asked what she was doing and without a hitch she explained to the cop that she was merely on the way to the train station to buy a ticket to visit several girl friends that she had in Franklin. Her street experience had taught her that if you have motion and a stated, intended direction then the police are more apt to accept you and your presence at the time you're confronted even in shabby dress and with virtually no money in your pockets. It worked and both parted different ways.

Our reporter had picked up on the Pennsylvania connection and found a brother, Frank Opinsky, back there but quickly had the impression that the family connection was more titular then blood. The brother hadn't heard from or about Mary for years although he had no hesitation to assume the body that was found, the victim of foul play, was undoubtedly his long lost, crazy, rebellious sister. And no, he wasn't about to make a trip there to see (or to claim the body) to find out for sure.

As a fellow ace reporter, just younger, my hat goes off to this enterprising news guy. The bulk of this story went to press in the Tuesday morning edition of the *Tennessean* still two days before the local The Review & Appeal would be published and with a deadline that had to only have given fourteen hours from start to cutoff (time). I wonder what the police would have done or been able to do without this. And just think that if the janitor hadn't overslept, Franklin would have had another perfect murder. For reporting purposes, the trouble with perfect murders is that no one seems to know how to keep track of their numbers.

There was one thing ace picked up, a heck of a coincidence, that momentary placed suspicion back on our itinerant deafly mute hitchhiker. Mrs. Beatty mentioned she was pretty sure Mary had some friends in Mars Hill (reported and printed as Marra Hill),

North Carolina. This struck a cord with the police and our bootblack's claim of being originally from Asheville only 19 miles away. But Oscar was not deterred and focused more on the Burge place and had sent his men into the area to "ask around."

My secret singing friend, gossip columnist, and mentor, Walter Winchell, quickly picked up on the story, wrote a blurb for his 800 paper daily column and spoke of this on his syndicated radio show. Walter, a consummate showman used his unique Vibroplex Lighting Deluxe Telegraph Key pad to generate fast Morse code that he sent as 900Hz tones and could be heard as background as he started his broadcasts with his signature, "Good evening Mr. and Mrs. North and South America and all the ships at sea. Let's go to press!"

The Sunday night/Monday morning drinking party at the Burge's couldn't and wasn't suppressed and was used as the "probable cause" to coral most of the boarders, seven men and three women, and haul them down to the station for extensive questioning and to search the place, "notorious for bootleg whisky and other vices." In their roundup and on Oscar's first Monday morning visit, no one noticed Mary's coat hanging on the peg near the door, the one given to her by Mrs. Beatty of Portland, and the one not found on her cold, mostly frozen body.

Meanwhile this ghastly event had spellbound the community for three hundred miles around and many in the larger cities that carried the story. People couldn't get enough information, which fortunately was coming fast under the bizarre circumstances.

The knife wielding, ex-convict, carpenter, Lewis Smith's picture being interviewed by State Highway Patrol Inspector, James T. gill hit the front page on Wednesday but the corresponding headline pointed in another direction: *Murder Probe Points to 'Party.'* The article went on to say the police were positive the victim hadn't been killed where she lay nor had she been sexually assaulted. Actually they said, "criminally," but that's what they meant.

The search at Betty's was fruitful. Sheriff Ewine Frasier and the his party of deputies poured over "that place of ill repute" and came up with two bloodied overalls hidden under a pile of dirty clothes, a blood stained hat in Smith's room, a good portion of the floor in a first floor bedroom, reportedly Betty's, had been vigorously and recently scrubbed, a chair and footstool upstairs had been similarly scrubbed, and Mrs. Burge was in the act of cleaning one of the curtains in her first floor bedroom when the raiding party entered the house. The later seemed unusual since the remaining curtains in that room seemed never to have been cleaned and all the other curtains in the house were dirty and still hanging. Clean and unused (but not new) bedding was in evidence but a through search of the premises and trash out back could not wield what they had replaced. Lab technicians were immediately called in (and they were going to confirm that the blood found throughout was human and the same type as the dread girl's. They were also going to find human blood on the window sash in Betty's bedroom – that Betty's cleanup had missed).

"Knife Artist" Smith, who had slashed a dozen men including the former Sheriff Charlie Fok as the officer sought to arrest him for drunkenness and for which he had spent two years in the state prison, stated that the overalls belonged to Sherman Burge and that his blood stained hat was because of his own nosebleed that "got misdirected." Further he stated that he knew of little else since he had become very drunk early in the evening, somehow had retired to his room, and that's also the reason he called in to work "sick" Monday morning.

Sherman said the workpants were his but that the blood was from his work, slaughtering hogs. Sergeant T. J. Fife said the cuffs were muddy and the blood spots looked as if they had been washed. Meanwhile, Mary's body was prepared and about to be laid out at the Bethurun, Henry & Robinson Funeral home in Franklin where scores of phone calls had swamped the place let alone the press and dozens of onlookers anxious to attend the viewing.

Thursday's news: Fingernail tips, clipped from the hands of Betty and Sherman were under going tests. Sherman had no explanation for the blood stains under his nails. Five other men and two women were released but another woman, another boarder, was been sought. "Wide publicity of the case only hours after she arrived has aroused unusual interest." Only nine shopping days left until Christmas. Hundreds and hundreds lined the streets outside the funeral home to pass through and view the "wandering waitress" victim. Viewing hours had to be extended so that the crowds would not become unwieldy or rowdy.

Friday: Police feel that the human blood of the same type as the victim's that was found on the window sash in Betty Burge's bedroom was convincing proof that the murder happened there. One knife, believed to be the (or one of the) murder weapons was found and held by the police. Drainage of the establishment's outhouse was in progress in an effort to find other weapons that may have been used.

Our falsely detained 30-year-old hitchhiker was finally given a free pass on his charges, several sustaining and free meals, a free haircut, new-used black lace and comfortable shoes, a free hotel room for his final night here, and bus fare for the next leg of his travels to Nashville. He pocketed the fare and found a ride north with no trouble the next morning and hasn't been heard from since.

Saturday: Mary Margaret Opinsky Dean was laid to rest in a white casket in the "potters field" area of Mt. Hope Cemetery in Franklin, an area reserved for those dying without means or friends. Highway patrolmen and Sheriff Frasier served as pallbearers. Simple and brief graveside rites were conducted by Dr. H. R. Sherman, Chaplain of the State Patrol. A single spray of two dozen red roses from an unknown donor were left behind with the card addressed to

Mary Rose Dean, a donor and former client not visited that late Sunday night by the rain soaked Mary.

Ironically, Betty Burge (60), son Sherman Burge (37), Bob Woodward (22), and Lewis Smith (47) were arrested on first-degree murder charges for her murder only minutes before the thin crowd said the Our Father to conclude the services. And investigators were "tight-lipped" about new "evidence found" in the old Golden case that could implicate (and convict) Mrs. Burge. Investigators were expected to interview John Golden at the State Prison who was serving his fifth year of a sixty-year sentence in the clubbing death of his wife Sallie. The later served only to fuel the frenzy flames of interest in the case as the Holiday spirit and talk of Christmas seemed to take a back seat (but big surprises were yet to come).

Sunday, December 18th: The Williamson County grand jury was to convene January 9th just after the New Year but Circuit Judge Wallace Smith, worried about the abhorrent attention brought by this case, announced that an "extra" session would be convened that coming Tuesday. The Sheriff's department leaked the information that the knife found in the Burge's outhouse that was drained was undoubtedly the actually murder weapon used to slash Mary's throat four times with anyone of the strikes being a fateful killing blow.

Tuesday, December 22nd: In the matter of the "wandering waitress murder" the Williams County Grand Jury indicted all four. Trial was set for Monday, January 16th. The Post Office reported that the volume of mail piling up would be a record. Canada's official hangmen – know to the public only by the pseudonym of "Arthur Ellis" was to have his busiest day in office next February 22nd when he would hang four men in one day.

Arthur Bartholomew English was a Brit who became the infamous "Canada's Hangman" in 1912 when he was officially offered the job. He hung over 300 in his career. He used the pseudonym of Arthur Ellis as an honor to his uncle in England, John Ellis, also an executioner. The Crime Writers of Canada present an annual, prestigious literary award titled *The Arthur Ellis Award*. (Us writers know about those things).

Sunday, December 25th: the Burge's spent Christmas in jail. Rumors fly that the prosecution would seek the death sentence, a first for a woman in Tennessee. Rumors also abounded about a possible first hand witness that would openly testify at the upcoming January trial. Everyone wondered if there was going to be a Christmas, Sunday night party at Betty's Place in her absence. James David Bennett, 23 died in a Nashville hospital, a Christmas victim.

Thanks to these events, the year ended on a bang-up business note for the two industries, the newspapers and the gin mills. The over one-hundred Ben churches continued to struggle, mostly secretly, whether this should be an open-forum, public, sermon-topic in light of the continuing ground swell and seemingly tight grip on virtually all of the congregates' attention. Fortunately the holy-holidays gave the majority of them an excuse not to bring it up. Finally, it was reported that several recent editions of the newspapers were missing along with the cookies and milk at several of the Franklin's houses after Santa's visit Christmas Eve.

Thursday, January 6th: It was announced that the first tobacco sale for the year would be held January 10th and that last season was officially declared as a sell out, "with all prophecies and expectation realized" and with Williamson County leading all of middle Tennessee in the sale of burley.

The Post Office hit a peak for the last year's activity. Real Estate set new records for the last year and for December. Last month's bank statements were "rendered" this day, earlier than usual. And the *Circuit Court Selected Its Grand and Petit Jurors*.

Thursday, January 12th: "*Selection Of Jurors Poses Problem In Burge Murder Trial; State To Ask Extreme Penalty*." "...with 323 veniremen having been interviewed only 4 have been acceptable to 'both the state and defense.'"

Friday, January 14th: Appropriately enough, the new movie, *Ambush* starring Robert Taylor and Arlene Dahl opened in the theaters. "Blazing adventure and breath-taking romance in the days when the West trembled to the redskin's war-whoop!"

The pre-trial war-whoop heard locally was from one, John Golden, serving sixty years for the murder of his wife, Sallie. A murder Betty B Burge still denied being a party to. John said, "Now she'll get hers ya'll just wait and see!" Of course he said it much louder than I could possibly write here and he said it quite often and to anyone who would listen. Maybe it was more of a whoop-de-do or at least a whoopee. Anyways, John was a whooping it up these days.

Monday, January 16th: Trial. An estimated (and incredible) fifteen-thousand people, far exceeding every man, woman, child and maybe pets of the Ben, gathered outside the courthouse, the square and the nearby streets in the biggest confluence of people this community had seen since the Battle of Franklin with two armies, 86 years before. Some had camped out from the night before. Many had called in sick to work, and hundreds and hundreds of school kids had played hooky to share the throng's excitement. And the crowd were not disappointed on this the first day of the trial of the century since Bobbie Woodard had turned states evidence and was about to lay out the entire story with every gory detail.

Security was caught by surprise and vastly inadequate but the crowd, thank heavens, was a perfect example of decorum and civility. Without any other means of communicating with the outside onlookers, the judge overlooked the inventive, volunteer relay-teams set up to take court events back out to the court house steps with public announcements of what was happening inside.

Even all the dozens of news media couldn't have possibly fit into the courtroom if they had tried. Fortunately for the crowd, the year was starting out as one of the best on record, with "spring-like weather."

Despite the prosecution's earlier doubts and fears, Bobbie Woodard was a compelling witness. Tall and lanky even emaciated with a somewhat reputable, soldier past and a heart wrenching disease; Bobbie had a long face with large ears and with the right one much higher on his head than the left. This last feature, his soft enunciation, and his slight lisp hushed the courtroom to dead silence so that every single word of his eyewitness account could be heard and absorbed. His nervous exaggerations of talking with his overly long arms and thin gangly hands seemed to hypnotize his attentive audience even further.

As the trial wore on women brought their knitting, a few brought quilting stuff, men brought newspapers and many, having learned their lesson, came with chairs of all kinds. It would have been interesting to know the numbers of crossword puzzles that were completed during the ordeal or not. A good portion of the crowd had brought lunch bags or baskets even on the first day. The many pocketed or brown-bagged whisky bottles in evidence were overlooked. With the obvious traffic jams caused in the immediate area from the first day, the locals avoided the area for blocks around enabling the those in attendance who drove, in-the-street parking, converting all to temporary parking lots, anywhere in the vicinity of the courthouse. Some enterprising street vendors were gearing up hoping for a very long trial but things were moving quickly

January 18th: The largest robbery in the nation's history, \$1.5 Million in cash in Boston, temporary took the headlines from the trial as Betty and son testified, denying any knowledge of, let alone killing the wandering waitress. The Mississippi River was on a rampage, cracking levees and flooding everything. And the Mighty Mo, the USS Missouri battleship was aground in a Chesapeake Bay mud bank. Loew's theaters announced the opening of a new movie this Friday, *Battleground* starting Van Johnson and Ricardo Montalban. But by now, Wednesday, everyone just knew it, the trial battleground, was virtually over but the wagering outside that was hushed in the first days now peaked with a vociferous frenzy. The greatest odds favored 25 years for Sher, and 5 for Betty. After his first day of testimony, it was expected that Bobbie would go free.

January 19th, Thursday: It only took forty minutes for the twelve-man jury to decide. This was in contrast to the estimated last forty seconds Mary Margaret Rose/Rosa Opinski Dean had that ended her life. Grandmother Betty and perspiring son were found guilty of 1st degree murder and whisked away to the state prison in what was cited as the quickest trip from courtroom to prison but not before shouting their innocence to anyone in earshot. "I had never seen that woman before we went to the funeral home," protested Mrs. Burge. And for the first time in the history of Tennessee, a mother and her son were to sit on death row. The date for electrocution was deferred pending action on a motion for a new trial made by B. H. Hagey, defense attorney and assisted by another Nashville lawyer, Russell Green. Bobbie Woodard was set free.

Despite the rotation schedule for the 15,000 in attendance, but because of the brief trial, less than half ever heard a word within the courtroom. It was a week to be remembered and one not to be forgotten by the news guys who continue to bring up a little know aspect or two to this day.

This was the same news day that a Chattanooga 26 year-old Negro man, Eddie Lee Williams received the electrocution death penalty for slaying another Negro in an argument over a $1 dice game.

In a fourth floor cell in the same prison, a 75-year-old cellmate of five years, shouted as to be heard, "She had it coming to her." The inmate was John Golden and he added, "If she had told the truth in my trial, she wouldn't have been in this trouble now!" thinking that her death-row-cell was more ominous than the one she would have had for the last five years.

Betty and son's fast trip to prison rivaled virtually every detective and murder magazine's rush to print their particular version of *The Wandering Waitress Murder* story of Franklin, Tennessee. Numerous trips to interview the prisoners for follow up stories only found the "still innocent" façades with them and it would be many years before Betty voiced the bitter, "If my son had only properly taken care of things," to a cellmate that any sense of guilt could be inferred. But then, and those words were reported; they could have been interpreted in several ways without further context.

By Sunday, January 22nd, the story had calmed down and the Hiss story was headlined. Alger Hiss, an aide to President Roosevelt, was found guilty of lying in his denial that he sold state secrets to Communist spies and was branded a traitor.

Monday, January 23rd: A little, inside, two-inch single column article noted that the Burge Home was sold to a R. N. Moore, who purchased the "ramshackle" place for $1,750 to pay for Betty's attorney fees.

No one seemed to notice until Betty's house was inspected for sale, that a wrecking crew posse had attacked all the walls and flooring in Betty's bedroom sometime after hers and Sherman's arrest and the time she deeded it over from jail to be sold to cover her attorney's expenses. No one could say exactly when the tenants had left the place or that they did after this enterprising but criminal activity. And no one could account for their presence whereabouts or their obvious absence from the community.

Of course when he heard of this, Oscar, our Johnny-on-the-spot Police Chief, had to investigate. When he was there the last time before the trial, the three more or less evenly spaced holes going up the wall but then patched and painted between virtually every stud in Betty's bedroom were obvious since they were done on the sloppy side of good-carpentry. But Oscar assumed it was an attempt to insulate the Madame's personal room from cold or noise or both. When he found a few dollars tightly stuffed in one of the wall cavities that the destructive vagrants or thieves had missed, it was theorized that frugal Betty had used these "savings deposit" areas rather than any of our several Ben banks probably having Sherman patch up any opening once she had filled it from a deposit-drop hole. Maybe she slept better among her loot.

Whether the previous, flown-the-coop tenants had had a field day or maybe a messenger sent by Betty from jail to retrieve some of it to keep her attorneys happy, Chief didn't know. But with no other resources, assets or recourse, the house was to be sold to meet the Nashville's attorney fees.

In February, Hagey and Green, defense attorneys for the Burges had their motion summarily denied for a second trial. Hundreds but not thousands came to this hearing including the two Burges but they were swiftly returned to prison, almost as fast as their first trip.

Wednesday, October 18th: the headlines read, *US READY TO FIGHT – TRUMAN.* It was on the front page, above the fold, that Governor Browning decided to commute Betty and Sherman's death sentence, "in agreement with the State's Supreme Court's recommendation." A 99-year sentence was put in placed instead. In the same paper but a different page, Guy D. Hicks of Curtis Publishing Co., presented Gov. Gordon Browning with a bound copy of the Tennessee edition of their holiday magazine. Presents all way round except I can't find that the smiling Governor commuted our dice game slayer, Eddie Lee Williams from Chattanooga.

One of the fallouts from this ordeal was that the very apt Tennessee reporter who broke the case, who obtained mounds of pertinent information, who enabled the paper to usurp all others but who didn't get his byline or any credit for any of his stories and who had his name summarily deleted throughout by a jealous editor who replaced it with the ubiquitous "a Tennessean reporter" quit his job, joined a bigger paper and went on to win a Pulitzer. I wonder if he saw this coming when he was in the middle of the story and purposely misspelled Mary's name as Kopinsky (rather than Opinsky) in one of the later stories – to get (a little) even.

This experience, exercise, has taught me several things. First, even small towns have their secrets. Secondly, it's amazing what one can learn talking to lots of people about the one item or event, that proverbial skeleton in the closet that everyone remembers, has opinions about but doesn't bring up since it has more than less been swept under the town's history carpet. Thirdly, well, maybe that'll eventually come to me.

Oh my God, as if forgotten: Betty Burge, prisoner #43081 was transferred to General Hospital from prison on March 26th 1958 and died there on April 11th, 1958. Ironically her paramour, John Golden died the same year within months of her. There are no prison records that they ever communicated in any fashion despite the eight years they shared the same housing.

Tennessee Prison Records, Volume 74, states Sherman, #43080 had his 99 years commutation from the death sentence on October 18th, 1950 then to a "life sentence" on January 14th, 1967 only to be paroled two days later on January 16th. Sher died June 2nd 1975.

Both Betty and Sherman share the same shade tree in Mt. Hope Cemetery, in G Section. Some refer to Mt. Hope as the Great White Hope place because it butts up against the separate Colored, Negro, African-American, Black cemetery, the Toussaint Cemetery that abuts it to the east. Both tombstones, Betty's and Sherman's are just to the south of the tree with Sherman's being closer and slightly uplifted by its roots.

Betty and her first husband, John, share the same headstone. All three are only a matter of yards away from Mary Margaret Opinsky Dean just further to their south but within shouting distance. And yes, I'm sure that *Peyton Place* received much notice in 1958, especially compared to the little notice I mentioned earlier, of a Mrs. Betty B. Burge's funeral.

Oh – the third thing; it just came to mind. It's hard to understand why our criminals get so perturbed being "sent up the river" at least the Tennessee "river" since our state ranks third in the most unsolved escapee cases in the nation. Only New York and California with their much, much higher prison populations have more. For those in the know, "Do the crime in Tennessee – and still have a good chance at freedom!"

What's in a name?

The guy, Abram Maury, who had set aside the land for the town, a corner of his 640 acre tract, divided the 109 acres into 192 lots, six poles by twelve. Now I had heard of hectares, chains, yards, perch (for volume), and roods as arcane measurement standards but never poles. Let me save you some trouble of looking it up – it's about a half acre (6 X 12 poles), which I found fascinating. I wondered whose pole it was that was used as the criteria. It sounded like something biblical as if someone used Moses staff as the standard in their time.

I also found fascinating that the lower town land often finds the Harpeth River flowing through it (read: flood plain) so I wonder if there was a town-tax-write-off that Abe was able to take for his generosity. I know that's applying one of today's concepts to ancient history. But I'm probably the first to bring this up – the town's folk didn't seem to want to "look a gift horse in the mouth" (at least until the next major flood).

Abe gave 88 by 88 yards for the proposed town square with the two intersecting central streets, Main and Main Cross streets (the later turns out to be our Third Avenue). These streets were four poles wide. And it sounds simple (but simple's good) that the bordering streets (of the 109 acre town) were called North, South, East and West Margins. Our Fourth Avenue was originally named Indigo

Street because of a blue dye factory that was build there. I wish it had remained Indigo. Colorful.

The 192 original lots each cost ten dollars but were (only) chosen by the "draw." Since the lots were of good size, it is curious to me, and possibly Abe, that virtually all the early settlers build their homes on the street line (as opposed to the middle of the lot or set further back). This was undoubtedly, at least to me, a custom brought over from the "old world" but I gather "the" reason is open for much speculation. Another curious item is that the North, South, (etc.) Margins streets weren't exactly that since the town tilts a good eighteen degrees toward the west but that nestles it nicely into the crook of the Harpeth River (an inverted U).

Speaking of inverted river U's, Nashville has one too, on the Cumberland. Both battles, Franklin and Nashville were (virtually) fought in these several miles-crooks. I wonder if the Unionists leaders purposely positioned themselves and troops up against the river knowing that soldiers having no apparent "retreat path" would fight harder. I'm not sure but it's a thought. By the way, don't miss the tiny Fort Nashborough on the Cumberland on 2nd Avenue in Nashville. It's thought provoking as a sight to see. One wonders how daunting or defendable it really was or whether that space designated as such was the real Fort at the time. Something doesn't make sense. But I have to warn you, you don't visit Nashville, Opryland, or the Franklin without being fully intrigued to the point of wanting to live here. The area, environs, people, places, and history are infectious, mesmerizing, captivating, and endearing. You won't be the same having been here. Remember: You've been warned.

And speaking of settlers, which you could become, there's a wealth of stories here also but not where I'll be going anytime soon except to say that at one point there was present the expected frontier crudity where preachers had their hands full trying to dissuade their service-attending parishioners from spitting their chewing tobacco juice on their sacred floors (and pews) and at that same time the so called "education" was believed "for only the rich" (and certainly not for the common folk). OK, so that's an insertion, maybe not so subtle but I had to place it somewhere.

Officer Garner, Oscar B., *gendarme extraordinaire*, quiet, non-assuming Franklin Police Chief, was an interesting man. Squared off shoulders, still in shape, always in proper uniform crispy pressed, and known for the jaunty way he wore his cap. He was in the police business for most of the century up until the *Wandering Waitress Murder*, the Burge case. So when he stated that Mary's murder was the most heinous he had ever witnessed, he said a lot. Of course he was slightly bending the truth to "play for the press," something more or less expected. As a very young officer he had seen something similar that I'll tell you in a minute.

The second most mutilated, water decomposed corpse-case he had seen was the *Farmhand Wife Murder*, the Golden case. He somehow missed the John Burge one as did everyone.

In the second one he knew in his heart that Betty Burge was a part of that despite her lies, despite her denials, despite her not going to trial along with Golden or being convicted as he was. With a lifetime of experience and countless cases dealing with humans of all types and backgrounds, you don't sit across from someone looking them square in the eyes without knowing whether they were lying to you or not and John Golden wasn't lying when he said Betty helped. Of course that wasn't hard evidence but it helped drive the search for what was needed to convict the guilty son-of-a-gun sitting across from you.

In his gut he felt but never had expressed it to anyone that Betty's first John, husband, might have met an early death but was far from proving it especially since it was one of those many cases that the bureaucracy expected to be a pass-through, a no-case-at-all. Sure it was hardly important in the scheme of Franklin-things, no one really cared, old ailing John was going to die sooner than later anyways and the cost of a good investigation, prosecution and trial would have undoubtedly been big, big bucks. Besides, forensics wasn't a science yet.

But that's not the way young Oscar thought things would be when he first joined the force. Police have a sub-culture all of their own due to the circumstances of their job. Most look forward to the correct implementation of law, protecting and contributing to their community, seeing Justice is done and the other righteous things instilled in their well constructed upbringing by usually upstanding parents. It's kind 'a like the ideals of marriage that each partner expects (but somehow doesn't come to pass). Yes there are the cases when an early injustice spurts one on to the force, in an effort to right such wrongs in life by being an instrument of such for all others but I'm talking the majority. It may be a little ideal and also narrow as life goes but thank God it has a good beginning.

Oscar was no different – but, and there always seems to be a "BUT." When you work with humans, deal with humans, and especially when you are reporting to a political bureaucracy filled with humans and with much different human agendas than your ideals, there's the inevitable chipping away, bending, compromising, conflicting orders, and wrong, very wrong mistakes that are routinely made. Just to learn that our laws aren't perfect, that many in office that should – don't care, that many are corrupt, etc. is disheartened at best, is typically disillusioning, and washes out many.

The biggest, defeating chisel on one's ideal moral fabric is the realization that you will never be in the unique position by yourself or ever have the adequate tools to completely fulfill your original mission but will always and forever be subject to life's and the office's limitations. Any ten, twenty, thirty year, or more veteran of the force that comes through this process is not unscathed, some descend into the very opposite from where they started, but the ones that survive with at least some of that original idealism is a true unsung hero and deserves a medal. Oscar is one.

Police Chief O. B. Garner was only a rookie officer when the second most Franklin-earth-shattering murder case unfolded, the infamous *Truett Moonshine Case*. With the name by which it's remembered, not the last name of the Seventh District Jurisdiction Law Constable and moonshine still raider/enforcer, Sam Locke who was killed – that tells you a lot.

Hopefully I've shown you the insular effect of a small town. That outcome is exacerbated by other factors such as customs, history, and environment and lots more. Compare a small town on Long Island or on the outskirts of Washington, DC with a small town in the southern part of the Appalachian Mountains. Hopefully the possible differences are obvious. Now lets look closer to our home.

Tennessee is an oasis state. As the definition goes, it's fertile ground where the green stuff grows and travelers can replenish themselves, recharge their batteries, and re-supply, a place that gives relief from troubling or chaotic conditions that serves as a launching pad for the next foray. But the trouble with oases is that most times they aren't appreciated until much later in one's travel. When finally at an oasis, one tends to think, "Gee, if it's this good here – just think what it will probably be like out there." And one goes on. Such thinking seemed to be indigenous to our adventuresome forefathers and that's why many missed the haven and peace they had here in beautiful Tennessee.

Tennessee, with its knobs, bluffs, hollows, traces, pikes, plush vegetation and milder weather, is a sliver state nestled in the middle of many with several directions to choose. It's easy to pass through and doesn't have the defining obstacle-boarders to corral it's own. Walk into the early Michigan and see what your choices were.

TN was a frontier back when it was easy to cross after mounting the Appalachians or facing the Mississippi. Our extensive river systems including the Cumberland River promoted the "forward" movement. Many that crossed "the mighty Miss" only to face the less plush west, and then the Rockies often said to themselves, "Why didn't we just stay back in bountiful Tennessee."

Those that settled here had to be resourceful for themselves since this was far from the coasts, politics, even the enviable "progress" that seemed to motivate the East to distraction. For those that settled here, the quiet good life was treasured and outsider-dictates were resented. Crafts, arts, customs, the ideals and demeanors of the "Southern life-style" and it's independent, gracious living were nurtured. And one of the felt-freedoms that this included was access to moonshine as it became to be called after the Volstead Act, which was also called the 1920 National Prohibition Act that the federal government saddled upon the nation. Actually twice Congress passed this law, the second time on October 28, 1919, by a two-thirds vote of both House and Senate in order to override the veto of an insightful President Woodrow Wilson who knew the "people" better than the congress.

But way before The Volstead, Tennessee had tried to legislate its own prohibition as far back as 1838 as did Maine in 1846 and the mountain dew stills had to be hidden in the woods out of sight and worked at night to be less obvious. Laws were only good as they fit into or benefited the accepted life-style and to many a Tennessean the right to moonshine was god-given for those "so inclined." Therefore by the time of The Volstead, Tennessee had lots of practice at this back-woods industry especially considering that the state didn't begin to have the resources to enforce any such laws. The United States Fourth Census in 1820 showed that New York, Pennsylvania, Ohio, and (little) Tennessee had more capital invested and employed more men in the production of "spirits" than any other states in the Union.

So it's probably fair to say that the "stills and moonshine" was an venerable institution in Tennessee.

Then there were those individuals that accepted the law as it was handed down. Law is law and for want of a better reason, Tennessee is part of the US and if that government decreed prohibition outlawing the spirit-stuff, "Well that's just the way it is." The later more or less defines one Samuel Claybrooks Locke who happened to have ended up with the title of Constable, Seventh District Jurisdiction Law Enforcement Officer, a title that if written vertically would almost be as tall as Sam. Sam was a big man with a little wife that was very adapt at churning out children. Sam, a simple and religious man, started out his law-abiding career like Oscar Garner as a Franklin police officer. But before I tell you more about Sam, let me add the following:

Generally there are three things that "unfit" laws do; first they are like a burr under the saddle that doesn't go away but builds up umbrage (at least), second they call into question whether the powers to be had you in mind when they made such a law, and thirdly they present some unsavory opportunities to those so inclined, namely and in this case – bootlegging. After all, when something is "prohibited" and several providers deem to withdraw even if that something is still in vogue – up goes the demand and with fewer suppliers - it's called opportunity.

If you don't understand, bootlegging is quite an extensive industry once started. Galvanized pipes, boilers, nipples, faucets, holding tanks, bushings, jars, axes, shovels, hammers and hand tools, sugar, rye, meal, etc., some three hundred items needed to set up a still let alone the workers, guards, trucks and vehicles needed for transportation, the distribution network – all before the next level, usually a wholesaler, before delivery to the numerous "blind pigs," speakeasies, as Al Capone used to call them.

Did I forget to mention the sickles, axes, saws, hand tools, ropes, shovels, and the extensive labor needed to clear, build and then camouflage the still plants or as they like to be called in nearby Tennessee, factories, as well as the accesses and egresses as well as a handy escape route in the event of raids.

Before there was our unrighteous Sam, there was our Jesse who lived up on Deer Ridge Road. Jesse Richardson was a legend and the whisky-scourge of the infamous, badlands First District. Jesse was a Federal Agent that knew the law and his community, meaning every knob, bluff and hollow in those parts of our western county. Maybe it was prophetic to be called the "western" part. Jesse with his dog, Tater, his 1920 Liberty 10B open Touring car, and his Browning automatic 12 gauge shotgun took to his surrounds to rid the area of those god-awful-illegal stills whose output were killing almost as many of his neighbors as those made to feel extra good or to profit from them.

It you recall, the First District, quite disconnected from the rest of the Ben until (finally) the New Tennessee Route 96 was build, was just a piece down the road from the Nash, an insatiable market for the moonshine. Liquor somehow seems to go with music better than candles, food, or virtually anything else and like Memphis, home of the blues, we're talking Music City Nashville. Amen. Anyways, Jesse's home was so riddled with "warning" bullets by the erring, moonshining neighbors so inclined to meet the needs of Nashville, that he called it his Cheese Factory, good for it's airing qualities in summer, drafty in winter.

Jesse was good, an inspiration to Sam Locke. But Sam, who was concentrating on the immediate area surrounding the Ben, was better. Sam left the Franklin Police department in January 1925 because of three reasons. First he wanted to do something about the bootlegging that the PD seemed to be catatonic or at least helpless. Secondly Sam had become very uncomfortable with what he had learned while working for the department namely the involvement of many town and county officials in the bootlegging industry either directly or indirectly including bribes and payoffs.

With this pervasive corruption as he had named it, the attempts to control and eliminate this blight on the community were virtually ineffectual from the departments efforts yet he (and they) still had to deal with the lawless effects it brought to the streets and alleyways of Franklin. He knew he would have to align himself with the Feds and an agency out of the area, namely Nashville, if he was to be effective in helping to eradicate this plague. And that's what he did – with a vengeance.

With only two weeks orientation to the Federal-way of doing things, Samuel Claybrooks Locke was sworn in as Constable and sent back with the mission to "dry up Williamson County."

Sam was solid and a big man. He was never bullied in the eight years of schooling he had and was always there to protect his sisters if needed. His family inspiration was his stalwart pappy, grandfather, who Sam was named after. His dear pappy was a miner over in East Tennessee that is until the methane explosion and collapse of that particular coal mine when Sam senior was working one Monday morning. Thirty-two other miners died with his granddad and oddly or miraculously enough one of the canaries those dead miners had carried into the mine with them to be warned of possible methane was seen flying out of the mouth of the very same mine by some of the rescuers going in after the explosion.

Sam was young at the time but had spent some time with his pappy who always had time for the youngster when he wasn't working underground. Sam's dad had been working in the mine too but wasn't on that particular, fateful day and picked up his family and went west soon after they buried old Samuel vowing never to work in a mine again.

Young Sam missed his pappy and spent a lot of time in front of the only picture of pappy his parents had brought with them, the one where pappy was wearing his Sunday bowtie the one young Sam inherited (since his father, superstitious, was never going to wear anyways). That and the fond memories were the only things that Sam had left after his pappy died. After that Sam Claybrooks (his mother's maiden name) Locke pretty much wore a bowtie everyday including as part of his Federal job outfit. He approached his charge of cleaning up the county as a business and dressed accordingly even on the raids deep in the woods.

Sam had a double barrel shotgun but only shot it in self-defense and had never killed or even wounded anyone. In fact he shot it off on several of the raids to scatter the workers rather than round them up thinking it was the owners that were really breaking the law and most weren't at the sites. It was a costly penalty in fines and loss of product and equipment just to destroy the operation. If Sam was successful in putting the owners out of business, the workers had to seek other employment anyways. Hopefully the destruction of their stills and the fines were going to be enough for the owners to re-think this unlawful, insidious and immoral business. "So says the law," as Sam often said to himself.

In less than a hundred days, bowtie Sam had successfully raided and destroyed an astounding six-dozen stills dumping thousands of gallons of the rotgut stuff. Reportedly he cost the Ben's Truett's, one of the most successful and ambitious family-syndicates in the business in this area, over $14,000 in fines let alone the costs of the dozen or so stills and the confiscated, destroyed moonshine. The trouble with running the Truett's out of business was that they'd been doing it long enough, had a very large customer base in five states and had the resources to "keep goin."

The more he succeeded, the more support bowtie received for his work from Nash and not just from the agency but from the many concerned law abiding citizenry of his county. Nashville called him leader of the Williamson County Flying Squadron, named after an elite force of Bureau of Internal Revenuers numbering about four thousand, formed into special tactically efficient units that were sent into the most ardently defying areas, usually big cities. But whenever anyone referred to the "bowtie" there was only one person that came to anyone's mind.

The Truett name was no small matter in the area. Henry W. and Sarrah Clampett Truett came to Hickman Country, Tennessee from North Carolina and established a fruit nursery on their farm. A son followed suit and established the very popular Rosemont Nursery in Nashville while another son, Alpheus (1823-1898) settled in Williamson County also setting up and operating a nursery.

Alpheus built a very large, graceful antebellum home north of the Harpeth River next to his glass-enclosed greenhouse that was used by Union General John M. Schofield for his headquarters during the horrific Battle of Franklin in 1864. At the time, the Yankee paymasters set up their "paying station" occupying the Truett greenhouse with its glass brought from Philadelphia via boat, oxcart, and horseback. The fragile greenhouse and its nursery stock were predictably destroyed during the ensuing activities. Fifty-one years later, after the demise of Alpheus, the family received $395 in compensation for the damage/loss from the Federal government.

Edwin Campbell Truett (1850-1932), son of Alpheus took over the business, the Truett Floral Company, thought to be the oldest business of its kind in the state. John H. "Grandpapa" Truett, Sr. (66), had farmed, hauled rocks for the city and owned the very popular livery stable downtown, near the square on East Main Street. He had been a city alderman for eighteen years. Son Neely (or Neeley) Truett (35) owned Tom Shine's Poolroom, a grocery store on Main Street and various homes including a reputed house of ill-repute in Hard Bargain that he reportedly frequented. John's other son, John "Papa" Jr. was also a Ben resident. Key to the bootlegging industry, the Truett's reportedly controlled the sugar, rye, and meal that went into the whiskey production in this area.

On Friday, March 6th, Sam led a raid on one of Truett's most hidden stills that happened to be deep in the woods on John Sr.'s farm. Owner and his son Neely had feared such a raid or had somehow been tipped off in advance and had given one of their workers, Jim Kelton, one of the John Truett Sr.'s shotguns with the instructions that, "If'n the bowtie sees fit to raid our still, ya'll are to put him down."

Fortunately Bowtie Sam knew the owners of the still versus the workers that weren't of much interest and gave one of those early warning shotgun blasts as he approached in the woods. Sam had also brought armed help as well, just incase there was a "waiting reception" for them. This scared the bejeezus out of the several workers including Jim Kelton who took to the woods in the opposite direction, using the shotgun to plow his way through brush and shrub not thinking twice about any consequences for scratching the same. This scenario in effect foiled the first Truett planned attempt on Sam's life.

Saturday, March 7th, Sam stopped into *The Review Appeal* in Franklin to update the paper on his week's progress including the Truett raid of the day before. TRA liked to run a week's summary since it was newsworthy especially in the numbers Sam and his crew were racking up. Besides, this had great appeal to the more law-abiding citizenry in the area. The TRA has run, as long as anyone could remember, a first line in small caps right under there heading at the top and on the first page that reads: THE LIBERTY OF THE PRESS AND THE LIBERTY OF THE PEOPLE MUST STAND OR FALL TOGETHER.

After reporting in to the TRA and calling in his report to Nash, Sam had a bite to eat at the Elite Café. Here he decided to take in the show at the Franklin Theatre. It was Friday evening and Ma Locke would be about the business of getting the children settled for bed and Sam knew he had the opposite effect on his many kids that loved him dearly.

Ma Locke had married Sam young and had provided several offspring right in succession but not without an emaciating effect on her with the result she had the look of a woman twenty years older than Sam. But Beatrice Henricks Locke was from good stock, was of solid moral character, a carrying, church going mother, and a supportive wife. Sam loved her dearly, even more than he had loved his pappy when he was young.

The Zane Grey story of the "vast open spaces" brought to the movies, *The Last of the Duanes* starring the famous cowboy Tom Mix appearing with his Wonder Horse Tony, had just opened at the Franklin Theatre. Sam knew it would be inspirational feeling he was all about cleaning up the Williamson County Frontier just as Tom Mix did in the old west. All this was observed by the Truett's followers who reported all of Sam's movements to Neely Truett at his grocery store.

When Sam finally emerged from the show he entered his 1919 Ford car to go home and Neely, watching from outside his pool hall, signaled Jim Kelton and Frank "Red" Cain waiting patiently in a car borrowed from the Truett's Livery. With this, Jim and Red took off in pursuit of Sam. The March night, still winter even if only mildly cold and with only a half-moon but cloudy, was mostly dark.

John Sr. and Neely had roughly berated Jim after his failed job on Friday and had been assured, "It wouldn't be happen'en again boss." Both Red and Jim had been working at the Senior Truett farm for the last two years with duties mostly associated with the stills including transporting the booze for the Truett's and "other tasks for the masters." Jim had come on board, quitting his county-road-building job, after John Sr. had bailed him out for having been caught running his own still over in Maury County. Red was the designated driver for this next mission this Saturday night laid out for them by John Sr. and son Neely the day before.

Sam on his way home and looking forward to a quiet Sunday with his family was busy thinking about the Tom Mix movie and his pappy, so he didn't bother to notice the car that overtook and passed him carrying Red and Jim. He was still thinking about the movie when he pulled up to his gated property. The wooden gate was to keep the couple cows in as opposed to a security thing. And he was still thinking about the movie when he stopped his car at his front gate leaving the car running as he got out to open it for the quarter mile trek back to his very modest, one story, four room, wood clapboard home near Boyd Mill Pike on the west side of Franklin.

Red and Jim had been at the gate several minutes before Sam. It wasn't locked, only tied close. The five-foot high, eight boards by twelve-foot wide gate was just a convenient car length off the road. Well hinged to the right, the gate butted up again a four and one-half foot stonewall to the left overgrown with bushes. Jim had gotten out with the Truett shotgun and had hid just inside the gate behind the bushes to the left so that he would be in a relatively close proximity to anyone attempting to open the gate. Red continued on up the road, pulling their car slightly off the road and out of sight so that Sam wouldn't notice as he approached his home.

Sam's car lights highlighted every step he took in front of his idling car, up to the gate and rope loop that held it shut since the rusty latch had given up that job a couple years ago. Sam was just bringing up his arm to unleash the rope to swing the gate inwards when Jim stood up, gun ready and pulled the trigger unleashing a one pound, 12 gauge shell with 10 lead balls, all but two striking Sam broadside in the neck and collarbone area, also shredding his bowtie. Dead Sam was thrown off his feet and swung to his left back toward his car. Not that a second shot was necessary but nervous Jim let go a second shot almost immediately striking Sam under the right arm while still in the air.

Hearing the shots, Red came back with the Truett car to find shaking Jim standing in the headlights of Sam's car over Sam's body still pointing the empty shotgun at his dead quarry and spouting something like, "I done did it, I did it, I done did the deed…" It seems the pint of moonshine that Neely had given Jim, "to calm ye nerves," that Jim had consumed on the way here from town and without sharing, wasn't enough and Jim was "rooted solid like'n a deer in de headlights. Stand'n there, a shak'n and a talking his fool head off" when Red approached.

Red made Jim put the shotgun in their car, mostly "to get'um moving," and then the two of them for some unknown reason dragged Sam back to Sam's car, driver side and propped him up behind the wheel as if he had just arrived at the gate. This was no easy task because the Locke's older Model T had the old center door so that Red and Jim had some maneuvering to do even inside the vehicle.

Red, carrying Sam by the armpits, became very bloody in the process, hands, overhauls, and shoes. They had closed the car door but didn't even take the time to turn off Sam's headlights or ignition, which would have been difficult due to the center door configuration once someone was in the driver seat. And now completely terrified out of their wits, the two murderers returned to their car and "skedaddled" taking circuitous routes back into Franklin, more for their nerves then for the reason that anyone was following them or would bother to investigate the shots, even this late at night. There weren't any houses in proximity that someone might just pull back the curtain to look out and there just wasn't any other traffic on the road this late on a Saturday night anyways.

But within a half-hour, another dead body, friends called him "J.J.," happened to be passing by care of Sam's friend, neighbor and undertaker, Henry M. Cotton. Henry, in no particular hurry, was transporting J. J. Hardison from his demise in Nashville back to Franklin and watched the Locke auto as he came down the Boyd Mill Pike. Henry was driving his 1921 utility Ford Huckster, wood exterior and canvas curtains in the back giving privacy to J. J. and with its canvas door. Henry thought it unusual that what appeared to be Sam's black 1919 Ford Model T remained stationary before the gate, lights on, engine running and nothing happening.

Henry slowed even more as he was about to pass by. That's when he noticed that someone seemed to be in the driver's seat. Maybe after a rough week, Sam had fallen asleep before making it home through the gate. Then Henry thought that maybe Sam had tied one on and only made it to his gate. But then Sam wasn't a drinking man so that didn't make too much sense. When Henry thought about Sam's work, undoubtedly making many enemies, he became worried and stopped his vehicle, backed up, and decided to investigate this unusual setting. Henry knew J.J. wouldn't mind.

Even in the dim light, Henry didn't need to open Sam's car door as he approached because he could see through the driver's window the body with the almost severed head that was most certainly Sam's. Henry raced back to J.J., not a very responsive traveling companion, and quickly drove to the very next neighbor who Henry knew had a phone and together they called the authorities, the Franklin police.

Just as the police were getting in their cars to investigate, excited Jim, who had been "talk, talk, talk'n" the entire way, and quiet Red, who couldn't seem to wipe the blood off his hands on to his overhauls – no matter how hard he tried, were pulling into town only from the opposite way. One of those Franklin police officers responding was a relatively new recruit who had pulled night duty, Oscar Garner. (Now do you remember Oscar?)

Red let Jim off behind Neely's pool hall and continued on to the livery to return the car with the shotgun in the back seat. Jim was anxious to tell the news but more importantly, to collect his $500.

Neely was there, of course, and with many more – more than usual. It seems Neely had let out the word that "somethun's brewing" and that all his friends should come on down to his pool hall. And they did thinking that where there was a celebration to be had, moonshine had to be close by. This made for a good Saturday night.

Neely saw Jim come in, just standing near the back door and looking around. Neely laid down his cue and came right up him but Neely's out-of-character, purposeful walk caught virtually everyone's attention and a wave of silence met the smoke filled room. "W'ere ya been? I'm been a wait'n. How'd it go?" he said in rapid succession before Jim could respond. "Well?" Neely continued impatiently.

"Ah, well boss..." Neely, thinking the worst cut in, "Come on boy!" Jim came to a worker's attention and started over, "Well boss, the deed's done, the work's finished and..." Neely interrupted again,

"Where's the car and gun?" Hoping he was going to say the right thing Jim said, "Well boss, Red took'n the car back to the liv'ry an I done left your papa's gun in the back seat." With that, Jim didn't know quite what to expect but he didn't see Neely reaching for his wallet. Instead Neely turned to the small crowd with his back to Jim and said in a commanding, loud voice, "Leroy, lock the front…drinks are on me ya'll. We gots some celebrat'n to do." A concerted "Yea!" erupted and Neely walked away to get a drink at his own bar.

Jim struck around hoping he could finish "his business" with Neely but after a drink or two, that seemed to have no effect on him, he figured that Neely was about the business of spending Jim's promised $500 on drinks for his consort of friends and wasn't about to pay Jim, at least tonight. So Jim, virtually unnoticed in the crowd anyways, quietly left out the back door and moseyed home.

Maybe he should have questioned the "reality" of being paid that kind of money for anything this side of robbing a bank for the Truetts but his thoughts had been in the direction that with such funds, he could "vamoose" out of here and set up someplace far away. Anyways it didn't matter; he had no real choice. Red and he had been warned in the "shed" where the two Truetts had laid out the plan for them that "if'n ya don't do the deed, ya'll get the same."

On the way, Jim couldn't help but relive the events over the last several days, kind of like a fictional movie. About half way home in the dark and cold, it occurred to him that John Sr. and Neely had probably put Jim up to this as "his turn." There had been four other bootlegging killings in recent months, not federal men but kind'a related to the moonshine thing. Jim wasn't sure about any of them and no one seemed to be talking but reviewing Red's actions tonight, Jim started to think that the Truett's had used Red to do "the work" before this and now it was Jim's turn. He wondered if Red, who had become uncommonly quiet over the last several weeks, had been promised something for the driving tonight but certainly not the $500 Jim had. But probably "somethun thou." Jim finally decided that such thoughts weren't helpful, that he found himself in with a "very bad crowd" somehow, and he decided that he better forget everything to date to be able to "live another day."

Jim was in bed if you can call an uncomfortable canvas cot such, by twelve-thirty and promptly went to sleep, a deep sleep, probably one of having done a good job for the boss-man. Red wasn't so lucky.

Red had taken the Truett car back to the livery and was about finding any clean, or near clean rag trying to wipe the copious blood off his clothes, hands, steering wheel (from his hands) and car seat. He was concentrating so hard on these areas that he never thought to wipe clean the floorboard, door or handles in and out or especially his shoes. In fact he had already wiped his hands and arms red, which were now a mixture of blood and black car grease from the rags he had picked up to use. This even carried over to his face, now slightly bloodied and smeared with grease. This happened because he went to wipe off the sweat.

Yes, Red was sweating profusely this March cold night. Finally he gave up and started walking home getting there just before midnight. There he continued his cleaning ritual but with cleaner rags and water, after shedding his overhauls and shirt, ready to discard both even if they were a major part of his paltry wardrobe. The Missus was awake but smart enough to play being asleep and even smarter not to ask any questions. Missy knew in her heart that like all the colored who were trying to survive, her husband was just doing "what he had to do whatever that was" in order to get by.

Red knew that he wasn't going to be able to sleep this night and went out to the outhouse to retrieve a pint he had squirreled away in the rafters from the last pay. Well, not exactly the last pay. He had gotten his pitiful pay in cash and swiped one of the many pints he had been asked to deliver when no one was looking. It was suppose to make up for the pay the Truett's should have paid but somehow neglected to do. It was suppose to be there for his upcoming birthday but tonight became more important than any other considerations. Besides, this way he didn't have to worry about sharing. However he did lose some of the precious white lighting just after his third gulp when he found it necessary to pour some down his soiled arms and hands, to cleanse the final remnants of that night.

Neely's party lasted until light started breaking over the knobs east of the Harpeth, outlining the shaded poolroom windows like prison bars. Some were asleep in various piles and an inebriated but still-standing couple was trying to focus on playing one last game of pool. Neely was slumped in his special lounge chair back in a dark corner where he usually "could keep an eye on things" unobserved. Tonight, err this morning, his eyes were closed and his Hard Bargain, negress renter, Alma Ferguson, snoring softly in his ear, minus panties that she never wore anyways, straddled him.

When Neely finally woke up he knew the first thing he had to do was call his dad about the news but somehow there was a serious weight on him and an empty pint bottle in his right hand that he didn't want to drop because, from experience, he knew it would shatter all over the floor. He could hear his daddy now, "that bottle cost money Neel, and ye can't afford to lose money, every penny counts." With that Neely, who figured he had hired-help to do any clean-up and who had heard one too many lectures in his now adult life, let the bottle go. It loudly shattered as predicted but also served as a wake-up call to the revelers still left from the night before including the now responsive seductress companion on his lap. Neely was lucky because he wouldn't have made such an impression if the empty pint bottle had been in the other hand and dropped because his big, 110 pound, red bloodhound dog, Fetch, who measured 27 inches high at the withers was sound asleep on the floor on that side of Neely's chair. Yes, Fetch who preferred beer to moonshine, was more of less drunk too.

"Daddy?"

"Yes, Neel, who else is goin'a answer this here phone at this here time on a Sunday morn?"

"Daddy, Jim did the deed. It's done."

"I knows it Neel, no thanks to you. Where's the gun?"

"At your's livery daddy."

"Get ov'r there, get it cleaned and get it back here pronto. And make sure our boys don't talk. Da ya hear me Neel?"

"Yes, daddy. Right away."

While Neely was making his phone call, the Franklin police and Nashville feds were burning up the lines. And with all the other gossiping phone calls being made throughout the Ben, the poor Sunday switchboard operator was about to call for backup. It seems bad news travels fast and sensational news travels even faster – especially in a small town.

And bootlegging in the county was never going to be the same again. Of course, there was no telling, at this point, what was going to happen to the price of what moonshine could get produced.

The reaction in Nash was probably predictable and was extreme. No one realized the country's dichotomy better than the prohibition enforcement officers and now someone had killed one of their own. But first, Sam had to be put to rest and that happened the following Monday.

Regen & (Henry M.) Cotton was the funeral director and since Sam had been a steward at the Methodist Church at Hillsboro, funeral services were conducted there by the Reverends J. B. Cheek and J. L. Stevens and with the revenue officers that Sam worked with as the honorary pallbearers. The supportive, sympathetic attendance was enormous, estimated at over 1,500. The Independent Order of Odd Fellows and the Women's Christian Temperance Union of Franklin took part in the gravesite ceremony complete with wife Beatrice, Sam's five children, three brothers and four sisters.

By press time on Wednesday, dozens and dozens of local citizens were contributing to a Rewards Fund for the killer or killers of Sam. $1, $5, even $100's were reeling in. Already the amount was over $2,000 and the contributor's list was published in the Thursday TRA. Conspicuous in their absence on the list was any of the Truett's or their businesses.

The frenzy continued to heat up unabated. It wasn't Red but Jim, who after not getting "his due" after several days back at work, feigned illness, stayed home, got slightly liquored up, was caught up in all the excitement, and started "a-brag'n." Once that cork was out of the bottle, there was no going back. Word spread first among his peers.

Also by Thursday, Nashville had started reacting with an impact seemingly foretold by the unusual tornado that just happened to hit Williamson County the night before where "hillsides (were) swept as clean as if a powerful broom had been employed..." was reported. They probably meant "the knobs, bluffs, and hollows" for hillsides.

Plans to permanently add two federal Nashville men to be stationed in Franklin were being arranged. Washington had approved and was moving Fred Snyder, noted member of the (real) Flying Squadron of the Federal Prohibition Department to Nashville with many added prohibition officers in tow. Fred was given a virtual carte blanche budget to accomplish his assignment: Lawlessness especially related to bootlegging and moonshining was to be completely rung out of

Williamson as well as the murderers and perpetrators of Sam Locke's death were to be brought to justice.

By the TRA's March 26th newspaper the reward monies had grown to over $4,000. Next to the same front page article was the announcement that "Chautauqua Here – On June 5th."

Rumors of Jim's possible involvement had now reached the Franklin PD. Raids and "roundups" began in earnest as what was described as "boatloads of revenue men" descended on the area and "truckloads of suspects" were conducted back to Nashville.

It was the TRA that broke the big news with the headlines, "OFFICER STATES COUNTY WILL BE ASTOUNDED SOON," Thursday, April 9th. Flying Fred announced in this interview that, "in no county in the United States, with the exception of Williamson County, Illinois had the United States government thrown as much of the official strength into a prohibition fight and the suppression of lawlessness, as in has of recent days into Williamson County, Tennessee."

This made me look up Williamson County, Illinois because I guessed it held Chicago, but I was wrong. It's almost as far as one can be from The Windy City and still be in Illinois. (Excuse the pun). It's in the very southern part of the state close to Kentucky with Marion as its county seat. And I'm shocked because I remember the very first article of the Sam Locke killing in the TRA, on the last page, continued from the first, which prophetically had another "Contributed" article next to it titled: "Williamson County, Illinois vs. Williamson County, Tennessee."

At the time I didn't pay attention to it thinking it had to do with "sister-cities" of some such thing trivial thing. But it ended in the second last paragraph with the words, "Towards unfortunate Williamson County, Illinois, an alternately sympathetic and outraged nation has expressed itself, in no uncertain terms. The eyes of the hundred million people have watched for months the unbridled strife in Herrin as disregard for the law stalks the streets or lurks in the alleyways with murder and outrage kindled of factional passion." Isn't there a saying about people throwing stones while living in a county made of glass?

The TRA article of April 9th continues: "The officers furthermore stated that a local chapter of a secret order, implying the Ku Klux Klan, is doing the cause untold good. He (Fred) said that many, many times has the order's membership brought information which led to the ultimate arrest of law breakers and persons implicated in the liquor traffic in the town and..." Wow! Pandora only thought that she had a "box." Actually it was a pithos (jar).

In the preceding days, eighteen determined revenue agents had arrested over thirty men, "both black and white." Neely Truett was included "for possessing intoxicating liquors." Jim Kelton, "colored, was arrested but the charge against him (was) not divulged." The article continued, "Never before has there been such a grand number of arrests in this short a time as there has been in the past few weeks...(and) a number of 'higher-ups' will be arrested and no stone is being left unturned..." Twenty-five "sensational" arrests involving some of the "notorious bootleggers of the county" were made.

To demonstrate the seriousness of their actions, a small accompanying article laid next to this one noting how four revenue men had stopped at the Franklin's Elite Café with three prisoners "alleged moonshiners" for a bite to eat on their way to Nashville. When they returned to their car a bystander remarked, "If he was told to get in the car and go to Nashville, that he wouldn't do it" whereupon one of the revenue men replied, "get in and have a seat." When the fellow refused, he got a Colt .45 "jammed against his mid-section" and took a seat. The article concludes that forty or fifty people had gathered around by this time "and 'mouth-music' was in order." I'm just not sure what that later meant, the nuance is lost on me but I doubt the writer was talking about lilting or the Gaelic, Puirt a beul. Anyway, Tom Mix was still playing at the Franklin Theatre, in this new "western" town.

The citizenry were becoming more and more outraged that is the law abiding, prohibitionists, clergy, and even those who had something to hide. Meetings of concerned citizens started to be held. Franklin High School near the Carter House entertained over a 1,000 such people who listened to clergymen, city officials, etc., with the result that a citizens Central Law Enforcement Association to act in support and as an auxiliary to the "officially constituted authorities" was proposed. After which, and in a twist to their direction, Dr. Gus Dyer, a professor from Vanderbilt University in the Nash, spoke about the need to repeal the Volstead as a way to solve the problems. This at least confused many with several leaving the gathering dumbfounded.

As noted previously, the KKK started right after the Civil War, founded mainly by veterans of the Confederate Army who wanted to resist the north's idea of "Reconstruction." It was also a vehicle to oppose the "invading carpetbaggers and scalawags." Incredulously, by the 1920's, the organization included approximately fifteen percent of the nation's eligible four to five million men, i.e., white and Protestant. White supremacy targeted Negroes, Jews, and Catholics.

With the news that a "colored" man had killed a "white" man let alone a lawman with the development that the citizens were willing to put a "Central Law Enforcement Association" into the hopper, the KKK started coming out in force to increase its presence in the county. A Memphis Klansman, Mr. Curtis, visited Franklin and spoke at an impromptu rally about the ideals, principles, and benefits of a strong Klan presents in the community. Membership recruitment and "information for interested parties" were available. Meanwhile "visits" to the "colored" to instruct them on "proper behavior" was being conducted throughout the town.

Violence reared its head a few days after the recruitment rally when five, reputed Klansmen, driving a 1923, dark colored, Buick, Model 45 Touring car kidnapped and raped Miss Willie Williams, a young black woman out on Liberty Pike, whipped her with a switch, and left her there by the side of the road with the treating message, "get out of town Bitch - if ya know what's good fer ya." Fortunately, they didn't have free access to Jim Kelton or an "old time hanging" would have undoubtedly been had.

To understand and fully appreciate what events happened next, one must put themselves in the "colored" frame of mind, in this time frame, and in particular Jim's. With this in mind, if you didn't think Jim's thoughts about being "drawn and quartered" were real and probable or for that matter many of the "colored" residents feeling the same way with having no involvement other then their skin color – you've missed a lot including the point. Of course the Klan's activity played into the Truett's position, deflecting interest in their possible involvement and add to this the residents feeling that they had rights contrary to the prohibitionists who therefore would support the Truett's out of default.

Jim Kelton's "confession" came late afternoon, Friday April 8th. Two "federal" officers had kept Jim in their car for more than four hours under intense questioning, driving around Williamson County continually passing by the scene of the crime. Jim kept steadfast adhering to his "I don't know nothin' boss!" Steadfast until late in the afternoon when the officers stopped by Sam's gate to play-act the scene as they felt it happened. One officer unlocked and stepped behind the gate lowering himself down out of sight. The other approached to unlock the gate with the first jumping up with his pretend shotgun, "BAM…BAM" proceeding to place the gun against the stone wall to the left dragging his partner, now on the ground, to their car and then trying desperately to wipe the supposed blood off his hands, arms and clothes before retrieving his gun.

Without another word the officers entered the car and started toward Nashville. Sweating profusely on this mild Tennessee spring day, Jim burst out, "Boss, stop, de car boss, stop de car! I'll tells ye everythin." And they did and Jim did.

The resourceful officers had gotten the scene mostly right but missed the accomplice, the livery car, and the involvement of some of Franklin's prominent citizens, the Truett's. Then they sat back spellbound as Jim unfolded the bigger picture of bootlegging in the county implicating at least a dozen other citizens and county officials to boot.

Of course it made sense that someone or some of means had to be involved for a man of little means to have a shotgun let alone lack transportation to and from the gate in order to pull the murder off and escape undetected versus being picked up walking back in to town with a shotgun. Then there was the motive, Jim had lost his still and was only working for another. Of course the promise of a hundred dollars to a man of no means made a lot of sense.

The Tennessean: "Immediate following Kelton's confession Nealy Truett, John Truett Sr., Frank (Red) Cain, J. M. Martin, Wallace Corson, Mays Mangrum, Newt Martin, Liza Parrish, negro, Eta May Murray, Nannie Gosev, negroes, were brought to Nashville by federal Officers for questioning…Neely Truett, Kelton, John Truett Sr., and Cain were arrested on charges of assault on Locke. At the same time warrants charging conspiracy to violate the national prohibition act and owning and operating illicit stills were served on J. M. Martin, Wallace Corson, Mays Mangrum, John Truett, Sr., and George Reese. Those arrested refused to talk."

The newspapers were selling out editions, reporters were scampering everywhere, the rumor mill ground out "more than one could fathom," the price of moonshine shot up, the blind pigs (speakeasies) extended their hours, discussions over the pledged reward monies hit fever pitch, the clergy clamored for calm, the Franklin Police Department geared up for "civil unrest," the basis of a vigilante "committee" to free the Truetts got under way, death threats abounded, the "colored" were worried about walking the streets, Locke's widow went public telling the "Story of Assassination," the prohibitionists went to marching, prophetically the salacious Dante's Inferno with "See Hell…(with) Thousands of uncovered souls floating through space each form visible for his or her particular sin!" opened at the 5th Avenue Theater in Nashville, Will Rodgers, America's humorist plugs Bull Durham chewing tobacco in the newspaper…two bags for 15 cents, and one Williamson County Sheriff decides it's time to resign and with probably good reasons.

Sheriff Wallace Crockett, publicly denying any culpability or involvement in the "county's liquor ring," stated his reason for resignation, "I have co-operated in every possible way with the federal officers who have been in charge of the investigation since the day of the murder. I have given them every particle of information I secured, have done all they asked me to do and have spared no effort, day or night to assist them.

"However a rumor has persisted that I have not co-operated with them at all, and in almost every issue of the Nashville papers it is stated that whatever has been accomplished in Williamson county has been done by federal officers unassisted...I am aware of the fact also, that enemies of mine in the county have been most interested in trying to find something in my record to criticize. No charges of official misconduct have as yet been made, and I here deny that I have ever been guilty of any such...Rather than be subjected further to the slurs and insinuations that have been cast upon me from certain quarters and rather than continue together with my family in the state of mind that we have been in for the past several days, I have concluded that I had much rather be a private citizen." Sheriff also offered that a number of citizens had "called upon him" last night stating that a group of Truett's friends were organizing a party to attack the jail and free the prisoners, prompting the Sheriff to return the Truetts back to Nashville.

We're here talkin' bout trouble,
Real trouble with a capital T
And that rhymes with B
And that stands for the Ben,
the Harpeth River City.

The Williamson County grand jury returned "true bills" charging first-degree murder against Jim Kelton, John Truett, Sr., and Neely Truett on April 17th. One was not returned against driver Red Cain but it seemed likely that he was receiving clemency in return for testimony against the other three. The trial was set for September at the Court House in Franklin. Meanwhile the feds vowed to conduct more raids until the county was completely cleaned of the bootlegging plight that some papers reported as "blight."

One such raid over in our infamous First District, near Jingo near the Davidson (Nashville) Williamson county lines was typical. On

Wednesday, July 24th three federal officers working out of the Custom House in Nashville located a large steam-still. Four men were working the factory in a hollow. The moonshiners had a team of mules for hauling wood and the whiskey. Three of the men were captured in the raid but the fourth made good his escape. The raiders found country ham, loaves of bread and canned goods meaning the foursome were "fixing to be there for a good spell." The still and its contents of approximately fifteen gallons of whiskey were destroyed along with six thousand gallons of beer, a virtual liquor river.

On top of the nearest bluff, officers discovered another seventy-five gallons of whiskey ready to be shipped out, which they destroyed with axes and shovels. The next day another steam-still was located and destroyed in the very same vicinity. And on the next, the officers laid in wait at still another dormant still and sure enough, with the other stills out of commission, four men soon came to "crank it up," Those four were captured and the three thousand gallons of beer found at the scene was destroyed. The stills in the First District woods seemed to be propagating and popping up faster then the Tennessee Nuttall Cottontail (rabbit).

Jim was in a whirlwind quandary. He knew too much, probably told too much, fingered too many people, feared for his life even if he was to get out and didn't know how to "play things." He tried to minimize things with, "Yous knows how a ignorat nigger is when he's got dat stuff in'im!"

"Who gave you the liquor?"

"Master Neely."

'Were you drunk?"

"Na boss. I wasn't zackly drunk, I jes had enough of dat there old licker to keep me from keerin' about anythin'."

Another problem was that he knew, or at least was pretty sure that the shotgun belonged to John "Papa John" Truett, Jr. and Jr. had never treated him badly so he was inclined not to tell this but to put the gun in John Senior's hands where he felt (the blame) belonged or at least Senior's house when in fact he had, as instructed, picked up the gun from Junior's house. Yet another problem was how the questions were asked of him, "Where you paid by the Truett's to kill the Constable?" Good intention but wrong question that he answered truthfully, "no" but without the $500 offer in the mix that put the onus back on him. Jim's waffling served to defeat his testimony. This and the color of his skin opened wide the "door of innocence" for the Truett's by any competent (white) defense lawyer doing his business before a (white) judge.

The powers-to-be decided to try Jim first and the Truett's after. Jury selection started with five hundred names on September 21st but by the 24th and 200 veniremen interviewed, only two jurors had been selected. By October 1st only six jurors had been chosen, a possible indication of the uphill battle for the prosecution. Meanwhile the curious crowds were building by the hundreds. October 8th, only nine.

October 13th, after an hour of evidence, speeches, and fifteen minutes with the jury, the verdict of first-degree murder "with mitigating circumstances and a recommended sentence of life imprisonment" was handed down on Jim Kelton in the "most notorious murder in the history of Williamson County." The prosecutors had hoped for the death penalty as ammunition going against the Truetts. Interestingly, the Attorney General prosecutor's last name was Neeley.

Jim Kelton's second "four hour dilemma" came during the Truetts' trial when the defense grilled him unmercifully (even without the merciful benefit of a pint). Reportedly that wasn't the case among the two thousand in attendance, at lease the ones outside that could "sneak a swill or two."

More details of the $500 were introduced. When Jim and Red had been taken into "the shed" on the Truett farm by John Senior and Neely, John Senior conducted the "meetin'." The plan was to have the other members of the "liquor ring" help with the $500 to Jim and also to blame the deed on Ellis Martin, owner of one of the many stills that had been raided by "bowtie." It was unclear if and/or how Red and Jim were to split the money, seemingly not a concern for the Truetts. Unfortunately, the already free and now cavalier Red's testimony was by no means a slam-dunk for the prosecution.

On October 19th the Truett's blunted the prosecution by "standing on their constitutional rights of refusing to answer any questions." The counsel clashed frequently over this alleged "right." The popular, prominent Franklin businessman, John T. Senior, sitting (white) prim and proper before the jury of (white) twelve men even denied owning any stills, much to the chagrin of the prosecution. This was repeated over the next three days.

On Friday, October 23rd, Judge J. C. Hobbs charged the jury but with a "twist" or two. First, the jury was to (re)try Kelton's guilt or innocence as the basis for the two Truetts guilt or innocence. Secondly, they had to disregard any evidence of bootlegging except as it contributed to motive. Thirdly, "one accomplice cannot collaborate the testimony of another. Forth, the jury was not to take liberties in supposing or inferring what the defendants would have answered in reply to questions about the liquor traffic of the county…

After twenty-seven hours of deliberation, the Saturday headlines of the *Tennessean* read: TRUETTS FREED, NEGRO GETS LIFE IN LOCKE KILLING. None of the Locke's family was in court when the verdict of acquittal was rendered. Next to this front page article was a picture and the news that "The Rt. Rev. Arthur S. Lloyd senior suffragan bishop of New York, will preach at the morning services Sunday at the Church of the Advent, Seventeenth and Edgehill avenues."

Seven months later, John Truett, Sr., John Truett, Jr., and Neely Truett were tried on violating the Volstead Act. Neely and John Jr. pleaded guilty and received two and four years. John Senior received a $2,500 fine. Other defendants like Buttermilk Thweatt were dismissed with fines of one cent. The Volstead Act was repealed by the Twenty-first Amendment on December 5, 1933. Jim Kelton died in prison in 1934.

I was returning some of the microfiche to my favorite and helpful Librarian, "Dorris-with-two-R's Douglass-with-two-S's" (that's one whole name), resident since 1959 when I overhead her talking about a bo-bettle with another patron in line ahead of me. I had heard of the aggressive cotton boll weevil, the scourge of the south but not this new predator. Since "Dorris-with-two-R's Douglass-with-two-S's" is easy to talk to, I asked.

I like bringing merriment to people, especially the people I like but I hadn't expected the outpouring from the expected-quiet librarian type. But then, who better to break the QUIET library rules than a librarian. When "Dorris-with-two-R's Douglass-with-two-S's" was through laughing she said, "You mean Bocephus."

"Well I guess so. It's the one that attacks the funny bone and not the cotton."

Calmer now, she asked, "Have you ever heard of Hank Williams?"

Proudly, I said, "Why of course. He's a legend and died in 1953," I added just for flare.

"Well I went to school with Hank Senior's step daughter, Lycrecia Sheppard Williams. Hank Junior got his nickname from when his famous father looked into baby Randall Hank Williams' cradle and said, 'Bocephus. That's my Bocephus.' And his name stuck. Why I even saw Junior in diapers but that was awhile ago."

It seems there was a TV ventriloquist dummy named Bocephus at that time. That touches my own funny bone and suddenly I had new visions of Hank Junior that weren't going to go away easily.

In talking about Alpheus Truett, I had mentioned that their greenhouse and nursery stock had been destroyed during the Union occupation of the Ben during the infamous battle and that fifty-one years later, after the demise of Alpheus, the family received $395 in compensation for the damage/loss from the Federal government. That compensation was more than that received for the decimation of the Ben's historic Carter property, which Fountain Branch Carter meticulously recorded.

It started in 1863 when the Union General, Gordon Granger occupied Franklin with 8,000 troops. Granger felt a fort on the north side of the Harpeth River, with a clear field of cannon fire south would be a strategically sound defense especially as regards the rail line. So Granger set about building a fort and had his troops remove the thirty acres of poplar, Elm and other trees that happened to be on Fountain Branch Carter's land. Enraged Carter set about measuring the axed stumps and recorded each to determine his actual loses.

But the losses didn't stop there. Occupying troops will be what they are and over the next several months, Fountain Branch lost four large mules, one mare, six hogs, ten large brood sows, fifty-six small port hogs, twenty-one head of beef cattle and one fine boar. Yes, it's probable that the Union troops ate well. Unfortunately, FB also lost two large barns, five houses, a cotton gin house, and a stable as well.

Then came the rag-tag army silently north up Columbia Pike even pass the bivouacked Confederate Army of Tennessee. General Jacob D. Cox commandeered the Carter house for his temporary headquarters. They occupied Franklin starting immediately to build substantial breastworks suing shovels, hands, lumber, timber, and anything they could put their hands on. Carter lost his cookhouse along with almost 4,000 feet of plank that had once enclosed his yards and garden. Eight plows were piled on to the fortifications.

After the five-hour battle, thousands of corpses, human and horses, (and dozens of rabbits) littered the land with corresponding Union and Confederate troops burying their comrades where they lay making the land unusable for tilling, planting, and farming let alone the unspent ammunitions and soldiering gear of all descriptions were left where they dropped. Of course there was damage to the dwellings and outbuildings left standing. Some of it can be seen today. And the breastworks, significant and miles long, was not dismantled but left behind as the Unionists fled north to join their comrades in Nashville. Written in longhand, FB's exacting list, several pages long and totaling more than $20,000 was submitted to the Union for reimbursement in 1865 following the war.

Carter died in August 1871 without being paid and another fifteen years would pass by when the twenty-one year claim was acknowledged and discharged with a check for $335. Divided among the six surviving Carters, each received $55.80.

I wish I could take credit for this information but another talented, readable, news and columnist guy, Hudson Alexander, has to be thanked. Thanks Hudson – don't stop writing.

There are two theories to arguing with a woman. Neither one works.

- Will Rodgers, American Humorous

What's In a Name – That Does Last Forever?

The county of Benton Tennessee was originally named for Thomas Hart Benton. Benton was important to me. He gave me my first sex education thing. Well you didn't expect the parents to be on top of that – did you? No, no pun intended.

I found Benton in one of my parents old books on the bottom shelf of the living room book cabinet back in the bungalow – you know, the bottom shelf made higher for tall books. It was an art book, *Art In America* (or something similar) that maybe my parents only looked at once, when new, and that had to be a long time ago. Maybe it was a good intentioned wedding present, shelved.

Benton was featured on the cover of *Time* magazine (1934), one that I had seen earlier on the bottom shelf in with the tall, hardbound books. It caught my attention because my parents didn't subscribe to *Time* or any of the other many magazines except two: *LIFE* and *Saturday Evening Post*, which had yet to be delivered on a Saturday (that I could notice and that bothered me - as a kid). I wished they had a subscription to *Popular*

Mechanics or *Scientific American.* (I know, they're expensive). Nana got *Field and Stream* and *Reader's Digest.* In RD she loved to read the regular feature, "The Most Unforgettable Character I Have Ever Met." She was mine.

Both (of their – my parents') magazines were a little "artsy." I have this on good authority, theirs. SEP was because of Norman Rockwell who some how (seemed) to paint all the covers. Now that had to be a prolific artist. And *LIFE* was artsy, not that I would know, because mom always caught the magazine delivery and went through it cutting out any "artsy" pictures (girls in bathing suits especially bikinis, pointy bra ads, Bettie Page pin up Queen, B-25 bomber nose-art, Yvonne De Carlo, Rita Hayworth, Liz Taylor, or Brigitte Bardot anything, etc.) before it was placed on the family couch for all to see – me mostly, even thou I wondered if it had anything to do with dad too. Na, he was never home – and could have picked one up at any of his many A & P stores in the, his, Scranton area, even for free (leftovers/returns). We didn't have a coffee table for such items being on the poor side of life – I, just not knowing it, was only a kid.

Yes, the mom-first-thing was a challenge and I was determined to catch the postman delivering the weekly magazine before mom. I really couldn't figure out how she did it, maybe had the postman deliver it next door to our friendly, neighbor-lady, Who-Who (that was her name) – to be picked up from her later? But she was lucky, I just had so many better guy-things to do that she got off (and always got the magazine first). Oh well – my first bout of censorship (but not the last).

OK, she was good. I never saw the August 1948 cover until I was visiting my good buddy next door. And the October 1956 just disappeared!?! (It's good to have good buddies next door – with an

uncensored *Life* collection in the cellar).

Benton was from Missouri, the "show-me" state. I liked that part immediately. He was born in Neosho. The reason I remember the state's logo and his birthplace was that I had put them into my memory as Me-No-Show. From there, the real name and logo wasn't a big leap. I'll look up his B-D dates in a minute.

Tom was classified as a Regionalist American Muralist. That title was too much. I just pinned him as an awesome painter. His painting sucked you into them. You didn't have a chance. And his figures had movement to them plus every one of his paintings told a story, especially his *Persephone*. I never understood the name or did I care. In fact I didn't look at the name the first fifty times I went back to the painting and according to the description, it was life size, 6 foot by 5-ish. And the real name, above, wasn't learnt until years later because in mom and dad's book it said the name was, *The Rape of Persephone*. That made me go back behind the haystack in the field across from the tree by the stream and the lecherous farmer who was sneaking up on what's-her-name – another fifty times.

The foliage was so real, moving in the slight breeze. I felt sorry for the mules hooked up to the wagon who could do nothing but wait. Her parts became beautiful even if I thought she was kind of ugly. To think a woman could be so uninhibited to stretch out and relax like that. Where were the mosquitoes? Where were such women? Missouri? Was there fish, Brook Trout, in that lovely stream next to her? The guys said that old men lost their sex drive, maybe not farmers? Anyways, when word got out – no other woman was going to face the consequences of being so "open" and free. Damn shame! Did the artist have to feel what he painted? Live the scene? I just can't believe how real that foliage was - OK, the parts too!

College brought back all these memories when we studied the Greek myth, the one that accounts for all of our seasons (and their changing) thanks to Hades, lord of the dead, and his lust for Persephone. I was glad I saw her first. The painting was better than the stoic myth.

There was another painting in that great book that I took, upon looking at it, to be attributable to Benton. It was an awesome fight, boxing painting. It caught my attention because after we got our first TV, oval and greenish picture (versus black and white that it was suppose to be), dad drove hard to get home Friday nights in order to see his favorite thing, Friday Night Boxing at ten o'clock.

Tie off, shirt and vest open, hopefully home in time to see the younger sister before bed time and to have a few minutes with his lady, mom, before getting a cold beer from the frig and settling in to "his" chair in front of the TV for the fights. Mom knew best not to bring up any problems when dad first got home and yes, I was usually (at least) one of those. I know she always was threatening, "Wait until your father gets home," but I quickly learned (being a quick study that I am – except for painting of naked ladies in distress, whether the ladies knew it of not). So I usually pulled up a kitchen chair near his special one to watch the fights too. He became visibly excited when they came on the screen and even more animated as each round passed, adamantly vocalizing coaching instructions even it they were never heard ring-side. He always had picked his "favorite" by the second or third round and cheered him on to the end, whichever way they went.

Actually I thought that two grown men in a confined space trying to beat the crap out of each other was stupid. What I was really watching was this man called Dad. I wanted to learn more about him, what made him tick, what he did, thought, and what he thought of me – at least before he learned what more I have done (or undone as the case might be. I was good at both). But dad always paid more attention to the tiny oval screen or an older male companion that came by to enjoy the fights with him and could talk the fights-talk. It didn't even matter that I would second (emulate) his excitement when something happened in the ring.

The fight painting, called *The Stag at Sharkey's*, and I have no idea what that means or why it was named that since a Sharkey wasn't any famous boxer that dad had ever mentioned. And Benton's dates are 1889-1975. Opps, I had missed his recent death for myself let alone the county for which it was named. Wow, he was old. Wait, how could the county be named in his honor? To the library we go. And it wasn't.

The man for whom our painter was named, Thomas Hart Benton, was his great-uncle who happened to be live just down the road in Leiper's Fork (once named Hillsborough I think). But when uncle's politics (anti-Jacksonism or being opposed to slavery or something) turned against the feelings of the locals, the Tennessee Legislature passed a bill that kept the name for the county but made it clear that THB wasn't the honoree but (and they must have searched for this) a local Benton County resident, David Benton, was the "real" exalted one. Don't bother looking up David unless maybe he had something to do with Benton Harbor, Michigan or whatever.

Wait, there's a THB quote that may have explained things: when the congressman was asked if he know Andrew Jackson, he replied, "General Jackson was a very great man, sir. I shot him, sir." There's got to be a good story there but I don't have time right now. We, the Ben, have another problem.

Another problem called - yet another flood. 1979. The year's not necessarily starting out well. For a town that has a mean temperature of 72° F, Tuesday January 2nd saw 11° with Wednesday getting seven degrees colder only to be followed by several days of rain causing flooding all along our Harpeth. Fourth Avenue North, Mt. Hope Streets, as well as Lewisburg Pike all saw traffic stopped in the early night hours. This was after a near record-breaking December rainfall month. Fortunately or unfortunately per your perspective, winter kicked in again and the flooding didn't develop as far as our 1972 flood. Ironically several suffered the weather to take a picture by the water pumping station on Lewisburg Pike which said, "No Vehicles Allowed," a sign that was all underwater except those three words. Chalk it off to small-town-humor, I guess.

The first week also saw another story, the deaths of three locals probably linked to bad moonshine. It'll be interesting to see where these investigations go.

Other than that, the Chamber elected eight new directors, our Aldermen are considering the pros and cons of a new plaza east, by the I-65 interstate, and the local bank promoted three to their officer status. And the wee-little wheels of our wee-small town continue. Oh hum. Life is good (here).

Then our competitor, TRA, carried one we didn't, the notice that they're going back to two issues a week. Damn, that could hurt us in the long run. We should think big – the Ben continues to grow. Franklin not only is attracting hordes of new people, it has annexed over 3,000 acres in the last few years. With a little effort and ad-salesmanship, we could go daily even replace the Tennessean locally with a UPI, AP, or even a Reuters hook up for the national and international stuff we don't have. I wonder how much they cost. I'll have to try and talk to Lance again, if he's not out (again).

That moonshine thing has been happening as long as anyone can remember here. Not as a tribute but more for an educational-informational matter, the County Archives have built a small replica, pseudo-still, in their lobby "for all things Williams County."

Being a little surprised, like finding some wax figures caught in the act of sinning in the Catholic Museum, I asked the receptionist there and that's where that comment came, "The moonshine thing has been happening as long..." She also added, "Just a few years back, my nephew couldn't get his dog to wake up and called his first cousin the Vet. 'Bring him over,' cus said. So Joe loaded the eighty-seven pound hound dog into the pickup and took him to see his cus. 'He's drunk!' was the diagnosis-es. Ya see, he had gotten into someone's sour mash back in the woods behind my nephew's house."

The Ben was home to the last bonded distillery in the county, the White Maple Distillery. Federally licensed, they opened operations in May 1901 with a whole two barrels a day production although they had bigger intentions, the warehouse could (reportedly) hold a thousand barrels. Tennessee total prohibition began in 1910, the last year of the distillery, and about ten years before the Federal Volstead Act (National Prohibition Act of 1919). But that may not have been the excuse for closing since the neighbors had had it to the point that they wanted it closed even if the Womack Brothers, owners, were going to supply them all free liquor, which never happened (or was offered).

It seems the sour marsh process gives off a putrid stench that stays in the air unless a regular gale comes along. And if that isn't enough, the business minded Womack brothers had a fair amount of insufferably noisy, squealing hogs penned there that took to the fat-producing sour mash residue like pigs. And the word is, that there's nothing worst smelling than a herd of drunk and fighting, smelly hogs cutting up something fierce at feeding time. Of course those same neighbors probably never lived downstream to the world's largest glue factory and nearby tannery when the creek was low and the effluent rich water only crept by at a snail's pace (like it did back in the G).

Yes, it ain't just a rumor, there were seven saloons on Main Street stretching up to and including our dear Public (round) Square by 1898. But if that number impresses you, there were 1.4 more in the allies and byways for every one of those official places in this little town only to be increased to 3X's when prohibition took place.

Reportedly, and we news guys seem to say that a lot, Hillsboro Road was the winner with four in a row, Shamrock Grill, The Coffee Club, Little Texas, and another that everyone seems to forget let alone getting or having been there. It may have been called The Chantilly Lady or such. They're all next door to one another, at the edge of town, toward Nashville. Well known to folks here and there and the challenge was to visit all four and still make it back home to Nashville (or the Ben). The next-day-test was whether you could accurately tell your companions what bluegrass songs the Fruit Jar Pickers were playing at the last place (whatever-its-name). If prohibition ever comes back I hope that exempt Friday nights.

Somehow the elimination of prohibition didn't seem to deter the local practice with these ally-shops continuing and being especially popular during the WWII days. Remember, Nashville was a rail-crossroads for the country so we saw our fair share of the "boys" in uniform.

As an addendum, the enterprising Womack's, having been educated by the likes of the infamous Jack Daniels of Lynchburg, Tennessee, owned one of those seven on Main as well as another in Nashville (but I can't get confirmation of how may of the speakeasies they also owned or were partners). Their place, the White Maple Saloon closed on May 23, 1903, the last legal drinking establishment on Main until Bennett's Corner (pub) opened in 1984.

Events put an earmark on this years April. Earmark – to mark the ear of a farm animal with a cut-out notch, a punched hole, a stitched or ear-perforated tag, or other symbol. Possibly the biggest drug arrest (and cache, three pounds of cocaine with an awesome "street value") happened here, right in little town, Franklin. This even knocked down, at least to a lower spot on the front page, the news that BGA, Battle Ground Academy, was going to go co-educational. Big city problems right here in Professor Harold Hill's little olé River City.

Then again, when one thinks they have the story of the year, just wait a ~~minute~~ month. Over seven inches of rain within 24 hours and an approximate $25 million in damages including over 150 residences trumps that April story. And that's what happened on Friday, May 3rd. Four hundred of our locals had to be evacuated, a lot for our small town. Ironically the same figure, four hundred, matched the miles of road damaged or destroyed. Such rains do a lot of damage to the agriculture in the area and this has reverberating repercussions in the area economy as well.

Our governor, Lamar Alexander flew in to view the devastation. Police and fire officials conducted many rescues. His visit and the waters make for a ton of picture possibilities. We just have to comb through the many for the best to place on our pages with the human-interest criteria being at the top of the list.

Fortunately there was no loss of life to report, just "things" lost. This makes our reporting jobs a lot easier trust me. No one really wants to interview a victim's family – trust me.

And speaking of human interest, what could be more interesting than our fast rising star, Dolly Parton. Dolly is a real person and the rains found her at the 77 year old mother of her manicurist. Really. Dolly liked the little house with the tin roof and the people who lived there, county folk that served the cowpen grown, three times cooked poke sallet (sometimes called Polk Salad like the 1969 song, *Polk Salad Annie*, written by Tony Joe White), deer soup, Real McCoy Mustard sauce, homemade country butter, corn bread, hog jowl, wild turkey, butter milk, peach cobbler, and pecan or potato pie. Dolly felt right at home there, reminding her of her roots and the home she was brought up in.

Dolly's Cadillac convertible was parked just across the little creek running by the house. The waters started rushing, quickly covering her car but fortunately not washing it away. Her husband, upon hearing the news, came with a wrecker to tow the ruined car when the waters were mostly receded but not so much that Dolly found herself having to wade to get to the other side. But not dissuaded, it was reported that Dolly asked to come back and maybe write some songs there.

No, I'm not going to look for or put a bid in on her soaked Cad. It's just not a news car and I would never be able to concentrate on reporting let alone driving, sitting in that same lovely, little, probably already warm seat. Besides, the Blue Fly would never forgive me.

Mentioning the BGA, Battle Ground Academy, as I did, an enterprising sixteen year old lad and student at BGA, Vance Ormes is responsible for the Ben having it's own community theatre. He pulled together family and friends and created the Pull-Tight Players just a couple of years before I got here. Their first production was *Our Town*.

Our competition picked up on the new drug problem and soon a new series of articles was appearing in their paper. The information was informative but the title (typically covering five columns with a two inch height), the author's picture, and the homey first word was what got attention. I'm referring to an enterprising, smart (or at least a good researcher) local law enforcer, Deputy Rick Eley and his weekly articles, *POINT BLANK* (complete with a black boarder and over a Sheriff's badge image). Consistently his first, introductory word was a (simple) "Hello." Hard to beat.

His youthful picture was Rick in uniform, holding a shotgun pointed near the camera with a woodsy background. He could have passed for a youthful Clint Eastwood. His confident demeanor impressed wishes on any observer of never wanting to go up against this kid. He had a pair of dark sunglasses casually attached to his shirt to add to his sober/pensive mood. For content I put Rick in the Spaghetti-Journalism area but this was like putting a GTO on the racing line with its expected affect even if it didn't have an engine.

This guy is cool, even his name. I was glad I didn't meet him in Journalism school. This is powerful stuff whether he was copying over the Declaration of Independence or a kid's book – this intro is so commanding that the info became unimportant. I immediately hightailed it to see Lance. "Lance…" waving the article in his face…"

"I know," he responded, "It will go away. The kid's reading from one of his training manuals."

"But Boss, the title and pict are compelling. We've got to do something. We have to counter this."

"Mark, it could just be needed filler on their part…but what did you have in mind," he said.

"Well, the Ben doesn't need more rote information, they need human interest stories. You know, Journalism 101. Let me try to find our own contributing officer and let him relate some of the hundreds of stories these fellows see on the job all the time." Then I added, "Even if I have to makeup and write the stuff myself," I didn't say to him – only to myself.

"OK, see what you can come up with. But it has to be original and can't seem as a counter-reaction on our part. You know the drill: we have to have at least six well-written and edited articles before we will think of running anything. And don't be surprised if this goes away before you can get the first one done." I thought he was through but added what I wanted to interpret as a complement to my bringing this to his attention, "Make sure we have a good title too."

I spent three days on this (and three nights in my thinking tub, with Port) and let it go. And I knew Lance would never bring it up again. When the competition wins, let them. Kudos TRA. Let them run with what they have and do (other) good work. Amen.

Whenever I get an inspirational flash, like the *Point Blank* one, and have to set it aside, I have to compensate for it or maybe it's substitution. Anyway, I found my (new) mission back in the barbershop. No I didn't really need a haircut, maybe just a trim, but I go there when I get a little depressed (ergo setting aside a good inspiration).

While I started out (sitting and waiting – something a guy has to get use to in virtually any barbershop) I found myself watching the TRA paper readers trying to tell how much time each would spend reading the *POINT BLANK* column (if any). Fortunately I overheard a conversation in progress, "It's too bad Ab Gordon or his daughter, Annie, didn't keep up the sorghum molasses tradition." If you want to see my ears "on point" just say something I never hear of before.

I (in my heart) knew the PB thing was over so I injected, "What's that?" There followed a respectful pause for an obvious (still new) outsider, followed by the predictable question, "You nev'r had any sorghum molasses, or sorghum molasses pie, cake, baked beans, or even the rich barbecue sauce?"

I knew it wasn't to offend, just introduce a new conversation so I simply led into it with, "No. Am I really missing something?" And when someone "bites" all that's left is to sit back and hear a soliloquy or two or three as the willing, participating natives unload their boyhood memories for you. I should have brought a stack of yellows. The barbershops must have taken over the rocking chair, cracker barrel, peanut shells on the floor, fireplace podiums sometime along the way.

"Whereas regular molasses is made from sugar cane (I knew that) and is kind 'a tasteless (I knew that too and had successfully avoided this despite Nana's many urgings). Our sorghum molasses is made from the sorghum cereal grass mainly used for stock feed. So I guess you nev'r had the prime kid-experience of sucking on a sorghum stalk. It's nature's premier candy." Wow!

I was listening intently because I wanted to catch the material but especially the name, sorghum. I swear it came out differently each time it was spoke.

"You can see sorghum all over the place. It kind 'a looks like corn stalks with the grain-clusters at the top. It's the third largest food grain, even used in beer. Some folk thinks it came from Africa.

"It's been a while but we had a good man, Ab Gordon out at the Shoals Branch. Ab and his daughter used to make the best darn sorghum molasses ever. And I think, Barney you can tell me wrong, that they were about the last to make it here yonder."

Of course I asked how.

"The olé horse mill idea. One sets up a press with three openings: one for the cane stalk going in, another fer it to come out and one for the pressed juice at the bottom. The horse powers the two crushing cylinders inside the press. This stuff on pancakes or biscuits would make anyone sit up and take notice. Trust me on this young man."

I liked the "young man" part and decided I had a mission: to find and try some of this southern, imperial stuff. Funny, one would think I would have already seen it in the restaurants for breakfast. I'm not one to not try a new thing or two. Except women – never mind.

But not to let the conversation dry up, I asked, "How does one make the pie?"

"That's particularly easy. Just mix five eggs, 1/3 cup of sugar and 1-1/4 cups of sorghum molasses into one's prepared pie-crust then leave until it's done." I think I knew what was coming but I participated, "Why?"

"Cause you don't want to go crazy doing the waitin, smelling all that good stuff comin from the oven." was the response. So I was right - but really wanted (but didn't) question why the two sugars. I might take a taste if I find a pie but I figure I had better not take a piece of two since I didn't have a field to plow or chores to do after having that much stimuli added to the system.

Wasn't it the Sugar and Molasses Act along with the Stamp Act that led to our American Revolution? I wonder if there's any sorghum molasses stills running along side any of our moonshine ones – to avoid any taxes. It seems there's a principle involved, maybe even an "American spirit." With all the wrongs to be addressed in the world and our own country, maybe this shouldn't be toward the top of the list. Gee, am I turning into a southerner or something?

My mission? Accomplished. It's around – one just has to look (hard).

They were right about the richness and I would call my Nana, if she was still alive, to tell her – the stuff's great and leaves the regular molasses far behind. By the way, I learned that the rich sorghum syrup pouring from the press described in the barbershop is next filtered through burlap and placed into a wood-fired cooker with the resulting pure bubbling golden syrup is then passed through another filter before it's bottled (or used).

This differs from my original thought that it was ready after the press as I concluded earlier. Also, some unscrupulous vendors use shortcuts but if you find the real thing (especially at stands along the back roads of Tennessee and Kentucky) you're in for a treat.

So maybe the "revenuers" don't bother the stands along our back roads. Damn, I should have asked if they had moonshine too (out of sight, maybe under the table). Naw – I probably would pass as a revenue-man in my Blue Tail. Oh well, another mission - another time.

Well, we're not out of the movie making business yet. Tommy Amato, EVP of General Audience Films of Studio City California is in town. He'll be speaking at our Rotary Club on the details of including scenes from Williamson County, our Rodeo and parade for possible inclusion in a new movie to be called, *Nashville or Bust*. The Director, Alex Grasshoff, is here too but with due respect, not nearly as flamboyant as Alan Holubar of our *The Human Mill* film but then maybe he won't go back to Hollywood and die on us either. Maybe I should remind him not to drink the water.

The film will be about two cowboys who are determined to make it to the Grand Ole Opry. Jesse Turner created the movie and stars in it along with our Slim Pickens, George Jones, Johnny Paycheck and Mickey Gilley. I happen to be in the lobby of the newly opened Opryland Hotel when who should come by with two gorgeous cowgirls, one on each arm, but the Mickey himself. I just knew right then and there that I needed a new pair of boots.

And while we're on a "media" role, July 13 will be our Darrell Waltrip Day. Darrell, of stockcar driving and Daytona 500 fame will be honored with a parade that will include the 101st Marching Band from Ft. Campbell. I hope they'll be selling popcorn.

Secondly, Television star Claude Akins of *Movin' On* across from Frank Converse, *BJ and the Bear,* and *The Misadventures of Sheriff Lobo* fame is in town filming some Spanish commercials. Of course I remember him best for his role in *Rio Bravo* across from The Duke (John Wayne). OK, so Angie Dickinson starred in the film too. I didn't go see him in the *Battle for the Planet of the Apes* of just a few years ago. The Apes didn't fit his cowboy image he engraved in me with his roles in *Wagon Train, The Big Valley*, and *Death Valley Days, The Rifleman* and *Bonanza*. Damn the 60's were good, at least for us cowboys.

Maybe too much knowledge is a bad thing. Claude Akins middle name is Marion. John Wayne was born Marion Robert Morrison. But maybe this doesn't spoil anything – maybe only news guys know these things. And maybe Roy Rogers was really born Marion Leonard Franklin Slye.

It's sometimes funny how things come together and as the story goes; Claude Atkins about ten years ago happened to meet one Jim Owen, originally from Robards, Kentucky, now of Franklin. Claude introduced him to the guitarist Chet Atkins and musician Mel Tillis.

Things really started to happen then and Jim has had about 100 chart records over the last many years including my favorite, *Louisiana Woman, Mississippi Man*. But Jim's idol has always been Hank Williams so he just had to do something about that. Jim took eleven months to write and record a ten-hour radio show on Hank Williams and it's already syndicated nationally and will air coming up January 1st of next year.

And I'm not done with the cleb thing. Remember Jeannie C. Riley, one of our county residents and more popularly known for the catching *Harper Valley PTA* smash hit written by another resident, Tom T. Hall, well guess who has agreed to be this year's honorary chairman of the local March of Dimes campaign. Her residence, the Harrison House, had never looked this good. Man, I'm ready to march to that tune. Oh sorry, Mickey (husband).

Oh my God, The Harrison house, south on my street south of town, I've been out front of it taking pictures, the house in which General Hood make the faithful decision to attack Franklin. "No I wouldn't put you on because it really did, it happened just this way."

Wow - our historic Carnton Plantation where the bodies of five generals of the Confederate Army were laid after the Battle of Franklin, the bloodiest…(you know - anyways, the Plantation) was given to the newly formed Carnton Association for Restoration and Preservation by

Dr. and Mrs. Sugg. The gift was for the mansion, the Confederate Cemetery, and ten surrounding acres. The announcement came at the annual Heritage Foundation Ball held on the grounds of Carnton. Gettysburg, watch out! Attention tourists!

The Decade is closing out with Clint Eastwood playing the part of Frank Lee Morris of Alcatraz fame. The movie is called *Escape from Alcatraz* and it's based on Frank and company's engineered escape, the only one to my knowledge, from that island prison in San Francisco Bay. The movie is based on the J. Campbell Bruce's non-fiction book. The small prisoner group went through the prison vents in the back of their cells, into an un-monitored utility corridor, up to the roof and down to the bay known for its unpredictable currents and cold temperatures. There they boarded a home made raft or rafts and disappeared into the June 11th, 1962 night never to be heard from again. The guards found makeshift dummies in their beds in the morning.

The name Frank Lee Morris caused some questions locally since we have a Morris Frank in Williamson County who is also quite famous but for a different reason. Our Morris was blinded when he lost his sight in a schoolyard fight at the age of 16. For perspective, people with handicaps at that time, the 1920's, had virtually no career opportunities except becoming sideshow carnies, performers, beggars, or working in sheltered workshops. Some blind people went on to college but when they got out, there were no options because the society they were re-entering hadn't yet opened to this or other handicaps.

Morris was read an article in the November 5, 1927 *Saturday Evening Post*, about Dorothy Eustis, an American dog trainer living in Switzerland who wrote that a school there was training German Shepherds to lead blinded WWI vets. Morris wrote her asking her to train a dog for his use. He wrote, "...Thousands of blind like me abhor being dependent on others. Help me and I will help them." Morris made his way to Europe the following year.

He received his first dog that Dorothy had named Kiss, but Morris changed her name to Buddy. When he returned to the states, Morris did the unthinkable and crossed the busiest street in New York City using nothing but his trust in Buddy. He had a mission and traveled the country, putting himself and Buddy to the test in every conceivable traffic situation. Frank and Buddy were a common sight in downtown Nashville for years. Frank successfully challenged the "no dogs allowed" codes on streetcars, elevators, and in restaurants. The concept of service dogs sharing space with humans in public places first gained social acceptance on the streets of Nashville thanks to Morris' persistence. Once the triumph of this was complete, interest and faith began rising in German Shepard's as Guide Dogs.

Eventually, Morris Frank started the nonprofit, Seeing Eye dog guide school now located in Morristown, New Jersey. Today they use Golden Retrievers, Black Labradors, Yellow Labs, Chocolate Labs, and Boxers as well as German Shepherds.

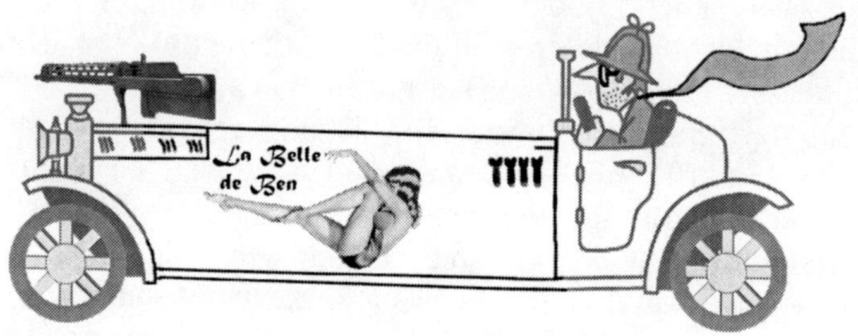
La Belle
de Ben

Don't Placards

Did they mean Tennessee? Or did they mean, "Don't Mess With Texas – Let the Volunteers of Tennessee Do It?

This decade sure has been different, at least for me. One note that it's ending on is worth mentioning. It's a catchy song by Dr. Elmo and wife Patsy called, *Grandma Got Run Over by a Reindeer*. The title tells it all (if one just adds a lot of eggnog). I love it and will probably wear out my copy by repeated playings.

Un-reverend tee shirts are making their presence know here abouts but I suspect they're more popular in the north. Listen to me now – like I've lived here all my life.

Oh yea, tee shirts. One of the ones that was popular (in the north) was *Jesus Hates The Yankees*. I got a kick out of that – maybe having been a former Dodger fan. You know, the Brooklyn

Bridegrooms? These resulted in lots of Jesus Hates knock-offs including one college one, *Jesus Hates Slackers*, much to erudite for the streets.

You'll be proud of me. Remember our brief discussion of Thomas Hart Benton, the influential painter (especially to me) and his great uncle namesake? Well I didn't want to leave it alone as much as I tried. Besides, I was truly at a lost on knowing how to pursue. That's when olé fate stepped in. I'll explain.

When I was doing the research on the Betty B. Burge murder I asked to see the only formal thing I could find that was ever written about it other than the newspaper accounts. The Special Sections in the library claimed to have a poetry book written by a local about the event. His name was reportedly Yates as I've already talked about.

I couldn't imagine that this was the only thing about one of the most significant criminal events in relatively calm Tennessee's history, at least in Williamson County. So I asked to reserve and take it out but it's so small they couldn't find it (at first) and I was given a take-out book by a Yates only another Yates instead. When I was flipping through it to find Betty (because it wasn't indexed) what pops out but Thomas Hart Benton, the local to Franklin, original Benton. I was shocked at the coincidence and then shocked again how life seems to pull things together.

T. H. Benton the eventual "Magnificent Missourian" and MO five-term, thirty-two year Senator has been credited with building his Tennessee roots but that's not the story of the local Mr. Yeats here in the Ben. From Yates' writing, it all started with his father, Jesse Benton, who had claimed the large Tennessee land grant while still alive and living in Hillsboro, NC.

Upon his death in 1801, widow Nancy Benton, 32, formed her own caravan and moved everything she thought she would need including her slaves and her brood of eight children to TN. Yes, I said 32 with 8 children. And slaves. The trek took two months and all she found was 2,500 acres of wilderness at the foot of the Highland Rim, astride the Natchez Trail just a little west of Franklin.

Immediately she set about clearing the land and building a substantial house. Her oldest, 16 year old son, Thomas Hart Benton helped her. Once this was accomplished and feeling the need for neighbors, she leased sections to other pioneers to start their own homes and build a log school, a log church, and several other community small buildings and named the place taking shape, Benton Town, which as it grew, was to become Hillsborough in honor of her NC home. Hillsborough became Hillsboro and was then renamed Leiper's Fork the current neighboring town of the Ben.

Thomas in 1805 at the age of 20 declared himself to be an attorney (like Andrew Jackson had done) and was admitted to the TN Bar. He grew to become a civic worker with influential contacts in Franklin, Nashville, and the state capital Knoxville (at the time). Three Franklin attorneys were especially helpful in his practice and were the opportunity to come to the attention of Tennessee's First Citizen, Andrew Jackson, who being impressed with Thomas took him under his wing.

In the spring of 1812 Andy asked Tom to take a "commission," get on his horse, and round up a company of voluntary reservists to help Colonel Andy defend New Orleans against the British. This Thomas did and with Andy, led the men down there.

But Tom, Andy and his men didn't see action on that first trip. It seems they got as far as Natchez, Mississippi (the end of our Natchez Trace) and were told to wait there by the commander of the Regular Army, General Wilkerson. Two months of waiting later,

Wilk said, "Take your men and go back to Franklin – we don't need ya" and they did, went home. But it wasn't over if you know your history and the historic battle to end the war three years later with Sam Houston there too.

You may know your history but I bet you don't know that Andy gave a brass cannon to Franklin for their participation in the (final) successful battle of New Orleans. I couldn't find the cannon unless it's one of the ones below our statue in the square but there is a small monument at Five Points that reads: On his return from New Orleans, Andres Jackson gave a brass cannon to Franklin. A part of his soldiery camped here on their way to New Orleans. Placed by Col. Thos. Hart Benton, Chapter, W.S.D. of 1812 (1917).

Meanwhile, Andy asked Tom to do the same thing the following year following Tom's first recruitment efforts. His task was to recruit another company to go fight the Creek Indians in Alabama and it was on this campaign the Three Stars of Tennessee, Andy, Tom and Sam, became closer in fighting for a common cause despite their distinct differences.

All were strong, intelligent, ambitious, aggressive, individualists of Anglo-Saxon heritage, self-educated that had been thrust into family responsibilities at an early age. Houston, born 1763, a heavy drinker, was a giant and had troubled times in most all of his "family" encounters. (Of course the arrow in the groin at Horseshoe Bend, Alabama where the three were fighting the Creeks may not have helped). Benton, born 1782, a teetotaler family man, was tall and husky. Jackson, born 1767, a devoted husband to his beloved Rachel, was tall, thin, even wiry and only a social drinker.

Jackson, as you know, went on to become the seventh President. Benton moved on to Missouri. Houston became the 7th Governor of Tennessee, the President of the Republic of Texas, and after Texas was finally annexed, the 7th Governor of Texas - the only person to ever have two governorships in two different states.

And here's a test, do you remember THB's quote when the congressman was asked if he knew Andrew Jackson, he replied, "General Jackson was a very great man, sir. I shot him, sir." Finally, I've got the story on that too.

As background, here are two more memorable quotes of Thomas to what I'll relate: "Nobody opposes Benton, sir, nobody but a few black-jack prairie lawyers. These are the only opponents of Benton. Benton and the people, Benton and Democracy are one and the same sir, synonymous terms, sir, synonymous terms." And secondly, "I never quarrel, sir, but I do fight, sir, and when I fight, sir, a funeral follows, sir."

It seems AJ hadn't heard the second one and Andy, in a downtown Nashville hotel, make a derogatory remark about Thomas's brother Jesse, named after their father. Thomas didn't take kindly to it and a (predictable) duel ensued whereby Thomas added to Andy's rattling "like a bag of marbles" with a lucky shot. THB was unscathed. No, a funeral didn't follow.

Going through the Ben one more time, I finally know what that special feeling is, a feeling I have never gotten any where else. It's like walking through an art museum. The buildings and homes here, many titled with their little black historic signs, are like a walk through history, each block is like a "period room," each place like a framed story all by itself. Each one is its own installation. And I like paintings that tell a story.

But unlike a stoic gallery, this is a vibrant living gallery even today with subjects, the residents, coming and going unaffected - even unaware of their roles or the history they trod or drive on. With the leaves, shrubs and trees that have seen a lot just standing there swaying to the soft Tennessee breezes daring you to ask what they have seen. This stops many a tourist - and brings them back as well.

One walks through the Ben and one walks through a timeless, living, continuing history, our own - and as far back as one cares to see.

I know I say (even threatened) to talk about the ubiquitous "colored" situation here. But as a recent, almost ten-year outsider, it's not really a "situation." But it's also not a topic that a northern boy coming south can fully relate too, even an ace-reporter one. Yes, I have studiously talked to many, many people (of both races) and read the literature that's available (and there is a lot). This included Rick Warwick's excellent *Williamson County In Black & White*, Williamson County Historical Society Journal #31, 2000 and many of Thelma Battles books. Thelma calls Rick and her the "Salt and Pepper Historians of Franklin/Williamson County (and rightfully so).

I think by now you know it is a pressing issue for me, one I would like to put my arms around. But: I wasn't here for the key times, like slavery, emancipation, reconstruction, desegregation…even the Civil Rights Acts of 1957, 1960, 1964, or even 1968.

All that I can tell you that it's becoming a non-issue, evolving as probably (hopefully) the rest of the country. Sometimes, in fact many times, we don't like it but the human condition seems to take its time about some things. So hopefully you're not disappointed but I must leave it here. I do encourage you to visit, walk the streets, and see it is "evolving" maybe even disappearing by the time you get here.

My Own, Just Life

It's truly fascinating, at least to me, how most things come together in more ways than one. I have to think that it's more then mere coincidence. Three small towns, all with Opera houses, floods, bootleggers, unsolved murders, minstrels, and a myriad of other similar legends, unique to each but seemingly with the same generic subjects. And now I receive something that ties together my southern-leaning Ben and my former Union V in a special way.

Do you remember in my last book that after the Confederate forces surrendered at Appomattox, President Abe gave a great celebration at the White House, complete with the United States Military Band playing on the front lawn and Lincoln called out from the balcony, "Play *Dixie*. We have captured the Confederacy, and now Dixie belongs to the Union." Of course he was just mistaken, it was always the North's (if not the world's at that point).

I just received a letter and picture from a former, Ohio friend back in the V. It came out of the blue, no pun intended. The picture is of a memorial in the V dedicated to Daniel

Decatur Emmett, the father of minstrels who had written the loveable song, *Dixie*. She had come across it by accident, figured that I had never seen it, that I might like to know of its existence, took a picture and sent it to me. I was even surprised she had my address. The memorial, a large brass plaqued rock started out, "In loving remembrance..." and was presented by the Daughters of the Confederacy, Ohio Division.

This is the last year of the glorious seventies. I'm not sure if I feel they are – glorious, maybe (just) interesting. I'm getting a pattern to my life, my pre as well as my adult life, all thirty plus years of it. It seems it is/has been chopped up into ten year segments. Ten years growing up in the B as a youngster, ten years growing up in the G until college and dad dying, ten years in the V before moving on to here and now there's a good chance I'll be moving on despite how much I really love this place but the reasons are seemingly compelling.

My landlord is retiring based on a very good offer for his store and building, and because of his failing health. I can't blame him except the new owners wouldn't be ruining his store as a going business but tearing down the building for whatever. I had offered, many times, to help him out in the store over the weekends but he had always gracious declined. His help hadn't been especially dependable so the no-shows on the weekend, a busy time, stretched him. Plus he was devoid of any family members to pass it on to – they all had their own lives even though there wasn't any doubt in my mind that he would have generously turned over the key and walked away – a gift for any one of them so interested. A really nice guy. Of course that type of business, more mom-and-pop, didn't seem to have longevity with all the new types of super stores popping up everywhere.

But the bigger reason for expecting to move on is that Lance died. I think I mentioned his frequent absences over the last six months, which didn't seem to matter too much. The team knew what he wanted and the Chronicle seemed to be running itself then Lance could pick up any pieces when he returned. It wasn't known at first why a guy that used to put in an inordinate amount of hours, and was passionate in what he did, would take any excuse for a vacation, sick day, or any leave of absence but with small towns, word eventually got out – he was ill. We all hoped it wasn't much but as time went on it seemed obvious, he wasn't doing well. And it wasn't anything that could be reported in the paper until his death notice, which appropriately took a lot of our first page.

None of us, except maybe C knew how much he owned of the business or what/who the silent partners were but now the details are coming to the forefront fast since continuation or termination is the big question on everyone's mind. Me too. I knew there are a lot of resumes circulating. I guess I should update mine.

As it turns out, C's parents own a slice of the business. Actually it seems to have been a family enterprise but C's parents are the only "owners" that are local, the rest of the family live out of town, one even as far away as California and I don't think that's necessarily good. It's obvious that Lance didn't prepare a replacement for this possibility even though I don't think he, as an eminently practical man, had delusions of living forever. Maybe six or so months isn't enough for one to realize that the next "assignment," up there, is coming fast.

Following the funeral, and that (of course) was played up a lot bigger than in *The Review Appeal*, probably predictably so, C and I met at the pub for our own saluting-toast to one hell of a great guy, Lance. There, at the funeral home, and in confidence, C said he had been approached by the family to take over Lance's position. My gut reaction was that he would be great especially with his education, quiet demeanor, and dedicated, talented work habits. He wasn't pushy, overly ambitious, listened well, took our opinions, etc. Unfortunately he said he didn't think it was a good possibility. Being close, and knowing we were talking about my future too, I couldn't leave this alone and asked why. C said two reasons, one business and one personal.

C's personal reason was that he saw this as an opportunity to try the big (city) papers. He liked, even loved the small town stuff but felt it wasn't very challenging. He, still not married but quite involved, a place I had never felt comfortable going, said that by moving on it would test the potentiality of the relationship. Furthermore but not that C wasn't his own man, this would be a good excuse to get out from under his parents "umbrella" as he put it. Having been over to their place for a few cookouts and having run into them socially at a few of the Ben's functions, it was clear to me that they weren't the interfering or overbearing type but then to any outsider – it probably didn't look good and I understood what C meant.

But it was the business reason I hung on to – after being shocked. C said that the family (owners) had been carrying the paper for the last two years since it hadn't been turning a profit. Now they looked to him to cover, turn around, and make profitable their investment. I, trying to see through my shock, thought that he just might be the man to do it even though I had no inkling that the paper had been in such a position. For myself I would do anything to help him knowing that a lot of times it's easier to work with what you have rather than face the next unknown. I was about to verbalize this when he, astutely said, "Mark, I just don't think I need that kind of pressure while trying to establish the next layer of my life!"

It wasn't a question. The alternative of trying to sell the paper with the obvious competition or the prospects of starting to fine a Lance-replacement with the inevitable cost cutting, etc. wasn't good, at least in my opinion. So it was clear, I was looking at moving on, just haven't made it crystal clear in my mind.

Wanting to understand things better especially since he was confiding in me, I asked C, "How do you think this happened C? How did the paper get into this fix?" I wanted to add a third question, "How was it kept so quiet?" but didn't since the first two were more important in the long run.

"It probably wasn't one thing," said C and continuing, "Lance's health may have been a longer problem then anyone realized. The TRA going to publishing twice a week after the first of the year didn't help. You know they scoped us on a bunch of stuff because of that and somehow paid for it with increased advertisement although I don't know this for sure. Maybe they're stretched too but will win because of our (paper's) predicament.

Maybe Franklin, with it's fantastically increasing population from everywhere isn't in the need for the homey news or maybe doesn't have time to bother yet – until they get settled in. I'm not sure. We seemed to have been doing everything we were before that worked. Maybe small town newspapers are in the throes of big changes, the likes we aren't seeing yet let alone understanding soon. Let's put it this way, Mark, if I was to try to fill Lance's shoes, I don't have a clue in what to do. And I'm saying that to you but would never admit it to anyone else, even my own family."

Damn, he's scared – too. A new place to replace my apartment, that I would have to get in any case, was going to be a really big problem. I can't really put money down on a house or even look at a one year rent/lease under these conditions. Maybe there was a reason I'm still single, able to go on. I know what C was talking about as far a testing his "relationship," every single guy I know that tied the knot has never left the place they first settled in to. A couple of these friends even lost jobs and ended up with a drive to the next one rather then moving and I don't know the real reason but am very suspicious it had a lot to do with the un-willingness of their brides to even consider it. It turned out to be "his" problem.

Yes, C was right; the TRA scoped us big time on the May flood earlier this year. The flood had happened on a Friday, after we had both published our Thursday's editions but they were ready with the Tuesday's whereas the news was old by the time we covered it the following Thursday. It was big enough that the governor, Lamar Alexander, had flown in with his helicopter landing right in our five points. Their (typical) first page news spilled over for several pages with pictures galore.

There was a little funny associated with the May flood, the Dolly Parton flood as we refer to it around the office. Our coverage, late that it was, seemed to be adequate (for old news) except the part I wrote about Dolly. The TRA had covered the story but I just couldn't let it go – to get zapped and Lord knows, Dolly is/was newsworthy. Yes I was about the only one pushing for it to be included and the team, in Lance's absence, voted it down, but then a little "filler" was needed at the paper was put to bed so it got revived – placed. Isn't it funny how things work out.

Dolly, the 154 cm, 40 inch bustline doll from east Tennessee has been heating up the country as well as the pop charts over the last few years. Back in '74 she left the ever (and still) popular TV Porter Wagoner show after seven years to strike it out on her own and her parting gift to Porter, her song "*I Will Always Love You*" really propelled her into the spotlight. I personally like her album of two years ago, *Here You Come Again* with the song "*Two Doors Down*." OK, so I didn't say anything about her bustline in my article but that wasn't the end of it – so to speak. And if Dolly can't ever live down her obvious assets (is that singular or plural – sorry) then I've got to move on just to avoid the faux pas made in my name.

If you recall, Dolly lost her Cadillac convertible to the flood and had to wade across the stream in order to return home. Well, TRA had said "…Dolly had to wade water above her knees to get across the creek…" whereas I said (changing the creek to stream and the following), "Dolly found herself wading across the swollen flood-stream with water up to her knees in order to join her husband who had…" No problem, right? Well the layout guys, who I may not be giving enough credit, placed the first part of my small article on our first page as needed filler and toward the bottom with the residue on the second (and yes I hate to be cut up – article wise). But they cut the article at, "…with water up to her (continued on page 2).

But they erroneously and at the last minute, put the few sentences left over on the third page so everyone reading my article was left with "that" thought - maybe not even bothering to look for the conclusion. You may think it's funny, even laughing, the entire town did (and may still be five months later – our office is, even sniggering at the funeral, I can just tell). Sorry, neighbor Dolly, sometimes resident of the Ben. But if it's publicity you want – god bless me (and them).

In passing, 154 cm is 5' 2". Can you imagine if she would have been 6'? Hey, no offense, she's a great gal. The TNDOT (that's the Tennessee Department of Transportation – I just like saying the initials) put a life size poster of Dolly in the Visitors Welcome station just inside the state border for everyone to have their picture taken with Dolly. I did and would show you but the light reflected off the cardboard and you can't tell that it was Dolly. On second thought and with the hundreds and hundreds of celebes we have in the state, whom else would they put there? Oh, yea, Elvis.

Dolly, a real down to earth (Tennessee earth) person met her husband Dean when she was 18 at one of Nashville's Laundromats. It was called the Wishy-Washy. As an ongoing Laundromat aficionado, I just love that. We don't see much of Dean or Dolly on the streets but her sister is seen here often.

In TRA's same, Tuesday-Flood issue and also on their front page, they again zapped us - with the 30th Annual Rotary Rodeo coverage that was also the previous Friday night. Maybe I had blinders as to what was happening over the many previous months, complacent just doing my usual ace-reporting job.

I had approached Lance when TRA first went to two issues a week saying we had to do it too nor was I the only one but I (or anyone) didn't get a hearing on the subject. God bless him, Lance just pooh-poohed it. Maybe Lance, god bless him again, was ailing already. He never impressed me as one to back down on anything and I remember being surprised at his seeming dismissal response but now that's history. Probably time to move on.

OK, so life is full of surprises. I'm talking about the check I just received, one bigger than a year's salary. Yes, I'm a writer – of books! Yes! But that's no all; my publisher sent a ton of mail along with the check. Guess he didn't want to part with either!?! Well, I dove into the mail even before thinking of cashing the check. Now it's your turn to guess about my mail.

I really wanted to see hundreds of "well-done-s, attaboys, more-more" maybe humble will go by the wayside. But what I received was hundreds and hundreds of proposals!?! No, the ones from Japan were subtler but not so subtle as to also be transparent. What is happening? Is that what murder-mystery writers receive – hundreds of unsolved cases? Is this were girls and dating are today?

After reading this, if you think you're going to see me on a book-signing tour – forget it! I'll get my agent to go in my place. I'll start writing history books. I'll think twice before giving up my day-job. Wait – maybe I could sell them, the mail. Is there fodder there? Yes, that was an attempted pun on the herd I've heard from.

If it wouldn't take too much trouble, I've removed my name and any mention of my book and send the batch to Dear Abby. She'd have a field day – well, with at least a few until it became old news. Is this were dating and girls have gone? I guess I already said that.

OK, so there were some pictures in the ones I opened and I'm not going to open any more. Where do you think I got the idea of cows and haystacks – and now I'll really be in big trouble. I'll deny it.

Maybe my first books will be sufficient and I'll have this one published post-mortem. Maybe I shouldn't think about giving up my day job – ever – or at least until the NY Times can report me married. Just kidding – about the Times and the institution.

I think my mail was all the same, more of less. I'll need a Japanese-English dictionary for some. What if those are Japanese well-done-s that I can't read? Probably the ones with pictures can be discounted. What if my books do really take off and they are translated into other languages? Well, French is OK, Italian too. Maybe Spanish and German is border. But Russian? Guess I won't worry about Sign Language. But Pashtu? Eskimo-Aleut? Doesn't India have 22?

Damn, is this check with or without taxes? New problems – and dilemmas. Does this mean I can quit my day job? Stay in the Ben and write? Should I think of investing in the paper? Buying my apartment building? Gee, it's a lot of money but not enough at the same time. I know what all the investment gurus say – I've written a few of those types of articles – "With any significant change in one's life, don't do anything radical for a year." And I know the same applies to the death of a family loved one.

I wonder if there's more money where this came from and why I didn't see it coming – maybe I'm not such a good businessman - even for my own affairs. Decisions, decisions. What and where will I be ten more years from now?

I got it! I'll buy myself a knob. OK, so only a bluff. Well then, maybe just a hollow. Gee, a hollow between two knobs – what image does that conger up? You didn't think of a fertile, green, idyllic pastoral valley?

But, is this check from the Japanese contract? Just one? Where is the accounting or at least a statement explaining these things. Maybe it's a pay off, a buy out, the last one I'll ever receive. Until I can talk to him, I'll just think of it as a monthly stipend but won't cash it until I do talk to him.

Gee, Japan. Now, in this my sequel, I've been talking about them. I wonder if this will sell – or ruin everything. Yea, that Post-Mortem was a good idea – I'll have to think serious about it. I bet my publisher won't like it.

I really liked my trip and Japan. Given the Catholic forgive-and-forget thing and with due respect to my WWII uncles, I never felt threatened and if there are some grudges held by the old generation, I clearly felt the new one wanted to know everything about us – in a good way. Maybe I should go back to school and take Psychology. Do they have such a thing as Japanese Psychology? In Japan?

Maybe I should just mediate like I was told the elder in Japan do or at least the monks. The trip seems like a lifetime ago. I came across this just by accident and now I forget what temple I was walking through. I think it was one that there was construction going on so we, my rep and I, had to detour through one of the Japanese gardens, they're everywhere, and for esthetic reasons, to commune with nature.

Anyway, while walking through this very well manicured oasis, I came across this round, obviously carved stone jutting out (up) of the pristine garden by a small water fall. Part of the falls was detoured to the stone via a bamboo shoot used as a pipe and a trickle was entering the square shaped cutout on the top of the stone. Looking closer I saw four characters that I assumed where Japanese carved in the north, south, east, west position. Knowing the everything in this garden had been placed with meticulous care and had a purpose I asked my rep, now my friend, what was it.

He said it was a tsukuba and I had him repeat it several times until I had it. Then I asked him, what is it and what is it doing here? "The temple monks use this when they wake up early in the morning to start their day." This gave me more questions than answers but before I could ask, he continued, "They would come to the garden to splash a little water on their face to start their day. Once their eyes were opened, they would pause and rear the inscription that you see around the stone."

I think he purposely waited, wanting me to ask the next question, which I did. "What does it say?"

He said that the four characters, *ware tada taru wo shiru* roughly translated into "What I have is enough," which was a daily reminder to the monks of being satisfied with what (little) they had.

Wow, what a life lesson. I just knew that this was going to change my life and I purchased a souvenir coin at the gift shop on the way out. It emulates the top of the humble small stone garden pillar and I wanted it to, intended it to, be a pillar of my future life, rocky or otherwise. (I know I know…once a punster always a punster).

Honestly, I don't intend to give up my day-job and deep down know it's time to start thinking bigger. Some professor, back in college, said that jobs, businesses, and careers are alike in that they 1. Change, 2. Grow, or 3. Stagnant and die. I didn't want to hear it at the time but it's haunted me ever since – since I feel there's a lot of truth in what he said. I've never since (or then) found that in any of the text books but I've been seeing it all around me.

So maybe I can keep a friend, thing bigger, and move on in one felt swoop (who ever said that first). C, a friend and thanks to his old school connections (and high academic credentials) has learned that there's something very big in the works, in our industry. Someone or ones, with hopefully big bucks, are thinking of taking on the biggest but staid papers in the entire USA. I'm talking competing with the likes of the New York Times, the Washington Post, and/or the Wall Street Journal, etc.

C's very excited and so is his (investing) family. The idea is to make a more compelling daily that reaches the average person with all the day-to-day stuff that they're really interested in (and not just what someone else has determined was "the news that's fittest to print" et al). And in color too – the daily.

This is a huge challenge, never been done. I, in all my imaginative career scenarios, could never have guess this was possible. And of course they're going to need some ace-reporters to accomplish the impossible. Wish I could find out more but it's kind of hush-hush for now. Anyways, I could continue my friendship, grow, and work on that Pulitzer after all. Wonder where they'll be located or maybe several key places throughout the country. I wonder if one can carve out a 12 or 15 block area for one's own in a big city.

One of my last thoughts: I remember the rules for Journalism from academia: One doesn't use prepositions to end sentences with. Also, always avoid annoying alliteration, attitudes and altercations. And above all, (that's eleven) don't start a sentence with a conjunction. Avoid clichés like the plague mostly because they're old hat. Finally please note that parenthetical remarks (however relevant) are (usually) unnecessary. But since I use them, these rules-to-write-by, every working day, I just didn't want to apply them to my own personal writings.

Mark Moiré

This is my third novel exploring my very own fascination with the American small towns, a dying concept and genre. And no, I don't pretend to be an expert on Japan (or anything including the subject of women). I'll also admit that my experiences can and will, undoubtedly, vary greatly from others while they may be in the same room, conversation, country, era, or even a small town.

I liked the time frame, the Seventies. And like the Fifties and the Sixties, I think the future will eventually treat them as unique segments in American history even with the reverence/excitement that it already treats the Roaring Twenties. The Twenties were just the Oldies and Goodies of an earlier generation.

The many and well seeded websites for Franklin, the town, battle ground, history, etc. made this book possible. I know the fantastic Natchez Trace Bridge wasn't completed until 1996 with the dedication by vice president Al Gore (of TN) and of course the Governor didn't land atop the 5-Points library that hadn't been build yet to check out the flood of 1979. I never have found that tallest radio tower in Nashville nor taken a picture of George Jones' biggest rocking chair outside his house on the east side of Franklin. I'm told it's a sight but given the choice that I should opt for George's Christmas display, reputed the biggest and best in all of Tennessee. Fortunately I happened at a book convention at the Opryland at the time of the music awards, or at least one of them. Seeing the country singers and celebes parading through the lobby after the show in their peacock best was a thrill, worth the trip by itself. I even saw Mickey Gilly in his finery that included two of the best looking cowgirls, one on each of his arms that I've ever seen in person.

As I've said before, I hope you'll agree that there is something very special about small towns and the people there. My goal is simply and purely entertainment. My characters and facts are mostly fictional based on some facts in the public archives of the town. I try to be imaginative and not autobiographical so don't bother asking that question if you happen to come across me on a book tour. That sounds optimistic doesn't it? And Johnny Seay's friend, Willie York, died in 1991. Johnny is living (and hopefully still writing and singing) in Texas. And yes, I do have a one square inch Tennessee plot in the vicinity of Lynchburg that I hope to visit one day so you can call me Squire Mark.

I know there's a lot more to unearth, to tell, and that new small town stories are beginning as I write this. Maybe you'll take up the genre-baton and tell us more about your experiences in them. If I can be of help, or just be a friend, don't hesitate to yell. The very best to ya'll (they still say that in Texas – and some parts of Tennessee).

Oh yes, boots? Yes, I wear them. If you're far from a western store, try CowboyBoots.com. That's not an endorsement, just a friendly tip.

Feel free to send me your comments via MARKMOIRE@comcast.net. If you've enjoyed this book, please look for my next one, one about life in another small town in the US (I'm just not sure where as I write these last words).

On second thought, it's been a long time since *Gone With The Wind* and Franklin is ripe for such an epic or two, maybe three. Yea, I like that. Maybe it's time for a best seller. I think I can…

Mark graduated with a degree in Journalism from the University of Illinois - now some time ago. Mark, his wife, Evita, and with their children, Eric, Elaine, and Samatha, currently live in Lodi, a very small, quiet, rural and friendly community in central Ohio – with lots of stories of its own.

⇐ New Territory – Franklin ⇒

Franklin, TN - Recent Awards and Laurels:

1,000 Places to See in The USA and Canada Before You Die, by Patricia Schultz

Money Magazine's Top 10 Places to Retire

Money Magazine's Top 100 Best Places to Live

Clean Cities Award (TN Department of Transportation)

Tree City USA

Great American Main Street Award

Preserve America Community (designated by First Lady Laura Bush)

Number One Small Town in Tennessee

Reader's Choice Award for Natchez Trace Parkway/Scenic Drive

One of Five Best Places in America to Antique Shop

Five National Register Historic Districts

Trip Advisor's One of Top Ten Hot US Destinations for 2007

Franklin, TN – Some of the Many Websites:

Andrew Jackson's Hermitage: www.thehermitage.com
The Carter House: www.carter-house.org
Carton Plantation: www.carnton.org
City Guide: www.city-data.com/city/Franklin-Tennessee.html
Cool Springs C of C: www.greatercoolsprings.com
Factory at Franklin, The: www.factoryatfranklin.com
Franklin C of C: www.williamson-franklinchamber.com
Franklin Downtown Neighborhood Assoc.:
    www.historicfranklin.com/DFA.html
Franklin Gov: www.franklin-gov.com
Franklin Historic/Heritage Foundation: www.historicfranklin.com
Franklin Is: www.franklinis.com
Franklin Jazz Festival: www.franklinjazzfestival.com
Franklin Life: http://c-dh.net/affiliate/franklinlife
Franklin Living: www.franklin-tennessee-living.com
Franklin On Foot: www.franklinonfoot.com
Franklin Police: www.franklin-gov.com/police
Franklin Tomorrow: www.franklintomorrow.org
Franklin Transit Authority: www.tmagroup.org
Franklin's Charge: www.franklinscharge.com
Harpeth River Watershed Assoc.: www.harpethriver.org
Historic Downtown Franklin: www.historicfranklin.com
Heritage Foundation of Franklin and Williamson County:
    www.historicfranklin.com
Jack Daniels Distillery: www.jackdaniels.com
Johnny Seay, Cross and Grave Ranch. Glen Rose, TX:
    http://johnnyseay.com
Lillie Belle's of Franklin: http://lilliebelles.net
McLemore House (Black American) Museum:
www.carnton.org/mclemore_house_museum.htm
Nashville's Parthenon: www.nashville.gov/Parthenon
Nashville Zoo: www.nashvillezoo.org
Natchez Trace Parkway: www.nps.gov/natr
O'More College of Design: www.omorecollege.edu
Opryland: http://www.gaylordhotels.com/

Pull Tight Players Theater: www.pull-tight.com
Renaissance Center, Dickson, TN: www.rcenter.org
Republican Party of Williamson Co. Tennessee:
http://williamsontngop.org
The Review & Appeal Newspaper: www.tennessean.com
Sweet Dreams Cookie Company™ Franklin, TN:
http://sweetdreamscookies.com
Tennessee Walking Horse Association: www.twhbea.com
Trail of Tears (National Park Service): www.nps.gov/trte
Wikipedia: Franklin, TN:
http://en.wikipedia.org/wiki/Franklin%2C_TN
Williamson County: http://www.keepwilliamsonbeautiful.org/
Williamson County Convention & Visitors Bureau:
www.visitwilliamson.com
Williamson Co. Fair: http://www.williamsoncountyfair.org
Williamson Co./Franklin Libraary: http://lib.williamson-tn.org/
Williamson Co./ Historical Society:
www.tngenweb.org/williamson/resources/histsoc.html
Williamson County Public Library (Franklin):
http://lib.williamson-tn.org/FRNK/wcplmain.htm
Williamson Co. Parks & Recreation: www.wcparksandrec.com
Willaismson Co. Today: www.williamsontoday.com
Williamson Herald: www.williamsonherald.com

Printed in the United States
147368LV00001B/198/P